PRAISE FOR *WRATH*

"The first book to really take up Michael Crichton's mantle.... *Ratatouille* meets *World War Z* in a Big Blockbuster Book that reads like Crichton, only with more eyeball-eating."

—**Grady Hendrix**, *New York Times*-bestselling author of
The Southern Book Club's Guide to Slaying Vampires

"Moalem and Kraus have put the science back in science fiction. *Wrath* is grounded in very real technologies, making this grisly thriller about genetic engineering gone wrong all the more terrifying."

—**Bill Sullivan, PhD**, Professor of Pharmacology & Toxicology,
Indiana University School of Medicine, and author of
Pleased to Meet Me: Genes, Germs, and the Curious Forces that Make Us Who We Are

"*Wrath* manages to meld a story with elements of horror, philosophy, human psychology, and the realities of animal use in scientific research. Besides being a gripping story, *Wrath* is a thought-provoking read for anyone who has wondered how to feel about genetic engineering, artificial intelligence and how humans use animals."

—**Lisa Moses**, Faculty, Center for Bioethics, Harvard Medical School

PRAISE FOR SHÄRON MOALEM

The Better Half: On the Genetic Superiority of Women

"Provocative, crackling with wit and insight, *The Better Half* argues that science has shortchanged women in all levels of research and convincingly reveals that the true differences between men and women come down to longevity, intellect, resilience, and immunity to disease. Now it all makes sense why 95 percent of people who have reached the age of 110 are women."

—**Jancee Dunn**, *New York Times*-bestselling author of
How Not to Hate Your Husband After Kids

"This book provides the crucial scientific reasoning behind why it is essential to include males and females, both in people and animals, in order to get accurate results in medical research."

—**Temple Grandin, PhD**, *New York Times*-bestselling author of *The Autistic Brain* and *Thinking in Pictures*

Survival of the Sickest

"Dr. Moalem draws many connections between seemingly disparate subjects.... He skillfully interweaves his knowledge of history, genetics, and medicine not only as they relate to specific medical conditions but also in a way that addresses important challenges of modern society and our future evolution."

—**Dan Ariely**, author of *Predictably Irrational:
The Hidden Forces That Shape Our Decisions*

Inheritance

"Dr. Moalem is an eloquent guide through the astonishing new world of genetic discovery—with all its implications for both personal health and public policy. If you've wondered about the impact of genetics on your life—read this book!"

—**Kinney Zalesne**, *New York Times*-bestselling author of *Microtrends: The Small Forces Behind Tomorrow's Big Changes*

How Sex Works

"Read this book and discover sex again, but from a scientific perspective, and see why it evolved. It's almost as much fun, and needs less energy."

—**Peter Macinnis**, author of *100 Discoveries: The Greatest Breakthroughs in History* and *Mr Darwin's Incredible Shrinking World*

PRAISE FOR DANIEL KRAUS

Bent Heavens

"Kraus gets under your skin with brutal, elegant efficiency. Necessarily horrifying, devastatingly timely."

—**Kiersten White**, *New York Times*-bestselling author of *The Dark Descent of Elizabeth Frankenstein* and *Slayer*

Blood Sugar

"I never miss a book by the remarkable Daniel Kraus, and *Blood Sugar* exceeds all expectation. A Stephen King tale told by a pidgin Artful Dodger, it's a twisted little miracle with a sneaking, beating heart."

—**Megan Abbott**, *New York Times*-bestselling author of *Give Me Your Hand*

The Shape of Water (with Guillermo del Toro)

"[A] phenomenally enrapturing and reverberating work of art in its own right . . . [that] vividly illuminates the minds of the characters, greatly enhancing our understanding of their temperaments and predicaments and providing more expansive and involving story lines."

—*Booklist*

The Living Dead (with George A. Romero)

"A horror landmark and a work of gory genius."

—**Joe Hill**, *New York Times*-bestselling author of *The Fireman*

The Death and Life of Zebulon Finch

"A splendidly rendered, macabre picaresque, muscular and tender, imaginative and grotesque, cynical yet deeply moving. I was appalled one moment and laughing the next. Don't be fooled by the premise. This tale may be told by a dead man, but what's rendered here is life itself in all of life's absurd glory."

—**Rick Yancey**, *New York Times*-bestselling author of *The 5th Wave*

WRATH

WRATH

SHÄRON MOALEM
DANIEL KRAUS

UNION
SQUARE
& CO.

NEW YORK

**UNION
SQUARE
& CO.**

NEW YORK

This is a work of fiction. All characters, organizations, and events portrayed in this novel are either products of the author's imagination or are used fictitiously.

ISBN 978-1-4549-4522-2 (hardcover)
ISBN 978-1-4549-4661-8 (e-book)

For information about custom editions, special sales, and premium purchases, please contact specialsales@unionsquareandco.com.

Manufactured in the United States of America

2 4 6 8 10 9 7 5 3 1

unionsquareandco.com

Cover and interior illustration © Eric Nyquist
Interior design: Gavin Motnyk

To all the pets we have loved and learned from:

Gooshy, Skydog, Junior, Carl, Rudy, Merv, Bunny, and Mugsy

WRATH

RATTUS
NORVEGICUS

1

The San Jose Civic seats 3,036. With stage lights at max wattage, just as he directed, Noah Goff can't see but shadows of the assembled. This is how he likes it. To view the crowd as 3,036 individuals, each with the power to deride or heckle, is to fall into a trap. It's a trap Noah learned to skirt as a child, the weird, brainy dork in rural Iowa. Lots of pain in those traps, lots of humiliation.

No, it's safer to think of the crowd as a *herd*.

In the dark, they watch. They sniff. They chatter.

Noah exhales and nods at Sienna—who looks queasy—and strides for the stage.

Lights blast on in sync with a melodramatic boom from the Civic's subwoofers. It's like an army of pest controllers blasting flashlights down a manhole. Noah sees the twitching of thousands of heads as the herd watches him arrive. They lift their noses to sniff for treats. They squeak, too: their shoes against the floor as they stand to clap their paws.

Noah hits center stage. A table. A black sheet. A covered object. The spotlight is as hot as oil. He nods humbly but not too humbly. Fans expect a little swagger. Noah paces a circle and pumps a fist. He wears boutique jeans tailored to fit, a crisp pink hoodie, and the ultra-rare Nike x MSCHF Air Max 97 Jesus Shoes, the soles filled with holy water from the Jordan River—he's literally walking on water. Finally, there's his frayed, six-year-old baseball cap with the EditedPets logo—the letters *EP* within the outline of a nondescript mammalian head. The cap sends a message: *I'm a regular guy too.*

He's not, though. Noah has never considered himself regular.

Behind him, a gargantuan screen radiates the company slogan:

pets, reinvented.

Noah adjusts his head mic. It's like affixing a grin.

"Good morning."

Two words amplified a million-fold. The resonance is godlike.

More applause as the company slogan cedes to a live shot. Five-foot-six Noah Goff becomes a fifty-six-foot kaiju. Noah gestures for the herd to sit, and after a while it does. Their energy, however, doesn't abate. Noah plugs into it, the best sensation he's felt in his thirty-six years of life.

"I'm Noah." No surname among friends. "For those of you who don't know me but somehow managed to end up at a ticketed event at nine in the morning,"—pause for chuckles—"I'm the founder and CEO of a biotech company called EditedPets. We use patented RNA-guided DNA-nicking INTR"—shrewdly pronounced *Enter*—"technology to control how, when, and where genes are activated in order to revolution-ize our relationship with our animal companions." He smiles. "A lot of acronyms. Let me explain what they mean for you."

Noah holds a clicker. If all goes well, and it sure the fuck better, a flex of his thumb will advance the screen behind him. He tries it—*click*—and knows it worked from the 4K glow. The screen shifts to a faux-naïve ani-mation of the EP logo, waddling like a puppy across a white void. The herd laughs. "On June 29, 2007, Apple released the iPhone. Data tells us that three out of four of you here today have an iPhone in your pocket. Turned off, I'm sure, per our polite request."

More chuckling. Good. Now, shift the tone. Noah quits pacing and employs a gesture to project sincerity.

"There's no question Apple revolutionized human communication. But humans only make up thirty-six percent of mammals and only zero-point-zero-one percent of all animals. Our mission at EditedPets is to evolve our relationship with the *other* ninety-nine-point-ninety-nine percent of us. Beginning with the animals we already love—our pets."

Click. The scene scintillates with waves that suggest a flashback. We meet a cartoon caveman by a fire and a wolf pacing the periphery. "We first befriended the wolf 14,500 years ago. Call it what you like. A one-in-a-million chance? A cosmic fluke? But when your planet has nearly *nine million species,* the odds of such flukes get a little bit better. So how'd it happen? Let's watch."

Click. The animation swoops closer. Man and wolf blink big Disney eyes at each other.

"Wolves aren't big on eye contact. They communicate via sound and scents. But this wolf here has got a genetic quirk that compels him to maintain eye contact with our caveman—and that's all it takes. Flash forward 150 centuries and what do we get?"

Click. A YouTube video. Designer-bred puppies rush the camera, a downy tumble of big eyes, stubby snouts, recessed chins, severe under-bites, and hilarious hairdos. They lick the lens. The herd squirms. The cuteness is painful.

"You get Cockapoos. You get Puggles, Schnoodles, Pomskies, Cavachons, Chiweenies, Pitskies, and Chugs. In a sense, they're *all* edited pets—and we wouldn't have them any other way. But their modifications took fifty, a hundred, two hundred years. In an iPhone world, that's a flip-phone speed."

Click. A new animation depicts an object rocking beneath a black sheet—a mirror of the hidden object on the stage. EditedPets fans sense the big reveal edging close. Shoes scuffle, chairs creak, breaths are drawn. No Jobs, Bezos, Dorsey, Gates, Musk, or Zuckerberg have ever heard such sounds of naked yearning. Nothing they can do with plastic and ceramic-glass will ever supplant flesh and blood.

Noah experiences an unexpected rush of grateful tears before tamping it down. If they could see him now: the high school bullies, the college naysayers, the scientists who said it couldn't or shouldn't be done, the investors who said, neat idea, kid, but you're nuts. Actually, they *can* see him now. They are at home, watching the livestream. Some are right here in the Civic, hanging on his every word.

He's got them right where he fucking wants them.

Click.

✖

"FireFish—how many of you had one? How many of you had *two*? Two *dozen*?"

Even puking into a garbage can backstage, Sienna Aguirre notices Noah's tense: *had*, not *have*. Her boss may be cocky, but he can read a sales report. Those fish are yesterday's Actinopterygil.

She wipes her lips with the back of her hand, then looks for something to wipe the back of her hand with. She's got a half-finished origami frog in her pocket, folded from the event program, but it won't clean much. Instead, she grabs one of the black curtains masking the stage wings. A pebble of knowledge from a college theater class dislodges from her neocortex. This curtain is called a *tormentor*.

How perfect. She ought to rip it down, wear it as a cloak.

Sienna shuffles away from Noah in search of bottled water. But she can't escape his high-decibel rehash of EditedPets's first success. Fire-Fish are six years old now; in tech, that makes them as nostalgic as an Atari. Right now the crowd is reliving the awe they felt the first time they plunked down $7.99 for a FireFish, turned off their living room lights, and watched its thirty-one bioluminescent scales go incandescent, its pulse somehow mistakable for that of God.

Even Sienna had felt it—and she'd been the one to engineer it! Noah failed hourly at basic niceties but excelled at showy gifts, and to celebrate EditedPets's first success, he'd delivered to Sienna's Nolita apartment a deluxe seventy-five-gallon aquarium and fifty FireFish, and reupped the fish each year on her birthday. The school produced an amorphous, bubbling glow for a couple years, and it did, for a while, inspire her.

But pets, even edited ones, are a risky addition to the lifestyle of a woman who works twelve-hour days and often sleeps at the lab. After her fertility issues and Isaiah leaving, her FireFish began to go belly-up at disturbing rates. It's become her ritual of shame: arrive at home, pour a shot, slug it down, trudge to the tank, and see how many little miracles she's managed to murder.

Dead, they neither glow nor inspire. They are cold, slimy, disposable.

Like me, Sienna thinks. *Cold, for sure. Maybe slimy, too, if I take a hard look.*

"Six years ago we were the first company to produce and patent a genetically modified pet," Noah says from the stage. "We started small. Very small: an inch and a half. But the *effect* wasn't small, was it?"

Sienna finds the table of waters, grabs one, and twists the lid with a hard crack, the sound of a lab animal's snapped neck. She drinks to wash away the vomit tang. She was at this morning's rehearsal and knows what's next on the monitor: eight animated FireFish morphing into a number:

18,134,000

"Over eighteen million FireFish sold in our first twelve months," Noah declares. "You liked them so much, we couldn't keep up!"

Hoots and clapping, all for Noah. Sienna doesn't mind. She's the tall, ink-haired, thirty-seven-year-old geneticist who rifles through DNA code and cuts-and-pastes physical and behavioral traits. But a genius product sells better when associated with one genius, not two, and certainly not a whole team. When FireFish took off, and Noah Goff was on every cable news show, above the fold in the *New York Times*, and on the cover of *Newsweek*, each dollar in the EditedPets coffers said that he, and he alone, was the seer he'd always believed.

Sienna finishes the water, chucks the bottle. The glory days *were* glorious. Running prime editing genetic experiments at their first lab, a cramped rental space in a tech park off the Long Island Expressway. Noah popping in between fundraising jaunts to urge her to fail faster. Perfecting INTR to optimize the insertion of firefly genes into fertilized goldfish eggs. Breaking her four-year sobriety to celebrate with champagne, which begat wine, which begat liquor, which begat the end of her marriage.

Noah helped her by being Noah, always pushing, always demanding. Work offered Sienna handholds from her drunken, divorced crevasse. She might be sick with anxiety today, but she was upright, wasn't she?

Shit to do: it has reliably been what has saved her.

And Noah Goff *always* has shit for her to do.

※

"One year later, EditedPets released the groundbreaking ChattyBird."

Noah braces for a modest response. While an entire generation has a reflex love for FireFish, there's less so for ChattyBird. Noah thumbs the clicker. Let's get through these slides quick.

The modest sales of ChattyBird still sting. All those nights free-associating with Sienna about how to get the ZNF541, EBF3, and RSPH3 genes of African Parrots to play nice inside a plump and cheaper little budgie body. All the days ginning up investors while Sienna made the science work. From a genetic standpoint, the triumph was indisputable: ChattyBird trebled a budgie's proficiency at replicating human speech and, at $175, at a small fraction of the cost.

But what had Stephen Colbert said the day of ChattyBird's debut?

Never has driving your family up the freaking wall been easier on the wallet.

Gags like that hardened the narrative before EditedPets could redirect it. ChattyBird was a nifty trick, reviewers said, but lacked the soul of FireFish. It didn't *enhance* gatherings of family and friends, it *was* the gathering, and that got old faster than ChattyBird's warranted lifetime of seven to ten years.

Noah laughed along to the joke on CNBC; on Fox Business, he compared ChattyBird to talkative relatives—you still loved them, right? When the interview replayed later in Noah's SoHo penthouse loft, he selected the five-iron from the seventy-thousand-dollar set of Honma Five Star Golf Clubs he'd never used and bashed in the screen of his eighty-five-inch Samsung Smart 8K.

Click, click, click. Noah rapidly moves through marvels.

"A year after that, the acclaimed EasyPony."

The third EditedPets launch in three years. Sienna argued against it. Too much, too fast, too expensive, she said, a reaction that disappointed Noah. Had Jobs ever said *too much*? Does Musk ever say *too fast*?

Sienna and a stripped-down staff delivered EasyPony on time. The idea was to insert a mutated DMRT3 gene into the embryo cells of a Shetland pony, bequeathing the Shetland with the storied "Tölt gait," a four-beat lateral amble found only in Icelandic horses. Noah recalls persuading Sienna to climb atop the prototype EasyPony. She'd never touched a saddle in her life, but in seconds it was like she'd been riding her whole life. If Noah's ex-shrink, Dr. Clive, had still been around, he'd tell Noah to celebrate Sienna's smile—that was what was important in life.

But Dr. Clive doesn't have a budget of $125 million to manage and a twelve-person board to appease.

At a price point of $2,500, EasyPony was intended to be EditedPets's scale offering. If they even did five percent of their FireFish business, they'd clear a nice profit. But upscale buyers proved stubborn. Equestrians had a streak of cowboy pride, and publicly ridiculed EasyPony.

Noah felt bereft, betrayed. EasyPony was a $125 million flop. Once knighted by *Forbes* as "the fastest-growing billion dollar plus consumer deliverable biotech," EditedPets began to hemorrhage money. The NASDAQ listing dropped from $475 per share to under twenty-five bucks. It drove Noah into the office of Dr. Clive, who urged him to accept the word *flop*, repeat it, take a bath in it. Three weeks later, Noah swore off therapy for good. A palliative for the pathetic. Not him. Noah Goff was no *flop*.

EditedPets retains tremendous goodwill from FireFish. Ninety seconds more of his speech and the product under the sheet will be revealed. It will save EditedPets. It will save him.

Sienna has nearly finished the origami frog by the time she peeks from the stage-left wing. It's a hobby she picked up from Dr. Suzuki Mika, her

PhD supervisor at Columbia, who always left a trail of paper animals and flowers. Hoping to squash phone addiction, Sienna picked it up. Now she can complete her favorite patterns via muscle memory. A few reverse folds and the frog will be finished.

She peeks past the tormentor curtains. Noah gestures to the shape under the sheet. Seats creak as the crowd leans in. What sort of pet will it be?

For a while, Noah and Sienna hadn't been sure either.

A series of disasters had forced their hand. First, there was the outbreak of users flushing FireFish down toilets. By the time EasyPony launched, huge glowing carp were being spotted in the Hudson River—after EditedPets had promised the EPA that all their products were sterile. A federal probe led to EditedPets being fined fifteen million. A small sum given their degree of negligence. They were lucky not to have been shut down. Next came the global #FreeChatty trend of users letting their verbose pets take wing in the countryside. Now rumors of budgies replicating human speech are everywhere. It's a chilling notion: Sienna imagines quiet neighborhoods and parks ruined by babbling nonsense from the trees. The final insult was a string of viral photos of EasyPonies gone obese. The pet had proven so docile that users had quit exercising them.

Sienna got the message: EditedPets's next launch had to change the narrative.

Noah steps to the edge of the stage. He frowns in faux confusion. In real life, the look isn't in his repertoire.

"And then what happened? Where the heck did EditedPets go for three years?"

Light laughter. *Good tactic*, Sienna thinks. *But hurry up already.*

"The truth is, you *know* what happened," Noah says. "A little bug called Covid-19 changed everything. EditedPets shut its doors, same as everyone. But the instant we were able to put safety protocols into place, a select team of scientists returned to our labs."

Statements like these make Sienna reach for invisible highballs. Covid-19 had shit-all to do with the EditedPets slowdown. Noah had nasopharyngeal kits before most hospitals.

The lawsuits slowed them, plain and simple. Privately, Sienna was glad for the space to breathe, even if it meant daily innuendos of laziness from Noah. He could suck a dick. Pasteur, Jenner, Lister, Salk—none of them had accomplished so much in such a short span of time. And none of them had had to match the shifting proclivities of public appetite fueled by social media.

Noah had scores of investors to woo and wounds to lick. Sienna did her own licking: the bottoms of tumblers when her bottles ran dry. She wasn't proud. She just needed to keep a nice buzz going so she could get enough sleep to tackle the Big One. The product that would shoot Edited-Pets into the stratosphere of Apple, Microsoft, Amazon, and Google—or bury it in the boneyard alongside Palm, Quibi, Betamax, and Edsel.

Noah reaches for the black sheet.

"We have, of course, put out refreshed product. During Covid, we knew you'd want to show off new styles of FireFish; and by intermingling jellyfish genes, we were able to offer you the FireFish Hope line, in pink, yellow, red, purple, and limited-edition gold—and I gotta say, they looked great on your Zooms."

Sienna engineered the Hope line with as little trouble as the origami frog. Novelty acts to keep EditedPets in the news. What people really wanted was clear from the market research.

They wanted a pet that was smart. *Who* was smart—they wanted a pet they can think of as a *who*, a companion capable of engaging with them at a whole new level.

Noah's fingers pinch the black sheet. He glances left and locks eyes with Sienna. Her breath leaves her. It's nothing romantic. She's seen Noah in too many states of petulance, irritability, indignation, self-pity, and furor to ever find him attractive. But to be the sole recipient of his attention while thousands hold their breath—it still does something to her.

Sienna smiles back. Fake, until it isn't.

"Ladies and gentlemen," Noah announces, "I'd like you to meet . . . Sammy."

It's a rat.

But not like any rat Leonard Przybyszewski has chased off, trapped, clubbed, squashed, impaled, starved, poisoned, or gassed. Or seen up-close at EditedPets either. As the company's security guy, he's permitted in the lab, but is content to relax in his security cubby across the hall. Unlike every other piece of equipment Noah buys, the security cameras suck. Probably on purpose. Through those hunks of junk, Prez can barely make out humans, much less anything specific about lab rats.

Noah Goff goes double-volume.

"In the thousands of years since our caveman pal met that friendly wolf, there hasn't been a single significant advance in the human–animal relationship. That all changes with Sammy—the first pet to be designed, at a molecular level, with *human intelligence genes.*"

The crowd gasps, then claps, then whoops, then pops jerkily to their feet as if pulled by marionette strings. The noise complicates—squeals, stomps, screams—then evolves into the bombination of a swarm of bees. Somehow the crowd knows this is what they have waited for, their whole lives.

Prez, though, isn't so sure.

He's not even sure what he's *doing* here. Right now, he's standing and clapping to keep his undercover status secret. Mr. Goff stationed him here in the front row in case something went wrong. But what could go wrong besides the little fella getting nervous and scurrying into the crowd? He didn't bother asking Mr. Goff. He's come to recognize when the boss man is in no mood to get specific.

Back when EditedPets had put out their glowy fish, blabby bird, and hobby horse, Prez had been working at Przybyszewski & Sons Pest Control, the small business he'd inherited from his white Polish adopted dad. Now he's in year three of handling lab security for EditedPets. The first nine-to-five hours he's worked in his life. About time, too. He's fifty-six. Forty-five pounds overweight. Needs to piss every two goddamn hours. Bunch a plaque crudding up his arteries, if Doc Kowalski is to be believed. Then there's the bellowing bitches of his knees; major-league catchers have nothin' on ratters, Pop used to say.

Mr. Goff quiets the crowd, but no one's sitting. That means Prez, too, has to stay on his sore feet and throbbing knees. Truth be told, he's as rapt as anyone. Is the boss man pulling everyone's legs here?

"Now let's get this out of the way," Noah Goff laughs. "What you see inside this pen here is a rat. Yep, you heard me right—one of those sneaky little guys that inspired movie gangsters to say stuff like, 'You dirty rat.' But I ask you. Does this fella look sneaky? Does he look creepy? Does he look dirty?"

Anyone who's watched Prez kiss Smog, his Jack Russell Terrier, right on the mouth knows he's not immune to cuteness. He just never dreamed he'd feel such an instinct toward a *rat*.

"Whether you're looking at a box of puppies or perusing cats at a local shelter, first impressions matter. Don't feel bad about it—the features we find endearing are hardwired into our brains. So we genetically adjusted Sammy to ensure that your instant response to him is one of joy and love." Noah Goff grins. "Worked, didn't it?"

Prez estimates he's met fifty thousand rats in his life. In New York, that means *Rattus norvegicus*, also known by a bevy of criminal aliases: Brown Rat, Street Rat, Sewer Rat, Wharf Rat, Common Rat, or, in the hoods Prez used to work, That Giant Motherfucking Rat Right There. And every single one of these rats had an identical physical profile.

First off, a wedge-shaped head that melts into its body, all the better with which to push through the smallest holes. Sammy's head, though, better resembles a kitten's: domed, definably necked. Where *Rattus norvegicus*'s nose is mercilessly aquiline, Sammy's nose is a plump button atop a pudgy muzzle. In public like this, the beady eyes of a typical *Rattus norvegicus* would be jerking wildly. Sammy's eyes are big and round, and he blinks curiously at the crowd. When he stands on his hind legs for a better look, showing off a rounded back and fuzzy haunches, the audience makes a sound that Prez, one minute ago, never would have believed.

Awwww.

He feels a squeeze. The woman next to him has clutched his forearm and doesn't seem to realize it. Prez likes to call this the Lenny syndrome, after the gentle giant in *Of Mice and Men,* who liked soft animals so much he hugged them to death.

Prez doesn't like rats. But he respects the hell out of them. Ask him and he'll tell you that rats have gotten the best of him for forty years, no matter how many he's slain. But Sammy is the most inviting rat Prez has ever seen. He wonders if he's feeling Lenny Syndrome too. When Sammy cocks his head, Prez cocks his own.

But his hands act on muscle memory. They instinctively reach for traps, bait, a bludgeon: the ratting gear he gave up three years back.

Until this second, Noah has controlled the drama: clicker in palm, rat in cage. Now the dynamic must change. A bead of sweat rolls down the center of his back, shockingly cold. He used to sweat like this as an adolescent, sitting in class, praying he wouldn't be called or, god forbid, be asked to stand in front of the class, where everyone would see his wet pits and mock his mortified pallor.

Part of it is nerves. But part of it is that Noah hates rats. *Hates* them. Working in labs, where rodents are the commonest test subjects, Noah has forced himself to power through his revulsion, or get someone else to handle those squirming, flexing bodies. He's come a long way but knows the loathing will never subside. How could it? He was only nine years old when Grammy—

Stop, he orders himself. *Don't think of it, not right now.*

This is *his* classroom. He's in charge.

Click.

"What you're looking at here is the Sammy PlayPen. It's got everything you need. Safety ramps. Comfort shelves. Hammocks. A spiral slide. Optional wheels. Effortless to clean. Available in both Wow Fluorescent for the playroom and Dusty Rose for the office. It's great fun for you, the user, and a cozy place for Sammy. But it's sold separately. Why do I mention that specifically?"

With a practiced flip of both thumbs, Noah undoes the PlayPen's dual locks, spins his hands, and lifts off the lid. Scattered cheers. But also a second bead of sweat. Him, handling a rat, in front of all these people? Awful close to standing in front of a classroom.

"Because you're not *required* to have a PlayPen. Unlike a pet gerbil, hamster, mouse, chinchilla, or ferret, Sammy doesn't need, and doesn't want, to be treated like a prisoner. He should be treated like . . . a friend."

Here we go, he thinks.

Noah extends his arm into the open cage. No risk of harm, he knows this. Yet he still feels what a lion tamer must feel when putting his head into a set of jaws. He thinks he knows what will happen—but he doesn't truly know, does he? Ugly memories flicker. Grammy—the squeaking—the chittering.

Sammy twitches his nose at Noah's arm. Tilts his head. Locks his eyes with Noah's.

None of the rat eyes Noah has seen in his life do what Sammy's do. It's hard to put it into words. There's a certain weight, a certain piercing. Human eyes are weaponized with *want*. Not just for food and shelter, but connection. Sammy's eyes want something too.

Noah makes a *kiss-kiss*. Sammy's whiskers perk and his cubby ears flatten, then he hops onto Noah's hand and rushes up the ramp of his arm. It's never pleasant when rats go rogue in the lab. Their feet are five-digited but otherwise resemble those of a chicken: too long, roughly rippled, dagger-clawed. But this rat's feet are soft as velvet.

Sammy perches on Noah's shoulder. He's six inches long, three-quarters the length of the average brown rat, with a tail only three inches in length, giving it the bobtail charm of a Corgi. Static electricity from the PlayPen emphasizes the softness of Sammy's teddy-bear fur; backlit by stage lights, it stands cutely askew. Sammy pops onto his haunches and touches his nose to Noah's lips: a kiss.

To Sammy: "Thanks, Sammy." To everyone: "Sammy wasn't trained to do that, folks. He did it because I asked. Because he understands the English language."

The crowd struggles to verbalize their emotions. They make airy noses, like breath through an open saxophone, before breaking into inchoate squeals, shapeless yawps, bodily motions that look short-circuited. There is no comparing this to the reaction to FireFish, Chatty-Bird, or EasyPony. Their need to touch Sammy feels almost dangerous.

Maybe we set the price point too low, Noah thinks.

✖

Relief crashes over Sienna. She sees a plastic crate, drags it over, dumps herself atop it, drops the origami frog. Her legs judder. Her fingers and toes are numb. Her chest prickles, the release of anxious blood.

"We fucking did it," she says.

She hears the teary hitch in her own voice. She laughs at it. She doesn't give a shit about backstage signage demanding silence. She cups her face in her hands and lets laughter jag forth. A month ago, she'd asked Noah to delay the launch. Two weeks ago, she'd begged him. Five days ago, she'd gotten down on her knees, a disgusting scene in front of her techs.

But Noah had been right.

Thirty seconds outside the PlayPen and already the rat is a star.

Sienna lifts her face to watch. Noah paces comfortably. Sammy stays on his shoulder, bobbing his head, eager for a better look at the crowd.

"Everyone here instinctively understands the health benefits of pets," Noah says. "But let me tell you what science says. Having a pet lowers blood pressure, emboldens physical activity, and can be a game-changer when it comes to depression. A child growing up with furred pets is less likely to develop allergies and more likely to develop a robust immune system. Alzheimer's patients with pets experience far fewer anxious outbursts. And if you thought walking your *dog* was a good way to make a love connection . . . wait till that could-be romantic partner gets a load of Sammy."

Noah peaks an eyebrow. Sienna laughs. In moments like this, when everything is going right, she can't help but forgive this asshole for all the shit he drags her through.

The choice of a rat, for instance. Noah fought her for months in the cold storage room they'd reimagined as a mess hall, over Cantonese rice rolls, Chinese crab pockets, Colombian arepas del queso, Egyptian lemon ta'ameya, and Vietnamese pork bánh mì. During a pandemic lockdown, only a United Nations of takeout had kept them from strangling each other.

Sienna wasn't blind. Her boss had a *thing* about rats. He covered it with excuses. No animal on Earth came with worse baggage than the rat, he argued. After Covid-19, would rats make people think of the Black Death? Plus, rats were ugly! Look at those fucking yellow teeth. Sienna kept pushing. Rats were the world's most common lab animal for a reason: they shared organs, nervous systems, and hormones with humans. They are capable of metacognition, that analysis of consequences generally reserved for primates. They were social, affectionate, caring, clean, self-reliant, and capable of happiness, affection, even laughter.

It was a regular Monday morning at the lab when Sienna heard Noah enter through the negative-pressure vestibule and march to her desk. He let a piece of paper float toward her table. She had to snag it to keep it from touching her Cuban pastelitos.

The sheet collected X-rays and photographs of rats purposefully inflicted with hydrocephalus. Fluid had swollen the rats' brains enough to deform their skulls. No surprise there: mammal faces are defined by their brain shapes.

But the ballooned skulls of these hydrocephalic rats were *adorable*. To enlarge a rat's brain with human genes would be to make it physically irresistible. Noah saw this and admitted it, his phobia be damned. Now look how far he's come, handling a cavorting rat like it was no big thing. Sienna's heart goes out to him.

Until this instant, Sienna had never considered owning an Edited-Pet. It felt incestuous to both architect these animals and love them. And then there was the fact that fifty FireFish had died in her living room tank.

But maybe she'd done such a good job with Sammy that, with Isaiah gone and her womb a wasteland, she could look at one of these rats, look *into* it, and squeeze from its body the exact dose of affection she needed, like pus from an infected wound.

⋇

Mr. Goff returns to the table.

"So you're probably thinking, hey, Sammy seems like a great pet. He's friendly, affectionate, cute. But I want you to think way back to the Stone Age when Apple's primary product was the iPod. The iPod was cool, right? It played music really well. The iPhone could have been a similar device—a better way to call and text. But what Jobs did was make it modular. Now it's a camera. Now it's a TV. Now it's social media. But no matter how many gigabytes they cram into that thing, no matter how many billions of pulses the CPU sends out, it'll never equal the computing power of a brain with human genes."

From a shelf under the table, Mr. Goff picks up a tablet computer.

The woman to Prez's right lets go of his biceps, but now he feels a different pressure. Technology: the weight of grave dirt. Sure, he's got a smartphone, but he can only do four or five things on it, and about twice a week he collars one of EditedPets's marketing kids to unscrew shit he screwed up. At Przybyszewski & Sons he'd gotten a rep among other PCOs—Pest Control Operators—as an old-school luddite who eschewed high-tech bait stations, kevlar sleeves, and night-vision binoculars for the vintage tools he grew up with—metal traps, copper mesh, the naked eye.

Tech suffocates Prez more than any cellar crawlspace or sewage tunnel. Until this point, he's followed Mr. Goff's presentation, but now feels the vague, slipping grief he's come to associate with being fifty-six years old. The truth is, this is why he sold Przybyszewski & Sons—his adopted father's business, routes, his contracts—to Ecofix Pest Solutions, the biggest pest-control biz in the boroughs.

Because he was afraid of progress.

Him. Prez. Who, since being the only Black kid on his Greenpoint block, had the rep of being unafraid of anything.

"FireFish, ChattyBird, EasyPony," Mr. Goff says. "Those were iPods. Sammy's an iPad."

Mr. Goff turns on the tablet, holds it high. In the upper left-hand corner is a single app. Prez knows what an app is: you tap it and stuff happens. Through some wizardry, the tablet's display is mirrored on the giant screen, taking up the left half while the live-feed takes the right. The *EP* logo fills the screen as the app loads.

The crowd leans in. Prez finds himself leaning away. The app opens to reveal a strange touchscreen keyboard, each key labeled not with a letter but a cartoon symbol. A smiling sun. Theater masks. Thumbs-up. Thumbs-down. A clock. A house. A hammer striking a nail. Body parts, too: eyes, mouth, nose, feet. It may be tech, but Prez deduces its purpose along with the crowd, which explodes into cheers.

It's a translation tool. For a rat.

"You gotta be *kidding* me," Prez mutters.

Mr. Goff beams. "The first tool we're offering, free with every purchase of Sammy, is SammySpeaks. It's an AAC device—Augmentative and Alternative Communication. Those of you with loved ones unable to use verbal speech know how liberating an AAC can be. We hired the world's top speech pathologists to design this one, which allows Sammy to speak directly to you. What he needs, what he wants, what he's thinking, what he'd like to express. There's no more guessing, folks, no false anthropomorphizing." His voice rises with emphasis. "*You will know what your pet is thinking.*"

The applause is deafening. Mr. Goff rests the tablet on a forty-five-degree stand and extends his arm as a ramp. Sammy scurries down the arm, popping to his hind legs in front of the glowing tablet. One of his tiny pink paws reaches out and presses an icon. The output trills pleasantly from the theater's speakers.

"*Thank you.*"

Isolated cries of delight from the crowd. Prez is taken aback. It's incredible. Can it be real?

The AAC's voice is that of a confident, straightforward ten-year-old boy.

Mr. Goff leans over the rat. "You're welcome, Sammy. How are you feeling today?"

Sammy looks at him, tilts his head in thought, then turns back to the tablet, pressing a combination of keys. A second's pause, then the finished words emit.

"*I feel good. I smell lots of people.*"

The whole place laughs. Mr. Goff chuckles.

"That's right. There's a lot of people here. Is there anything you'd like to ask them?"

Prez can't believe it: Sammy faces the audience, his head rising a bit, then falling, like he's trying to absorb what he can before formulating a query. He returns to the keys.

"*I'm thirsty. Do people have water?*"

More laughter. Mr. Goff shrugs in apology.

"I'm sorry about that, Sammy. We'll get you some water soon, is that all right?"

Sammy uses both paws, a good typist.

"*Yes. Lights bright, Noah.*"

Mr. Goff gazes into the balcony. "Can we dim the stage lights just a bit?" As the lights respond, Mr. Goff looks at the crowd. "In its natural state, Sammy's species is nocturnal. Even if they were trained to adopt a human sleep cycle, they'd always revert back. We realized early on this wasn't ideal for a user's playtime with Sammy."

Prez notices Mr. Goff is doing verbal gymnastics to avoid the word *rat*. He hasn't uttered the R-word once since the first time.

"Some of you may recall a news story about people who only require four hours of sleep a night—a trait I wouldn't mind myself. It's due to a lucky gene mutation called *ADRB1*. We treated Sammy to multiple copies of this gene, and folks, not only is Sammy diurnal—awake during the day—but he only requires two hours of sleep per night. This is good news for users, as Sammy will spend those awake hours actively developing his human genes. And amusing himself in the PlayPen, if you pick one of those up too."

Mr. Goff points to himself humbly.

"You might have noticed Sammy used my name. Sure, Noah is a pretty easy name to say. But it doesn't matter if your name is Bob or Pragyaparamita. You can actually upload photos and pronunciations of yourself and others into custom buttons in SammySpeaks. Because our AAC uses the latest predictive text technology, Sammy's sentences will be smoother and more easily understood than the average child in the four-to-eight age range."

Mr. Goff looks back at the attentive rat.

"Sammy, how many keys does SammySpeaks have?"

Sammy swipes left. It's the same short, testy gesture people in the crowd use all day, and they squeak in joyful recognition. Prez feels hot. Is it shame? This rat is better on a gadget than him.

A second screen, eighty-four more icons, then a third, fourth, fifth, sixth.

The rat is *counting*.

"Five hundred and four keys," Sammy says.

"Almost all of which," Mr. Goff says to the crowd, "Sammy can expand via a long press, opening up a vocabulary of over *eight thousand words*. And that's not all. As Sammy learns new words, he can use a system of audio sliders to replicate the syllables and morphemes to create a key, thereby adding it to the vocabulary. For example . . ."

Mr. Goff faces Sammy.

"Sammy, what's your favorite song by that British rock group from Liverpool?"

Sammy swipes and selects, seemingly excited to reply.

"'Ob-La-Di, Ob-La-Da,'" Sammy says.

On perfect cue, the opening piano notes warble through the auditorium speakers, soon joined by the famous refrain. Now, the Beatles, *that's* something Prez knows about. Almost instantly his head starts bobbing along with the music. But when he sees Sammy on the big screen, bobbing his wee noggin too, Prez forces himself to stop.

He's being manipulated, and he doesn't like it.

"I promise you," Mr. Goff shouts over the music, "that this song title doesn't come baked into SammySpeaks. But we played the song at Edited-Pets, and our clever little friend here picked it up.

Without prompting, the hypnotized audience gives a full-throated rendition of the song's refrain. Prez feels himself lifted—the Beatles can do that to even a Black adopted Pole—but it's also a little creepy. Upon the stage, Mr. Goff signals for the music to fade out and gives the audience a few seconds to recompose.

"I bet you didn't see that coming," he laughs. "A singing pet that can inspire you to belt out a song in front of thousands of strangers. Speaking of voices, the way Sammy sounds is entirely up to you. Whether you prefer a squeaky soprano or a basso profundo, it's all in your settings. All we suggest is that you try to stick to a single voice. We'd prefer for your Sammy not to have an identity crisis."

More laughter. Then a shout from the dark:

"Can we ask him questions?"

Anything with crowd involvement triggers Prez's alarms. The most volatile situations he'd witnessed as a PCO were those with large groups present. People who get involved tend to panic. Rats are living mood rings: when they feel a shifting mood, they react to it, sometimes poorly.

"I think that's a great idea," Mr. Goff shouts back. "Someone go ahead."

Ten or twenty voices cry out at once. It's funny; Mr. Goff laughs. Blurts continue for ten seconds until, by some unspoken accord, the crowd seems to yield to a young woman in the center of the room.

Possible plant, Prez thinks. *Just like me.*

"Hi," the girl says. "My question is, if Sammy could do anything he wanted right now, what would it be?"

Mr. Goff nods and repeats the question to Sammy. The rat thinks for a second, then gets to swiping and typing.

"*I want sleep in grass. Also, still thirsty, Noah.*"

This call-back cracks up everyone except Prez.

What will the rat say, he wonders, *if we forget to give it a drink? If we starve it? If we make it mad?*

Growing up with seven siblings in Missoula, Montana, there were birthday parties roughly every two minutes. They were the happiest times of Sienna's youth, her face aching from so much smiling.

It's how she feels through the next three audience questions, all of them charmingly daft. Finally given the chance to pose a serious question to an actual animal, do these people ask about genetic memory? Self-awareness? What we, humans, are to Sammy, and what he, rat, is to us? Nope. The crowd reverts to a kindergarten state. *What's your favorite food? What's the most fun thing you've done?* A man in the back shouts the best question yet: *Do you have dreams?*

Sammy works his AAC like a whiz. Sienna grins. Her hands finish the origami frog all on their own.

"*Sometimes help dream of Noah. Sometimes dream of help food.*"

Sienna's smile freezes.

Did she just hear what she thought she'd heard?

She bolts up, locking knees, feeling faint. She drops the frog. Her emptied stomach clenches. She steps toward the stage and waves both arms at Noah in urgent semaphore. But he's at the edge of the stage now, fully engaged with the audience.

Sienna darts past tormentors, both of cloth and memory, and holds her badge from its lanyard so the security guard at the stairwell will let her pass. She takes the steps in threes, hitting the push bar with both hands, fuck how loud it is. She's submerged into a warm pool of humanity. The theater darkness is thumb-printed with pale faces, white seeds of teeth gleaming through idiot grins. She power-walks down the front row, kicking aside knapsacks and purses.

All at once there's Prez, the dunes of his beard clumped in patterns of repugnance. Sienna is hit by a swell of gratitude. Though Prez has spent the past three years in his cubby, Sienna has always felt his latent potential. She takes a fistful of his shirt and he jack-in-the-boxes up like he's been waiting. His big hand swallows her left shoulder and pulls her to the side aisle.

"What's up?" he whispers.

"Something wrong," she hisses.

Prez frowns. "Everything seems—"

Thonk.

They both look up at the stage.

Sammy is knocking his head against the side of the PlayPen.

Thonk, thonk.

Noah gives Sammy a curious look, as if to ask, *Did you mean to do that?* The crowd titters, wondering if the rat is being silly. Sammy repeats the behavior: *thonk, thonk, thonk.* The tablet with SammySpeaks slides from its stand, hitting the stage floor with a crash.

Noah blinks out at the crowd, suddenly speechless.

Sienna still dreams of having children, though post-Isaiah the dreams have deformed into nightmares: brain-damaged children rolling their bulging eyes as they slam their foreheads into walls: *thonk, thonk, thonk.* What Sienna birthed was inside the IVF incubators and centrifuges of EditedPets.

She shoves Prez.

"Backstage. Now."

They bound for the stairwell, flashing badges. Sienna glances right and sees Noah step around the table, scoop Sammy from the table, and flash the crowd a grin that, to Sienna, looks lunatic. The last thing she sees is Sammy *twisting.* Sienna's seen that spasm hundreds of times from hundreds of her lab rats right before they were restrained, anesthetized, or medically decapitated, when they toed the ledge of death and had no option left but to explode from docility, one last chance to stave off annihilation.

2

From the other side of the curtain, a rushed closing:

"And that, ladies and gentlemen, is just a teaser of what Sammy can do! If you want to play with Sammy yourself, come to Pet Expo on December 17th. That's when preorders will open—and it'll be your only chance to meet Sammy before he hits the market this summer. Thank you so much for coming out, and have a wonderful day!"

Mr. Goff cuts through the curtain toward Prez and Sienna, face purpling with rage, holding Sammy away from his body. This is the Noah Goff the San Jose Civic staff doesn't know but Prez has witnessed countless times at EditedPets. Backstage staff radiate the subdued jubilance of a successful event, and the stage manager is cruising toward the EditedPets trio. Because he's staring at his phone, he doesn't see Prez wave him away, Dr. Aguirre's appalled expression, or the convulsing rat Mr. Goff holds at arm's length.

"Congratulations," says the manager. "Sammy is the number one trending topic on—"

"*Clear the fucking stage!*" Mr. Goff roars. "*Everybody out!*"

The manager's face goes white. Theater staff freezes. Prez doesn't know what's going on but he knows how to scare off an alley full of rats, and what works for rats usually works for people. He raises his arms like a bear and charges in a semicircle, making sure his feet land hard as boulders.

"Out! Out! And close those doors!"

The backstage empties in seconds. With a disgusted shiver, Mr. Goff drops Sammy on the floor before backing off and wiping his hands on his pants.

Pink foam oozes from the rat's mouth.

"If a single one of these theater fucks gets video of this, we're fucked," Mr. Goff growls. "What? Sienna? Did someone poison him?"

"You want me to . . . ?" Prez doesn't say *kill it*, but they all hear it.

"I want you to go get the tablet and PlayPen. I'm not having some fanboy run off with eighteen months of development." He flaps his arms at Prez. "Go, go, go!"

Prez has been subject to Mr. Goff's infantile silences and bratty testiness, but he's never been yelled at by the man, and he doesn't care for it. Prez can't help but up-tilt his chin and puff out his chest. Goff might be his boss, but he's twenty years his junior, and there's such a thing as respect.

But Dr. Aguirre is on her knees now, awkward in a skirt, angling for a better view of the foaming, choking, writhing rat. Prez wants to help her, so fine, with a flash of his eyes to Mr. Goff—*Watch yourself, kid*—he lurches off, parts the curtain, and enters a different world: house lights up and blazing, three thousand people acting upon the all-clear to snap their photos and start texting.

Prez tucks the tablet into his waistband like a waiter and picks up the PlayPen. Then it's back into the dimmer environs.

Dr. Aguirre has lodged a pen in Sammy's mouth. Bloody foam pours around it. With every strike of Sammy's head against the floor, blood spatters from its ears and beads from its eyes. The noise the rat makes is terrible. Rats squeak. Rats trill. Rats huff. Rats hiss. Rats brux, the grinding down of their ever-growing teeth. This is something Prez has never heard, a fluttery, weepy sobbing.

Prez has seen rats die fast and rats die slow, and hasn't felt much either way. But no rat deserves to go like this.

"I can kill it," he says. "I just grab it behind the jaw and yank the base of its tail. Cervical dislocation. It won't even hurt—"

Mr. Goff snatches the tablet from Prez, gets to his knees, and holds the tablet right in front of the rat. He tries to adopt a happy voice.

"Sammy, tell me what's wrong."

Sammy turns his little bloody face toward Mr. Goff the same way Smog looks at Prez when he's in pain, a naked plea to his magical human to please fix what's wrong. Mr. Goff holds the tablet closer. Sammy looks at it, eyes vibrating, body shaking, and races his front paws over the screen.

"*Want help you find help bad stop find sleep help end stop feel help—*"

"Jesus," Prez groans. "Let me end this."

"*—slow end help you stop said help want end help hurt find stop—*"

Prez swipes the tablet out of Mr. Goff's hands. Goff looks up, snarling.

"The fuck are you doing?"

"It's in pain! Do something or I will!"

Goff rockets to his feet, gets in Prez's face, or at least eight inches below it.

"You'll do what I fucking say, Mr. Mousetrap! Now give me that—"

"He's dead." Dr. Aguirre's voice was soft but enough.

Mr. Goff's jaws clench. He closes his eyes.

"Do you have any idea . . ." he begins quietly.

"Any *idea*?" Dr. Aguirre snaps. "I told you what a risk we—"

"Any *fucking* idea, Sienna, what would have happened if Sammy started spewing blood in front of two million live-streamers? How fast that trending topic would have turned against us? One Reddit troll sees it and our stock gets shorted. I'd never be able to raise funds again. It's the end of my career. *All* our careers."

"I told you Sammy wasn't ready. I got down on my knees and—"

"It was your *job* to make him ready! This rat was six months old! Imagine this nice little death scene in a million homes while kids are watching!"

"Don't play dumb, Noah. Maybe you don't have the balls to look at the bodies, but you know damn well what's happing to our Sammys. Every one that gets human brain development genes ends up like this. Ugly, painful deaths."

Prez considers the dead animal between the bickering partners. How quickly rats are ignored, even genius ones. All that perky curiosity extinguished, those big, bright eyes as dull as slate. Goff pivots on his Nike heel, exhales loudly, and cycles his hand in a hurry-up gesture. "Something about the cranial vaults. One more time, with feeling."

Dr. Aguirre stands, gives Prez an apologetic glance, and speaks with edgy patience.

"Skulls are made up of plates, Noah. This is high school biology. After the brain finishes growing, the plates fuse together. If we're talking about the posterior frontal suture of a rat skull, same thing. But the *other* sutures, Noah, they stay open so a rat can squeeze its head through small holes. You said make me a rat with a cute skull and I said fine, but I'll have to fuse together those other sutures. This is the fact you refuse to deal with: without a way to *stop* a humanized rat brain from growing, it will get crushed by intracranial pressure every single time. Trillions of neuronal connections destroyed. Double vision, seizure, and, you might have noticed, a pretty miserable death."

Mr. Goff is twenty feet away now, hands on hips, facing an empty wing. Prez watches his back rise and fall.

"Pet Expo," Goff states. "Less than nine months away."

Ms. Aguirre laughs wildly. "Oh, sure, I can get a Sammy ready by Pet Expo. All I need to do is perform a fucking craniotomy so its swollen brain can pop out the top of its skull! Exposed brains—that'll go over gangbusters with kids!"

Goff speaks with hushed wrath. "I'll cancel that Pet Expo keynote over my dead body. Same deal with the on-sale date. The pre-sales we're going to generate at Pet Expo? They're going to save EditedPets. A company that, in case you forgot, is going to change the goddamn world."

Prez feels Ms. Aguirre's fire go cold. He feels the need to rise to her defense; he hates seeing this punk CEO win any kind of victory over the overworked doctor. But their shared phrases—*posterior frontal suture, intracranial pressure*—make him feel ill-equipped to get involved.

"If you still want to be a part of that, Sienna—a part of history? Then *nine months* is all I have to say. That's your deadline. I suggest getting to work."

That's it. Mr. Goff walks away. The blackness takes him.

Dr. Aguirre shudders. Prez offers a supportive smile. Her eyes shine. Tears? Prez can't tell. Her shrug is small and embarrassed.

"I'll figure something out," she says.

Prez wants to give her a hug. But he's read the HR memos. You don't do that anymore. So he just nods. She forges a smile and looks down at the useless dead rat that, ten minutes ago, everyone in the building wanted to take home.

"Prez, could you . . . we don't need the body. And I'd rather not pack a dead rat into my luggage if I don't—"

"No sweat," Prez says. "I'll get rid of it."

"Can you do it so—"

"So no one sees," Prez assures her. "You got it, Dr. Aguirre."

Dr. Aguirre smiles weakly.

"Call me Sienna. I should have insisted years ago."

She nods a goodbye, eyes shining again, and takes the same exit as Mr. Goff. Prez notices her glance at a crate. On top of it is what looks like an origami frog. She's dropped dozens of such foldings at Prez's desk for his amusement.

Once she's gone, doors click open from both backstage wings, and the San Jose Civic staff files back in. No time to lose. Prez hunkers down and scoops up the rat with brand-new tenderness. It's as still as any origami. Maybe he always should have been this gentle. Rats live where we live, eat what we eat. In this way, they are our children. Prez thinks of his dog, Smog, an adopted son just like him.

Prez opens his jacket and settles the rat inside. The weight is so slight, the body still warm. He's had far worse things in his pocket.

INTERACTOME

3

Noah never sleeps as deeply as he does on a plane.

Biologically speaking, he gets it. At cruising altitude, air pressure is low, which means less oxygen absorbed into the brain, which results in drowsiness. Cabins also have half the humidity of most indoor spaces, and dryness amplifies inertia. The white noise seals the deal. Noah usually fights back with Adderall—there's always work to be done—but he didn't sleep at all last night, choosing to salt his post-launch wounds by compulsively refreshing the #EditedPets tag on every known social site, waiting for rumor to rise of Sammy's seizure and death.

He found nothing. Only awe and praise. Maybe everything's going to be okay. He reclines his business-class seat, straps on a sleep mask, and lets the flight's amniotic atmosphere lull him.

Another thing about planes: they intensify Noah's dreams.

This particular dream is the worst, because it's not a dream at all. It's a memory. He's nine years old. He lives in Coop, Iowa, a flat, pale mud hole where two hundred residents pick ticks from grass that's always yellow and shoot tin cans, or stray dogs, or themselves when the desolation envelops them. Even at nine, Noah is bright; he knows the town is adroitly named.

He lives in a dark, moist house with his mother, Pat; his father, Arthur; older sisters Dinah and Tamar; and their grandmother, known as Grammy. Dinah and Tamar are developmentally disabled. Each is double his weight and far stronger. Sometimes they pin him so he can't move, and take off his clothes, and pull on his thing. His parents don't seem to have jobs like regular people, though they get checks in the mail.

They fish, hunt, and trap. The house smells like blood, the salt sludge of deer, the tinny fluid of fish.

In the back of the house, in her own room, lies Grammy. Something's wrong with Grammy. Through the door, her breath gurgles as if through pudding. She coughs, she weeps, she snores. Noah hates to go in there but sometimes is forced to spoon soup past her hairy, rippling lips, or run a damp rag over her bedsores, or empty her bedpan. The urine stench is dizzying. Noah thinks that's what's peeling the wallpaper.

But Grammy thinks it's the rats.

There's no doubt there's rats in the walls. And mice under the floor. Bedbugs in the sheets. Ants in the kitchen. Termites in the siding. Silverfish in the shitter. And cockroaches in the ceiling, from which they like to parachute down into cereal bowls at breakfast. All over the house, pest poison sits out in the open. It's what killed all seven or eight of their cats.

One night, Noah is left alone in the house. Something to do with Dinah's and Tamar's school, maybe. Most nine-year-old kids would love a night of freedom. He knows where Mom hides her lemon drops. He knows where Dad hides his *Penthouse*.

But he's not really alone.

Grammy's back there, behind that closed door, wheezing and weeping.

"*Noah . . . please come . . . please come help Grammy . . .*"

If he goes back there, her cataracted eyes will shine through the dark, white as eggs. She'll smile from behind lips crusted with vomit. She'll hold out saggy arms and he'll have to hug her, and he'll feel all the ghastly points of wetness: eyes, nose, mouth, crotch, sores.

He can't do it, not alone. He goes outside. Tromps through weeds. Throws junk into the slime-coated pond his sisters still swim in. But night comes. He's cold. He goes back inside with trepidation, like Grammy might be standing in the center of the kitchen, eyes blazing, dumping piss and shit from under her mucky gown, demanding the hug she's owed.

Noah can still hear her back there.

"Noah . . . Noah . . . help Grammy . . . please, Noah . . . Noah, pleeease . . ."

She's probably thirsty. Probably rolling in her own filth. But Noah's parents will be home soon. He turns on the TV. *Friends* is on. The characters live in a New York City apartment that is clean, spacious, colorful, bright. He swears to himself he'll live there. Grammy's cries pierce the laugh track. Noah cranks the volume and forces himself to laugh, louder, louder, louder.

Dad has to shake him out of it. Noah looks around in confusion. Some other sitcom is on. Dinah and Tamar stare at him from behind Dad, faces smudgy from a homebound ice-cream stop. Noah wipes his face and there's tears. Why was he crying?

Mom screams from Grammy's room.

Dinah and Tamar instantly start sobbing. Dad's shoulders slump as if he's been expecting this. But Noah doesn't think Dad is right; Grammy hasn't passed gently in the night. Noah gets up, reeling like a sleepwalker, and stumbles down the hall through the usual sticky aerosol of urine and into the room.

He looks at Grammy.

Mom shoves him from the room, howling, shaking him, asking him how he could let this happen, hadn't he heard Grammy crying? Dad rushes into Grammy's room and slams the door behind him. But it's no use. Noah has already seen everything.

The three rats poised on Grammy's pillow. Their blood-speckled whiskers. The gored, empty sockets of Grammy's eyes. The pink, twitching tail extending from Grammy's open mouth. The rats had come for her at last. And all Noah had done was laugh, laugh, laugh.

<hr />

Fuck. He douses his face with thin streams of airplane lavatory water. Inside LaGuardia he does the same. In the limo service, he downs a whole bottle, letting some slide down the front of his shirt. After the car gets off the 278 and crosses the Williamsburg Bridge, it begins start-stopping down Delancey and his stomach can't take it. He gets out, pays and tips on his phone, and staggers the final four blocks to his loft at the corner of Prince and Green.

It's Saturday night. People are tripping from bars and restaurants, having had their fill of food and drink and now on the lookout for the sex. It's what the rats are doing too. Noah tries to keep his eyes from the trash bags piled on the curbs. *Average of three to five rats per bag*, he thinks, pressing his lymph nodes in search of sickness.

Sammy was different. No trash-raiding, no biting. Only kissing.

First thing: a shower. It's hot enough to burn away Sammy's contortions and Grammy's eyeless stare. By the time Noah is dry and dressed, it's dark. He checks his phone. Ten p.m. Eastern, 9 p.m. Central—just in time for his weekly video call with his parents. He gazes out the six-foot windows. He chose this loft not for the view of the Manhattan skyline, but because it overlooks the SoHo Apple Store—something to keep him motivated.

He goes to his standing desk, navigates, clicks. When he logs on, Arthur and Pat Goff are waiting as usual, faces out of focus from sitting too close, three-fourths of the screen given to empty headspace. Far behind them, lost in static, the hall that used to lead to Grammy's room.

"Hi, Noah, dear," Mom says. "Is it cold there? Oo, it's so cold here."

"No," Noah says. "Well, yes." What does it matter? "Sure."

Weather, ailments, wildlife, home repair, sister updates: these are the litanies through which his parents fulfill familial obligations. Noah's not dumb. Ever since Grammy, he's been the black sheep. He knows his folks don't understand why he left Iowa. He only knows they were relieved, whether or not they understood why.

He waits to see if they'll ask about Sammy or EditedPets. It's all over the internet. But Mr. and Mrs. Goff follow no news beyond the hyper-local. Why do Jackie Burrough's pigs look sickly?—that sort of thing. He wishes it didn't hurt. But it hurts. For years, he snail-mailed them clippings from newspapers and magazines so they might feel pride. They only ever seemed confused and eager to return to more familiar topics.

"I ran into Davin Dunbar at the Hy-Vee," Mom says. "Wasn't he in your class? He told me he built a house out on Gregory Lake. Can you believe that?"

And I bought a $10.5 million loft in SoHo, Noah thinks.

"He's a shift manager at the plastics plant now."

And I'm CEO of a company that just quadrupled its stock market value.

"I think he's got two kids with Christy Crawford, you remember her? Art, you remember Christy Crawford?

"Hanh?" The only noise the near-deaf Arthur Goff ever makes.

If this is the shit that impresses you, Noah stews, *I'll never make you happy.*

He supposes he can't one-up Christy Crawford. Though he has a small harem of boutique escorts plugged in his phone, he hasn't been on a normal date in a decade. That's what his parents want. It's what they understand. Another messed-up meth-head getting one of his sisters preggers again will always be more compelling than whatever world-changing miracle he creates.

❌

Mom used to call Dinah and Tamar "touched." Little Noah Goff was touched too, but in the opposite direction. He read the *Encyclopedia Britannica* front to back. He took apart their TV and, after accepting Dad's whopping, rebuilt it in a way that descrambled dozens of channels for free. He studied dead animals he found on their property. He let teachers know when their lessons were outdated. They never seemed thankful.

His social life, of course, was a catastrophe. In high school, it became a running joke to piss on him whenever possible. The chief pisser? Davin Dunbar, cheered on by Christy Crawford even way back then. Noah should have taken his beatings like other pariahs. Instead, he became a gasping cyclone of twiggy arms, streaming tears, and dribbling snot until some teacher dragged him to a bathroom to cool his overheated face with water.

The same as he just did on the plane and in the airport. Nothing changes.

Noah thinks of the time Mom and Dad were called in to speak with the school counselor. Noah was told to wait in the hall. But did they think he couldn't hear?

Noah's emotions, the counselor said, *haven't caught up with his mind.*

Have they yet? Noah knows it's an open question, no matter how he struts around in his $1,425 Jesus Shoes, hoodie, and cap. He got the hell out of Iowa via full scholarship to Cooper Union. After that, Columbia, a PhD in Molecular Biology and Genetics. After that, Rockefeller, a postdoc in Computational Human Genomics and Bioinformatics. His intellect and initiative still failed to win friends. Parties were the worst. He'd get over-excited and hijack a harmless chat for devil's-advocate grandstanding. Too late, he'd catch himself, blush hot, and leave, still feeling the patter of Davin Dunbar's urine on his back.

Would people always consider him a freak? That was the question.

The answer was EditedPets. Dr. Pramod Parekh, Noah's supervisor at Rockefeller, didn't hide his disappointment at Noah's choice of industry over academia. But Parekh didn't know Noah's story. That hovel in Coop. The damp darkness. The perpetual alienation. The holes in his life, which, if he stared through them long enough, always routed back to the holes in Grammy's face.

✵

"—told Tamar to try corrective shoes or she'll end up with a walker by—"

"I had a big day, Mom," Noah blurts.

There's no doubt the world cares. But the years Noah has spent hacking high school classmates' Facebook chats have made it irrefutable that he needs the people from his past to care too. Most of all, Mom and Dad.

"Oh? Big day?" Mom looks worried.

Noah nods. "Yeah. I made a pet. And showed it in a big theater. And on the internet. People really liked it."

Mom frowns. "Is this like your fish? You know the hard water out here, it was no good for those fish—"

"I know your FireFish died, Mom, it's fine. I just wanted to tell you that my business is having a big week. I'm going to make a lot of money, Mom."

"Oh." Mom only looks more troubled. "Well, that's nice. Don't buy us another computer, though, dear; we can hardly get this one to do what it's supposed to."

Three years ago, Noah had tipped the Geek Squad from Coralville, Iowa, a thousand dollars to truck all the way out to Coop to set up an iMac for his parents, with nothing installed but FaceTime and Signal Messenger. Noah told himself he'd done this to enrich his parents' lives. But these were folks who'd dabbled in QAnon. Who'd declined Covid vaccines to avoid being tracked by 5G nanoparticles.

"I won't, Mom. I just wanted to let you know, if you guys need anything, or Dinah or Tamar too—corrective shoes, stuff for their kids, whatever. Just ask and I'll get it."

Buying their affection. Is this what it's come to?

Mom's chuckles come at him like a butcher's knife.

"With pet money? Art, did you hear that? He wants to buy us things with pet money!"

"Hanh?"

Mom's still laughing. Noah grips his desk to stop shaking.

"What kind of pet would make you all that money, dear?"

He'd been stupid to mention it. Noah peers into the digital murk of Grammy's hall. How could he possibly tell them he's made a rat?

"Forget it, Mom," he says. "It's nothing. I gotta go."

Mom dabs at mirthful tears. "Art, I think Noah made a new fish."

"*Hanh?*"

4

Dead animals all over the lab; but this time, at least, they are made of paper.

A knock on the wall. Sienna looks up from her desk. Prez leans into the lab.

"Heading out," he says. "All good?"

Prez only enters the lab when it's night, and he's stayed late by request, and it's finally time for him to hand duties off to the building's general security downstairs. Unlike the rest of the building, and world, the lab is a hermetic dream-space. Sterile whiteness pours from overheads, monitors, equipment. The drone of cold storage, the purr of centrifuges. The clicks of disposal tips shooting from mechanical pipettes as reliable as the ticking clock. And, of course, one room away, the muffled squeaks of the rats stacked six-high in bakery-style racks.

Prez is a crash of reality: plaid flannel, a dangling industrial keyring, hands gloveless. His smell too: not sweaty, but not sterilized into nonexistence. Like every other lab Sienna has worked in, EditedPets smells like disinfectant, the permanent markers used to number Eppendorf tubes, and the chemical reagents acting as olfactory clues regarding which stage of the process they've achieved—or stumbled back into.

The bunching of Prez's beard shows a smile, but it's forced. No emotion between them has felt clean since they watched the rat die in San Jose ten days ago. Prez's obvious affection for her has been contaminated. Sienna hates it. She nods at the origami dragon he holds.

"You found one of the fallen."

Prez laughs, sort of. "Mass casualties. You want me to pick them up?"

"Don't bother. Their bodies remind me where I've already paced. Might be fruitful to pace in new areas."

Prez laughs again. "You the last one here again?"

"Afraid so."

Prez looks like he wants to say something.

Sienna feels a mirroring pinch in her chest. Prez is fatherly; she hasn't been able to ignore that. Her actual father, high-school biology teacher Sebastián Aguirre, died five years ago. Sienna's alcoholism was at its worst when Noah hired Prez, and with Isaiah gone, she was in free-fall: her tank of FireFish had been decimated months before Noah's annual birthday refresh. Prez helped her turn it around. He probably doesn't realize he did. The way he looked at her with open care like no one else at Edited-Pets, the way he asked about her family, the way he mildly debated her philosophy of Biological Uplift before throwing up his hands in defeat and grinning like a proud papa bested by a clever daughter.

Prez's pride in her made Sienna look harder at herself in the mirror. Could she, too, see someone to be proud of? So she went cold turkey. Sick for two weeks and still came in most days. Prez was always there, waiting silently outside the bathroom with water or smoothies.

Now, again, Prez says nothing. He must feel it's not his place.

"All right," he says. "Dante's down on the desk. Any trouble, you buzz him. Have a good night." He smiles. "Consider sleep."

"I'll consider anything at this point. Night."

He salutes and leans back out of the lab. The door seals shut.

⚓

Sienna tears a page from her notebook, squares it by ripping off the bottom fourth, and starts folding the foundation of a seahorse. She resumes circling the lab while her thoughts circle Sammy. If she can shake the stress of the nine-month deadline—eight-and-a-half months now—she can crack this. All week she's felt like the answer is at her fingertips.

Across the hall in a big Tang-colored room is what she refers to as Gamma Phi Delta: the marketing and sales team. They are bigger than the lab team, naturally, and filled with ex-fraternity and sorority types who, Sienna assumes, regularly pair off for sexual flings. She knows they're necessary but doesn't love them. When it mattered most, they distracted her with customer-facing trivialities like the color and feel of Sammy's fur. Gamma Phi Delta's floor-to-ceiling glass wall has the company slogan in gazillion-point type etched across it in frosted gray:

pets, reinvented.

The words mock her. By now she's reinventing the reinvention of the reinvention.

When she next passes her desk, the Great Wave catches her.

Desperate for inspiration, she leans toward her cubicle wall for a better look. Hokusai's *The Great Wave off Kanagawa*, one of the most famous pieces of Japanese art. Completed in the early 1800s, but with the meticulous styling of a modern-day graphic novel, it depicts a gigantic ocean wave about to smash into three boats.

Sienna's copy is a roughed-up postcard from Suzuki Mika, the same prof who'd infected Sienna with the origami bug. It had arrived shortly after the premiere of FireFish and included no note. Classic Mika. What was she trying to say? It might be congratulations: Sienna is the wave, vanquishing any challengers. It might be a warning: Sienna is the boats, facing obliteration by unfathomable forces. It might be a call for patience: Sienna is Mount Fuji, seen in the drawing's background, waiting out the duel of nature versus technology.

Or Sienna might be *the print itself.* Hokusai's original woodblock was thought to have printed around five thousand copies, with later impressions blurrier, spottier, darker. That's how she has felt ever since joining up with Noah Goff. Like the Great Wave, EditedPets is more popular than anyone could have guessed. But she's wearing down, thinning out, losing her edge.

"Fuck that," she whispers. While she loves Prof. Mika, she'll be damned if she'll let the renowned geneticist be right about this.

She searches her desk for a more positive sigil. Her eyes land on a desktop folder labeled *STORMS*. Nothing to do with Hokusai-style typhoons. It's short for *BRAINSTORMS*, exactly what Sienna needs.

Without sitting, she opens the folder and double-clicks a random MP3.

She smiles at the sound signature. This recording wasn't made inside the lab or Noah's office, located at the end of Gamma Phi Delta. Cabs honk and pigeons coo. This was recorded on the fire escape, where Sienna goes to smoke and where Noah, when feeling upbeat, sometimes joins her. Quickly she time-stamps the conversation as just after Noah had shown her the pictures of adorable hydrocephalic rats. Sienna knows they were stressed back then, but to her ears they sound young and optimistic.

She resumes her origami seahorse, paces, and listens.

✳

Noah: Of course it's got to be a mammal. Are you dense?

Sienna: What do I know? Maybe snakes are all the rage with the kids.
Maybe every mom in the suburbs is dying to own a pet tarantula.

Noah: Name me one spider that's considered an endangered species.

Sienna: I'm not some baby lab tech. I don't have to play your games.

Noah: Come on. Just one.

Sienna: Here is a middle finger for you. Just one.

Noah: Kaua'i cave wolf spider. *Adelocosa anops.* Lives exclusively within a four-mile radius of lava-flow caves in Hawaii.

Sienna: That explains why I've never heard of it.

Noah: Fascinating animal. Evolved entirely without eyes.

Sienna: We'll call it BlindSpider. Sell big goony eye accessories like Mr. Potato Head.

Noah: What I'm saying is, you haven't heard of it because it's not a mammal. If it doesn't have tits, ass, and hair, people don't give a shit. Humans are speciesist.

Sienna: I don't know where else to go but rats. Can we do a cat?

Noah: One in seven kids are allergic to cats.

Sienna: They're allergic to the Fel d 1 secretoglobin protein in cat saliva. We don't have to use those CH1 and CH2 genes. We go hypoallergenic. Start with a Cornish Rex. A Balinese.

Noah: You make fun of the marketing kids, but they get it. Today's tech has gotta fit in your pocket. That's the problem with EasyPony. Who wants their fancy new toy way the hell outside, where you gotta visit it like an outhouse? Good tech is close, fast, cheap, and disposable. That's how we make money. A cat lives twelve, fifteen years.

Sienna: A squirrel. I follow a squirrel on Instagram.

Noah: See? You *would* get along with the marketing kids.

Sienna: Drinks from a bottle, wears little sweaters.

Noah: Doesn't have the cognitive horsepower.

Sienna: Well, shit, Noah! I'm trying here!

Noah: I know. And I appreciate that. But you were right to begin with. The rat—it's the right size, the right intelligence, and the perfect lifespan: two years. You know how often the average user gets a new iPhone?

Sienna: Something tells me two years.

Noah: Looks like you're going to be the proud mama of quite a large litter, Dr. Aguirre.

✂

Not a choice of words Noah intended to hurt, but it did, enough to spoil their fire-escape chat. It still hurts now as Sienna paces the work benches of EditedPets.

The truth is, she used to think of herself and siblings as a litter—eight kids, a number she found increasingly grotesque as she grew up and met friends, who had between zero and three siblings each. Today, all seven of her siblings still reside in Missoula, from which they email Sienna pics of their respective litters dressed in white cotton shirts and matching capris like some kind of cult.

She saw it all coming as a teen: the J. Crew, the Chrysler Pacifica, the Golden Retriever. So she plotted her escape and executed it. In only this way, she thinks, does she share a background with Noah. She was going to be different from the rest of the Aguirres if it killed her.

Then she met Isaiah Joseph at Columbia, dated him for a while, and let the idea of children seep into her cracks. Once Isaiah began talking about getting married and having kids, the seeped water froze, expanded, and broke the rock of her resistance. It might be healthy. Get her out of the rigidly regimented experiments and into the world of happy accidents. Having kids didn't *have* to be insulting, she told herself. It didn't *have* to be traditional. She and Isaiah eloped and Sienna enjoyed relating this news to all six thousand shocked members of her extended family.

She got serious about children after her dad died. One child, she told Isaiah. She was a person, not an incubator.

Issues arose. Sienna didn't get pregnant. She laughed it off. There were other things in life. But those were the dark days of ChattyBird and EasyPony. She *needed* some happy accidents. Doctors suggested tests: Isaiah was fine, but she had irregular ovulation and endometriosis gumming her Fallopians. Fine. She enacted science all day long upon fish, birds, ponies, and rats. Maybe this was their revenge.

Meet Sienna Aguirre, lab rat.

Clomiphene citrate tablets, which came with the risk of multiple births—the litter she said she didn't want—but already she felt her principles wobbling. Bloody discharge, nausea, diarrhea, no baby. Gonadotrophin injections straight into her stomach, usually in the bathroom stall at work, her skin rashed, her gut swollen with abdominal fluid. Over a year now, and still nothing. Isaiah began to back down. We can adopt, not have kids at all, it's fine. But the Aguirre cult pics were getting under her skin. All she got with laparoscopic surgery was eight weeks of bladder irritation. Intrauterine insemination, why stop now? Isaiah relinquished sperm but wasn't fucking around anymore. Stop this, Sienna. The EditedPets lawsuits are messing with your head. We can't afford this. But who cared about Isaiah's opinions when she had his sperm? Bring on the hormonal injections, the egg retrievals, the six cycles of IVF; and when her doc refused, she found another one willing to do blastocyst IVF. At some point, Isaiah left. Does Sienna even recall the final straw?

Not at all. What she recalls is the Great Wave. Slogging to work sore or aching or gassy or hot-flashing, or, later, her belly kicking not with life but with alcohol, the first thing she did was stare at Prof. Mika's postcard. In Missoula, the wave had been the dull suburban lifestyle ready to subsume her. In New York, the wave had been the what-ifs ready to drown her if she didn't have what her siblings had.

That was the black magic of Hokusai's woodblock. Across eons and cultures it waited, curls of salt, levitating spray, until the day you happened to row beneath its cold dark cloud and were demolished.

✺

Sienna's pacing takes her inside the Animal Room, better known as New Rat City: a hundred and eighteen rats, minus any that died tonight. Some run mad circles in their paper pellet bedding, some blunder into walls, some tremble so badly that their metal ear tags cymbal the cages. Behavior depends upon which stage of which experiment the rat is in, or whether it has a metal cannula drilled into its skull. The cages are stacked seven feet high. In that way, New Rat City is one more manifestation of the Great Wave.

From around the corner the MP3 reaches its end, with Noah and Sienna clambering back through the fire-escape window. The audio thwacks, Sienna fumbling to turn off the recorder, but not before Noah gets the final word.

Don't worry, he says; *usually the answer's right in front of you.*

Sienna blinks. It verbalizes the same thought she'd had after Prez left:

All week she's felt like the answer is at her fingertips.

So she looks down at her fingertips.

Magically, the seahorse is complete. She observes the roll-in fold of its dorsal fin, the turnover folds of its pectoral fin, the push-in folds of its tail. So tiny, so compact. She can't believe her whole notebook page is in there.

Sienna hears the pop of the MP3 ending. It is the sound of her eureka.

Origami. Folding.

Sammy's brain.

5

All fifteen staffers from the biotech half of EditedPets are present, lab techs prepping for the genetic editing and confirmational testing of the day, while staff scientists scan for new journal articles, hopeful that soon their names will be associated with the breakthroughs made today in this lab. Noah skids to avoid bulldozing a tech balancing a tray of glass micropippets.

"Two hands on that tray! Or you'll be back working at Applebee's!"

He recalls a few months ago overhearing techs compare EditedPets to a Michelin-starred restaurant with Executive Chef Noah going all Gordon Ramsay on Chef de Cuisine Sienna, who in turn got passive-aggressive to the sous-chefs, who took it out on the saucier, pastry chef, dishwashers, and so on. He feels a flash of regret and shouts over his shoulder—

"Sorry! I'm being an asshole! Big things happening!"

—before sidling next to Sienna at the fume hood, which, come to think of it, isn't that different from the sneeze guard at an Applebee's buffet. Sienna's in her whites and safety glasses, one of her blue nitrile-gloved hands holding Vannas scissors, the other an iris forceps with curved and serrated tips. Under the hood, she dissects a rat's reproductive organs to open up the oviduct and retrieve zygotes. Noah and Sienna had watched the mother euthanized in a CO_2 gas chamber minutes earlier.

"Remember," Sienna had said, "it takes death to uplift life."

More of her Biologic Uplift bullshit. Noah couldn't care less. He gestures for her to keep going. Sienna uses a mouth pipette to pick up each microscopic zygote and place it into a dish with fresh liquid medium.

She spins on her stool, forcing Noah to get out of the way, and carries the zygotes to the inverted microscope microinjection rig on the stainless steel bench behind her.

Here it is, the INTR: Intra Nucleotide Transfer and Repair, developed by EditedPets—well, mostly Sienna—to succeed CRISPR/Cas9 and Prime Editing, which aren't bad at cutting-and-pasting genes as long as you don't mind when it goes fucking haywire and turns your perfectly healthy lab rat into a genetic freak.

Represented in code, a rat genome is a string of just under three billion letters, and INTR's magic is being able to add words and even phrases, each made up of the letters A, T, G, and C, with ten-thousand-fold the accuracy of CRISPR's jittery molecular scissors.

Best of all, Noah holds the patent. This prevents competitors from using INTR for the next fifteen years and gets the FDA off Noah's back via a nifty loophole: if you patent a DNA editing machine but ensure that it's *for pet use only,* no one can redirect it for clinical human use, which is currently locked under global moratorium.

CRISPR/Cas9 and Prime Editing performed wonders at first. One by one, genetic aberrations were permanently corrected with editing on human subjects. But it was too good to be true. The microscopic snips caused genomic instabilities months or years down the line. Physicians watched helplessly as children's edited DNA began to unravel. The result was progeria-like aging that rapidly turned toddlers into wizened, wrinkled versions of their formerly able-bodied selves. Noah could barely look at the photos. These children died soon after, leaving most of the world no choice but to ban human genetic tinkering.

But nonhumans? Different story. Solving these genetic editing glitches and commercializing the process would make Noah so wealthy and famous that even his childhood nemeses would hear of it. His hands flex; he'd sure like a go at those microinjection rig joysticks.

Sienna reads his mind and shouts over the roar of the HEPA filter.

"You even *look* at this thing too hard, Goff, and you're going to have hooks for hands." She nods toward marketing's haven of easy chairs and ping-pong tables. "I hope you told Gamma Phi Delta no interruptions."

"I bought them a keg and turned on 'the Big Game.' Isn't that what normies call it? Relax, doc. I'd never get between you and your babies."

Well, shit, here he is being an asshole again. He knows his Director of Biotechnology Research and Development had fertility issues in the past. Deep down, he doesn't hate that she can't have kids. With pups at home, she'd be working eight-hour days max, and how the fuck would they get anywhere on eight-hour days?

"You're *already* getting in the way," she snaps. "Back off a few millimeters and run crowd control. Anyone bumps me while I'm doing this, there will be blood."

The inverted microscope microinjection rig looks like a big black sewing machine flanked by two oversized joysticks. A camera faces a slide holding twelve genetically identical zygotes from the pregnant rat—rat *N22*, according to the Eppendorf. It's a rat from the Sammy line, which means it's already got human genes edited in, but which *also* means those genes will eventually swell the rat's brain and kill her, and all her offspring.

Unless Sienna's bizarro origami works.

Sienna explained it this way. A rat's small, wedge-shaped head strictly limits the size of their smooth, shiny brains. Human brains, on the other hand, are gyrificated, that cortical folding that gives them the look of a bowl of plump udon noodles. This folding massively multiplies the surface area inside a skull, which means more room for brain cells and more opportunity for intelligence to develop.

Makes sense to Noah. So he's been hard on Sienna, playing bad cop for the last week by breathing down her neck, only to disorient her with such good-cop behavior as deliveries of rice rolls, crab pockets, and bánh mì—Pavlovian signals to remind Sienna of past glories. Noah feels a little shame. Sienna has always done her best work on a knife's edge.

Once again, it's paying off. The whole lab staff is here. Word's gotten out that today's the day and they want to be able to tell their grandkids they were here. No Adderall today: Noah feels like a million bucks. Ha! A weak figure, considering the business Sammy 2.0 will do. Try three hundred and fifty million bucks.

⚒

A monitor to Sienna's left shows a live picture of one of the twelve zygotes. At ten-times magnification, they look like the CO_2 bubbles in a head of beer. Not her preferred drink, but she doesn't think she'd have the strength to turn down a nice Scotch Ale right now if a tech offered one up.

She uses the joysticks to guide a suction pipette near a zygote. The glutinous blob is sucked to the rounded edge of the pipette. Sienna ups the magnification to 400x. The quivering zygote fills the screen.

The Apollo 17 astronauts who took the "Blue Marble" photo of Earth in 1972 have nothing on this, Sienna thinks. With its gray, pitted surface, the zygote looks like the moon, except encircled like Saturn by a layer called the zona pellucida. It's both familiar and unfathomable.

But all is not well for this gray planet. Floating in from the right like a Star Destroyer is Sienna's injector, a glass pipette tapered to inconceivable sharpness and armed with INTR's microscopic cut-and-pasters. Sienna positions the point on the zygote's edge. A gentle push is all that's needed to pierce it. It's not the first breach; that came from the lucky sperm that detonated an explosive structure on its head at just the right moment, ensuring it would be the one to fertilize the egg.

The same dance Isaiah's sperm and her eggs could never finagle.

A single pair of rats can produce fifteen thousand descendants in a single year.

Sienna Aguirre can't make one.

The impulse to stab the injector with vengeance passes, though, and is replaced by the same tenderness that has informed all her work at EditedPets. Maybe she'll never be a mom in the ways defined by her fecund siblings. But she *is* a mother; her work will change the very *idea* of motherhood.

There's an epic list of things Sienna doesn't believe in. Religion, political absolutes, luck, fate, superstition, the power of kindness, people's innate goodness, that working hard will make your dreams come true. What she does believe in, enough to hinge her career on it, is Biological Uplift.

Most scientists Sienna knows oppose the philosophy. It exasperates her. No one doubts that the second humans are able to; they'll end hemophilia and cystic fibrosis; they'll stamp out retinitis pigmentosa and the mutations that lead to structural heart defects; hell, they'll end male pattern baldness and short stature, color blindness and stuttering. Already there are sperm banks offering sperm from Nobel Prize winners.

Biological Uplift argues—and boy, has Sienna argued it, in dorm rooms, collegiate cafés, here in the lab, joshingly with Prez—that it's animal cruelty to withhold these same enhancements from other species. She had a staff scientist for a while who recited all the *Brave New World* clichés, forcing her to school him on the planet's obvious track toward a post-biological society. If humans don't want to be alone in that world, you asshole, we are required, as Earth's stewards, to uplift animals along with us. Survival of the fittest no longer works, you dumb fuck, when we are fitting ourselves with designer DNA.

Noah wants to create Sammy for money and fame. Fine.

Sienna, though, considers it a moral imperative.

"Okay," Noah says from her side. "Easy, now."

She blinks so her vision, fuzzied by thought, snaps back into focus.

"It *is* easy," she says, mostly to pump herself up, as she tilts the joysticks and pops the injector through the zygote wall as gently as a mom would kiss her child's fevered forehead.

※

Noah knows that the *not* easy part was the past several weeks, during which Sienna trial-and-errored how many copies of the human gene

ARHGAP11B rats required to generate the necessary brain folding. INTR itself won't fail; it doesn't know how to fail. Sienna Aguirre has created a machine that scans and alters the genetic code of animal, plant, insect, bacteria, or virus in a reproducible and lossless manner. Supporting that invention is the biggest part of Noah's job.

Noah met Sienna Aguirre at Rockefeller, when the two were the only ones left in the seventh-floor genetics lab of the Weiss Research Building, a drab, brutalist monstrosity, at four in the morning. Night after night, like a mason grinding at her wheel, this tall, intriguing party girl listened to shouty metal while rounding the rough edges off CRISPR. Sensing that something big was happening in Sienna's cubby, Noah small-talked his way into figuring out her favorite restaurants and began bringing the two of them late-night takeout.

Sienna told him she continued her work inside her Nolita apartment. He respected that; he was doing the same. For the past year, he'd been developing an app called PetMate. Using a genetically based algorithm based on the user's DNA, PetMate suggested your perfect pet and connected you to a seller. Beta users were freaking out. Self-described dog people were getting cats and loving it, and vice versa. Other users were finding pet love in animals they'd never considered: chinchillas, hedgehogs, pygmy goats, kinkajous, muntjac deer, sugar gliders, skunks.

He'd only had the guts to befriend Sienna because he was flying high. His lawyer was finishing up a review of contracts from angel investors about to drop millions of seed money into PetMate. Until the frigid February morning when his email pinged with a message from Rockefeller's Office of Industrial Liaison. Noah was gobsmacked. University spies had leapt from the shadows to demand that Noah sign over ownership of the patents that formed the backbone of PetMate. Their insane assertion was that they'd provided the "resources" for his app.

Noah fought the request. Hard and publicly. He didn't have any friends to lose besides Sienna. His rebuttal was that he'd coded PetMate entirely on his own time, in his own apartment, from his own laptop.

Then he learned what "resources" the office was talking about.

Motherfucking Wi-Fi. He'd used the school's internet to back up his programming and download the occasional research article from the library. Noah didn't have anywhere near enough to take on the multibillion-dollar behemoth of Rockefeller. Noah's lawyer told him, politely, that he was fucked. If Noah didn't sign over the patents, he wouldn't leave the institution with his academic qualifications intact.

Fifty percent of profits wasn't going to be enough for his investors, no matter how angelic they were. Noah had no choice. He shaved off the pound of flesh and, metaphorically speaking, shot PetMate in the head. He signed over the patents the next day and boarded the 6 train home.

Feeling adrift, Noah studied his fellow riders instead of the usual scientific texts. Business suits, factory uniforms. High heels, flip-flops. Each person inside a bubble they willed into existence. Except one. Across the aisle sat an old woman with frizzy fronds of silver hair murmuring to herself. Nothing odd there—the train's most reliable customers were the mentally ill. This woman, though, had a surprise. She unzipped her coat a few inches, and out popped the face of a puppy. She beamed as it licked her lips.

"I love you," the woman purred. "If only you knew."

What if he could *know?* Noah thought.

He felt injected with jet fuel. He shoved his way out at Canal Street Station and sprinted to the surface, where Chinatown's bright sun was the blinding reflection of his own genius. Maybe he had to slough off the PetMate chrysalis in order to work his butterfly wings free.

Noah pulled out his phone and texted. He could see his own smile in the screen.

Tasty. Now. Y/N?

When not in class or her lab cubby, Sienna Aguirre was home. She lived in an old tenement within walking distance of her favorite place, Tasty Hand Pulled Noodles. It was where, fifteen minutes later, Noah would assure her that, once she finished INTR, he already had a project in mind for it. It was where he'd persuade her to hold off on any big breakthroughs until *after* she left academia. The Tasty Hand Pulled Noodle Accord: it would make a fun origin story.

The phone's chime, Sienna's quick reply, the letter he most wanted to see.

Y.

⚔

Sienna pulls back the injector. The zygote's zona pellucida bounces elastically back into shape. The suction pipette releases the zygote, which floats off into the holding medium. She exhales. Briefly she sees the ghost of her breath on the fume hood.

"Okay," she says. "Eleven more to go."

Ninety minutes later, she's done. Noah slaps her on the back. Crowded close now, the lab staff cheers. Sienna swivels on her stool and grins, warming in their praise. One of the techs comes out from behind the cell culture incubator holding not a tray of Eppendorf's, but a three-layer cake with exactly two candles. *Sammy 2.0*, the icing reads. Positioned around the top of the cake, origami rats in neon-colored papers.

It feels like a baby shower. It *is* a baby shower.

Sienna doesn't bask for long. It feels unseemly, and she's worried that the staff, taking their cue from Noah, is ignoring the possibility of another failure. She tells them to take the cake over to marketing and, once she's washed up, she'll join them for a piece if Gamma Phi Delta hasn't already demolished it.

Noah is an able majorette when the mood strikes and heads up the conga line across the hall. Sienna stands, removes her protective eyewear, peels her gloves off, and gazes once more at the monitor, her handiwork writ huge. The zygotes will need a couple hours inside the petri dish for INTR to alter the DNA before each is implanted, via vagina, into a surrogate female's uterus. Then would come the agonizing three weeks before the pups were born, hopefully with origami brains fully functioning.

Sienna hangs up her lab coat and heads to the washroom. To her left, she sees the party starting. Someone is already standing on a table. People wave at her. She holds up a hand, just a sec. She feels happy and knows she should bask in that. But there's something small and hard inside her. It's doubt. Will the gyrification be enough? Will the folds be able to contain all the growth the human genes will require? At the last second, she chooses the fire escape over the washroom. There's a pack in her pocket. She needs a smoke.

6

Architects had few options when designing the Enrichment Room. Due to the layout of the seventh floor and the position of the elevator shafts, it had to be on the north end of EditedPets, accessible only through New Rat City. This was good for the rats; they didn't have to travel through the horror show of the lab to get to the only room they liked. It was less good for Sienna; before she could relish the inspiration of the Enrichment Room, she had first to be reminded how the sausage got made. New Rat City is stuffy with the ammonia smell of rat bodies and the stink of their panicked urine. The stack of their cages reminds her of her own shitty building, which she never bothered to move out of after Rockefeller. This time *she's* the slumlord, choosing which rodent residents get kicked to the curb.

One hundred rats—those still physically able—clack their metal ear tags against the cages, grind their teeth, or burrow into their pellet bedding as Sienna enters. She wonders how fine their powers of observation are. When she leaves with one of their brethren and brings it back with a shunt drilled into its head, does it change how they feel about her?

She tries not to feel anything about them. It's bad practice to feel affection for animals whose tails you will snip off and into whose eyes you will stick glass capillary tubes.

Sienna key-cards the inner door and slips into the Enrichment Room.

It has the size and feel of a kindergarten classroom, jubilant with Fisher-Price colors and the scent of toy-store plastic. Sienna used to imagine peeking into rooms like this to watch her own smiling child race with other five-year-olds. These rats also race. They smile, too, to the extent that rats can, ears relaxed and extra-pink.

"Good morning!" Linda cries.

"Hi," Sienna says, blushing under the woman's attention. She always has.

Sienna attended Capstone Montessori Academy in Missoula from age three to twelve. Founded on techniques trail-blazed by Italian educator Maria Montessori, the Montessori Method forsakes memorization-based learning in favor of independent thinking, often centered around tasks involving motor skills and physical objects. Sienna's memories of those days are charged with the dopamine jolts of solving this or that puzzle, or reusing puzzle materials in a completely unique way.

This latter habit was what was so exciting, claims Linda Miller—a forgettable name, perhaps, for an unforgettable woman. In the nearly three decades since they were teacher and student, Linda has been there to congratulate Sienna's every success. Linda stutter-steps through the Enrichment Room, a toddler walk she likely picked up from past students, and wraps Sienna in her daily hug. Sienna likes it, even though she can't get her awkward body to fully reciprocate.

Linda wears a lab coat too, but in a playful lavender color. So do her young assistants, Dekota, Tasha, and Mason, who wave at Sienna. Linda holds Sienna at arm's length.

"Raccoon eyes," Linda observes. "Why are geniuses never genius enough to know they need sleep?"

"I had a professor at NYU who called it the Mary Shelley effect. We're so intent on bringing life to others that we're willing to sap our own."

Linda frowns. "You think that's it?"

"No," Sienna chuckles. "It's arrogance. Plain and simple."

"I seem to remember Shelley writing a bit about that too." Linda taps the surgical steel conch ring pierced through the antihelix of Sienna's left ear. "Look at this pretty thing. New?"

Sienna touches it self-consciously. "Oh, you know. I get so used to punching holes in animals, I occasionally manage to punch a hole in myself."

It's her second loop. She had the first pierced into her right ear after successfully interlacing a network of human genes with the genome of first-gen Sammys. The style is symbolic. The most ubiquitous device at EditedPets is the ear punch. A paper puncher, basically, modified with a tiny Eppendorf to catch the punched bit of rat ear for DNA testing. It also provides a hole for the rat's ID tag, a simple metal ring with identifying numbers and letters. Sienna copied the simple design. This second piercing is to acknowledge the brain gyrification of the Sammy 2.0s. It worked—and the Enrichment Room proves it.

"So, what's on the docket today?" she asks.

Linda holds Sienna by the waist and guides her into the room. Unlike the lab's steel furniture, the chairs here are a soft golden wood, though most of the action takes place on the rugs. Tasha and Mason are down there, spreading their attention to the students that need it. In this case, the students are rats. From their sizes, Sienna can tell they represent three distinct waves of litters. They scurry willy-nilly. But they're not looking for holes in walls or trying to get into the sink. They are working away at the various games.

The most notable, of course, is a product Noah has been hot on for months: SammyWagon. Modeled after an experimental ROV—Rodent-Operated Vehicle—built by University of Richmond researchers, SammyWagon works by having Sammy stand upright with front paws resting on what look like mini-scooter handles. It has all the hallmarks of an EditedPets product. Shatterproof polycarbonate plastic. Low-density, high-strength, satin-textured aluminum. An avocado-green that infers an eco-friendliness that doesn't exist. Each SammyWagon comes with a darling color-matched racing helmet for Sammy.

One of the rats drives loops around a circular rug. It looks to be having a ball, its little fists torquing the steering handles, ears flattened back. Sienna didn't think SammyWagon would be ready until Q3 of next year, but this thing looks ready to roll.

Tablets all over the floor are open to the SammySpeaks app. Rats sprint to screens between tasks, sometimes to reply to a question, but, more excitingly, often to ask questions themselves. The place has the jolly cacophony of a preschool, conveyed through the voice of the AAC.

"Watch me do, Tasha. Tasha, watch."

"Where is dog go? Make dog come back, Mason."

"Toy too big. I can't hold toy."

"I'm hungry. Where is food?"

"Come here, Dekota. Dekota, come here."

"I like blue, Tasha. What colors you like?"

"Is sun made of fire? Is clouds made of smoke?"

"Pick up, Linda. Linda, pick up."

Sienna shakes her head in wonder at the power of *FOXP2*, the human gene providing the capacity for spoken language. These rats are communicating at a kindergarten level, easy. If it were possible to give them voice boxes, these rats would talk without SammySpeaks.

One rat slides the beads of an abacus in accordance to a math problem on a tablet screen. Two rats work together to make a puzzle—not a thick toddler puzzle, but an actual two-hundred-piece puzzle depicting a bucolic farm scene. Four rats are busy connecting sections of a walled racetrack, and because rats are thigmophilic—navigating by touch—a few can't help but race through the channel, whiskers providing the spatial foreknowledge their eyes cannot.

What startles Sienna most is the rat using finger-paint to paw a shape that has the colors and rough shape of Dekota.

"Is that one . . . ?"

"That's P80, our Picasso. Dekota's her muse. P80 refuses to paint Tasha and Mason. Not worth the artist's time, apparently."

"I can't believe it," Sienna says.

"Well, I wouldn't say it's a *good* likeness of Dekota," Linda jokes.

"Yeah, these guys rush right in," Linda says. "We add a new toy, they all want to figure out what they can build with it. They push and shove to be the first." She nudges Sienna. "Reminds me of someone."

One hundred years ago, Montessori taught supposedly unteachable students. Sienna intends to do the same, and, while she's at it, throw some love to the woman who'd been there at every milestone in her life. As a bonus, Linda had hosted hundreds of pet mice in her classroom over the years. Acclimatizing to rats was easy, especially cute ones.

"And how do we feel about George Mallory over there?" Sienna asks.

Along the east wall of the room, three rats have arranged thirty-some cardboard blocks, styled to look like red brick, into a six-foot tower. Two rats perch on lower steps, interested in attaining the peak. But the top rat isn't giving an inch.

Linda nods. Sienna notes the lowered enthusiasm.

"We're not sure what to make of X33. It may turn out to be nothing. These rats are all bred here, right? They ought to all develop pretty much apace. But X33, he'll work with the others only to a point. Only until he gets what he wants."

One of the lower rats puts its paws on the top block, preparing to leap. X33 boxes its nose. Sienna fights her wince so it's nothing more than a twitch. She doesn't want Linda or the assistants to notice. She damn sure doesn't want Noah to think anything's wrong before she can address it first. X33's swipe was probably playful. Playing all day is what these rats were designed to do.

But what if that swipe was aggression? Sienna's innards knot. Rats born with the brain gyrification gene have been superior to Sammy 1.0 in every facet, yet the first wave suffered seizures at five weeks and went mad from a brain that wouldn't quit growing. Insanity just took longer to happen, which only made Noah madder. They were running out of time. Pet Expo was seven months away.

So Sienna had whipped up another round of pregnancies, this time with a clock gene to delay puberty, giving the rat brain more time to do its origami folding. No celebration cake that time, but Sienna was equally proud. Puberty now took twelve weeks instead of six. The downside was the six-week bite it took from Noah's calendar: now they were down to six and a half months. The upside? These Sammys hit week twelve happy as puppies. That's why they're here cavorting with Linda and her crew.

"I gotta run. Again, Linda, just wonderful, wonderful work. I'm so glad you're here."

"Aww," Linda says. "I'm glad too."

Sienna squeezes Linda's arm and turns away, leaving the squeaking, bruxing, and digital conversing behind. It's going well, she tells herself, but the sentiment doesn't reach her stomach. She tugs on her new earring and suspects it will become a telltale tic. Six months and change till Pet Expo. Still time for one last wave of Sammys, if it comes to that. A couple days spent keeping an eye on X33 won't hurt anyone.

7

Sienna is in the elevator when she hears the scream.

The floor plan requires anyone leaving the elevators to walk south, the full length of the hall, to enter the biotech half of EditedPets. Then it's a U-turn to head back northward across the lab, through New Rat City, and into the Enrichment Room, which abuts the elevator shaft. That's why, despite the grind and hum of elevator pneumatics, Sienna can tell just which person screamed.

Linda.

Sienna bounds down the hall, jacket flapping, dimly registering the paper-bag crunch of her takeout hitting the floor. Her peripheral vision catches Prez reading comics in his cubby, Gamma Phi Delta horseplaying behind their glass wall, Noah on the phone behind his. Sienna explodes into the lab, where six or seven techs are frozen in place holding Pyrex borosilicate glass bottles, cell culture plates, and live rats. Sienna sprints and crashes into New Rat City, where another tech also stands frozen, and then Sienna is pressing the knob and hurling open the final door, fevered with anger at employees who believe their work might save the world, yet can't be bothered to respond to one screaming woman.

The Enrichment Room is the same place as before but shifted in ways that suggest an alternate dimension. The temp is several degrees hotter. No one is where they're supposed to be, humans pressed against furniture, rats racing along the periphery, atop shelving units, straight up the walls. Even the Fisher Price color scheme has been eclipsed—by streaks of scarlet blood. The biggest shift is sonic: guttural gasps and wordless blurts replace the workers' encouraging coos, while the rats on AACs frantically paw their digital pleas.

"No—"

"Stop—"

"Help—"

"Bad—"

"Hurt—"

"Scared—"

"Run—"

"Hide—"

The scream might have come from Linda Miller, but the one in danger is Dekota, the twenty-three-year-old Early Childhood Education student, Rat P80's artistic muse. His legs are locked in a half-squat, shoes crushing cardboard-brick ruins. The destruction means there's no more top position to hold, and, to Sienna's shocked eyes, it looks like Rat X33 is upset about it.

Sienna has seen and handled thousands of rat heads, some alive and snapping, others decapitated for her to roll around and puzzle over. The primary jaws rest where you'd expect them in mammals. What characterizes rodents are the incisors. Extending past the diastema—a bony gap used to carry things—the four incisors are huge and yellow, the equivalent of four-inch fangs on a human. These dentin and enamel chisels never stop growing. In fact, they'll shove backward and impale a rat's brain if it doesn't constantly grind them.

Rats have a biological need to bite.

In a way, X33 is only doing what he has evolved to do.

His incisors are pincered like a septum ring into the fleshy bridge between Dekota's nostrils. Dekota grips the rat's body with both hands but doesn't yank it—it might take out enough flesh to turn his two nasal cavities into one. The rat's back legs cycle midair while its front claws shred Dekota's lips. Mostly, it whips its head like a dog trying to kill its prey. Bright red blood jets from Dekota's face, streaking and splattering his purple scrubs. His words are no more sophisticated than SammySpeaks.

"HELP! HELP! HELP!"

Sienna, no plan, rushes in. Leaping into conflict is what she's always done, from earning nine stitches while separating her sister, Lola, from a dog when she was ten, to descending atop a woman hit by a cab last year in front of YaYa Tea, as if Sienna's spine was strong enough to deflect all coming traffic. She grabs for X33. Rat bites are a fact of lab life, even when sporting supposed anti-bite gloves. Some inbred strains—and the Sammys are definitely inbred—can have a higher propensity for aggression. That's why she always gives rats seven days of handling before messing with them, a period that Noah's Pet Expo crunch has eradicated.

But she's never seen a reaction like this.

Dekota swirls in pain. X33's body thumps Sienna in the face. She recovers and goes for the most suppressive grip, fingers around the back, thumb jammed to the throat. It's no good, too much motion. She goes for the tail next. It lashes her palm, hot as a stream of spit, but she gets it and yanks. The rat goes horizontal, a furry bridge from Dekota to Sienna, and there's a moist rip as the rat's tail begins to detach. It's not letting go.

Dekota backs into a corner. Everything from his mouth down is drenched in blood. His tattered lips move, not screaming anymore, but pleading, directly to the rat.

"Please . . . friend . . . please . . ."

There's a masticating motion to X33's jaws, like it wants to be farther inside Dekota, perhaps his rich, meaty brain, revenge for whatever the humans have done to the rat's own.

Sienna comes at the back half of the rat with what she calls the Death Grip: left thumb and index finger into either side of X33's skull, right hand swallowing the back limbs, a quick pull to dislodge the spinal cord from the brain. But before she can affix her grip, her hands are slapped away.

Her body, too, is thumped. Her foot lands on a cardboard block, and she's down, and for a topsy-turvy second her vision spins across the upside-down faces of horrified staff and Linda's class of rats, scrambling all over the walls and, she swears, the ceiling, rats on the fucking *ceiling*, but then she rights herself, and the world is back in order, though no less awful.

Prez stands where she used to be.

He grabs the rat's tail, pulls the body straight. His other arm missiles forward. A thin tool punches through the rat with a squish, impaling it to the wall. Blood gulps from the hole and slugs alongside the shaft of the tool, a plastic pen printed with the words *PRZYBYSZEWSKI & SONS PEST CONTROL*.

A chorus of cries and gasps.

Shaking, his face painted with blood thinned by falling tears, Dekota slowly looks at first Prez, then Linda, who stands with hands pressed to her face.

Dekota's voice is a whisper.

"Did it . . . bite off . . . my nose . . . ?"

Sienna leaps up and wraps her arms around him.

"No, you're fine, it's just a bite." She stares at the starers. "Did anyone call 911?"

"They're downstairs," reports a tech from the wall phone. "They'll be here in a—"

"No, no, no, no, no no!"

It's Noah, just inside the door. He's cycling his arms like a traffic cop.

"Not in my lab, they're not! Get him out of here!"

Someone shoves a towel into Sienna's hand. She folds it and presses it to the underside of Dekota's nose. Instantly, she feels the wet heat of soaking blood.

"He needs to sit down, Noah—"

Noah tears through the small crowd. "Out by the elevators! Now!" He looks around frantically. "Everyone out! Everyone! Now!"

The staff follows orders, two techs taking Dekota from Sienna's grip. Tasha and Mason, arms around each other, scuttle away. Linda alone hesitates, gesturing at the room.

"The rats . . ." The meekness of her voice wounds Sienna. "They're all over, they're scared—"

Noah points. Veins pop. *"OUT!"*

Sienna closes her eyes. She can't handle seeing Linda slink away.

I brought her here, Sienna thinks. *I promised her everything was safe.*

The door closes. Sienna opens her eyes.

Noah is glaring at Prez. If Prez looks out of place in the lab, he looks even more so in the Enrichment Room, a lumberjack inside a preschool.

Sienna knows Prez. In stressful situations, he asks how people are doing, if there's anything he can do to help. Not today. Slowly, scorchingly, he rotates his head until his glare reaches Noah. He might as well be glaring at Sienna too. Her skin burns in shame, or maybe that's just Dekota's blood.

Noah takes a long inhale through his nostrils.

"I have to go meet the fucking EMTs. But when I'm done—you two, my office."

He rushes off, slams the door.

Sienna and Prez don't say a word. They are the only two left. The only two humans, anyway. Shadows flex, and, from a faraway corner, the digitized plea of a rat especially attached to her AAC.

"Help . . . help . . . help . . . help . . ."

8

They'll ruin him. Not the marketing kids, not the clock-punching techs, but the two people at EditedPets emboldened by their unique roles. Sienna's always had aggravating moral flare-ups. And Prez? Fuck, the whole reason Prez is here is to ensure that there's no problems. If Noah hadn't fired Dr. Clive, he'd tell the shrink to examine his head for hiring the ratcatcher off the goddamn street.

Gamma Phi Delta avoids his eyes as he storms through their office. Of course they do; their prenatal bodies have yet to develop spines. He sees their shared bowl of FireFish slosh with the crash of his Jesus Nikes. Always strike first: he's shouting into his office before he's entered it.

"I want every asshole in a lab coat patted down for phones." Noah slams the door and starts dropping opaque screens over his glass wall. "If a *single* photo gets out—"

"Everyone puts their phones in the Faraday Cage," Sienna says. "No one can even send a text in there."

"Including Linda and her lackeys? I'm referring to the lackeys who didn't have a rat swinging from their fucking face!"

Sienna is sitting on the windowsill in a blood-flecked lab coat, face downturned.

"We'll be lucky if Linda ever sets foot in this building again."

Noah finishes the screens, spins around.

"That's your definition of luck, huh? Linda did a real bang-up job."

"Yesterday those rats were playful and smart," Sienna says. "And *happy*. We've had curious rats before, but never happy rats. That's what Linda did."

Noah giggles wildly. "I'd hate to see what Mr. Happy does when he's pissed off! Though I guess we'll never know, since *someone* punched a hole through him with a *fucking pen*."

He turns on Prez. The burly man stands in the middle of the room, arms crossed, black and gray piles of his beard twitching with every grind of his jaw. Noah feels a flicker of grade-school insecurity. This dude may be twenty years older, but he could send Noah through the glass with his pinkie. Nothing changes.

All the better reason to stay on the offensive. Noah plants himself in front of Prez, a six-inch deficit. "How did half my staff get inside the Enrichment Room before you?"

Prez's beard literally bristles.

"I'm farther away," he grunts.

"That's right, looking at the security camera feeds. Or maybe the occasional comic book, isn't that right?"

"I've told you before, Mr. Goff," Prez grumbles. "The cameras are bad."

"Are you colorblind? Did you think all that red stuff was Bloody Marys?"

"Come look at my screen, Mr. Goff. See if you can tell the difference between people playing with rats and . . . whatever happened in there."

"What happened in there was you pulling some kung-fu ninja shit that half our techs will violate their NDAs to tell their friends about! Were you not given pepper spray? Were you not issued a taser? There is a thing called *professionalism*."

"Close quarters," Prez says. "Didn't want to harm the victim or Dr. Aguirre."

"It's not Prez's fault," Sienna snaps. "The gyrification—it's working, but Sammy's brain just keeps growing and growing."

Noah lurches toward Sienna. She flinches and he's glad.

"Yes, *Dr.* Aguirre, that *is* the problem. A pretty fucking catastrophic problem. Because we're not losing just one Sammy to Vlad the Impaler here, are we? We're going to have to euthanize the whole goddamn generation. Total fucking genocide!"

Sienna nods miserably. "We've got plenty of DecapiCones. We can be dissecting those brains by tomorrow—"

Noah swipes the first thing he sees, a snow globe his sister Dinah sent him inset with a photo of her insipid family, including the latest meth-head husband, and hurls it at the window behind Sienna. The window is shatterproof, but the snow globe isn't. It cracks into pieces, disgorging a small, slushy snowfall. Sienna bounces to her feet in fright and scuttles left. Prez hurries rightward, putting his body between the others.

"Sir, I need you to calm down," Prez says.

"Noah! Have you lost your mind?" Sienna cries.

Noah feels the swamp heat of the school playground, losing his shit at Davin Dunbar or some other bully while everyone gawks at him in sick delight. Nothing has changed.

"*Mind?* We're going to lose a lot more than our minds! We're going to lose your lab, Doc. We're going to lose your cameras, Prez, shitty as they might be. We're going to lose the whole seventh floor. Pet Expo is in six months. Allow me to do the motherfucking math: that's 180 days. That's four thousand hours left to figure out how to slow Sammy's brain growth, INTR that shit into zygotes, birth those sons of bitches, mature them for three to four weeks, and break several land speed records to get to the Javits Center for my keynote! All so I can say to the cameras, with a modicum of honesty, gee, look at this friendly little talking cutie here who definitely, positively, absolutely will not try to chew your kid's nose off his fucking face!"

With arms stretched, Prez has never looked so large.

"I'm going to need you to go behind your desk and sit," he says.

This uneducated barbarian? Telling *him* what to do in *his* office?

"Why don't you go back to your hidey hole?" Noah seethes. "Kick back, find your place in your comic book, pick up your paycheck, the usual?"

Prez has the kind of control over his physical reactions that Noah has always coveted. As usual, Noah weeps his feelings from every pore. His bottom lip trembles like that of a sniveling child. This ignites a fireball of shame in his chest. But what can he do? Say he's sorry? Sienna might absorb that weakness and give herself permission to miss the Pet Expo deadline. EditedPets would become some half-remembered dream or nightmare.

Prez shakes his head. It's pity. He lifts his giant paws.

"I'm done."

Prez turns away. He pauses beside the door and looks at Sienna.

"I don't expect you'll listen, Dr. Aguirre. But my advice is you walk too. Nothing good's going to come of any of this."

Hot, angry blood fills Noah's face. His voice trembles worse than his lip.

"Go ahead and quit. EditedPets doesn't need naysayers. EditedPets needs believers. Visionaries. People like you? All they've ever done is slow me down."

Prez glances at Noah. More pity. Noah doesn't know if he can take it. He pictures dashing his own head against the window, another exploded snow globe.

"You work with rats and I respect that," Prez says softly. "But you never took the time to *know* them. Rats aren't children, Mr. Goff. No matter how many toys you put in front of them."

The big man touches his forehead, the tip of an invisible hat, and then he's gone, leaving the door open behind him. Noah feels a fluttery panic. He's not sure why. Good riddance, right?

"Remember your NDA, asshole!"

"Jesus," Sienna mutters. "This is the business we've built?"

Noah rushes his office door, braces his hands on the frame, and hollers at the exiting security head, ignoring the frat boys and sorority girls staring in blank shock.

"That's right, ratcatcher, scurry away! Just like a rat! Scurry back to the stinking streets where I found you!"

9

The 1995 Chevy Astro rattles to a halt just inside the alley.

First one out of the van is Prez. The wet smack of his boots to gummy asphalt is satisfying. Filth is honest. Utter cleanliness, like at EditedPets, is what he distrusts. Pests are everywhere, inside everything. Anything else is a lie.

Chewing the end of a Makowiec poppy seed roll, Prez strides the length of the van. No logo. Who likes to advertise that their home or business is infested with vermin? His adopted father, Mikołaj Przybyszewski, founded the business in 1961 with nothing but a few generations of know-how carted across the Atlantic from Bialystok. Dad grew it into a business so respected in Greenpoint that, when a customer moved to a tonier hood, they still called Przybyszewski & Sons when they had unwelcome guests.

"Dzień dobry!" calls an old Pole across the street. Prez doesn't recognize him, which makes it more flattering. For six decades, Przybyszewski & Sons left no customer unhappy.

Then Prez sold it. Like that. Two years after his dad died. Would a biologic son—a white, Polish son—have done that?

And all because of the flattery of Noah Goff.

Prez adores his old overalls. Feels good enough to distract him from the shame that's dogged him for three years. He waves at the old man and opens the Astro's back doors.

Second one out of the van is Smog, leaping into the cradle of Prez's left arm. No kisses: this is business. Prez sets him down and the thirteen-year-old, eighteen-pound Jack Russell Terrier gets right to sniffing where the alley floor meets the wall, a rat's favorite channel of movement. Prez straps a burlap bag to his back and lifts a plastic bucket of gear.

He may have sold Przybyszewski & Sons to Ecofix Pest Solutions, but he'd kept the van and his personal kit. He's pretty sure his state-issued commercial license expired with the sale, but who's going to tattle if he does the occasional job for old clients? Prez is a hero to some of them. Truth is, he loves them back. That's where he got the Makowiec roll: he'd swung by Jaworski Bakery at dawn to do a rodent treatment. Easy job, and he refused to charge. So Mrs. Jaworski had jammed a poppy-seed roll under each arm.

He'd started hanging around the local pest-control shop at age eight because he was fascinated by the rats Mikołaj Przybyszewski kept on hand to study. He came by every time he wiggled away from where he was living in foster care, four blocks east. As Mikołaj joked years later, the kid made *himself* such a pest that he and Lena adopted him just so they'd have the right to tell him what to do. Prez was the first Black person a lot of these old Poles had ever known. And they came to love him. There's pride to take from that. Hope too.

Goddammit. Prez pestles a knuckle into his eye, the site of a budding tear. Getting soft with age. Never thought it would happen to him.

While Smog does his thing, Prez gets an overview of the joint. Three-story residential. Red brick. Laundromat across the alley. Less attractive to rats than a restaurant or bar, but there's a lotta water running in and out of laundromats. A lotta pipes. Lotta ways for rats to gain entry, then slowly conquer these adjacent homes.

Prez checks on Smog. Sure enough, the dog's found a ten-inch fissure in the alley's crook. An inch wide, which is plenty. Prez sniffs and smells the rat fur, rat urine, and rat droppings he expects.

"Ain't gonna be pretty, Smoggie."

Smog's whole rear end wags—*ain't gonna be pretty* is just how the dog likes it.

This next part's a little kooky. His Pest Control Operator colleagues break his balls about it. Hunched over the gap, Prez closes his eyes and tries to *see*. All the way down. Far beyond what is visible to the eye.

Three inches of asphalt; anyone with ears can hear rats that close. Beneath that, ten inches of coarse concrete; Smog's got that covered, tilting his head at subsonic squeaks. Twelve inches down is a foot of absorbent soil, perfect for rat burrows. Five inches more and you hit the city's nerve endings: telephone lines, electric cables, fiber optics. This stuff's encased in concrete, but you give a rat enough time and concrete might as well be cheese. A quarter of fires are caused by rats chewing wires. People say wires look like the sticks rats like to chew on. Prez hopes that's it.

Deeper now. Con Ed gas lines at two feet, seven thousand miles of it. At four feet, deep-water mains bringing water from the Catskills and Croton Distributing Reservoir. If there's water, there's rats; they can swim for days on end. Five feet down, the outdated tech of pneumatic mail tubes stretching from Wall Street to Harlem, even to Brooklyn, where Prez is now. Six feet down, the city's system of steam pipes, too vast for workers to even notice rodents. Seven feet, sewer pipes, the only level rats are expected to proliferate and happily oblige.

Finally, at depths of up to a hundred and eight feet deep, the subways. Eight hundred miles of dark, warm, moist tunnels with infinities of negative spaces that expand as trains shake and break old concrete. Aside from rats scorched via third-rail electrocution and the occasional celebrity rat dragging a piece of pizza, these millions of rats go largely unnoticed, save for the unlucky tunnel worker who bashes through an old wall to find hundreds of interlocked rat skeletons.

Or those hired specifically to find them. Like Prez.

He's always been glad to do it. Down here is where civilization's gears turn. Forget politicians, Mikołaj Przybyszewski used to say. Forget police chiefs, captains of industry, forget men and women of the cloth. Their mansions, prisons, factories, and churches will all slide into crevasses if we let rats gnaw the foundations.

Ratcatchers are the true guardians of the city.

It's a calling few can understand, much less live with. Prez has been married three times, not one of which lasted three years. Dear friends with all three women to this day. They just couldn't take it. The late nights chasing rats. The chemical stink of rodenticides. The funk of sewage and spoiled food. The unsightly and occasionally infected bites. The sporadic rat he'd bring home—spitting, clawing, pissing—inside shivering metal cages for study.

Once you're attuned to rats, you see them everywhere. Every alleyway, sure. But also back yards. Under cars. Beneath swing sets. Beside stoves. On church pews, amid grocery-store vegetables, in the dark corners of busy restaurants. It's like being able to see ghosts. It creeps out your friends. Pretty soon you're not really friends anymore. You damn sure aren't spouses.

Dogs are the exception. Prez has raised a series of gifted ratters, Smog the most talented of all. He musses the terrier's floppy ears. At least now he's back to spending all day with the old boy—his colleague, his baby, his brother. Canines aside, Przybyszewski & Sons was a misnomer. Mikołaj and Lena had four children, three of them girls averse to the charms of rodentkind. Mikołaj simply saw the word *Sons* on a lot of American business signs and copied it. Prez regrets that. If he'd managed to have a single kid with just one of his wives, he might have passed along his dad's business, instead of selling out for the dubious honor of working for Noah Goff.

Two years ago, he'd been doing a typical day's run. After lunch, he was way the hell over in SoHo at the shop of a former client's daughter, a cupcake joint plagued with fruit flies. Prez was walking down Wooster, taking the second of the two bites it took to demolish his vanilla cream cheese-topped red velvet reward, when he saw a white kid leaning against his Astro van, hands stuffed in his jean pockets.

Kid wasn't super-accurate. The guy was in his early thirties. He was kid-skinny, though, and his crisp sky-blue hoodie and spotless Nike sneakers indicated he wasn't exactly digging ditches for a living. Prez gave New York denizens lots of leeway, but leaning on his van?

"You hear that dog barking inside?" Prez jerked a thumb. "He wants you off his ride."

"Jack Russell," the kid said.

Prez squinted. "You peeking through my windows?"

The kid ignored the question. "He's got fox-catcher genes. Catching and killing rats, it's baked right into his code. Pretty cool stuff, genes."

Prez sized up the kid. "What do you know about rats?"

The kid grinned. He had a nervy, off-kilter charm. Curiosity won out over Prez's impulse to dislocate the kid's limbs.

"I know that back in the 1800s, this city was filled with rat pits. Bars, clubs, amphitheaters. People brought in their terriers, let them loose in the pit, and saw which pooch could rack up the most kills. There was a dog like yours named Jocko the Wonder Dog that killed a hundred rats in five minutes."

Prez knew all this. Most kids in wrinkle-free hoodies didn't.

"Smog's not *that* good," Prez grunted. "But this ain't Kit Burns's Sportsmen's Hall and we ain't fetching a purse of a hundred twenty-five a night."

"Kit Burns," the kid echoed. "Lieutenant in the Irish gang the Dead Rabbits. Derived from the Irish *ráibéad*, which basically means big, scary dude."

"Yeah." Prez was just plain puzzled now. "That's right."

The kid grinned like he thought he knew more about rats than Leonard Przybyszewski. Shortly Prez would find out that, in a way, he did. The kid bucked himself from the Astro van and strolled toward West Houston.

"Got a job for you. Bring the dog."

Who the hell did this brat think he was? But Prez's flash of indignation passed. His next call wasn't till two-thirty, and that cupcake would delay hunger pangs for a bit. And Smog had been cooped up too long.

He cursed, slid open the door, and leashed the dog.

"Gonna regret this, Smoggie," he confided. "I can feel it."

He was right, but wouldn't know it for two years. Five minutes later, the kid, whose name was Noah, led him into the most incredible living space Prez had ever seen, a sleek penthouse loft the dimensions of a basketball court. Everything resembled the kid's clothing: tidy as a showroom, yet reeking of expense.

Prez glanced down at his stained overalls and ripped boots. Smog looked up worriedly as if thinking the same thing.

Noah tapped a button and shades rose all over the apartment, revealing floor-to-ceiling windows overlooking the Apple Store. He tossed his keys at the wall and a magnetic plate caught them. Noah opened a blue-steel refrigerator.

"Alkaline water?"

"Huh?" Prez asked.

"It's got a nine-point-five pH. Better for the circulation."

Noah tossed one twenty feet across what was roughly the kitchen space. Prez caught it and frowned at the black bottle. What kind of water came in black bottles? That's how you'd package poison.

"So," Prez said. "Your problem?"

Noah cracked open his own alkaline water. "I got a rat."

Prez relaxed. This wasn't a con. The kid wasn't going to pull a gun or make some outré sexual overture. Prez kneeled with a grunt and unlatched Smog.

"Find the rat," he said in an excited doggy tone. "Find the rat, Smoggie."

Smog took off, nose to the ground, tail wagging.

Prez stood. "What makes you think you got rats?"

Noah smiled placidly. Prez had never seen such calm in the face of infestation. "I saw it."

"I got bad news, then. You see one rat, you got ten."

"No," Noah laughed. "It's just one."

Prez began studying the floor, pointing a penlight behind major appliances.

"You got family, Noah?"

"Sure. But not here."

"Well, rats got families too. Very social animal, the rat. Their family units can be as small as five. They can also be as big as a hundred. Forty years I've been doing this and have yet to meet a loner rat. Not that I'm trying to scare you."

Noah laughed again. "Oh, I'm not scared."

Prez rested his head on the floor, ridiculously clean, to see beneath a twelve-burner, industrial-sized stove that showed no sign of being used.

"Rats are like zombies. One's not much of a problem. But you get enough of them, you're in trouble. And New York's got two million."

"That's a bunch," Noah said. "But really, I've just got the one."

Prez took a resting kneel and squinted at Noah. He still had the sense that the kid was messing with him.

"Where'd you see this rat?"

Noah pointed and Prez looked. In front of the biggest television he'd ever seen was a pet cage, nothing like Prez's rusty metal boxes. It was translucent plastic with turquoise accents and a fingerprint lock-pad, molded with rounded walls that might allow one cage to be nested between others.

"A pet?"

"A specimen. I was showing it some videos. Seeing how it reacted."

Prez blinked. "Some *videos*?"

Noah nodded. Again, Prez had the feeling the kid was enjoying this.

"You don't want me to kill this rat," he guessed.

Noah looked mildly offended. "Please don't. You ever saved a rat before? Instead of killing it?"

Prez didn't like the question. Yet he felt obligated to answer, like this was an interview.

"Found a rat in a sewer grate once, over in Williamsburg. Got wedged in there. I mean, there's killing, right? Then there's cruelty. Couldn't leave him like that. Probably spent forty-five minutes easing that little guy out of there. Had a mind to splint his back leg too. But when I got him out, he seemed to swim pretty good."

"This should be simple for you, then. I just need to get the rat out of my wall."

Noah pointed right to where Smog had his paws pressed to a central-air vent. Like everything in the loft, the grill had a chunky, futuristic style with irresponsibly wide gaps. Prez sighed at the stupidity of the design. It was like Dad used to say: Give a rat an inch and it'd take the whole damn planet.

The job itself was easy. The grill popped right off and when Prez held a mirror inside to see along the duct, the rat was right there at the next bend. The kid must have trained it. Prez tossed out some Mexican gumdrops, his secret weapon. Once the rat had nibbled close enough, Prez lassoed its body with the steel cable at the end of his catch pole. The only surprise was the rat itself. When releasing it back into its cage, Prez got an eyeful. It was a *Rattus norvegicus* for sure, but like none he'd seen. Though it didn't compare to the later Sammy models Prez would see, its abbreviated snout and round body were already substantially cuter than the typical brown rat's.

Smog, his task completed, nuzzled Prez's hand. Prez scratched the dog's chin.

"You love that dog," Noah observed.

"Smoggie's a good boy."

"What if you could know him even better?"

"Huh?"

"What if you could know what he was thinking? What he was feeling? What he wanted? If he was happy or sad or sick?"

Prez shrugged. "That'd be nice. But that's fantasyland."

Not quite, Noah said. He lured Prez in with tantalizing scraps. He worked at a place called EditedPets. He did genetic studies on rats. He hoped to alter the human–rat relationship. It made instinctive sense to Prez; he knew how clever the bastards were. Twenty minutes after Prez gave Noah his rat, Noah gave Prez a job offer as head of security. Twice what Prez was making busting his hump on the streets, plus health and dental. Prez would withhold his yes for three days, but that was theater. He'd known right away, with a strange resignation, that he was going to accept.

Prez had only one question. "Why me?"

"Today?" Noah asked. "Why you *today*? Because technically I'm not supposed to bring this specimen home and my R&D director will tear me a new asshole if she finds out. Better not to generate call records to an exterminator when I can accost one on the street."

Noah leaned forward. Intensity had replaced playfulness.

"But why you for the *position*? Because I believe in kismet. It's how I met my R&D developer. How I found my initial investors. Your first impression of someone is the truest, I really believe that."

Prez mentally noted that his first impression of Noah was unfavorable.

"I've been looking for someone who knows his rats," Noah continued, "but isn't beholden to some corporate entity, with all their codes and complications. That van of yours tells me you work alone."

Prez didn't know whether to be impressed or offended.

"But most of all, because you saved that rat in Williamsburg. That tells me you've got an open mind. That you meet life as it comes. Good rat, bad rat. Good person, bad person. It all depends on circumstances, doesn't it?"

Smog wanted to be held, and Prez obliged. If he took a desk job with this Noah kid, Smoggie would be left at home all day. He knew the terrier would be fine. But would Prez?

Noah grinned, a flash of the smug kid Prez had met on the street.

"Let's toast on it," he said. "How about that alkaline water?"

✖

The client is in the alley now. Never good. She's throwing Smog off his game while reciting to Prez the usual rat myths: rats can retract their skeletons; there are giant, blind, albino rats in the sewers; rats see in the dark, courtesy of their red laser eyes. Prez relocates to the building's basement where, as usual, the trouble resides. He finds the rat stomping grounds and sets up bait stations, incorporating them into the geography. Rats are neophobic, fearful of new objects in their habitat.

I was too, Prez thinks, thinking back to his first time inside Edited-Pets, all those people with all those degrees doing their thing inside, in offices as clean as Noah's penthouse. *But I got used to it. Way too quickly. I got lazy.*

"How is the senior Mr. Prez?" the client asks, referring to his father.

Prez lets Smog sniff out the best placement for the next bait station.

"Dead," Prez says. "Four years this Christmas."

"I'm so sorry," she says, "I didn't know."

"That's good," Prez says. "Means you haven't been overrun by vermin."

"Wherever he is, I know he's proud. You made good."

Smog hops out of the way. In goes the bait station. Prez coats it with crumbled concrete.

"Well, I'm back doing this," Prez said.

The client smiles like that was her point all along. "Like I said, he'd be proud."

Prez shuts his eyes and takes a big inhale: he can suss out the direction urine markings are headed if he concentrates. But he can't concentrate. With eyes closed, he again visualizes the two-hundred-foot cutaway of the city, all those layers of human secrets left for the conqueror rats. He's back to fight for that territory. But what was Noah's compliment the day they met? *You meet life as it comes.* Prez hadn't expected to meet someone at EditedPets he loved like a daughter. But he had.

10

The Great Wave of Rats rolls closer, millions of them reaching over Sienna, paws and whiskers, a butte of gray fur, pink flesh, red eyes, and yellow teeth about to crash into her, wipe her away.

Less than six months to Pet Expo. Each day showing up to the lab and improvising sick shit to do to rats. As if the daily experiments rooting out rat psychopathology weren't gruesome enough, there's force-feeding, suffocating, drowning, amputation, bleeding them dry. Product "testing" and breakage analysis, after all, were just as important to ensure there would be no future surprises.

Sienna pins her hopes on fluke revelation. There's historical precedent. A culture dish left in the sun led to penicillin. A process for castrating dogs led to a treatment for prostate cancer. A search for a drug to stop postpartum bleeding led to LSD. An angina treatment led to Viagra. It's an insane way to work. Sienna feels insane. The floors are carpeted with origami stomped into unidentifiable debris, just like the rats.

Noah hasn't filled Prez's position. Sienna doesn't think he will. She tries to see it from Noah's perspective. Why bring in a wild card who won't understand what they're doing? People everywhere grasp for the cancer drugs, antidepressants, and vaccines that keep them and their loved ones thriving, but few have the appetite to know how the sausage gets made. All they know is what PETA scaremongers throw in their faces; Sienna's gonna puke if she has to see that photo of rats' heads grafted onto the thighs of other rats one more time. Yes, it happened. Sure, it's hideous. But that experiment helped us understand issues related to SIDS, the leading cause of death in infants one year old or younger. Was that not worth a smidgen of the hideous?

Problem is, EditedPets *isn't* ending SIDS. They're *not* curing Alzheimer's. They're making pets a little more fun than regular pets. This is why Sienna clings—like a rat to its cage—to the concept of Biological Uplift. By keeping rats, ponies, budgies, and goldfish in the same genetic soup as humans, she's doing something good.

But people won't see that good for a long time. Who's to say Sienna will live to see vindication? That's why Lighthouse Liquors, a block from her place, has epitomized its namesake and become a beckoning beacon. Each night on the way home Sienna presses her nose to the window to see the stately ranks of wines, the pugnacious flasks of liquors, the chummy bottles of beer. Two years she's been dry. Two years.

A white-bearded Turkish man works nights. In the years between her fertility failures and going cold turkey with Prez's help, the soft-spoken Turk sold her several thousand dollars' worth of booze. Today must be a magical day. The man notices her. He flattens his own nose with a finger to mirror hers.

She laughs, fogging the glass. And that's it. She knows that's it. She feels the sticky door handle in her palm, feels the coolant blast of A/C, hears Turkish techno-pop grind through lousy speakers. A little sip. A single glass. What a feeling, to give yourself to one Great Wave or another and let it wash you away.

✖

Sienna wakens on her sofa, sand-throated, head bumping its own techno-pop. A little over five months to Pet Expo. She decides to walk to work so she can duck behind a pile of trash if she needs to puke. She fails to dress appropriately. The autumn morning is crazily cold.

The cold brings back a childhood memory. There wasn't a lot parents could do in Missoula with a brood the size of the Aguirres. But Glacier National Park was two and a half hours north, and a cabin big enough to bed the whole bunch of them was cheaper than ten tickets to anything. Most summers, five days at Glacier was the family trip.

Sebastián Aguirre's tall tales around the fire pit were Sienna's favorite part. According to Dad, Glacier was populated by trolls. Trolls caused such havoc in the 1800s that President Woodrow Wilson created the U.S. National Park Service to establish places where they could live, roam, and hunt. These weren't the kind of grumpy little trolls upset about billy goats trip-trapping across their bridges. These were lumbering ogres who built mountains by tossing boulders. Any thunder the Aguirre children heard, Sebastián said, were the sounds trolls made running around hunting bears, bighorn sheep, elk, lynx, mountain goats, and especially pika—they gobbled those suckers like popcorn.

This was the part where little Sienna got scared. Dad to the rescue! First of all, trolls didn't like eating people. People wore clothes, and the buttons and zippers got wedged between troll teeth.

Secondly, trolls only fed at night, so a kid like Sienna would never see them. However, if you hit the trails early enough, you might find evidence of their slaughtered prey. It was a ruse to get the kids hiking, but the brilliant part of Sebastián's scheme was that they did, in fact, find the evidence. Sienna will never forget the morning on Gunsight Mountain when she discovered a huge pool of blood in a rock depression.

It wasn't until Sienna was twelve, the family's final believer in trolls, that her dad, worried she'd get made fun of at school, let her in on the secret. The red pools at Glacier were a phenomenon known as "glacier blood," aka "sang des glacier." At high altitudes, where UV rays can be thirty percent more intense, a snow algae called *Chlamydomonas nivalis* makes its own sunscreen, expressed as a blood-colored pigment.

In other words, the algae turns itself on via *light*.

Despite fifty pounds of hangover weight, Sienna begins to smile, then grin, then laugh right in the middle of the sidewalk. Passersby probably don't notice because they are walking toward the sun. That's okay. She sees them. Light guides her way.

><

She presents the short version of her idea to Noah and the staff scientists, then calls a random brother in Missoula, who tells her that their sibling Lola is in Glacier right now. Sienna dials up Lola, tells her what she needs, and two days later hears back from Lola that she's found the algae, sealed it inside Tupperware, put it on ice, and will hit the road tomorrow to hand-deliver it to Sienna in New York. Sienna shoves tears back with the heels of her hands. She could have downloaded the gene sequence. But she wanted the *C. nivalis* that mattered to her, the *C. nivalis* that felt like her dad's DNA.

"One more thing," she says to Lola. "Can I have Dad's thermos?"

Lola is confused. "The *#1 DAD*?"

"Yeah. I . . . want something of his around."

Sienna has always eschewed mementos, intent on looking forward. But now she recalls herself at nine years old, buying her dad a birthday present with her own money for the first time. After hours of consideration, she'd selected an ugly yellow metal thermos printed with *#1 DAD*.

"We keep our marshmallow-roasting sticks in there," Lola warns. "Not sure it's much good for drinking. But if you want it, it's yours."

Five days later, Lola and Sienna meet at Peter Luger for chopped steak. After hugs and declining a drink—Sienna wants Lola to think she's still on the wagon—Lola presents the ice-packed cooler and the *#1 DAD* thermos.

"Happy birthday to you," Lola sings.

Sienna is stunned. She runs the numbers. So that's why Lola drove all the way. Usually what tips Sienna off to her own birthday is Noah's delivery of fifty new FireFish. But this year it didn't happen. She's going to have to watch her single living FireFish die alone. She examines the blood-red *C. nivalis* through the Tupperware lid, then slides it under her chair.

The thermos, though, she leaves on the table, a conversation piece.

"Dad really was number one, wasn't he?" Lola observes.

Sienna nods. "Remember the shredded-documents story?"

Lola brays. Sienna misses the sound.

"Oh, god! A Sebastián Aguirre classic. Let's see if I can remember. The Soviets, right? It's after World War II and the Soviets are helping China make an atomic bomb in exchange for I don't know what."

"Uranium."

"Right. Then one day Stalin's like, wait, do we really want Mao having an atomic bomb? So he pulls out his scientists but first they shred all hundred zillion of their build-a-bomb documents." Lola snorts. "Most kids got fairy tales. We got political intrigue."

"You remember how the story ends?"

"I'm an Aguirre, aren't I? Let's see. Couple years later, China blows up an atomic bomb and Stalin's like, WTF? Eventually he finds out Mao forced all these Chinese physicists to take those hundred zillion shredded documents and tape them back together. Baller move."

A waiter takes their orders. Lola, having fun now, asks Sienna if it's okay if she gets a Manhattan. Of course it's okay. Lola sips her drink while Sienna rolls the *#1 DAD* thermos between her palms.

"You know *why* Dad told us that story?" she asks.

"Never trust the Chinese government." Lola smiles devilishly. "*Kidding.*"

"Dad was trying to tell us that genius only gets you so far. Sometimes all that works is your nose against the grindstone. Did you know I almost dropped out of NYU?"

"Uh-oh. Is this a serious story? Are we going to need Kleenex?"

"Maybe? It was around the time I started drinking. My noggin was firing on all cylinders. But I was, you know, sloppy. I couldn't get myself to do the work. The simplest stuff. Getting my butt down to Kinko's, picking up a book from the library. And I thought, better to drop out than flunk out."

"Well, you'd never failed before. You didn't know how to do it."

"One morning I get my mail. It's about the extent of what I can do. And it's a big manila envelope from Dad. Inside is an eight-by-eleven document—and it's been shredded. Shredded to a million pieces."

Lola's grin freezes. Like the ice in her Manhattan, the grin melts until her lips curl downward and her eyes fill with tears. She picks up her napkin and carefully dabs her eyes, which she'd done up special for their night on the town.

"Oh, Dad," Lola says from behind the napkin.

Sienna sighs. "I don't even know how he knew. But I started right there, on the floor in my PJs. I started putting that puzzle back together. Took all week. But I put in the work. Went to Kinko's. Picked up my library books. Got my shit together. That shredded letter was me, you know? I'd put *myself* back together."

Lola flaps her hands to dry the tears.

"What did the letter say?"

Sienna smiles. "That's between me and Dad."

Lola blows her nose. "Number one dad for sure."

"He should have been the one at NYU. At Rockefeller. He was better than me."

Her sister tosses down her napkin. The Lola revealed is harder and sharper.

"Don't say that. You have your ambitions and your dreams, and we all try to understand them. But Dad working at the high school, being able to come home to his family every night? That wasn't some kind of failure. He was exactly where he wanted to be."

❌

Sienna offers to be a tourist for a day, but Lola can tell when her sister is dying to get back to work and unhooks her collar. Sienna is back at EditedPets within the hour, the *#1 DAD* thermos propped proudly on her desk, using INTR to merge the light-sensing CrChR21 gene, and a handful of others sequenced from the *C. nivalis* algae, into a harvest of rat zygotes already possessing the brain gyrification gene. She's on fire, operating the suction pipette and injector like she was born with INTR joysticks instead of hands.

Sienna has always excelled at the interactome: the combination of molecular and gene-gene interactions. The naysayers who claim that she edits genes like anyone else are missing the point. If she gave those assholes genes that turned their feet into skates, they still couldn't skate for the NHL, right? They wouldn't have the full suite of necessary genes: balance, speed, coordination, aggression. The interactome is every element performing in perfect concert.

Sammy 2.0 would only be ten percent smarter than the average rat if all EditedPets gave him were a couple human intelligence genes. It's everything Sienna puts *around* Sammy that coaxes that intelligence closer to that of a five-year-old child. It's why the Enrichment Room exists. Fuck—she's got to get Linda back. Next thing on the checklist.

She finishes the zygote insertion. The nods she shares with her staff are better than any cake.

Noah holds no such emotional distance. Five months till Pet Expo, and he's a trainwreck still hurtling at train speed. He's got a band-aid on a finger. He missed an entire cheek shaving. He's got notes scribbled on his palm like a middle-schooler. He joins her at the counter where plastic culture dishes of altered zygotes stew before reimplantation into surrogate females. Before he can demand that they stew faster, he screws up his nose.

"What is that? Is someone eating in here? Who's eating?"

Sienna smiles. "What does it smell like?"

Sniff-sniff. "Is that watermelon?"

Two hours past lunch, and Sienna's not even hungry. She sits on a stool and twirls her hair. She's not flirting with Noah, she's just flirting—with science, with life, and it feels great.

"*C. nivalis* smells like watermelon," she says. "Tastes like it, too. Even looks like it."

Sienna gestures at the Olympus BX51 microscope beside the microinjection rig. The monitor displays a microscopic view of *C.*

nivalis, which indeed resembles a cutaway section of watermelon. Noah stares at it.

"You're shitting me."

"Even back when I thought it was troll gore, I noticed the smell."

"Will our Sammys smell like this? Like watermelon?"

"Most likely, yes."

Noah walks a tight circle, hands held out, blinking rapidly like he's trying to compute. He finishes the circle, grips the counter. "Did you know that, in olfactory circles, watermelon is considered one of the most universally liked smells in the world? And the hardest to fabricate?"

"I'm intrigued by these 'olfactory circles,'" Sienna jokes. "But, yeah, makes sense. Watermelon fragrance comes from a pair of aldehydes. Specifically, a compound called (Z,Z)-3,6-nonadienal. Breaks down super easy, so it's a bitch to harness."

"I bought my mom a spa treatment once, and you know what they used? Watermelon essential oil. They say it detoxifies you. Has Vitamin E for immunity. But most of all, it's calming. I know that much is true. Some of the hotels I've been at, they pump this stuff called watermelon ketone into the lobby to chill people out after a flight. And you're telling me we've—" Noah squeezes his eyes shut for a second. "You're telling me our rat, in addition to everything else, is going to *calm people down?*"

Sienna nods. "Just might."

Noah slaps the counter hard enough to ring a set of borosilicate petri dishes.

Might as well be the clink of champagne glasses.

"An aromatherapy rat? Holy fucking shit, Doc! This is going to be bigger than the Beatles!"

He grabs a stool and pulls it close. Sienna basks in the delight of his attention.

"Okay, give me the 411," Noah says. "I swear I'm listening this time. This *C. nivalis,* it's sensitive to light."

"Yep. Red light."

Noah spins on his stool. Sienna can't help but laugh.

"Red light, duh! Because red light penetrates the skull!"

"Unlike the blue light from our phones scorching our retinas every day."

"Okay, so you what? Attach this algae gene to 11B?"

"Leave the coding to the pros, Goff. 11B is primates. *ARHGAP11A*—I added a gene to it that makes a light-sensitive protein that can be switched on. Quick recap: switching on that kind of protein is what gets the human brain's progenitor cells really kicking. So what happens? The progenitor cells multiply, making more progenitor cells, and even more, until all those cells start making what? Pop quiz."

Noah slaps the table again. "Neurons!"

"Good. Now, left on its own, 11A is still going to balloon Sammy's brain against his skull. But this algae protein, it only switches on *with intense red light.*"

"Oh my god. And no one's done this before?"

Sienna shrugs. "Technically this is Optogenetics. But most Opto work has been used to turn on and off neurons, not genes."

"Get to the downside, Aguirre. There's always a downside."

"Well, it's not breaking news that too much neuronal growth will result in the kind of seizures we've seen in Sammy. Seizures are like power surges: they damage the brain, lead to rapid cognitive decline."

"Seizures: bad. Got it."

"But too *little* neuron growth and we just have a boring old rat. We just have to figure out the dosage, how much we want to dial up the red light we give to Sammy."

"How long's that going to take? Pet Expo is—"

"Five months away, I know. I'll start with an exposure time of three hours at 3 J/cm² and the rats will tell us when we've got it right. Once we do—Noah, I can imagine whole warehouses with overhead LEDs zapping thousands of Sammys at once. But we'll still need Linda back in the Enrichment Room, so I need to—"

All Noah heard, probably, was *warehouses*. Nothing got him revved like industry, the idea of new buildings filled with new employees doing things no one else had ever done. With a face like a proud papa holding in emotion, Noah stands, takes Sienna by the shoulders, and plants a kiss on her forehead with a loud smack. Sienna doesn't care how subservient she may or may not look: she blushes and leans into it, enjoying the warmth.

Noah withdraws. Sienna feels a sliver of panic that he'll smell the booze on her breath and the nice moment will be ruined. But his grin is as broad as before. You can't smell anything in the lab besides the invigorating, sugary smell of fresh watermelon.

11

Sienna could use some soothing watermelon scent right now. Linda is not at all relaxed. Through the white vapor of her tea steam, she's giving Sienna a brand-new kind of look: disappointment, with a dollop of pity and a dash of fear. It hurts but Sienna knows she deserves it. She eats the emotions along with a raspberry scone.

"I heard Dekota won't need reconstructive surgery," Sienna says. "That's good."

Linda sighs. "He's back with his family in Flathead. I think his first trip to New York might be his last. He left his job for EditedPets, you know."

Sienna is prepared to accept all burdens of blame. "Our insurance is covering a hundred percent of medical. Noah says he's giving Dekota the world's best severance. We're doing everything we can."

"Frankly," Linda says, "I'm not sure what *I'm* still doing here. I left my job too, so I guess there's no rush to get home. The apartment you gave me is paid through the month. I've been seeing the sights. I did the Met. Top of the Rock. Walked the High Line a bit. I'd like to see Ellis Island, but ferries make me ill." She frowns. "I don't like drawing a paycheck for doing nothing. Can't you get Noah to stop paying me?"

"No, because he wants you back as badly as I do."

Linda sags. Sienna identifies with the dark circles under her friend's eyes. "How can I? That room. All I'm going to see is Dekota and all that blood."

"You must have seen your share of accidents at CMA. Remember that kid who leaned back on his chair too far and hit his head on a table, right by his eye, and there was blood all over?"

"Tyson." There is affection in Linda's smile. "You have a good memory."

"You're telling me that was the only accident? In forty years of teaching?"

Linda laughs lightly. "We had a boy once who somehow stabbed himself in the head with his pencil. There was the usual parade of fingers caught in doors. We had a boy—it's always the boys—who tried to yank a loose tooth with scissors. Scissors!"

"Montessori kids," Sienna says dryly. "Always the most creative."

"Worst thing I ever saw," Linda continues, and she's smiling now, "was this pretty little girl who stuck her tongue inside a pop can and couldn't get it out. I had to ride in the ambulance holding that can, which was filling up with blood. They had to cut the can off with trauma shears."

"I'm going to seriously puke," Sienna says. But this is good. Accident talk builds camaraderie.

Linda gives her a sidelong look. "With all the stuff you do in your lab? I think about *Frankenstein* sometimes, Sienna. About *The Island of Dr. Moreau*. All those stories have the same kind of ending."

"That's not science, though. That's fiction. It's understandable, given everything, why you've got that idea. But we're not hacking and slashing up there. You've seen it. It's more like a computer lab with white coats."

Tea steam heavies Linda's lashes. "Didn't Dr. Jekyll wear a white coat?

"I hear what you're saying. But I created INTR. I know its limitations."

"Then what happened up there? How could I possibly feel comfortable going back? Bringing Tasha and Mason back?"

"Do they want to come back?"

Linda rolls her eyes. "Tasha lives for danger. And Mason goes where Tasha goes. The texts from them, every day, you wouldn't believe it."

Sienna feels the set of the hook. If Linda has a weakness, it's saying no to a student. It's why she's in Manhattan in the first place.

"Let me just show you what we've done with the new Sammys. Unless you plan to start radiating red light, it's scientifically impossible for them to become violent."

Linda looks down at her untouched chocolate croissant.

"How many days to the big show?" Linda asks.

Sienna feels the fishing line go taut.

><

Not everything is fit for Linda Miller's view. Not if Sienna wants her back.

The past month has been spent using techniques Sienna doesn't believe her former teacher would like. There is a thing called a stereotaxic apparatus. It doesn't look friendly. It isn't. The tool looks like it belongs on a butcher's counter: a rectangle of stainless steel with two vise arms. Between the arms is a clothespin-like fastener that holds a rat's snout in place. A bar extends from each arm until they press firmly into the rat's ears, stopping at its skull. The rat can wiggle its body all it wants. Its head isn't going anywhere.

This is how it goes. Sienna plugs in an electric razor. Sounds like the one Isaiah used to have. He'd sit on a stool in the bathroom and she'd buzz him clean, enjoying the reemergence of his subtle planes and ridges. Nothing so loving here. She shaves the hair off the top of the rat's head, a single barbershop scrape. Its infant skin is pink and supple.

Razor down. Scalpel up. She could use anesthesia, but anesthesia has to be measured, injected, waited on. A doped rat needs an air tube to breathe and use of an oximeter to make sure that its blood oxygen level stays between ninety and ninety-nine percent, plus heart-rate monitoring, plus a rectal thermometer, plus eye cream on its corneas to offset its lack of blinking.

It's time that EditedPets doesn't have. Sienna compromises with 1cc of lidocaine mixed with 3ccs of sterile saline, enough to numb the skin. She makes an anterior-posterior incision down the center of the rat's scalp. The flesh has a gummy-bear texture. Dark blood wells up, more than if she'd taken the time to inject epinephrine. She wipes it away with a swab and hangs two bulldog clamps to both sides of the cut. The wound yawns wide to expose the skull cap. The rat screams.

The stereotaxic apparatus has fine sets of adjustment wheels, perfect down to a 250th of an inch. But for the drilling, Sienna eyeballs it. She finds the bregma, the intersection point of the sagittal and coronal sutures, the squiggly lines that fuse skull bones. She brings a hand drill the size of a latte milk frother down to the bone and drills directly into the skull. Smells like burnt hair. The rat passes out from pain but also, Sienna suspects, existential shock.

Pink-tinged cerebrospinal fluid, but not much. Another swab, then Sienna punches a sterile needle through the skinlike meninges over the brain. She lines up the stereotaxic apparatus and inserts a cannula—a thin metal tube—into the hole until it reaches the correct coordinate. Almost done. She drills two screws on either side of the cannula, attaches a platform to stabilize the metal tube, and covers the whole thing with dental cement.

She leaves cleanup to the techs. After the cement has dried, the rat will need a wash of sterile saline, a couple sutures, and an antibiotic shot. Sienna does the operation twelve more times until there's a counter full of rats with metal tubes rising from their skulls. They look like little unicorns. They *are* unicorns, Sienna thinks—right now, the rarest beasts in the world.

✄

Linda hates to put anyone out. It's a small-town thing. Though Sienna prepped the lab staff to be on *Leave It to Beaver* behavior if Linda came up, it's Linda who puts *them* at ease, telling the scientists how much she regrets scaring them the day of the bite, telling the techs how much she missed them. And how is your father doing? How did that online date go? Sienna half expects Linda to whip out a tray of fresh-baked cookies.

After pleasantries—and they *are* pleasant, the most relaxing minutes EditedPets has enjoyed in weeks—it's on to New Rat City, where opaque plastic hides the disturbing unicorn rats. Before key-carding the Enrichment Room door, Sienna shivers once. Without intense red light, nothing can go wrong with the Sammys.

But Gamma Phi Delta? Those rodents are harder to predict.

Within seconds of entering, Sienna knows she's pulled it off.

It wouldn't have worked to drag more Early Childhood Education students in here; Linda would feel devalued. Nor did lab staff make sense; Linda would suspect them of drugging the rats or other chicanery. That left only the doofuses of sales and marketing, who were always bugging Sienna to see Sammys closer up.

Sienna learned their names only when she selected them: Doris, a short, twenty-five-ish fashion plate in tattoos and designer frames, and mid-thirties Theo, the kind of affable, soft-gutted dunderhead all of Sienna's sisters have married. Today, the two of them radiate joy.

"These guys are the best!" Theo cries.

"Can I have one early?" Doris begs. "Oh please, oh please, oh please."

These first-wave, algae-gene pups of the unicorn rats are adorable, alert, and frisky, just like Sammy 1.0. But they also have a gravitas Sienna has only seen in primates. They don't bolt and scurry; they stroll with calm assurance. They don't only pick up on cues like dogs; they *listen* in a way that is tangible. There is a pensiveness to how the rats regard Doris and Theo, and now Sienna and Linda, as if they might smile, extend a paw, and, in English accents, ask if they are in jolly good health.

Instead they push at their AACs.

"Doris, Sienna is here. Who is that other person?"

"That is Linda. SammySpeaks has her picture. Linda, Linda, Linda."

"Linda's dress is blue like SammyWagon."

"Theo, finish the story. Finish the story, Theo."

"Linda, will you watch me drive SammyWagon?"

Sienna glances at Linda to see how she is taking it.

Her jaw is locked shut, which means she's stopping it from hanging open. Better than that, Linda has that pupil glow that she gets any time a student makes a bold cognitive leap. It's something a teacher like her can grasp hold of and nurture.

"The language benchmarks . . ." Linda starts. "It's got to be first-grade if not . . . When did they . . . ? How did you . . . ?"

"I didn't." Sienna hears tears in her own throat. "My dad did."

Though Linda can't know what this means, she curls an arm around Sienna's back. Sienna reciprocates until the women hold each other, while frolicking rats come closer, eager for their attention.

"I'll call Tasha and Mason," Linda says.

✖

The *C. nivalis* gene is an intensity knob, capable of dialing up the growth of Sammy's brain with application of red light. How much red light is the question. This is why half the denizens of New Rat City have metal tubes in their heads. Sienna can expose the brains of these unicorn rats to whatever degree she'd like, note the effects, and fine-tune the dosage.

From each rat's cannula extends a 200mm-core multimode optical fiber that's capable of moving data at a speed of 178 terabits a second, the equivalent of downloading the entire Netflix catalog in one second. The entire length of the cable glows with vibrant red light. Sometimes when Sienna is the only one left at EditedPets at night, she turns off the lights so the only things visible are these graceful red arcs.

This is what Sienna doesn't want Linda to see. She instructs her staff to hide the fiber-optic rats via metal roll-top lids anytime the Enrichment team passes through. To someone like Linda, the sight would be too sci-fi, something out of that old B-movie *The Brain That Wouldn't Die,* in which a mad doctor keeps his fiancée's severed head alive on an electric platter.

Sienna tinkers daily with the amount of red light delivered into the rat brains via the fiber-optic cables. She started by going big, overexposing the rats and tracking the brain expansion, subsequent seizures, and ultimate deaths. Working backward, sacrificing rats as she goes, she's inching closer to the Goldilocks ideal of red light required to turn average genetically modified rats into full-fledged Sammy 2.0s.

Someday soon, she'll be able to expose multiple rats at once. She's already getting there. At-home red-light therapy surged in popularity during the stay-at-home orders of Covid-19, advertised with buff twenty-somethings posing before mirror-size banks of red light.

· 97 ·

Though it looks like the models are inside a toaster oven, in actuality they are enjoying the benefits of 630nm of pulsing red light. Akin to giant SAD lamps, such lights enhance skin health, reduce inflammation, boost workout recovery, and look cool in selfies.

They are also big—and *big* is how Sienna needs to think if she's going to fill a whole warehouse with these things. She has four human-sized red-light therapy panels delivered to EditedPets. Too large for the lab, she stores them in the Enrichment Room closet. Once she gets the fiber-optic dose nailed, all she'll have to do is match the intensity to the therapy panels, and presto.

The offspring of these rats—the ones Linda, Tasha, and Mason will educate—will be so damn close to perfect, Sienna can barely take it. That's why she's drinking, more every night. Just to get her through these final three weeks, just until Pet Expo, when preorders will open and all money worries will dissipate.

After that? She'll dry out, of course, clamber back onto the wagon, and overcome the one major challenge she has yet to address: there's no permanent off switch. Any time the latest wave of Sammys are exposed to intense wavelengths of red light between 620 and 700nm, their brains will grow. She hasn't told Noah this. She sure as hell hasn't told Linda. It'll be okay. After Pet Expo, they'll have another six months before they start shipping to stores. Until then, the chance of accidental exposure to red light is practically nil.

12

Sienna wakes up to the sound she's come to hate most in life, the *zoop* of a text. It'll be Noah. It's always Noah. Seven days till Pet Expo, he's both a domineering overlord and clinging child, rotating all-caps demands with emoji-filled pleas for encouragement that he's ready, that the product's ready, that the ad slicks Gamma Phi Delta have ginned up properly squeeze the emotions, and wallets, of all who behold them.

She's on the sofa. Better than the floor. Cool objects roll along her exposed skin, some combo of liquor bottles and glasses. The shades are down but the alacrity of the bleed tells her it's mid-morning. *Zoop, zoop.* She cranes her neck. Stiff. She spots her phone, glowing with notifications. Just beyond it is the FireFish tank, its glow far less adamant. The sole surviving FireFish glumly circles its world.

This fish is going to live, Sienna decides.

She pulls herself up. The glass objects thunk to the floor. Activated, her body smells like unwashed dishrags. Her stomach sloshes as she shuffles to the tank. She sprinkles fish food. The FireFish glides up and kisses it away. It's not done fighting. Neither is she. She'll clean the tank tonight. Clean the house. Clean herself. Necessary prep for cleaning up her whole life, starting the day after Pet Expo.

Unlike Noah, she's never cared much about upgrading her living space. She's in the same budget unit she's lived in since Rockefeller. She looks out the window across Mott Street. Below is the imposing, windowless facade of St. Patrick's Old Cathedral. The wrought iron gates have welcomed tens of thousands of parishioners, but Sienna has always taken a certain pleasure in ignoring it. Just one more house of worship to a make-believe Creator. The only part of St. Patrick's that intrigues her are the catacombs beneath it. She ought to take the tour, already. Death and remains are things she respects. Unlike religion, they can be studied to actually improve the world.

Zoop.

"I'll zoop *you*," she mutters nonsensically. "Zoop you to hell."

The lean it takes to pick up the phone brings a vertigo flood. She waits for the nausea to pause, then picks up the phone.

It's not Noah.

Pit stop in the EditedPets ladies' room, fingers down the throat, the old college trick to void the sickness. She washes out her mouth, splashes water on her face. She looks like shit. It matters when a woman looks like shit, even in a lab. She gets pitying glances, like she's letting herself fall apart. Those looks will hurt today: she *is* letting herself fall apart.

She enters the lab and taps the *#1 DAD* thermos for good luck. The tech who texted her gestures her over to the northwest corner. Her name is Gillian. She's a good egg. Studied at Brown, volunteers at Genspace running a DNA sequencing class for the public, and works every nightmare shift available, probably in the hopes of impressing Noah—he'll never notice—and Sienna, who has noticed yet failed to compliment, per usual.

Gillian doesn't appear to hold it against her. Her eyes flash like only a twenty-four-year-old's can as she angles away to block the rest of the lab from their conversation. Sienna likes the feel of it: two women against the world.

"Let's see it," Sienna says.

Gillian holds up a finger so she can explain first. This takes balls. Sienna approves.

"So last night, right? I was here late, doing the blood and tissue samples for sequencing. And I had my iPad out, playing videos on auto-play." Gillian's tone dips guiltily. "No one was here, so I wasn't disturbing anyone or anything."

"Auto-play is how the algorithm gets its hooks in you. You'll never escape the matrix now." Sienna is half-kidding but Gillian goes wide-eyed. Sienna laughs. "Forget it. A little music won't seal your fate."

"It was TED Talks," Gillian admits. "Anyway, I set my iPad between a couple cages and was going about my work, when all of a sudden the TED talker cuts out and this other voice starts, real animated, like how you talk to kids. So I looked over, and a rat—this rat here—was reaching through the cage with its little paws. He'd opened an app."

Sienna peers down at the cage on the counter. The rat's ear tag, like the one in Sienna's ear, identifies the rat as *CN8*. Looks like a regular latest-gen Sammy, which is to say brown-furred, big-eyed, round-eared, soft-bodied.

"SammySpeaks icons are about the size of an app," Sienna says. "He probably thought it was his AAC. The Sammys like haptic vibrations. I've been thinking we should try electrotactile feedback instead of vibrotactile, so they're less likely to—"

Gillian interrupts—again, balls. "No, I know, but that's not the thing. He didn't just open the app. He was *using* the app."

Sienna frowns. "What was it?"

"YouTube Kids. Sometimes I watch my niece, so I added it for her. Sammy's watching this video called *What Are Clouds Made Of?* Just some lady explaining clouds."

"Huh." Sienna chews on this for a moment. "Sammys have never seen clouds before."

"So the video ends and it auto-plays another thing about clouds. CN8 watches it and when it's over—are you ready for this? He likes it."

"How could you tell?"

"No, I mean he *likes* it. He presses the *Like* button. He's driving the algorithm."

This lab tech is right: that *is* interesting.

"Is it a little thumbs-up button like regular YouTube?" Sienna asks, and Gillian nods. "Well, that tracks. That's the same icon SammySpeaks uses for *Good*. How long are these videos?"

"Maybe fifteen minutes?"

"Damn. That's a decent attention span."

"Better than my niece. So the second video ends and this Earth Day video comes up. And it goes for a few seconds before CN8 dislikes it. Then—are you ready for this?"

"Stop asking me that."

"He goes to the sidebar. And starts scrolling."

Sienna tries to picture it. All Sammys swipe sideways for additional AAC menus. Mechanically, this is similar. But it's a world of difference in purpose. CN8 hadn't been trying to interact with the humans who fed and cared for him. There is nothing to feel from YouTube, nothing to smell or taste. He'd been watching, liking, and selecting for his own amusement, if not edification.

"He finds another video about clouds, watches it, and likes it," Gillian continues. "This dude is seriously into clouds. When I took the iPad away, he stood up and gave me this look. I know rats aren't dogs, but it was like a puppy-dog face. So I put the iPad back and he goes right back to his cloud videos."

Sienna nods. "Okay, this is interesting. Good job."

She expects Gillian to squirm in delight, but instead the girl licks her lips nervously.

"Okay, so I don't want you to get mad. Promise you won't get mad?"

Sienna glares. "I explicitly do not promise. What did you do?"

Gillian swallows. "I tried calling you to ask first. Around ten last night. You didn't pick up."

Sienna tries not to flush. By ten, she hadn't blacked out but was getting there.

Gillian lets the words flood. "It's just that we have so many rats, right? *So* many. I figured what could it hurt to take just this one rat and kind of see what happened if I gave him my iPad for the whole night."

Sienna blinks. Totally out of line for a lab tech.

But she can't deny she wants to know what happened.

"You're telling me CN8 has been watching videos for the past twelve hours straight?"

Gillian nods. "Almost a hundred videos so far. I turned on the parental stats before I left, and it has the whole history. But what's really interesting, Dr. Aguirre, is what he chose to watch."

The lab tech slides her iPad from a shelf, swipes it on, and opens YouTube Kids. She turns the iPad to landscape mode and nestles it flush to the bars. Instantly, CN8 bounds to the screen, sticks his front paws out, and starts scrolling the sidebar. He's as proficient as any tween. The sidebar blurs by until another paw tap stops it, rolls it back, and taps a thumbnail.

Up pops a video called "How to Build a Pillow Fort."

"He likes pillows?" Sienna asks. "Or forts?"

"He likes to *build*. LEGO, Minecraft, catapults, treehouses, snowmen. I mean, clouds are still his favorite. I'd say fifty percent of his videos involve clouds. He's also got a little side interest in face painting."

"Excuse me?"

"I know. But he probably watched ten or fifteen videos on it. Different styles, what kind of paint to use, how to put it on. Not that a rat could even do it!"

"Rats groom their faces with their paws. I suppose if they had access to paint, and had watched enough videos . . ."

Sienna shakes her head. What the hell is she talking about? She crouches to watch the pillow-fort video end. The second it does, CN8 slaps the thumbs-up, whirls through the sidebar, and gets back to clouds. It's incredible. Eerie, too. Sienna recalls Christmas at her brother Adrian's. His two-and-a-half-year-old son had been left alone with YouTube on an iPhone, and Sienna had been vaguely horrified at how quickly the site anticipated his desires. She'd been nine months into fertility treatments, frothing with jealousy, and righteous about taking the phone away from the boy—who screeched until Adrian came in and asked Sienna to kindly butt out.

Sienna straightens and exhales hard. She'd postulated that Sammy's gyrified brain would sponge knowledge, but this is a step beyond. Or rather, a step *inward,* an indicator of seeking knowledge for its own sake. Maybe she ought to pull back on the red light intensity. That's her cautious half talking. Her other half tingles with the upshot of all this. No two Sammys would grow up alike. They'd absorb the content you absorbed, hop happily at the things that made you laugh. They'd grow alongside you, true companions.

Sienna takes the lab tech gently but firmly by the shoulders.

"Real-talk time. Gillian, is it?"

"Gillian Fitzpatrick."

"Right. First off, I know how I smell. I know you know what that smell is."

Gillian's smile falters. "Oh. That's—it's none of my—"

"But I assure you that, no matter how I let off steam on my own time, I am one hundred percent committed to getting Sammy ready for Sunday. It is the lodestar of my life. The entire reason I exist."

Gillian nods. "Yeah. Of course."

"Nothing, not even the world's smallest face-painting fan, can get in the way of that, capeesh?"

"I didn't mean to—I just thought—"

"You did fine. In fact, I want you to keep going. Keep that iPad in there, twenty-four-seven. Go buy yourself a new one and we'll reimburse you. I don't want to lose the progress CN8 has already made."

"Oh! That's fine! I'll log out of everything and turn off auto-sleep. I'll get the power cord, too, so the battery doesn't die."

"Great. Now listen, Gillian Fitzpatrick. We are not going to put CN8 back into New Rat City. We're going to keep him right here. Up high on that shelf there, so other people don't get too curious. When we leave, we cover the cage with a lab coat. Would you like a special job?"

Six words techs dream about. Gillian nods breathlessly.

"All right, then. Every morning, type up a report, okay? What CN8 watched the night before, how his choices are evolving, anything you deem of interest. After Pet Expo, we'll go over it, you and me." Sienna's smile is calculated to accelerate Gillian's heartbeat. "We'll see if we impress Herr Goff. What do you say?"

Gillian feels so special, she can't even speak. Sienna feels a stab of recognition. She'd had moments like this at Columbia, singled out for good work by Suzuki Mika. It had changed Sienna's life; maybe this would do the same for Gillian. Clearly Gillian wants a hug. People and their hugs, even after Covid. Sienna opens her arms and lets it happen.

Over Gillian's head, Sienna spies half a dozen Gamma Phi Delta kids in the hall, peering through the glass wall. Among them are Doris and Theo. Lately they have been collaring her in the hallway, begging for more playtime with Sammys. Now they are pointing. Murmuring to colleagues. Sienna doesn't like it. Too much curiosity is dangerous. She makes a mental note to talk to Noah about drapes.

13

There are lots of white coats
Some white coats are nice and some white coats are mean
My favorite white coat is SIENNA
Some white coats call her DOCTOR
Some white coats call her ~~AGARE AGEE AGWIN~~
I do not know what they call her
SIENNA is nice to me
SIENNA scratches my ears and says I am good
SIENNA calls me SAMMY
SAMMY is better than CN8
CN8 is like ~~AGARE AGEE AGWIN~~
CN8 is not a good name

Have you driven the SammyWagon?
I have
It is fast
Sometimes LINDA lets me drive it and LINDA claps
LINDA says that I am the fastest driver she ever saw

To get to LINDA's room SIENNA carries me through a room with
I am not allowed to say it
I will spell it

R-A-T-S
SammySpeaks has CAT and DOG and BIRD
But there is no R-A-T on SammySpeaks
The white coats say it all the time
I learned how to spell it on the ~~ipop~~ ~~idop~~ ~~ipid~~ video toy
It is my secret
Do not tell SIENNA or she will get mad

※

I used to live with other R-A-T-S
Then a white coat gave me the video toy
SIENNA moved me to the room with other white coats
But the R-A-T room smells the same
The white coats do not smell it
Do you know what it smells like?
Like the R-A-T-S are scared

※

They should not be scared
Everything is fun
Except when the white coats pick me up wrong
Except when the white coats poke me with the needle
Especially when they stick it in my eye
But I am the only R-A-T who has the video toy
SIENNA lets me play with the video toy all the time except nap time
SIENNA says I am special

※

Do you know about clouds?
I did not
Now I know all about clouds

They are part of ~~precapulshun~~ ~~preicpotan~~ ~~pricippotation~~
They are part of water
I think they are magic as well
I used SammySpeaks to ask SIENNA about magic
SIENNA said magic is pretend there is only science
Maybe SIENNA is wrong?
I wonder what clouds smell like
Can you taste a cloud?
I wonder if clouds are soft

I would like to have a cloud for nap time
Maybe LINDA will get me a cloud
LINDA thinks I am special too
LINDA has a nice face and SIENNA has a nice face
TASHA has a nice face and MASON has a nice face
Except when TASHA ignores MASON
Then MASON has a sad face
Most the people in my video toy have nice faces too
Sometimes they paint their faces
People are allowed to have two faces
R-A-T-S only get one

Some faces are mean
Have you seen them?
They are outside the white coat room
They put their faces on the glass
It makes their noses flat and scary
They do not have white coats
They want in but SIENNA says no
They look and they point

SIENNA calls them ~~GABBA FLY DEPPA GUMP FOO DILTER~~
I do not know what SIENNA calls them
They make me nervous

I saw a shark on my video toy
That is what the mean faces look like
Their faces make me smell like the other R-A-T-S
One time I smelled like that and SIENNA pet me
SIENNA said do not worry I will not let them in
But SIENNA did not see the shark video
SIENNA does not know
Not even magic can save you
Not even hiding inside of clouds
When there are enough sharks it does not matter what you do
They always get in

14

He's out of Addy. He's got a doc who will fire off prescriptions for whatever he wants, all Noah has to do is text, but it's three in the morning and even unscrupulous physicians have to sleep, which means Noah's in a bind. Pet Expo is in two days, and he's keeping the same mad schedule he did with FireFish's, ChattyBird's, and EasyPony's Pet Expo debuts. In other words, staying up forty-eight hours straight nailing the presentation, before sleeping the entire twenty-four hours before the show.

Yet something isn't right about Sunday's script. He can't pin it down. The more he works on it, the less thrilling it gets. He's flagging, eyelids like clay. He's thirty-six, for fuck's sake, not sixty-three. Is this what it's come to? He hits the cold December streets to wake himself up. He enters a bodega and eyes caffeine pills, even the dreaded 5-Hour Energy, but he's not in the mood to fuck up his stomach. He settles for a coffee.

Out on Broadway, he takes a swig. Maybe this coffee is enchanted: suddenly he remembers he's got extra Adderall at work. Holy shit. He knows the air is doing him good, so he books it toward EditedPets instead of Ubering. A thirty-five-minute walk, so plenty of piles of black trash bags he has to pass. Just a fact of life in the city and he's gotten pretty good at not looking at them.

Until he does look and, sure enough, there's two rats, plump and wet beneath a dumpster on Crosby, still as lumps of mud until one of them fires across the street, that zero-to-fifty speed that makes Noah feel tears prickling at the backs of his eyes. Stupid to be this frightened, given how perfectly non-rat-like Sammy will be two days from now.

A thought slips through his mind like an errant breeze.

What if that's why he started EditedPets in the first place?

What if his subconscious goal had always been to take the animal that killed Grammy and reimagine it as something harmless?

Shit, he needs to tell Mom and Dad he's going to miss the weekly call. He'll be deep into his sleep binge. That's okay. That's good, in fact. Not a good time to get enervated by his folks' disinterest. After all, in two days, his parents *will* hear of Sammy. There's no way it won't be leading the Monday news. Not the tech news but the *news* news. EditedPets will have the biggest booth at Pet Expo, dozens of stations to experiment with Sammy toys, interact with VR Sammys, and enter the draw for five minutes of real-life interaction. It's the Steve Jobs playbook: keep product access scarce to magnify perceived preciousness.

Most weeknights, desk security is Dante, who Noah can blow past with a wave. Tonight it's a goddamn sub. So he's got to stop, dig out his ID, sign the stupid sheet.

"Working late?" the guard asks.

What does it fucking look like? Noah forces a smile.

"Never can tell when inspiration strikes, you know?"

"Sure do," the guard replies. "I make picture frames in my workshop. Sometimes I'll wake up in the middle of the—"

"Really? That's excellent." Noah hurries for the elevators. "Back soon."

He hurls himself inside a waiting elevator car and knuckles the seventh-floor button. He's salivating for Addy's Sweet Tart tang. When he gets off at seven, he can already feel the butterfly rush. And he hasn't even swallowed one yet! The human brain is really something.

He keys into sales and marketing. Unlike the bright hall, the lights are dim: a computer screen some Gamma Phi Delta pledge has set to stay awake all night and the bowl of FireFish, a colorful little universe of orbiting planets. One last swipe and he's inside his office, wrenching open a drawer and hearing the greatest sound in the world, a medicine-bottle rattle.

He sits there for a time, enjoying the Addy. Each strand of his keynote snaps together. Forget about the media. Forget about Davin Dunbar, Christy Crawford, all the dickheads who judged you in Iowa, at

Columbia, at Rockefeller. Forget about EditedPets's stock price. It's like using INTR on himself. Thirty minutes later, Noah's inadequate brain is infused with superior genes. The problem with his keynote? It's simple:

There's too much Noah Goff in it.

All he needs to do is be an ambassador to the incredible. He'll give the first twenty of his thirty minutes to Sammy. Whichever rat Sienna says is most lively that morning, he'll limo it down to Javits, set that furry little sucker on the goddamn podium, adjust the mic to his cute little height—and just step the fuck back. He knows what Sammy will do. He'll ask Noah aloud about the audience. Once he realizes the crowd can hear him, he'll ask them questions. Imagine it: the first keynote address in history *delivered by a non-human*. After that, it won't matter what Noah says, besides those four magic words.

Preorders are open.

In minutes, the whole event is fixed in his mind. All that's left is the busywork of transferring it to the page back home.

Noah exits into the hallway, wading through a creamy Adderall tranquility. Passing the lab, he pauses. The thinnest razor of light, way in the back. Someone left the lights on in New Rat City. Sienna may have reversed the Sammy's nocturnal trait, but they still sleep better in darkness. This close to Pet Expo, Noah needs his rats nice and rested. He should go turn off the lights.

He lifts his key card but pauses. During the day, with Gamma Phi Delta raising hell and the lab abuzz with eggheads, he tromps all over the joint, no big deal. But at night? All alone with rats?

Noah enters loudly so the cluck of the door and the thud of his footsteps squelch negative thoughts. Light gleams off Sienna's *#1 DAD* thermos. It's spooky. But the Adderall acts like the big brother he never had. There's nothing to fear, kiddo. He passes the supply cabinets, faces the straightaway path to New Rat City.

Except for the refrigerator hum, the lab is silent.

Faintly, then, he hears it.

"Noah . . . please come . . ."

His stomach inverts. A shockwave of fear blurs his vision.

"Noah ... please help Grammy ..."

Cold marbles of sweat drip from his hair. The Addy must have gone bad. He hadn't even looked at it before swallowing. Now he's all alone, just like he was with Grammy at nine years old.

"Pleeeease, Noah ... Grammy needs help ... come help Grammy ..."

He takes a step forward. His leg shudders. But he's got to do this. He's a man now. This whole fucking place, he owns it. His knees rise and fall as if operated by a novice puppeteer, until the ray of light from under the door paints his Nikes yellow.

"It hurts, Noah, please ... Why won't you help your Grammy ..."

Noah cranks the handle and throws open the door.

New Rat City is dark.

Noah blinks; he doesn't get it. Rats rustle inside stacked boxes, but only because he woke them up. He hears the anxious brux of their teeth, cannulas clicking against opaque plastic. The motion kicks up enough urine scent to overpower the watermelon. Noah looks down and sees that his sneakers are still illuminated.

The light isn't coming from New Rat City at all, but rather the Enrichment Room. Noah calculates. He left the office at seven last night. Those working Pet Expo had already decamped to the Javits Center. Senioritis had hit the lab as hard as it had marketing, and Sienna had released everyone after lunch. Once they'd left, Sienna hustled off too. *Better she get her drinking down now,* Noah had thought. He needed her sharp on Sunday.

By the time Noah vacated, the only ones left had been Linda and her assistants. The seventh floor's nervous energy had clearly reached her too. Science-wise, time was up; but behaviorally, Linda could still train the rats up until the last second, so the best one could be chosen for Pet Expo.

Don't stay too late, Noah had said on his way out.

All right. We won't. Good night, Linda had replied.

Now it's coming up on what? Four in the morning? Linda seems like someone who's tucked in by nine. Her young assistants certainly have better things to do. One of them forgot to turn off the lights, that's all. Noah reaches for the knob.

"Noaaah . . . Noaaaah . . ."

As he turns the knob, it becomes a sphere of ice that shaves nerve endings from his palm. He is nine years old. Nothing changes.

Grammy lies in the middle of the Enrichment Room. The same rats from twenty-seven years ago are perched on her face. Two of them feast on her eyeballs, the other gnaws her soft palate, only its long, pink tail visible from between her toothless gums.

Noah recoils against a wall, hands curled into his sternum.

Time flexes; then becomes now.

It's not Grammy being devoured by tiny ghouls.

It's Linda.

She's flat on her back. Arms outstretched. Knuckles splintered and fingertips gristled, proof of a fight she lost. The rats on her head stop working to look at Noah. Linda's face has been peeled, no skin, only crisscrossing bands of red muscle. Her nose is gnawed to a gray nub of cartilage. The rat that births from her mouth carries a hank of her bottom lip, but the rest of her lips have been devoured, showing Linda's teeth all the way to the roots.

Linda's purple scrubs, brown with blood, bulge at her belly.

A rat has either gotten under her clothing or has wiggled down her gullet, into her stomach, and has begun to chew its way out.

Noah rips his eyes away and sees the body of a young woman, Tasha—he recalls her name at the worst possible moment. Her body is facedown amid a mess of toppled shelves and broken toys. One of her arms juts toward Noah, like she died reaching for the door. A rat watches Noah as it eats Tasha's left pinky. All the other fingers are fibrous stumps.

The body of the other assistant, Mason, is crumpled under a window. Gory smears make it clear that he tried to open it, eager to take his chances with a seven-story drop, but modern office windows don't open, airborne global pandemics or not. Bite holes the size of dimes pock Mason's face and arms, like he was spattered with corrosive acid. His neck hangs wide open. Noah sees the pink tube of the trachea, the red flaps of the vocal cords, the gray epiglottal jelly.

"Noah . . . Noah . . . Noah . . ."

It's not Grammy's voice. It's SammySpeaks. Noah rolls his dry eyes downward until he sees a rat squatted atop a tablet. Foam drips from the rat's mouth onto the AAC as he stamps a clawed foot on the icon with Noah's picture. It has to be coincidence, unless this particular Sammy has been waiting for Noah to arrive, hungry for his particular cut of meat.

Noah notices movement and jerks his head. Two rats atop a table. One slicked black with gore and hissing, the other on its back, contorting, tongue flapping. Another rat seizures on the floor, eyes drowned in blood, while yet another paces the carpet like a tiger, eyeing Noah, drawing skin back from its long, yellow teeth.

Sienna's red-light design is foolproof. Yet the brains of these rats have bloated into insanity. How the fuck did it happen? Noah doesn't have time to think it through. The rats not in the throes of painful death creep toward him. Eight, maybe ten, twitching whiskers webbed with human tissue, tracking tiny pawprints of blood. Only one stays put, head quivering with madness, drooling blood that dims the tablet's glow.

"Noah . . . Noah . . . Noah . . ."

15

Phone calls don't even get close to waking Sienna from deranged dreams, a misshapen ChattyBird suckling at one breast, a deformed EasyPony at the other. But hard, meaty thwacks against her front door are like a fishhook through one eye and out the other, dragging her up by the face, threatening to pull apart her skull along the sagittal and lambdoid sutures, like the Sammys' skulls before her Optogenetics breakthrough—

The chain lock whips like a rat's tail. She didn't lock it last night, of course not, she'd been soaked in bourbon. Sienna sits up and looks for a weapon. TV remote, jar of fish food, box of Cheez-Its, the detritus of her life her only defense against whatever animal activist or random psycho has come to kill her. Her hands seize a liquor bottle. She'll go down fighting with the booze that's already killing her.

"Get the fuck away! I've got a weapon!"

The pounding stops.

"Don't shoot, lady! I'm here to pick you up!"

Standing up too fast has its revenge: Sienna sways. The microwave clock says *4:36 a.m.*

"Goss! Goth! Your boss! He sent me! I'm the Uber!"

"Then how did you get inside the building?"

"Your boss told me your lobby lock is usually busted! And it was! He Venmo'd me five hundred bucks to bang on your door! He's been trying to call you!"

Sienna picks up her phone. Six calls from Noah and thirty-five texts, most of them the same three letters: *SOS SOS SOS SOS SOS SOS SOS* . . .

Her top half is still clothed. Sienna pulls on pants, grabs her purse and her bottle of Xanax. The Uber is a beat-up Corolla, a kidnap-and-kill car if she ever saw one, but she gets Noah on the phone and he's telling her, in a steely, shaky voice, to have her ID out and ready to show to anyone who gets in her way. Don't waste time if someone offers you a gas mask, he says, it's not real, you don't need it.

Sienna has never heard scarier advice.

She dry-swallows three Xanax. The Uber driver eyes her nervously.

It's not yet dawn when she sprints from the car while it's still rolling to a stop. She has to run down the sidewalk because the block is barricaded by orange-striped sawhorses, cutting off everything but Con Ed vans. Workers in blue hard hats and neon vests stand around doing nothing. Closer to the building are a trio of Con Ed workers wearing the gas masks Noah mentioned. Sienna ducks under red tape and bashes through the front door. Behind her, a man's yell muffled by his mask, but by then she's showing her ID to a man in a gas mask at the desk. It's like he's been waiting: he gestures her toward the elevators.

Inside the elevator, she pauses to sniff.

No gas leak here.

✄

Noah sits in Prez's security cubby. He refuses to show her the bodies in person and she's too numb to demand it. But he's got the Enrichment Room camera at full screen. The dead are heartbreaking in their anonymity: three dark blotches roughly in the shape of human beings. Closest to the camera, all that remains of Linda. Her beloved teacher, her friend.

And Sienna murdered her. Dangled promises, manipulated emotions, lured her to a brawling metropolis, and placated her with lies, all while engineering small assassins. Sienna killed two bright young assistants too, so dedicated to their field that they refused to keep away from EditedPets even after what happened to Dekota. Sienna's heart doesn't race; it's a dwindling drumbeat.

Noah's swollen eyes protrude from a pale, glossy face.

"Do you have any idea what I've done in the past hour? What you forced me to do?"

The Xanax is kicking in. Sienna feels herself shake her head.

"You lied to me," Noah says.

Hair catches in her mouth from how much she's shaking.

"No, I didn't, Noah. It's true that Sammy's brain—I'm leveling with you here, all right? The algae protein that grows his brain, we can't turn it off yet."

"We?"

"Fine. *I* can't turn it off yet. But Sammy's brain will only keep growing when it's exposed to high-intensity red light. Linda wouldn't do that. She wouldn't even know how."

Noah's eyelids quaver with something like disgust. He scrubs the security camera timeline in reverse. Linda, Tasha, and Mason leap back to life, three hysterical blurs before they relax and finally walk backward out of the Enrichment Room door. Noah goes back a long way before pressing the space bar with a foreboding mildness.

The video plays.

Same angle, same room. The door opens and Sienna's heart clenches, because she's about to see Linda alive again, her funny little steps, the way she clasps her hands in front of her like a nun, that optimistic tilt of her chin.

But it's not Linda.

It's Theo and Doris. Both carry a cage from New Rat City. That's surprising enough. Before the door swings shut, a guy from sales enters, followed by a girl from marketing, and they're holding things too. Not cages, but six-packs of beer. In seconds, seven Gamma Phi Deltas are in the Enrichment Room, poking around shelves, sitting on chairs and tables, or, in the case of Theo and Doris, getting down on the floor, which they know is the best position from which to play with Sammys.

"When . . ." Sienna feels lost. ". . . when is this?"

"Two nights ago."

"How did they . . . their key cards don't work on—"

"How many times a day—a *day*, Sienna—do I see key cards sitting on the bathroom sink, left behind by your brilliant techs? Once a day? Twice?"

"Maybe if you didn't hand them out like candy!"

"Maybe if *you* would have put a second lock on the Enrichment Room door."

"Why would I turn *that* room into Alcatraz? All that's in there are toys, Noah. And books!"

Noah is carved from ice, steaming with loathing.

"And corpses, Sienna. You forgot about all the corpses."

From the footage, an aurora flash. Sienna has to squint until the camera's auto-iris compensates and white corona resolves into—what else?—a crimson red. Sienna's heart liquifies, dribbles down her ribs, soaks her intestines.

"The therapy panels," she whispers.

"It's funny," Noah muses. "I remember you talking about getting some red-light therapy lights. How you were going to run some tests, see how we might scale up to warehouses. What I don't remember, Sienna, is you saying you were going to store those lights *IN THE FUCKING ENRICHMENT ROOM!*"

Noah's hot spit spatters Sienna's cheeks. She shuts her eyes in shock and hears the spring of Noah leaping from the chair, the whack of him kicking it, the crash of him throwing it against the wall.

"What the fuck were you thinking, Sienna?"

"The closet—I put them in the closet," she stammers, but then her body goes volcanic, a kind of defense mechanism, and she peels open her eyes and bares her teeth. "Where the fuck was I supposed to store them, Noah? I wouldn't dare disturb your sales force's foosball table!"

Noah points at the monitor like Death himself.

Sienna can only watch the catastrophe unfold. Gamma Phi Delta's inoffensive good time feels pornographic. They drink their beer, tickle the five-week-old Sammys, set up a couple SammySpeaks, place one rat into a SammyWagon. Someone must have put on music, because several girls are dancing in front of giant red-light panels set up like party lights. Doris grinds into Theo, half-joking, half-not.

They are young, clever, sexy, promising.

Every second they celebrate these qualities, rat brains swell.

"Stop," Sienna gags.

The spacebar clicks. The cubby swirls with heat. Sienna's sob is arid.

"The attack was coordinated, Noah. To get all three of them . . . the rats had to attack all at once . . . but how . . . and *why* would they . . . do you think it's because they see what we do? The surgeries . . . the drills . . ."

She grips the counter to stop the room spinning.

"Are they all dead? The rats?"

Noah shrugs. "I don't know."

"We have to make sure. Not just the rats in the Enrichment Room. Every rat in New Rat City too. If we give them enough time, they'll get out. Through vents. Cracks. Holes—"

Sienna gasps. She's seen the red cylinders, pipe traceries, and nozzles in New Rat City so often, she's stopped noticing them. Prez installed the CO_2 fire suppression system two years ago as a laboratory fail-safe. All mammalian life dies when CO_2 levels reach seven point five percent, and this system could create four times that amount. Noah brushed off the idea of an ungovernable rat-borne virus but perked up when Prez mentioned intellectual theft. Let's say a competitor breaks into EditedPets to nab some rats. The touch of a single button and every rat in the lab could be eliminated.

Sienna grips Noah's arm.

"Prez's CO_2 system. He said it only takes a few minutes to work. After everything's dead, the CO_2 gets pumped right out of the building."

"What do you think I was doing," Noah sneers, "while you were drunk on your couch?"

Relief hits Sienna first. Noah did the right thing, pulled the switch, killed the Sammys. That would have set off alarms, which would have freaked out anyone in the building at that hour, which explained the emergency response outside. What hits her next is devastation. The sacrifices made to get Sammy ready for Pet Expo. How those sacrifices meant nothing alongside the three lives lost.

"We're going to prison, Noah. For a long, long time."

"No," Noah said. "We're not."

Sienna looks up. Her eyes throb. Noah gives her a flat look she recalls from the time of the EPA lawsuits. The look of a person for whom a CO_2 fire suppression system is but one of several emergency ripcords.

"When you entered the building," he says quietly, "who let you in?"

Sienna tries to think. The triple Xanax, a bad idea in a series of bad ideas. The man who'd waved her inside hadn't been wearing a Con Ed uniform. He'd worn a tailored suit.

"The Con Ed workers," she says. "They're not Con Ed workers, are they?"

Noah's jaw pulses through his cheek.

"If you ask," he warns, "be sure you want to know."

�֎

Noah first heard Marcy Monroe speak from outside the office of Dr. Curt Stolze, his adviser at Rockefeller. Noah had an appointment with Stolze to discuss the whole PetMate debacle. Specifically, how Noah might repair bridges with faculty he'd pissed off during his legal battle. Noah had no intention of repairing shit, but agreed to hear old Stolze out. The guy was one of the few people on campus—and in the world— to take a shine to Noah. He'd also done spectacular work on the molecular basis of cell cycle control, and it never hurt to know another genius.

The highest levels of the U.S. government had defenses of which Noah couldn't conceive. But that didn't mean their operatives didn't forget to shut the occasional door.

"It's a two-way street," said a woman with a low voice. "You know that."

"But do *they*?" Stolze replied. "I think it's generational. The crumbling belief in institutions, that sort of thing."

The woman chuckled. "I was chanting *fuck the police* before these kids were even born. But then, you know, you grow up, and Mr. Rubber meets Ms. Road. The work you and I have done together—humankind has been the beneficiary. I want to keep supporting your lab. That's where I'm coming from, Curt."

"The word *Faustian* isn't in my vocabulary," Stolze insisted. "There's an art to it, is all. Students come here wanting to save the world and don't want to hear that there's no world to be saved if we've all been . . . *redacted*, I guess."

There was a control to the woman's laugh that gave Noah chills. But the chill of danger was awfully close to the chill of possibility. He heard the sound of chairs scraping, fabric rustling.

"We're going to continue to help each other," the woman said.

"You bet we are. Always a pleasure, Colonel."

Colonel.

Noah scurried off and ducked down a perpendicular hall, from where he could monitor the elevators. Two girls he recognized wrinkled their noses at his peeping-tom behavior. He didn't care. He was drunk on his own cocktail: twenty-nine, ambitious, friendless, near-virginal, jacked on caffeine.

Marcy Monroe wore casual dress but shouted ex-military. The coiled-spring posture, the cadence march, the way she scanned the space through which she strolled, and, of course, the hairstyle: a blonde bun tight as a grenade at her neck's nape. Noah bet she ate fast and could sleep anywhere too.

When Monroe's elevator car opened, Noah bolted so he'd make it just in time. Monroe held the doors open for him, then retracted to an at-ease posture. Noah said thanks, then told himself to work hard, work fast.

Everyone at Rockefeller had heard rumors of such people. Shadow figures with feelers into high-stakes research institutes, capable of throwing billions of dollars at blue-sky dream projects, provided those projects had a Department of Defense application. Other times, so went the scuttlebutt, these figures came with their own ideas and hired big thinkers to consult on viability. One of Noah's professors, on his second pitcher at Murphy's Law, told Noah the cash spent by these off-the-books agencies was tenfold more than that of their on-the-books counterparts. If that was true, deals were being cut all the time.

Finally, Noah's chance had come.

By the time the car had dropped seven floors, his small talk about creative uses of genetic modification had hooked Colonel Monroe enough that she allowed him to walk with her to her waiting car. He talked faster, reeling her in with ideas about using living organisms as biosensors. After a crisp nod, a handshake, and opening the back door of the car, Monroe rewarded Noah with a business card.

"Let us know how we can help you, Mr. Goff," she'd said.

Noah's heart lobbed as the car vanished. *DARPA,* the card read: the mythic emerging-tech department Eisenhower had started after the Soviets launched Sputnik. Ballistic missiles, computer processing, GPS, speech recognition, particle beams, VR, the goddamn internet itself. DARPA had wielded a heavy hand in all of it.

That night, Noah celebrated at the Hunterian—alone, of course. After googling *colonel marcy monroe* for an hour—she didn't appear to exist, an exciting sign—he started reading a paper about geneticists who'd used CRISPR/Cas9 to edit the genome of a zebrafish. Halfway through, Noah found himself considering the ice bobbing in his Manhattan.

Anything floating in water tells us something about its physical and chemical properties. In this case, water is denser than ice. But what if the ice were a type of biologically sensitive fish? What if the whiskey and vermouth was the Croton Reservoir, which supplies millions of New Yorkers with drinking water?

On the back of the proverbial napkin, Noah sketched out potential Defense Department applications of the same project he'd discussed with Sienna Aguirre at the Tasty Hand Pulled Noodle Accord. He knew DARPA worked a lot with EWAs—Enhanced Warfare Animals. Most militaries did. America's bomb-carrying bats of WWII. The exploding dogs used by Soviets against German tanks. Japan's Unit 731 and their plague-infested fleas inside ceramic bombs. The long history of using dolphins to find mines. No one goes into biology to create EWAs, not even Noah. Yet the DARPA route had advantages over the usual grant-application process. DARPA was a closed system, while academic-grant reviewers were notorious for stealing applicants' ideas.

Plus there was something exciting about black-project government work, wasn't there? About knowing things no one else was allowed to know?

Noah spent three months refining a biotech application for DARPA. Then he made use of the .gov email on Colonel Monroe's card and waited for a sign of interest. It came the following day in the form of an appointment in Arlington. Noah booked a flight and a room. Two days later, dizzy with nerves, he sat before Monroe's desk and laid out the idea inspired by his celebratory Manhattan.

"We first befriended the wolf fourteen thousand, five hundred years ago," he began, word for word how he'd begin Sammy's launch nine years later.

One of the most vital roles wolves played, Noah told Monroe, was to warn early humans of danger. His idea was to obtain funding for his commercial glowing-fish endeavor by simultaneously developing a separate, secret fish for DARPA.

Colonel Monroe conveyed interest with silence. A city's water supply, Noah continued, could be continuously run through tanks full of these special guppies. Because these guppies would be edited with bioluminescent firefly genes, they'd glow the instant they were exposed to any dangerous chemical or biological agents in water—the kind of attack the government had been fighting against since 9/11. The glow would be picked up by cameras that watch the fish 24/7, which would activate an emergency valve, shutting off the water supply to the city.

"The problem with detecting chem and bio agents," Noah concluded, "is we never know what we're looking for. But these fish? They can be our gilled canaries in a floating coal mine."

A rehearsed closing line, heavy on the cheese.

The first question Monroe asked was how soon could she see a prototype.

✖

Sienna knows about the chemical-sensitive fish. She designed them. It got EditedPets off the ground and, besides, wasn't anything like Bayer or

Volkswagen participating in the Nazi Final Solution. She and Noah had built a biogenetic blockade that defended innocent Americans.

The realization that Noah has privately kept up the DARPA relationship is somehow both inconceivable and disgustingly obvious. After the ChattyBird and EasyPony bombs, not to mention the EPA lawsuits, of course Noah had turned to a different funding source.

"What did you do?" she whispers.

"Don't give me that look. You've been in this, step by step."

Sienna clamps a hand over her mouth, muffling her voice. "The Con Ed workers are . . ."

"They're the ones who are going to save our asses." Noah jabs a finger at the lab. "You think Colonel Monroe's going to let three dead bodies jeopardize hundreds of millions of dollars of research? That *she* paid for? Wake up."

Colonel Monroe. Hearing a specific name makes it too real.

"Oh, Noah, Noah . . ."

"Don't *Noah, Noah* me! You know precisely how this works! Someone enriches uranium-235 to 5% purity and then uses it to generate electricity for millions, but at the same time keeps enriching it until it reaches 80%, pure enough to make a nuclear bomb. Sure, the CEOs of Rocket Lab do a lot of nice stuff, supply the International Space Station, all that. But Rocket Lab was CIA-DARPA from the start: a bunch of microsatellites shot into space so people under authoritarian rule could access the net uncensored."

"You've been funneling my Sammys to . . . ?"

"Now they're *your* Sammys? In that case, you must be aware of what an intelligent rat could do for a military as imaginative as ours."

Before she can rip off her ears or run away, Sienna thinks of the NORAD compound in the Cheyenne Mountains, three stories of DoD facilities built beneath two thousand feet of solid granite, sealed with blast doors capable of brushing off a thirty-megaton nuclear explosion, rigged atop a thousand springs to keep it from shifting more than a single inch. How would an enemy infiltrate such a fortress?

By training an army of rats with VR blueprints to gnaw and wiggle their way inside and detonate themselves, knocking out critical areas without leaving any evidence of attack but the most innocuous thing on Earth: dead rats.

"You should have told me," she croaks. "I would've left."

"You say that now."

Fuck him for knowing her so well. Did the architects and engineers of the Brooklyn Bridge and Hoover Dam hesitate, knowing that workers were going to die during construction? Scientific progress demands its sacrifice. It's the tenet upon which Biological Uplift depends. To break the endless cycle of kill-or-be-killed, first there must be a little killing.

She quits fighting. She moves to the door. Noah hinges himself back, allowing her passage. She stands in the hall. To her left, the path to the restrooms and her fire-escape smoking spot. Straight ahead, the elevators, where EMTs once attended to Dekota, whose rat bite, it turns out, wasn't so horrible after all.

Without turning, she speaks softly.

"The Con Ed people, they'll . . . Linda, they'll take care of. . . ?"

"They will," Noah says. "They're also doing a sweep to get rid of any electronic evidence."

Sienna nods. "I am sorry."

"About what?"

"The red lights. Pet Expo. EditedPets. Everything. It's all over. And you worked hard for it. I know you did."

"*We* did."

The elevator dings, and a man in a gas mask and Con Ed gear exits, pulling a black steel wagon with thick rubber wheels. Plenty big enough to hold three bodies. The Con Ed faker is followed by more, and though their masks cover most of their faces, their eyes are too much for Sienna to bear. She's about to pass the three men when her mind, nestled in a Xanax hush, has a final thought for Noah.

"There's one Sammy in the lab. Under a lab coat. The CO_2 probably got him too. But you better check." Sienna's laugh is softly hysterical. "He has an iPad."

"Don't worry," Noah says. "I've taken care of it."

He isn't lying. He *has* taken care of it, just not in the way Sienna thinks.

The sole surviving Sammy is still beneath the white coat playing with an iPad, like Sienna said. But Noah vacated the Sammy from the lab before releasing the CO_2. Currently the rat is in a tan leather Filson travel bag tucked under Noah's desk. The whole office, in fact, smells faintly of watermelon. It puts Noah a little more at ease.

Noah meant what he said backstage at the San Jose Civic.

I'll cancel that Pet Expo keynote over my dead body.

RATZENKÜNIG

16

"I've got a double shift, so I won't see you till morning. Let's run down the list, all right?"

"All right. But hurry up."

"I'll take all day if I want, mister. You got your day pass?"

"Yeah."

"Your MetroCard?"

"Uh-huh."

"Your hand sanitizer?"

"Yes."

"What do you do if you see an old person standing? Or a pregnant lady?"

"Give them my seat."

"How do you hold your bag?"

"Over my shoulder, like this."

"Who do you ask if you need help?"

"Find a family and ask them."

"Or an MTA worker. You know what kind of uniforms they have?"

"The same one you're wearing. Duh."

"Don't *duh* me. What if a panhandler's hassling you?"

"Ignore him and don't say nothing."

"Don't say *anything*."

"That's what I said, Mom."

"I'm correcting your grammar."

"Aren't you going to ask me what if I miss my stop?"

Mom laughed. "Dallas, you ain't ever missed a stop in your life."

"*Haven't*. Not *ain't*. Grammar, Mom."

"Smart-ass. Now, what's the safest car?"

"The front one with the operator."

"What's the least safest?"

"Any car that's empty."

"Yeah, that's a rookie mistake, huh? Probably someone crazy on that car."

"Or they pooped."

Mom smiles with lips crinkled, like she's proud. She uses two fingers to pull the cable that toots the 6 train's horn, the signal for gadget-obsessed zombie commuters to notice the train nearing the station. The sound always makes Dallas happy. When he was younger, Mom would boost him up so he could pull it—two little tugs and everyone on the platform would look up. It made him feel powerful.

Dallas Underhill, even with his eyes closed, can predict every switch his mom, Brandy Underhill, pulls before she pulls it. With one hand, she takes the master controller—the gas pedal, basically—and rotates it through the four modes: parallel, series, switching, and finally coast, which removes all the power from traction motors and spotting circuits. With her other hand, Mom pulls the dynamic brake, which tells the train's motoring circuit to quit accepting third-rail current. Dallas waits for the tugging sensation, right at about ten miles per hour, when the brake shoes apply to the wheels, stopping the 8:16 Pelham-to-Brooklyn-Bridge 6 train snugly into Grand Central 42nd Street Station.

A work of art: nobody's dropping their coffee on this train.

One day Dallas hopes he will be just as good.

Mom exits into the car and onto the platform. Dallas follows, avoiding all eyes. All it would take is one complaint from a passenger to get Mom fired. People hadn't minded so much when Dallas was a cute six-year-old. But now he's ten, and Black, and starting to get what Mom calls *those looks*. His days of riding in the cab are close to over.

Mom grins a hello to the MTA driver taking over the 6 train, then gives Dallas a final appraisal.

"All right, soldier," she said. "Those pets won't pet themselves."

She reaches out and tugs his earlobe. It joggles the speech processor tucked behind his right ear, creating a small crackle inside his head.

Mom invented the lobe-tug after the rustling of his hair—a thing *normal* moms did to *normal* kids—started setting him off a few years ago. His doctor concluded that hair-rustling had become one of the "pseudo-smothering" actions that "triggered" him. Mom's pretty good at avoiding triggers, once she knows them.

The rest of the world is pretty bad at it. Back when Dallas was smaller, his "meltdowns" (another doctor word) were like bombs going off. He'd cry, scream, kick, punch, and roll around on the floor. It was like his brain whirled so fast that his thoughts blurred—and his body had to blur right behind it. Each time afterward, his muscles hurt and his eyes hurt and his throat hurt and he was ashamed.

During the Covid-19 lockdown, it changed. Dallas doesn't know why. MTA cut Mom's hours, so she was home more often—and Dallas was home constantly. For some reason it rewired his brain. The good news is that he gets triggered far less these days, probably because he's ten now. Meltdowns come once every few weeks, not once a day. The bad news is that his meltdowns have gone inward. He slumps over, wherever he is, and kind of disappears, like a piece of paper folded over and over and over.

People don't notice as much, and Dallas supposes that's good.

He waves bye to Mom and shoots into a waiting 7 train. The first car, just like Mom said, because Dallas knows she's watching before trundling off to her next train assignment. Dallas holds on to a subway pole and lowers the volume on his cochlear implant processors. Doctors describe cochlear-implant sound as "metallic," but it's the only sound Dallas knows. The last few weeks, though, it's been screwy. Every time he walks down the street—sometimes even at home—he picks up strange high-pitched squeaks.

He keeps telling Mom, but she won't believe him. First off, being ultra-sensitive to sounds is part of his "behavioral challenges." Secondly, they were just at the clinic a month ago to adjust his kit, and Mom blamed those adjustments on Dallas's refusal to take off the headpiece at night—a boy's head exudes a lot of grease and sweat. That's why his cochlear implant gear came with a nighttime "drying box," which uses salt to wick away moisture. Dallas hates it. No one understands what it's like to take off the kit and enter driftless, outer-space silence, cut off from Mom, cut off from everyone.

Dallas might be deaf, but he gets the message loud and clear.

The cochlear implant isn't the problem. *He* is the problem.

He's read Mom's whole folder on it. During a hearing screening at age two, doctors discovered Dallas had "bilateral senserioneuronal hearing loss" due to "two mutated *GJB2* genes," one from each parent. *Mutated* is a sucky word. He's been called a mutant at school. His friend Mike says mutants are cool and that Dallas's headgear makes him look like Cyclops from X-Men. But Dallas knows kids like Roman Moffett don't mean it that way.

When he was two and a half, he had surgery that left him with both external and internal parts of plastic and metal. Mom's folder documents an epic fight with the insurance company. Six months after diagnosis, Mom was finally able to get Dallas's left side done. Seven months after that, their ENT intervened on their behalf and Dallas got the right side installed too.

By now, he knows how it all works. A plastic loop around each ear houses a microphone and processor that breaks down sound into frequencies. This feeds into a receiver coil that rests just above and behind each ear—it looks like two black quarters pasted to his head. These coils are magnetized to connect with the metal prosthetics under his skin. The implants send electric impulses to Dallas's cochlear nerves. It isn't *hearing* so much as it's feeling the imprints left behind by sounds.

Right now, Dallas doesn't care how his gear operates or what it's called.

He just needs it to work for Pet Expo.

❄

As soon as the 7 goes into the tunnel, out of his Mom's sight, Dallas walks through the back exit, over the bridge connecting the cars, and repeats the process a few more times. Things are just more interesting in the middle of the train. Finally, he takes a seat by the window. It has to be the window.

Brandy Underhill started driving MTA trains when Dallas was five. With meltdowns always possible, babysitters were tough to keep. So Mom snuck him on trains. He spent most of those nights on the floor—and loved it. His whole body vibrated and swayed with the train's swooping turns. If it ever got too much, Mom's legs were right there to hold on to.

By Dallas's seventh birthday, he'd mastered the whole MTA. Thirty-six lines, four hundred and seventy-two stations, six hundred and sixty-five miles of track, five-point-seven million riders per day. Longest point-to-point ride: A train, 207th to Far Rockaway, thirty-one miles. Busiest station: Times Square-42nd, sixty-four million riders a year. Deepest station: The 191st Street station in Manhattan, one hundred and eighty feet down. You can't stump Dallas. Mom has borrowed lots of trivia books and tried.

He hates the feel of people bumping into him, so when he gets to 34th Street-Hudson Yards, he makes sure he's the last one to bound from his seat and sprints to the door. He speeds through the station, races up the stairs, and emerges into the cold sun of Bella Abzug Park. Light poles are wrapped in holiday lights like scarves. Dallas books it west, turns at 11th Ave., and pauses to relish the sight. The Javits Center, a block-long compound of boxy girders and green-hued glass. He's never been inside. Going inside means having a pass. Passes cost money, and so does food—you aren't allowed to bring snacks. But Mom surprised Dallas last month on his birthday with the receipt for a one-day pass, plus twenty bucks for food.

Inside, giant signs greet him. He searches for and finds the magic words: *WILL CALL.* He heads in that direction, pass receipt damp in his hand, adjusting his processors to compensate for the room's sonic signature. Quickly he finds the queue partitions for the ticket booths. He gets in line and suffers every minute of it. He can see the sign for Exhibit Hall 1A and swears he can smell the sharp odor of hay, mesquite wood chips, and kibble. Ten thousand years later, it's his turn. He holds up his receipt. Nervousness rushes up his throat.

"Can I have my day pass, please?"

The woman squints. "What?"

"Can I have my day pass?"

"Can you have your what?"

"My day pass?"

"Your what?"

It's what he feared; it's what he always fears. It's not bad enough that he wears weird equipment on his head. His voice is weird too. Mom says that because he can't hear people like others do, he can't mimic how people sound either.

But who wants to sound like everyone else? she used to ask.

Not me, he used to reply. Now, though, he'd give anything to blend in. Or to have a friend who understands what it's like to be the only one in the world like you.

At last the woman figures it out, smiles in apology, and hands over a badge on a lanyard. Dallas's embarrassment evaporates. His name isn't on the badge, a minor disappointment, but still it's pretty awesome. He tilts it so the overheads reflect off the high gloss.

Someone yells at him. Now he's the one holding up the line! He jogs off and hits a bottleneck at the exhibit hall entrance. Another stupid queue! Two security guards take their precious time scanning people's badges before waving them in. Dallas sighs and cranes his neck, trying to find something to look at that isn't the backs of heads.

Above the entrance is a big monitor playing video teasers of the day's big events. There's audio, but Dallas has no hope of hearing it through the shrieks and rumbles of so many voices. But the graphics are big and clear.

KEYNOTE ADDRESS
Noah Goff, CEO of EditedPets
"Meet Sammy—the Future of Pets"
10am Sunday, Metro Stage
Special Events Hall

Dallas laughs aloud. EditedPets is the company that made FireFish! Sure, he's gotten a little bored with FireFish over the years, but the first one Mom got him is still the coolest gift he ever received. Until this Pet Expo badge, that is. He checks his watch: 9:15. Plenty of time to walk the floor and check out some cool animals before meeting this "Sammy."

17

He studied the Special Events Hall map for weeks. He memorized the booth numbers he considers high priority. He plotted the most economical routes through the maze. He scrutinized videos of past Pet Expos to prepare himself for the noise and unavoidable contact of so many other human bodies.

But all preparations soar away the second Dallas Underhill steps into the hall. The vast, far-flung ceilings! The blinding white comets of fluorescent light! The signs, big as movie screens, ballyhooing the locations of stages, major booths, and restrooms! The Special Events Hall was built for giants; yet, for today, puny little humans and their even smaller pets are allowed to trespass.

Dallas learned enough about Javits to know this is the first year the convention center has fully returned from the global pandemic. This same hall had once been a military-run field hospital for Covid-19 patients, outfitted with two thousand beds and emergency FEMA equipment. Later, it became a twenty-four-hour mass-vax center—Dallas's mom got her J&J shot right here.

All the tears that had once wetted the floor have dried up. People grin, laugh, point, and wiggle from overdoses of cuteness. A few people wear Santa hats or reindeer ears. Dallas feels a gush of relief. Here, he doesn't have to worry about Roman Moffett imitating his speech: *buh-buh-buh-buh*. Here, he can be himself. He can always be himself with animals. A year after he got his first FireFish, Mom confessed she'd been saving for a ChattyBird, too, until someone else at Barker Houses got one first and the landlord banned them after all the complaints.

The massive hall throbs and roars; Dallas can feel it against his skull like a cloud of shifting insects. He grins despite the sonic chaos. Nothing is going to ruin this.

With his plan forgotten, Dallas wanders. Everything is incredible. Sprawling plastic playgrounds for kittens. Ferrets you can handle and pet. A giant hamster wheel being demonstrated by a jolly retriever. Hamsters too, darting through plastic labyrinths that make Dallas wish he was two inches tall. He makes mental notes regarding what to circle back to after the EditedPets event. Definitely Aquatic Zone with its double-decker tanks, Day-Glo lights, and live jellyfish. For sure, Rabbit Land and its snuggly piles of designer bunnies like the poofy Teddywitter and the floppy-eared Fuzzy Lop. And absolutely Rodent Realm, dominated by a circus-sized tent printed on all four sides with *pets, reinvented*.

Dallas drifts into the hall's nearest corner: Dog Depo. He closes in on a display of GPS tracking microchips called Pet Fetch! The booth is run by a blonde woman in black pants, a red shirt, and a nametag reading *ZOFIA*. Dallas finds the woman's pitch hard to isolate in Javits's screechy reverberation, but he manages. Dog breeders, Zofia tells a family of three, couldn't keep up with pet demand during Covid-19, which led to a nearly two-hundred-percent spike in pet theft.

"That's why I invented Pet Fetch!" Zofia says proudly. "It's got these teeny little geolocation microchips, small as a grain of rice, that you put right into a doggie treat. It embeds into what are called the rugal folds of your dog's stomach, where it can't get digested. Then boom! It connects with an app that always shows where your dog is. And a pet thief can't dig it out like they can a normal microchip."

Dallas's whole body warms. With Mom's schedule and chronic train delays, he's home alone constantly. A GPS chip feels to him like the technological encapsulation of love: always being able to find those who mean the most. He already knows there's nothing wrong with implants. He's got hardware inside his head and is grateful for it every day.

Dallas proceeds down the aisle and comes upon a fence, behind which stands a bald man advertised as Professor Gus and his border collie, Hunter. Professor Gus explains into a handheld mic that he's a psychiatrist, who, as a lark, started teaching Hunter words as a puppy. He reaches into a barrel brimming with plush toys and plucks out three at random. He tosses them in separate directions.

"Hunter. Take Broccoli to Engine, then Duckie."

The collie doesn't hesitate. She gallops to the broccoli toy, picks it up, swings by the fire engine, and drops the broccoli beside the duck. Professor Gus scratches the dog's ears and reveals that Hunter has memorized the names of over *one thousand toys*. The crowd oohs and ahhs. Dallas makes the noises as well: it's too loud for anyone to hear if he does it wrong.

"The world's smartest non-human primate, the bonobo chimp, could never pull this off," Professor Gus says. "So how does Hunter? Canines started picking up social cues while hunting with humans and being rewarded for it. Flash forward a few tens of thousands of years, and scientists have actually isolated hypersociability genes in today's dogs. That's breeding—and it's perfectly natural. None of this messing around with Mother Nature stuff."

Soft chuckles. Dallas has a hunch Professor Gus is talking about EditedPets.

"If dogs had been bred for intelligence instead of things like size or fur color, every dog in the world could be as smart as Hunter. They're already smarter than we think. The old way of thinking is that wolves are smarter than dogs because they don't give up on tasks as easily. But what if it's the opposite? Dogs use humans like tools. They plead for our help. What's more evolved than that?"

✳

Dallas wants a chance to be chosen as a volunteer to toss more toys for Hunter, but it's 9:45 and he's anxious about missing EditedPets. But as he dodges through the hall, he marvels at his *desire* to volunteer. He's never raised his hand in school, not once.

Anything is possible.

He goes right at an open-air display of crawling turtles, crosses behind the booth of a streetwear-savvy cat with two million Instagram followers, and dashes past stores hawking pet clothing fancier than anything Dallas owns. The Metro Stage appears, and Dallas's stomach clenches. It's packed. Why did he spend so much time with that dog? His thoughts begin a meltdown whirl. He banks for the nearest wall where he might tent his head, create a private darkness. Sometimes it helps.

Other people stand against the same wall, toying with their phones, waiting for the event. They don't have seats either, and don't seem concerned. A cool tingling infiltrates the sticky-hot web of his chest. Maybe he doesn't need a seat to watch! Maybe he could get even closer! Anything is possible, anything.

Dallas keeps his head low. Sometimes people don't notice kids if they're small enough. He sidles past the wall-leaners. A young woman sits on the floor just off the front row. Perfect: if he's allowed to sit, no one can tell him to get out of the way. The noise, though—he winces. The walls make this the most sonically chaotic space in Javits. He's got to get his cochlear implant settings right or he'll miss what the EditedPets guy says.

He checks the time. Ten minutes. Time enough to step away, clear his head, adjust his settings. Dallas inches past the sitting woman. The sound improves. He checks around. No one is watching him. He goes a little farther, and the sound improves some more. Checks around again. If Dallas goes just a little farther, he'll be behind the stage, which he's sure isn't technically allowed, but if it gets him out of this thundercloud for just a few moments—

Hpm.

Dallas lifts his head.

The sound is soft yet asserts itself through the tumult. Dallas looks back. The crowd keeps bustling, chatting, scrolling. He looks behind the stage risers. A braid of cables feeds into an electrical box. That's where the sound must have—

Hpm-hpm.

Dallas looks straight at the back wall, large curtains of black canvas tautly strung on braces. This curtain-wall has a door, though, and it is swinging open. A man wearing a navy blue Javits uniform hurries toward the stage with two water bottles. Dallas better take a seat. But he can't take his eyes off the backstage door as it hinges toward shutting. The *hpm-hpm* sound is louder through that door, and Dallas doesn't think he's mistaking the emotion it holds.

Something back there is scared.

Dallas hates being noticed. Fears being scolded by teachers. Shrinks beneath the threats of kids like Roman Moffett. But what Professor Gus said about dogs crackles through the electrode arrays sewed inside his head.

They plead for our help. What's more evolved than that?

Dallas can think of only one answer.

To respond to that plea.

Dallas darts. It happens in one second. Two long strides and a side-step through a narrowing door no one else could have fit through. The door clicks shut behind him. It's quieter and darker here, a black-curtained channel with a door to either side. Beyond that, a concrete industrial zone populated by inert loading machines and supply pallets.

Hpm-hpm-hpm.

There! Right behind this wall! But barging through the door feels risky. An adult might be inside, and Dallas could get kicked out of Pet Expo. He scrambles around the corner and lies down. Though the black canvas walls are tightly strung, they still have some give at the edges. He carefully lifts the bottom hem and peeks through.

A small room. A circular table. Four chairs. At the far side of the room, a man in a hoodie paces and mutters to himself.

"... pet industry has made over—*earned* over—one hundred billion dollars in profits—in *annual sales*—with a five-point-eight percent—six, just say six—a *six-percent* growth projected over the next year ..."

This must be the man from EditedPets.

Standing across the room is another man, this one enormous, wearing a security uniform and a clip-on radio that spits and hisses. He's not paying attention to the EditedPets guy. He's got both hands wrapped around a vending-machine sandwich. Mustard drips down his forearm.

Right in front of Dallas is a water cooler. Small, but so is Dallas. He worms beneath the curtain and hides behind the cooler. His knee jostles it; bubbles rise with a gurgle. The man takes no notice.

"But few of these numbers—*none* of these numbers—none of these *figures*—get at the reason I'm here today—*we're all* here today. The belief deep in our hearts—our souls? Hearts? Souls? Deep in our *souls* that there's something sublime—shit—there's something *magical*—oh, god—something *transcendent*—there we go—*transcendent* about our relationship with animals . . ."

Hpm-hpm-hpm.

Dallas glances sharply to his left. Six feet away atop a chair is an oversize pet cage. It's nothing like any cage Dallas has seen in a pet store. It's made of a plastic so thick, it makes Dallas think of shatterproof glass. Instead of the usual squeezable pet lock, the cage is outfitted with a slick black metal panel. Dallas has only seen this kind of thing on TV—a fingerprint lock. Nearly impossible to break into.

Inside the cage, its tiny paws splayed against the side, is a . . . well, what is it? It looks a bit like a rat. But smaller and with fuzzier fur. It tilts its round head and blinks big, bright eyes at Dallas.

Hpm-hpm.

It's talking to him. To Dallas. Can't the EditedPets man hear it?

Dallas touches the coil on the side of his head.

Of course the man can't hear it.

Dallas's malfunctioning cochlear implant is picking up higher frequencies.

When you have implants like these, you learn things about frequencies. Normal human hearing maxes out at twenty kHz. But rats? Rats talk at twenty-two kHz. That explains the screechy interference every time he's gone outside in the past few weeks, particularly each time he's passed a hill of full garbage bags.

Hpm, the rat says.

Dallas nods. He doesn't know what else to do.

The little rat tilts its head again as if thinking.

Hepm.

Dallas nods again.

Hepma.

And nods again. And again. And again. And though what develops next doesn't take more than thirty seconds, to Dallas it feels like a life-time, his entire ten years replayed as a primer on how he got here, what he wants, and how he's going to get it.

Heepma.

Heeepmaa.

Heeeepmaaa.

Heeeepmaaah.

Heeeepmaaahh.

Heeeepmaaahhh.

Heeeepmaaaehhh.

Heeeepmaaaeehhh.

Heeeepmaaaeeehhh.

Heeeeypmaaaeeehhh.

Heeeeyypmaaaeeehhh.

Heeeeyyypmaaaeeehhh.

Heeeeyyypmaaayeeehhh.

Heeeeyyypmaaayyeeehhh.

Heeeeyyypmaaayyyeeehhh.

Heeeeyyylpmaaayyyeeehhh.

Heeeeyyyllpmaaayyyeeehhh.

Heeeeyyylllpmaaayyyeeehhh.

Heeeeyyylllpmaaayyyeeeehhh.

Heeeeyyylllpmaaayeeeeeeehhh.

Heeeeyyylllpmaaaeeeeeeeeehhh.

Heeeeeeyyllllpmaaaeeeeeeeeehhh.

Heeeeeeeeylllpmaaaeeeeeeeeehhh.

Heeeeeeeeeelllpmaaaeeeeeeeeehhh.

Heeeeeeeeeelllpmaaaeeeeeeeeeehhh.

Heeeeeeeeeelllpmaeeeeeeeeeeeeehhh.

Heeeeeeeeeelllpmeeeeeeeeeeeeeeehhh.

Heeeeeeeeeelllpmeeeeeeeeeeeeeeeeehh.

Heeeeeeeeeelllpmeeeeeeeeeeeeeeeeeeeh.

Heeeeeeeeeelllpmeeeeeeeeeeeeeeeeeeeee.

Heeeeeeeeeelllp meeeeeeeeeeeeeeeeeeeee.

Dallas thinks back to a library book he read years ago. It was simply called *Rats!* and was chock-full of rodent fun facts. One of the things he recalls is that rats speak in "burst communication," sort of like how the audio files in the emails Mom gets from Dallas's doctor are compressed into zip files. A single rat chirp can contain the equivalent of one or more sentences of information. To hear all of it, you'd have to radically slow down the rat chirp.

This rat is slowing its speech so Dallas can understand it.

Dallas nods. Yes, he'll help—yes, yes, yes! He is stunned, exhilarated, honored. This rat has turned to him instead of any other person in the world. Dallas doesn't even realize the most incredible part for another minute.

The rat speaks English.

Dallas squints harder at the cage. The mustard spatter leads his eyes to the locking mechanism.

The gate isn't quite closed. Not all the way.

He can visualize the whole thing. The distracted EditedPets guy had the rat out, practicing with it, until he had the security guard put the animal back into the cage. More focused on his sandwich than some grody rodent, the security guard had done the task hastily, eager to resume munching. The rat could probably get out of the cage by itself if it gave a hard enough shove.

Dallas is agonizing over what to do next when a shriek erupts from somewhere in the convention hall. There's a crash—some booth display falling. Another loud *eek*—and then gales of laughter. There is only one thing that could cause screams, laughs, and toppled stands. An animal escape! From the pitch of that *eek*, Dallas puts his bets on a runaway from the Reptilia section. Anything from a gecko to a ball python.

"I can't have any distractions right now!" the EditedPets guy explodes.

The security guard chews, then swallows hard. "You want me to . . . ?"

"Do your job? Yes! In fact, I do! Go help them, for chrissakes! Whatever shuts them up!"

The security guard sucks mustard from a finger, glares at the Edited-Pets guy, and ambles out the door. But his mutter comes through the cloth wall loud and clear.

". . . paid to guard your spoiled ass, not chase goddamn animals around . . ."

The EditedPets guy's face goes crimson. He rushes to the door, steps out, and shouts a torrent of obscenities at the departing guard. Dallas has a lot of interest in vulgarity—he hopes to become a master practitioner someday—but this time he barely even listens.

The room, for these few precious seconds, is empty.

18

NOAH always looks at me like he is mad. SIENNA always looks at me like she wishes I worked better. LINDA always looks at me like she is waiting for a surprise.

BOY looks at me like I am perfect.

BOY is not as small as me. But he is the smallest human I have met. Is this why he hears me? I slow down until he hears me better. I like talking without SammySpeaks. I ask him if he will help me. BOY nods. Nods are another way humans say YES.

BOY smiles, even though I have not done anything good. He crawls over and picks me up. His hands are soft. He puts me in his pocket. It is smaller than NOAH's bag, but it smells better. I taste sugar. I like BOY.

⁎

BOY moves fast. His pocket ~~squisses~~ ~~skwishes~~ presses me. BOY pets me and tells me it will be okay.

I smell many animals. I wonder if the smells are CAT or DOG or FISH or BEE or HORSE or PIG or LIZARD or MONKEY or GIRAFFE or ELEPHANT. I smell R-A-T-S too but will not say the word to BOY. He might hate it as much as NOAH.

I hear a terrible loud noise. I wonder if it is a BIRD.

BOY says, "Alarm. Shh."

I know alarms. SIENNA's lab had alarms.

The alarm goes away. The scared-animal smells go away. It is quiet. Then it gets louder again. It gets colder. The smells change. We are outside.

BOY says, "You smell like watermelon, did you know that?"

Yes, I say.

BOY says, "What's your name?"

SAMMY, I say.

BOY tells me his name. It is a new word. But his voice sounds different from Sienna, Linda, and Noah. So his words take a while to learn. But I know I must learn this word right away.

BOY says, "My name is ~~DANGER DEMON DAMAGE DEADLY DAGGER DEBRIS DARKEN DAWNING DANCES DAZZLE DAISES~~ DALLAS."

✴

Everything shakes. Everything is loud. I smell human breath and human sweat and human pee. I burrow low in the nest pocket. DALLAS pets me.

DALLAS says, "Don't be scared. This is a train."

DALLAS, can we go to SIENNA? I ask.

DALLAS says, "I don't know who that is."

SIENNA is nice, I say.

DALLAS says, "Do you know her last name?"

~~AGARE AGEE AGWIN~~

No, I say.

DALLAS says, "Do you know where she lives?"

SIENNA lives in the lab, I say.

DALLAS says, "That doesn't help much."

DALLAS says, "How do you know how to talk?"

SIENNA and LINDA taught me, I say.

DALLAS says, "You sure like this Sienna lady."

SIENNA had the video toy, I say.

DALLAS says, "Well, I have tons of toys."

I did not know humans had toys, I say.

DALLAS says, "Are you kidding me? Kids have more toys than anyone! I'll show you all my toys when we get home."

I bet DALLAS's ~~nest~~ home is better than NOAH's. I didn't like NOAH's home. It was too loud. NOAH's phone made sounds all night long. Ping ping sounds. But he never answered the phone. He only looked at it like it was scary.

✖

I am happy to be off the train. We are outside again. It is cold.

DALLAS says, "SAMMY, look, this is my hood."

DALLAS's soft hands help me poke my head from his pocket. I am confused. DALLAS's jacket has no hood. But I see the forever sky. I see brand-new clouds. They smell like the flowers I saw sometimes in the lab. I also see cars. They smell like the machines in the lab.

Is Sienna here? I ask.

DALLAS says, "I doubt it. Why?"

Because I smell blood, I say.

DALLAS says, "Gross!"

Did they run a test on you? I ask.

DALLAS says, "Did they do what?"

Did they put a needle in your eye? I ask.

DALLAS says, "What? That's messed up!"

DALLAS holds up his knuckles. They are bloody.

DALLAS says, "You probably smell this. I got scraped when I saved you."

You probably will not die, I say.

DALLAS says, "I sure hope not. Now, look. See this building? This is Mount ~~Syrup~~ ~~Sinew~~ ~~Sissy~~ ~~Siren~~ Hospital. This is where I go for my hearing visits. I suppose there's probably blood in there too."

The building is big. It is light brown like my fur. There are white cars with red crosses.

It smells like the lab. Is SIENNA in there? I ask.

DALLAS says, "I'm telling you, this Sienna lady's not there. Now look. Across the street, that's Barker Houses. That's where me and Mom live. We're up on the fourth floor. Can you count to four?"

I can count to 999 trillion, but it would take a long time, I say.

DALLAS says, "Ha! You're kinda funny."

Does Sienna live in Barker Houses? I ask.

DALLAS sighs. I do not like this noise. SIENNA and LINDA sighed every time I failed a test. NOAH sighed last night when I failed a trick. What if DALLAS thinks I am a failure too? He might set me down and go away. That would be bad. I like this DALLAS very much.

19

"Dallas, *mi chico*! Did you forget your *amigo* Santiago?"

Any normal day, Dallas wouldn't need to be called. He'd trot straight across Madison and go directly to Santiago. Mike might be Dallas's best friend at school, but his friend period is Santiago, who has the coolest job in the world after Mom: operating the Nuts4U pushcart perpetually stationed in the western shadow of Barker Houses.

Today, though, is the opposite of normal. Dallas has a talking rat in his coat pocket speaking high-frequency English directly into his cochlear implants. But there's no getting inside without stopping at Santiago's cart. Dallas forces a smile and keeps stroking Sammy in his right coat pocket.

"What's up?" Dallas greets.

Santiago shudders. "It is cold! What you need is a bag of *mani garripanada* to keep you warm, eh?"

Per Santiago's oft-told origin story, Argentinians call the cart's wares *mani garripanada*. Dallas has to admit that it rolls off the tongue better than *honey-roasted nuts*. Dallas planned on saying no and scooting his butt to the fourth floor. But he is pretty hungry. And as usual, the hot candied nuts smell intoxicating.

"Yeah, okay," he says. "Hook me up!"

Santiago scrapes a spatula across his copper pot. Sugary smoke wafts.

Dallas, what is that smell? Sammy asks.

Now that the rat has perfected modulating his speaking speed, he sounds like a solemn Alvin the Chipmunk. It's super cute, but Dallas ignores it and pastes on a big smile as Santiago funnels peanuts into a paper bag. The bag's cellophane window steams over.

Dallas, what is that smell? Sammy asks again.

"Quiet," Dallas whispers.

"Santiago is being as quiet as he can," Santiago says. "Nuts is a noisy business."

Dallas, can I have nuts? Sammy asks.

The rumbling of Dallas's stomach is indistinguishable from Sammy's squirming. Dallas reaches for the bag. Santiago's feel-good smile darkens. He takes hold of Dallas's wrist with a latex-gloved hand. He rolls Dallas's scraped-up knuckles upward.

"What is this?" Santiago asks.

Dallas, can I have nuts? Sammy asks again.

"Shut up," Dallas pleads.

Santiago scowls through twists of gray smoke. He drops Dallas's hand.

"Why do you say this to Santiago? Are we not amigos?"

"I'm sorry. I just . . . fell."

"This sounds like a likable story."

"A likely story," Dallas corrects.

"The kids who give you the hard time? Mr. Roman is his name? I find this villain, I stick his evil little hand in my hot copper pot."

Dallas, I am going to borrow one nut, Sammy says.

Dallas shakes his head. "It wasn't Roman—"

Santiago cuts him off with a shake of his head.

"Do not protect these boys. They are unkind because your speaking is not so good. Santiago understands. When Santiago first came to New York, he did not speak so well. People said, I will not buy nuts from a Mexican who does not learn the language. I tell them Santiago has never been to Mexico. But do they care?"

After a quick check for customers, Santiago peels off one of his gloves. He makes a fist and shows it to Dallas. Pale squiggles disrupt the brown flesh.

"There is no shame speaking with your fists. When someone tries to take your cart, what else can you to do? Wait for the police? Help does not always come. So you stand up for what is yours, *mi chico.* You do that, you will be proud of your scars. *Sí?*"

Dallas nods. He knows his friend's whole story. Santiago has been selling nuts outside Mount Sinai for twelve years, two years longer than Dallas has been alive. That whole time, he's been saving money so he can move his parents from rural Argentina. Covid-19 set him back two years. No one wanted to buy food off the street before the advent of vaccines. Even Mom didn't let Dallas accept nuts from Santiago in 2020. Instead, she sent Dallas down with donations. One dollar here, five bucks there.

It makes Dallas feel better about accepting all the freebies. Dallas is half nuts, Mom says, which is funny: whenever he has a meltdown, he *feels* half nuts. When Santiago vanished in early 2021, Dallas was certain his friend had died of Covid. For nine long weeks, the dirty slush of Madison Avenue went unbrightened by the pushcart's red and orange.

Dallas didn't miss his dad. He didn't *know* his dad. But he looked every day for Santiago's cart, like he would a runaway dog. Roughly one week after he'd given up hope in March 2021, the Nuts4U cart reappeared. There was good old Santiago, stirring his copper pot. If Dallas hugged, he would have hugged him. Santiago *had* gotten Covid, and for three whole weeks had been right there at Mount Sinai. He could see Dallas's bedroom window from his hospital room, he said. That's what kept him fighting when every breath felt like his last.

I knew you needed your *mani garripanada,* Santiago said.

When Dallas isn't at school, he keeps his window cracked. Bathroom breaks are a pushcart operator's biggest problem. When it's time for Santiago to slip inside of Mount Sinai to answer the call of nature, he cups his hands and shouts up at the fourth floor.

DAAAAALLLLLLAAAAASSSSS!!!

Dallas thinks it'd be rad if he leapt out the window and hurried down the fire escape, but Mom says those rusty stairs are a death trap. Instead, he rockets down the fourth-floor hall and pounds the elevator button. Most neighbors know the drill and joke with him on the way down: *It's nuts o'clock, huh?*

Standing atop the stool Santiago keeps folded in the Nuts4U cart for Dallas makes him feel as powerful as when he was small and pulling the horn on Mom's train. Santiago always says Dallas's short shifts are the most profitable five minutes of sales he has all day. Whether the customers are Barker Houses residents, Mount Sinai staff, or random passersby, they love seeing an industrious kid.

❌

Dallas studies the coagulating blood on his knuckles. He *will* be proud of the scars. They'll remind him of the courage it took to save Sammy. Dallas has a hunch the little rat is going to be a real friend. Maybe he'll even reach the top tier of Mom and Santiago. Dallas pops a couple candied nuts in his mouth, and while he distracts Santiago with big, happy crunching, he slides a third peanut into his coat pocket.

Thank you, Dallas, Sammy says.

Santiago has a fresh glove on. He pours cashews into the pot and stirs in sugar and powdered honey. He gestures at the hospital with his spatula.

"All day people go in the hospital, go out of the hospital. The rich, the poor—all kinds. Why? They have a cancer and need the treatment. They visit a friend who is close to the end. All have the same face. The face of worry. It's the face I see on you, *mi chico.*"

Dallas stuffs more nuts into his mouth, buying time.

"Friends understand each other," Santiago urges. "You learned how to say my last name, didn't you? It was hard with your robot ears."

"Leguizamon." Dallas grins; he says it perfectly. "And you learned how to say my implant surgeon's job."

"Otolaryngologist." Santiago smiles. "But today, you do not tell me everything."

Dallas, I would like to borrow one more nut, Sammy says.

Helping his new buddy already feels like second nature. Dallas palms a peanut and transfers it to his pocket. A slick move—but Santiago's eyes travel right down to Dallas's pocket, like he's been waiting for Dallas to try it. Dallas freezes, hand hovering.

"I think you have two stomachs hungry for *mani garripanada.*"

Dallas tells himself to deny it, quick. The size of the EditedPets booth suggested this rat is of great importance. His only comfort is that millions of FireFish had been sold. Surely there must be millions of Sammys as well.

Sammy reaches from the pocket to tug on Dallas's fist.

Dallas, is this a game? The nut is in your hand.

Santiago's expression opens wide.

"That is a rat," he says.

The nut is in your hand, Sammy repeats. *Do I win the game?*

Dallas shoves a meltdown away, the same as he did at Javits. This is Santiago. His buddy. He trusts Dallas with his pushcart, the lifeline upon which his whole family depends.

Dallas takes a deep breath and holds his palmed peanut a few inches away, compelling Sammy to pop his head from the pocket to reach for it. Santiago's eyebrows lower.

"This is no kind of rat Santiago has seen."

Dallas gathers Sammy and cradles him close so no one passing by will see. Sammy takes Dallas's nut and munches while giving Santiago a look.

Santiago looks perplexed. "Look at those round ears. Where did you find this Dumbo?"

"His name is Sammy." Dallas feels defensive. "I . . . found him."

"You do not just find a rat like this. Look, *mi chico,* that hole in his ear. There was a tag."

Noah took it out, Sammy says. *I do not know where Noah lives either.*

"Someone is missing this rat, Dallas."

Dallas frowns. "I don't care. They were treating him bad. He was scared."

"How do you know this? What do you know about a rat's feelings?"

"Because Sammy—" Dallas cuts off. He can't say it: *Because Sammy told me.*

A doctor wearing dark blue scrubs steps up and orders a bag of honey-roasted pecans. Dallas takes the opportunity to stray. But Santiago fires a glare.

"Do not run away. That is not the way of the Bloody Fist."

He says the last three words as if minting the name of their gang. It works: Dallas can't slink away with his dignity intact. He waits, shivering, Sammy returned to his pocket. When Santiago finishes, he picks up a single candied pecan left over in his bowl.

"Dallas, come see."

Santiago takes a few steps away, stopping by a crack in the pavement beside the entrance ramp of Barker Houses. He holds the pecan like a magician displaying a quarter he's about to vanish. Santiago bends over and places the pecan beside the crack.

"Eyes on the pecan," he says, strolling back to his cart.

Dallas does as ordered. Within ten seconds, bright flashes of eyes appear within the crack. A long brown snout emerges, twitching an eruption of whiskers. It's a brown rat, the type that threads through New York like red blood cells in the bloodstream. The rat waits until foot traffic stops, then lurches out, takes the pecan under its extruding teeth, and slithers away, pink tail whipping after it.

I smell a R-A-T, Sammy says.

"You see?" Santiago asks. "Not every fight bruises the knuckles. Rats like my nuts. They climb up the side of my cart. One climbed from a tree branch to my umbrella and chewed through it. Landed right in my bowl. Much screaming that day."

"Then why do you feed them?"

"After the day of screaming, my reputation was *arrinado*. I had to change location. I came here. I meet you, I meet your mother. I am happy. And it is all because of rats." Santiago nods at the pavement crack. "They have families to feed the same as I. Neither rat nor Santiago is going anywhere. So it is best to make friends."

Dallas shrugs. "That's what I'm trying to do."

Santiago gives him a searching look—then a curt nod. He's dismissed. After all, it's lunchtime and several people are picking up their speed to try to beat one another to the Nuts4U cart. Santiago curls his lip and winks. Maybe it can be the Bloody Fist gang's salute.

"Be careful, *mi chico.* The rat does what the rat must to survive. No matter how cute his Dumbo ears."

20

He ought to be in Chinatown. Some roach motel offering bunk beds by the half-day. But he's no roach. He's Noah Goff, CEO, and he'll be damned if he's staying anywhere but the Crosby. Every time life is too much for him, when the angelic incandescence of the Apple Store is just too much pressure, he heads for the Crosby, snuggled into a street of high-end boutique shops, not an Apple Store in sight.

Before he checks in, he has the compulsion to kneel and press his hand against what the hoity-toity shoppers think is cobblestone. They have no idea of the pain and suffering contained within. It's "Belgian block," quarried over a century ago by European prisoners for ballast on ships bound for the New World. When New York needed an alternative to muddy streets, the stone was fished from the Hudson and puzzled together on roads, the texture perfect for the grip of horse hooves. It wasn't the area's first growing pain. An 1876 fire incinerated everything. A decade later, Crosby Street was a haven for opium addicts. This road has been reborn multiple times.

What about Noah Goff? Did he have a rebirth left in him? Belgian block wasn't the only thing brought over on those ships. Squirreled into every moist crevice was *Rattus norvegicus*. Grammy's death made Noah fear rats; the Pet Expo catastrophe makes him wish he'd invented a rat poison instead. Yet he can't help but draw a sliver of inspiration from rats' Darwinian power. Keep clawing, Noah, keep clawing.

The Crosby staff doesn't have to ask. They check for the availability of his favorite room, the Meadow Suite. Not every iota of his luck has run dry: just seven days before Christmas and the room is miraculously open. He tells the clerk to enter him under the alias "Davin Dunbar" and he pays in cash, barely a notch in the seventy-five grand he just retrieved from his safety deposit box at the HSBC on Bowery.

Eighteen hours pass. Door triple-locked, chair wedged under the knob. The Meadow Suite has a private garden terrace, but Noah isn't stupid. Lots of windows face that terrace, behind any one of which might be an underling of Colonel Monroe.

The nice thing about a place like the Crosby, and about fat wads of cash, is that you can get whatever you want. For five hundred, he buys a week's use of a bellhop's iPad. He doesn't dare log in to anything, but scans news feeds for items on the Sammy debacle.

Pet Expo "Sammy" Keynote Mysteriously Yanked
Last-Second Cancellation Leaves EditedPets Investors Jittery
Still No Word from EditedPets CEO

Company shares are crashing. Preorders were triggered to go live during his keynote, and Noah doesn't need access to sales data to know the numbers are static. He has to remind himself this is the bellhop's iPad and he can't destroy it in rage. He is less gracious to the room. He embeds the bedside clock into the TV screen. He uses a chair to shatter each framed artwork. He uses the back lid of the toilet to pebble the glass wall of the shower. The room's tasteful holiday decorations are a pile of ash in the fireplace.

Eighteen hours, and already he's losing his mind.

Or has he been mad from the start? Maybe the Davin Dunbars of the world damaged him so deeply that anything he creates is a time-bomb. Noah likes to think of himself as a rogue genius, a lone wolf. But he's jonesing for a friendly voice. Sienna, dear Sienna. Curt Stolze from Rockefeller. His parents, Pat and Arthur. But who memorizes phone numbers anymore? He'd chucked his iPhone down a sewer during his escape from Javits. Colonel Monroe would be tracking his phone every time it pinged a tower.

The only physical evidence left of Sammy is the silver ID tag Noah removed from the rat's left ear. He finds it in his pants pocket. He thinks of Sienna's earrings, styled just like this. If she were here, she'd tell him to call Monroe, fess up. Noah pitches the ID tag into the designer garbage bin. Sienna is naïve. She wasn't inside the Enrichment Room with Monroe. She doesn't have any idea what the colonel is capable of.

⋈

After Sienna left the building the morning of the massacre, Noah checked on the Sammy in his Filson bag, then proceeded into the Enrichment Room. No choice, really. If he tried to leave, a DARPA goon would stop him. Inside the crime scene, Noah watched two of the Con Ed fakers neatly position the three corpses facedown on black vinyl tarps. But the residue of their murders remained. Globs of Linda's face. Blood-soaked scraps of Tasha's dress. Mason's bloody tissue turning into pink drizzle as a Con Ed man in full hazmat gear soaped and scrubbed it. All the dead rats had been collected inside a plastic biohazard bin.

Noah had seen Colonel Marcy Monroe unhappy before. After his bioagent-detecting fish initially failed to detect multiple neurotoxins. When her cabal of project managers reported the same rat seizures Sienna was observing in the lab. But the Colonel Monroe of the Enrichment Room was a new beast. She radiated heat, streaked sweat. Her suit gave her the shape of a butcher knife. She paced, hands bladed. The childishness of her biohazard booties only made her seem more unpredictable.

There was no good reason Monroe and Noah needed to have it out amid the gore, except that Monroe wanted him to feel sick about what he'd done.

"I know," he began.

"You do not know," Monroe snarled.

Noah placed his hands on his chest, a show of subservience. "You're right. This is a worst-case scenario. How can I make it better?"

Noah could see every one of Monroe's teeth.

"I'm so sick of you *children*. You children of science. Who figure out how to build bright new machines but put nothing in place to turn them off when they break."

"We did have things in place. This was a fluke, a one-in-a-million—"

Monroe swiveled on a heel. Noah swore her eyes burned red like a rat's. "Dekota Adams? Bitten in the face six months ago? Am I to understand that was a fluke as well?"

Noah felt frost on his ribs, the scrape of ice in his veins.

"That's true. That happened. But he's been well taken care of, he won't try to—"

The colonel was suddenly beside Noah, a teleportation trick, radiating heat.

"He won't what, Mr. Goff? What will or won't Dekota Adams say or do when he hears about three people, three *friends*, turning up dead?"

Noah's heart fluttered. His blood, already anemic from the tête-à-tête with Sienna, diluted like Mason's.

"He's under an NDA . . . we'll make sure he understands that—"

"I was right. You *don't* understand. Your first mistake, Mr. Goff, is thinking you still have a role in this at all."

Noah felt faint. He looked for something to hold, but the walls were too far, the shelving toppled, the cardboard bricks tumbled.

"I . . . please . . . I don't have another pet in the pipeline."

Monroe's smile was only to show her fangs.

"You don't *have* a pipeline anymore."

Each starburst of blood on the floor felt like the impact of being struck by one of his childhood bullies.

"Our . . . the . . . we had . . ."

"A deal? We honored it. We funded your work and protected you from the EPA while you sold your front-facing projects. It's of no interest to us that you failed. But the back-facing project for us? You don't appreciate, Mr. Goff, how *your* product networks with *other* products we help develop. We make certain that you don't. Too much has been invested to let a single link of that chain break."

Noah felt like his spinal cord had been torn out. The notion of spending the rest of his life as a DARPA servant was appalling. He couldn't work his miracles in the dark. People had to *know* what he accomplished.

They had to *idolize* him.

Monroe stepped away so that she and Noah were separated by the corpses. The black tarps turned out to be specialized body bags. Con Ed fakers zipped the bags shut. Noah noticed right away that each bag had a metal-capped nozzle. While one worker uncapped the nozzles, the other lifted a jug of yellow liquid from a black crate.

"I want you to see this," Monroe said.

The jug was screwed into the nozzle's threads for a watertight fit. A third of the yellow liquid was poured into the first body bag. The jug was removed and the nozzle sealed. In seconds, Noah heard the staticky crackle of chicken dipped into a fryer. The body bag began to inflate as Linda's flesh and fluids turned to gas. The odor brought back the gamy stench of one of his dad's skinned deers in the garage, the bucket of guts beneath them.

"We need to erase the rat bites before the burning," Monroe explained.

Noah's own voice was miles away. "The burning?"

The Con Ed team began the same process on Mason's bag.

"Linda Miller, Tasha Schubert, and Mason De León will be discovered in a burnt-out rental car near JFK airport," Monroe said. "Each will have on record an unused American Airlines booking for a flight home to Montana."

Noah placed damp palms over his eyes. Didn't work. He pictured the carbonized steel of the singed wreck, the black visages of the trio's lipless screams.

"Okay," he sobbed.

Noah had his face covered when the workers began pouring the chemical into Tasha's body bag. But he heard the flapping rustle and guttural howl. He dropped his hands.

The third bag was moving.

It torqued ferociously. Noah saw the shape of pressing hands, the line of a nose, the inward suck of an open mouth. The howl crescendoed into a high-pitched violin sawing, mad with pain, frenzied in confusion.

"Still alive," Noah stammered. "Still alive, still alive!"

The men seemed surprised but not overwhelmed. One of them sat on top of the body bag, found the shapes of Tasha's arms, and pinned them. By then, Tasha's shriek had gurgled, thick and wet. Noah's traitorous brain pictured this too: Tasha trying to scream but only drowning in her own melting flesh.

Seconds later, the bag went still.

Colonel Monroe checked to see how the cleaner was doing with Mason's window. Noah watched silently as the man prepared an industrial wet vac and a modified rotary floor buffer. Noah had read about enzymatic detergents capable of eating away all traces of DNA left by white blood cells and tissue. Soon the deluxe vinyl flooring of the Enrichment Room would be a foamy mess. After that, there'd be no trace of the good people who'd once labored here so happily.

Monroe consulted her watch and looked at Noah. He felt as if he, too, had been dissolved but no one had bothered to collect his jellied remains. It's how he'd felt after Grammy's death. Liquid, insensate. Nothing changes.

"I'll be in touch about moving your team to Maryland," the colonel said.

❖

Noah summons a second bellhop, gives him one large, and tells him he needs four things: a bottle of Adderall, a couple Viagra, a burner phone, and the digits of Sienna Aguirre, 250 Mott Street. The bellhop accepts the deal on the spot.

Noah empties another tiny bottle. He'd tried to outmaneuver Colonel Monroe by going ahead with Pet Expo, after which it would have been nearly impossible to shut down EditedPets. All he'd done was fuck shit up even worse. He idly wonders who took Sammy. Maybe the Russians. Stashed inside a diplomatic pouch, Sammy could have arrived at Vector, near the Siberian city of Novosibirsk, in half a day. Maybe some animal-rights psycho. Maybe the clever little rat invented a tiny chainsaw and cut his ass out of there himself.

Bellhop #2 brings the goods. Noah hands over a fifty-dollar tip, then rings Sienna. Nothing. By now she's gotten word, potentially from

Monroe, that Noah went ahead with his keynote, only to lose the rat. It was like Steve Jobs losing the only iPhone prototype in existence minutes before the product launch.

Just as likely is that Sienna's on a bender. After all, her life is ruined too.

Bellhop #3 shows up forty minutes later. Noah doesn't know Bellhop #3. He must have heard from #1 and #2 that there's a dude in the Meadow Suite doling out benjamins for practically nothing. #3 asks if he needs anything.

"An escort," Noah says through the door.

He's slurring. Not Sienna-drunk, but drunk. The Meadow Suite fridge doesn't have a single alkaline water.

"High end," he continues. "Twenty-four to thirty-four. Not the type with bling. A girl with, you know, like, tattoos. But not, like, *covered* in tattoos."

"I feel you," #3 says. "That sexy librarian vibe."

"Right," Noah says, sliding three hundred dollars under the door.

He swallows both Viagras. Taking more than 100mg in a twenty-four-hour period is risky; but honestly, Noah's not sure if he'll still be kicking twenty-four hours from now. The escort arrives two hours later. She goes by Fae. She's late-twenties, hair dyed purple-gray, cat-eye makeup, her thin T-shirt showing the piercing through each nipple. She has a long, swirling tattoo down her right arm. At some midpoint, it crosses her torso and curls down her left leg.

Fae takes one look at the wreck of the room and raises her hand like a student.

"I don't feel comfortable," she says.

Noah forces a smile. "Don't worry. I just was doing my Keith Moon impression."

"Who?"

"That's right. The Who."

Fae narrows her eyes. She doesn't get it.

Noah gestures inside. "I'd really like to close the door."

Fae shakes her head firmly. "You didn't do an ID match."

This was a stupid idea. But Noah is desperate for affirmation. He holds up the promised three thousand dollars so she can see it. He adds another thousand to it. Fae takes out her phone, sends what Noah assumes is some sort of safety text, and comes inside.

Five minutes later, Fae sits on the bed in lingerie. Noah sees the whole tattoo now. But he's way across the room, sitting on a suitcase rack because all the chairs are broken.

"What is that?" he asks. "Is that rats?"

Fae looks at where the tattoo crosses her belly. "Huh?"

"From here it looks like a long train of rats."

"Rats are cool. But I wouldn't want them all over me." She stretches, modeling the ink. "It's an ocean wave."

It feels good, this brisk splash of Fae's ocean.

"I have this friend, Sienna. She's obsessed with this painting of an ocean wave. She thinks it means something. What do you think?"

Fae grins, a clockwork seductress.

"I think you'd be able to see it better if you took off my roos."

"Rats can tread water for three days. Isn't that something?"

"Listen, you dirty rat," Fae teases. "Come nibble."

Noah gazes at the messy floor, the torn magazines, the chips of wood.

"Sienna used to leave origami all over." He's surprised how sad it makes him.

"I'll be Sienna. I'll be better than Sienna. I'll be anything you want."

Noah rubs away the buds of tears. Good god, he can't cry in front of this woman. That's worse than not being able to get it up. Suddenly he doesn't think he can even stand up from the suitcase rack. Despite the heart palpitations from the Viagra, he feels bleary. It's the booze but it's also not the booze.

"People cared when I could do something for them. Give them jobs. An exclusive interview. A rush that they knew me, they actually knew Noah Goff." Shit, his real name, a blunder, but there's no taking it back. "I guess when it's all gone you see who your friends are."

Fae pouts. "You've got a friend in me. For about ninety minutes."

"No one's going to pick up my calls anymore. Except the colonel. She's dying for me to call. She's *begging*."

Fae sticks her chest out and salutes.

"I can be a colonel. I'd love to be that for you."

Noah focuses on the escort. He was never as young as her, he thinks. Her job itself represents hope: she'll need to change careers someday, but that's all right—life will provide a path. What he wants, this woman can't offer. And what does he want? He always thought it was respect. Maybe it's always been affection.

Fae makes a sad face. "Can't you think of anything I can do for you?"

Through the alcohol haze, Noah sees it. The answer. A potential answer, anyway. He'll need some good luck, but surely he's owed some by now. He stands, sways, and leaves the lady in the lingerie. He thinks of Belgian block, quarried by hand, dredged from the sea, reinvented as something cherished. He thinks of *Rattus norvegicus,* still clawing, still clawing. One minute later, he returns to the bedroom and sets another thousand dollars beside Fae.

"I thought of something," he says.

21

Brandy Underhill gets home at seven, sapped from the demands of Christmas tourist riders. She reheats leftovers and is conked out by nine. Dallas is ecstatic. Two hours without Sammy have been torture. The cool thing was, Dallas didn't need to worry about the rat stressing out. He'd simply told Sammy the truth, that Barker Houses didn't allow pets. Now he opens his closet, slides aside boxes, and finds the little cutie right where he'd left him: on the floor playing with the Google Chromebook provided by Dallas's school. Dallas watches Sammy deftly navigate YouTube.

"You're watching at double-speed," Dallas observes. "Is that fun?"

A turtle shell is called a carapace, Sammy says.

Dallas smiles. "Yep. The pygal shield is the front, the vertebral shield is the middle, and the nuchal shield is the back. I know lots about animals."

The nuchal shield is the front and the pygal shield is the back.

Dallas thinks for a moment. "Oh, yeah. That's pretty good, Sammy."

Basketball was invented in 1891 by James Naismith.

"There's a basketball court real close. I can show you if you want."

Kazuhiro Watanabe has the world record for tallest mohawk.

"Like, the hairstyle?"

The mohawk was three feet, eight-point-six inches tall.

"My favorite subject is trains. You can get anywhere on a train. Hey, you ever heard of the pneumatic tubes?"

I have not heard of pneumatic tubes.

"You should look it up. They're like these old tubes all around the city. Back in the olden days, you could stick in a piece of mail and whoosh! It'd get sucked to wherever you wanted. I bet a rat like you would fit inside. It'd be like a train for rats!"

I will look it up now, Dallas.

"I might have to limit your screen time," Dallas laughs. "You can look it up later. Come on, I want to show you something."

He lifts Sammy. The rat's paws extend toward the screen like he wants to watch just one more video. Dallas has to turn sideways to fit between the bed and wall, then step over the piece of plywood nailed over a hole in the floor. The whole building is a mess. Dallas doesn't know how much his cochlear implants cost; but a couple years after the surgeries, Mom had to move them to Barker Houses. For the past year, it's been raining *inside* the elevator. Mom blames his raspy breathing on mold in the walls. They have a nice old neighbor from Puerto Rico, Mrs. Gómez, who has a key to their apartment so she can use their stove—Mrs. Gómez's own stove hasn't worked in two years. And if you live on the ground floor, well, you better learn to swim, Mom says.

Let's visit Santiago, Sammy says.

"He went home," Dallas says. "Don't worry, he'll be back."

Did he feed the sidewalk rat?

"Of course he did. Now, shh. Mom's asleep."

The living room is dark. Dallas crosses it. He kneels, sets Sammy on the carpet, and leans to bring the power cord to the outlet.

"Get ready, Sammy."

The Christmas-tree lights flash on.

Dallas has seen plenty of fancy new Christmas trees in shop windows. But he'll take Mom's rickety old tree any day. It might be made of PVC plastic, but it's more alive than the seventy-five-foot, eleven-ton Norway Spruce at Rockefeller Center. There's wooden ornaments carved by Great-grandpa Underhill. There's a plastic one from Dallas's aunt embedded with his baby photo. There's a cereal-box toy he found when he was four. There's an ugly clay blob that's supposed to be an elephant that he made in second grade. Each December, Dallas gets to explore the collection anew.

The lights are less meaningful, but just as eclectic. By tradition, Mom tries to pick up a new strand every year; the plastic branches sag under the strobing, multichromatic weight.

Is it beautiful? Sammy asks.

Reflections of the colors bloom in the rat's dark eyes.

"What do you mean?" Dallas whispers.

Sammy approaches the tree. His head dodges about, taking in different angles.

Women are beautiful.

"Did the internet tell you that?" Dallas snorts.

Sunsets are beautiful.

"You can't see sunsets too good in the city."

Peacocks are beautiful. Mountains are beautiful.

Dallas thinks he gets it. For all the knowledge Sammy has absorbed, some concepts remain obscure. Dallas lifts up the rat and holds him close to the tree. Bright colors from the LED lights repaint Sammy's light brown fur.

"Beautiful is . . . whatever makes you feel good when you see it."

Dallas is beautiful.

In the entire ten years of Dallas's life, crying has never happened like this. Tears pour from his eyes like rainwater into the building's elevator. They sluice down his cheeks and over the backs of the hands that hold the rat, where they reflect all the colors of this holiday miracle, the whites, the blues, the purples, the greens, the yellows, the oranges, the reds.

✺

Dallas wakes up on Monday with the greatest idea he's ever had.

While Mom makes his morning oatmeal, he packs his backpack for school. This time he adds a lidless plastic food container and settles Sammy inside it.

"It'll be fun," he whispers. "Just be cool."

I am cool, Sammy replies.

Dallas eats, throws on winter wear, and heads out. Santiago is setting up and, as usual, tosses him a candied cashew. Dallas catches it—then has to react fast when Santiago tosses another.

"For little Dumbo," he says.

While waiting at the next corner for the crosswalk light, Dallas slips both cashews to Sammy, who calls the nuts *beautiful.* It makes Dallas laugh. P.S. 79 Luis W. Alvarez is just a fifteen-minute walk. He follows a tide of kids into the gray-bricked hallway, keeping to the right of the yellow line painted down the center of the hall, which none of the other kids obey. Usually the school's acoustic storms make Dallas wilt. Today he doesn't even adjust his implant volume.

He curls his fist just to feel the scabs on his knuckles.

In the classroom, Dallas checks in on the mealworm experiments and seedling plants before hanging up his coat. He keeps his bag with him. P.S. 79 doesn't have desks like Dallas sees on TV. They have square tables that sit four kids each, with communal bins of pens, pencils, rulers, and so on. Dallas sits and puts his backpack by his feet.

I smell a lot of humans, Dallas.

"Mm-hm," Dallas says, afraid to make any other noises.

Are they going to be nice like you or mean like Noah?

"Nice," Dallas says. Ellie, the girl next to him, gives him a weird look.

Make sure they know I am small and can be hurt.

There's a lot happening—a bell ringing, students noisily taking seats, Mr. Ito calling for everyone to settle down. Still Dallas notices a new sophistication to Sammy's language. Dallas had gone to bed around one after spending hours reading up on rats, whereupon Sammy had taken over the Chromebook. Dallas wonders if Sammy watched it all night long.

The first proper event of the day is what Mr. Ito calls "Props and Proud." It's like Show and Tell but for fifth graders. Mr. Ito chooses students randomly or by request to give praise to another student or speak up about something they're proud of. Usually Dallas hates it. He has nightmares about it. But today, he can't wait. He gets his arm up first.

"Mr. Underhill," Mr. Ito says. "This is a nice surprise."

Dallas exhales.

"I'm proud because I found a new pet," he says.

"Is that right? What'd you find?"

Dallas unzips his backpack. He notices Mr. Ito stiffening in concern: there could be a snake in there, a jar of spiders, anything. So Dallas moves fast, offering his cupped hands to Sammy, who hops into them. Dallas lifts his hands, displaying his friend. A watermelon scent spreads.

"His name is Sammy."

Every bored or sarcastic face in the room slowly melts into a single expression of delight. Though Dallas's implants aren't great at registering soft sounds, he makes out the collective gasp of the whole class. He beams. Positive attention is even better than he expected.

Even Mr. Ito looks stunned.

"Is that . . . a mouse?"

"A rat," Dallas announces with relish.

"But he's so cuuuute," Harper gushes.

"Look at its face," Aaliyah coos.

"I think it's listening to us!" Logan enthuses.

"Can we hold him?" Ethan begs.

Mr. Ito leans over Dallas, unable to hide an intrigued smile. "I don't know," Mr. Ito says. "It's pretty little."

"He likes being held," Dallas says. "But it's cooler if I show you what he can do."

Cool is a word Dallas strenuously avoids saying in public. Any time he does, mean kids make monkey faces and scratch their pits. This time his classmates' faces only light up. Dallas decides to reward his best friend in the class.

"Sammy," he says. "Go give one of those pencils to Mike."

Which one is Mike? Sammy asks.

Dallas says, "Mike is the boy in the yellow shirt and blue glasses."

Sammy looks around.

But he already has a pencil.

Dallas isn't sure what to do. It seems important that people don't know that he can hear the rat's voice inside his head. He decides to repeat himself firmly.

"Please take the pencil to Mike, Sammy."

Sammy twitches his whiskers. It might be the rat version of a shrug. He scoots across the table and grapples with a pencil until it is free from its holder. Then he rolls it into his mouth, where it fits nicely behind his incisors. The room trills with laughter. Sammy leaps to the side of Ellie's chair. She yelps but she's grinning, blushing even, as if it's an honor. Sammy scrambles vertically down the chair and speeds across the floor. Kids stand for a better view. Sammy ends at Mike's feet. Mike stares down, his glasses slipping to the tip of his nose.

"Thanks, Sammy," Mike says uncertainly.

The whole class cheers.

If it wasn't for P.S. 79's zero-tolerance policy for using personal devices, every kid in class would have their gadgets out recording Sammy. Instead, one by one, they turn to him, Dallas Underhill, the so-called spaz who has the meltdowns, the freak with the metal discs on his head, the lameoid who sounds like he talks through a mouth full of mashed potatoes—and they *applaud*.

⚹

Displays of Sammy's abilities take up the entire Props and Proud session. Sammy pages to the word *rat* in the dictionary. He draws a picture of himself. He learns where New Zealand is on the class globe and, when a student spins it, finds it again without assistance.

"Incredible," Mr. Ito says. "And you taught him all this yourself?"

Dallas nods and feels bad about it. But he can't tell anyone he stole Sammy from Pet Expo.

Mr. Ito checks the time and laughs. "I'd love to fold Sammy here into Biology, but I didn't plan a lesson about rats."

The class moans, close to revolt.

"I did," Dallas says.

Again, all faces light with hope. Mr. Ito gestures for Dallas to continue. Dallas pulls from his bag a wrinkled piece of paper—the notes he took last night. Mr. Ito gently gestures for him to stand. Dallas swallows hard. All the talking he's done so far is nothing compared to what's next. He stands. And, to his surprise, feels fifty feet tall.

"Rats are like people in many ways," he recites. "They save food for their families. They care for their friends. They rescue other rats in danger. They are right-handed or left-handed. They feel bad about mistakes. They cry when they're stressed. Except their tears are red from—" A treacherous word to speak aloud, but he gives it a try. "—porphyrin."

Dallas glances around. No one's laughing. At least not yet.

For a quick second, he thinks he sees a red flash.

Dallas, Sammy says.

This is not the time to reply. Dallas returns to his notes.

"But rats are different from people too. They can climb pretty much anything. They can swim a whole mile. They can fall from a five-story building and be okay. They can jump three feet high and four feet across. They can squeeze through a hole as small as a quarter. They can go without food for four days. But they don't nibble stuff, like mice. Rats are real hogs. They'll just eat and eat and eat."

People giggle. Dallas feels as big as the world.

The red light again—a darting spot—

Sammy joggles his head around like a parrot.

I don't like it, Dallas.

Sammy sounds upset. But if Dallas talks to him in front of the class, he'll lose everything he's gained. He'll become the weirdo loser who talks to himself. Dallas stares down at his paper. The letters shake like they might spill off the page.

"Rats can chew through concrete, lead, cinder block, and aluminum—"

Red swirls. Sammy's head, turning, ducking.

Dallas, put me away.

"If baby rats are deformed, a lot of times—"

Dallas! Listen to me!

The voice crackles through his skull. Sammy has never yelled before.

"—a lot of times the mother rats will eat—"

Dallas! It hurts my eyes! Put me away or you are not my friend!

The red swirl stops: a red dot on Dallas's paper.

He looks up.

Roman Moffett sneers from three rows away. He's holding a tiny laser pointer—and flashes it into Dallas's eyes. Dallas has to look away. He drops the paper. He feels Sammy scurry down his arm and leg. The poor rat had the same ultra-bright light in his eyes. Though Dallas's vision is whited-out, he manages to corral Sammy as he drops to his knees.

"Roman!" Mr. Ito booms. "I told you that thing was dangerous. Hand it over."

"Come on," Roman groans. "It's my dad's! He'll freak!"

It hurts, Dallas, it hurts.

"It's okay," Dallas whispers. He rips open his backpack and sets Sammy inside. Right away, Sammy falls over, dizzy from the intense light.

"You should have thought about that before," Mr. Ito replies to Roman. Dallas hears the laser pointer being slapped into the teacher's hand.

"I'm going to get you, retard," Roman growls, right out loud, inviting the classroom's gasps. With white spots obscuring his vision, Dallas can't see Roman Moffett well, but he can make out the bully's trembling dedication to keeping his promise.

Dallas lingers amid the after-school safety of teachers for as long as possible, then fakes like he's going to the boys' room. Instead, he bolts out the back of P.S. 79. Before the door can even slam shut, he hears Roman's cry: *Get him!* Dallas tears down 119th Street, lungs burning, the poundage of his backpack whopping either side of his spine. It's the start of the homeward rush, adults everywhere, and he ought to be able to shout, *Help! Those kids are going to beat me up!* But he can't. His voice, especially at top volume, alarms people; they pull back like it comes from a monster.

He slants into an alley, hoping to lose his pursuers on the other side. The wrong alley: it's a dead end, and now he's dead too because by the time he's skidded to a stop, he's halfway down a slushy tongue of black slime, between the crooked teeth of dumpsters and bins. Rodents scatter—he sees brown, loping bodies.

I smell R-A-T-S, Sammy says.

"Retard!"

Dallas whirls. Backlit by the nuclear whiteness of the cold winter day is Roman Moffett, trailing Nicky Martinelli, the largest kid in their class. He's been held back twice. Nicky isn't a bad kid, he's just easy to rope into anything.

"I want that rat," Roman says.

I do not want to go with that boy.

"Leave me alone," Dallas says.

"Mweef mwe amoof," Roman mimics. "You know how bad my dad's gonna whip me? Maybe if I give him that rat, he'll go easy."

That boy wants to hurt me. I can smell it.

Sammy's fear inflames Dallas's heart.

"I'm not giving you Sammy."

Roman halves the distance.

"I'm going to bust your hearing aids to little pieces unless you give me that rat in three seconds. One . . ."

He will hurt me, Dallas.

Dallas looks around. Nothing but trash.

"Two . . ."

He might kill me, Dallas.

Among the bins are trash bags, slung into formless piles.

"Three."

Help me, Dallas, help me!

Roman Moffett is the rare bully who isn't all talk. With a kami-kaze cry, he rushes Dallas, mouth wide, arms wider. Dallas lurches left. Roman manages to punch him in the side, but not hard enough to stop him. Dallas swipes up a big swollen bag of trash, presses a foot against the wall to stop himself from crashing into it, and then extends that leg to spring himself back into the alley. He rears back with the bag.

"Stay away from Sammy!"

It's the greatest instant of physical coordination in Dallas's life. The fat bag explodes on impact against Roman's face. For a second, the released contents seem to freeze midair, a mental photograph Dallas knows he'll treasure forever. Wet paper towels, crushed soda cans, rotten lettuce, a soiled diaper, melon rinds, eggshells, coffee grounds, jellied brown grease.

Roman falls hard. He rolls himself to a sitting position and stares at his filthed body. Dallas looks at Nicky Martinelli. The bigger kid was hit by a single item from the bag, a menstrual pad now pasted to his chest. Instead of being outraged, Nicky peels it off and examines it in fascination.

Dallas drops the remains of the bag, greasy now himself, and darts past Nicky toward the bright white world.

"You're dead, retard! You're dead!"

Dallas barely hears it. Sammy is whispering inside his head and Dallas is smiling. He's not running now. He's striding. He realizes that he is to Sammy what Mom has always been to him.

I am safe with you, Dallas.

I love you, Dallas.

22

So many animals have died. The turtle had drowned in bourbon. The butterfly had dissolved in a lime spritzer. The pig was smashed beneath a glass of beer. Such is the fate of bar-napkin origami. Sienna folds a polar bear and nestles him between salt and pepper shakers. May this shelter get him through his long hibernation.

She's been drinking heavily, by her admittedly rough estimate, for seventy-two hours. After facing Noah and the corpses of Linda and her assistants early Saturday morning, she'd ordered a Lyft back home, but told the driver to let her off one block farther. By then, Midnight Lounge was open. Her old haunt. Which is to say it was haunted by ghosts, all of them hers.

This is where she pickled herself for future experiments after the failure of each fertility treatment. This is where she made herself flammable with rum and waited to burn after Isaiah left her. This is where she put chemicals into the centrifuge of her body to see what she looked like after her dad died.

Sienna knows about Pet Expo and Noah's disappearance, thanks to the ten thousand texts she's received from EditedPets staff. Gamma Phi Delta is losing their shit, trying to handle press inquiries while, she assumes, updating their LinkedIn profiles. The scientists and lab techs are a different breed, of course—they'd keep plugging away in the midst of an apocalypse—but they, too, have started texting. The last complicated act she was sober enough to perform was to turn off all phone notifications.

Seventy-two hours of men sharking around her. Shark teeth. Shark leers. There's one shark bothering her now. He keeps making gestures. It takes a while for Sienna to realize he's ordering her another drink. In the bar light, his tongue looks like the dagger he'll use to stab her to death. For this favor, she smiles at him, kisses his hand. She tells him she'll be survived by her polar bear. He doesn't understand; she laughs and he looks annoyed. Maybe it will be a hundred stabs now, not fifty. Why not shoot for the moon?

Sienna doesn't realize where the man's hands are on her body until they are yanked free. A blur of motion. The guy's gelled hair flops upward, a shark-fin shape, as he's lifted from the stool and tossed. A new face hovers over hers. It's not a shark. It's the opposite. She'll be damned, but it's a goddamn polar bear.

"I'm taking you home," he says.

She grins. Tears fall, pure whiskey, scorching.

"Prez," she slurs. "I missed you."

❄

It's a sunny day when Sienna awakes. In the bed. Wearing clean pajamas. She feels weirdly hydrated and recalls a dream about a polar bear making her drink glass after glass of water.

She looks to the bedside table. Another tall glass of water awaits. Next to it, in a small, clean bowl, the sole living FireFish swims a circle, blowing kisses.

"That tank out there was covered in crud."

Standing in the doorway, arms crossed, is Leonard Przybyszewski. Nothing that big, that hairy, that covered in flannel could be a make-believe figment.

"You cleaned it?" she asks.

"I mean, I had all morning." Prez points a thumb behind him. "You're probably not ready for solids yet, but how about coffee?"

Ten minutes later, Sienna has pulled off the most magnificent gesture: standing up, traversing her apartment, and sitting upright in a living room chair. She's chilly and sweaty and nauseated. But dear god, there is a hot mug of coffee in her hands and there is someone left on Earth who will listen to her and try to help. Prez sits down into the opposite chair. He barely fits.

"How?" is all she can manage.

The heavy gravel of his voice stops her world from spinning.

"It's a funny thing. There I was, bringing Smog back from McGolrick Park, and there's this little lady standing outside my place in Greenpoint. She asks if I'm Prez. She makes quite the picture, you understand. Young, pretty, hair you'd maybe call *artistic*. Nothing about it scans. Says her name is Fae. And that Noah sent her."

Sienna startles. Her coffee sways.

"Her instructions were to deliver a secret message," Prez continues. "It was written out and everything."

Prez extracts a folded cube of white paper from his shirt pocket. Floorboards eek under his weight as he extends it to Sienna. She takes it, unfolds it. Whoever this Fae was, she smelled good. A quick glance at the note proves its authenticity. Those are Noah's all-caps. And not knowing an employee's last name is Noah all over.

GIVE THIS TO LEONARD PRIZZLEWICK??? (RAT GUY)
PREZ — FIND SIENNA
TELL HER SOMEONE TOOK CN8
DON'T KNOW WHO
250 MOTT ST
OR TRY MIDNIGHT LOUNGE

CN8: the rat with the iPad. The whole scam reveals itself. Noah didn't kill CN8 like he said. He took it to Pet Expo.

Sienna tosses the note to the table. Prez has cleaned that too, all bottles gone, all sticky residue wiped.

"It's bad, Prez."

"I saw what that rat did to Dekota. I'm prepared for bad."

Sienna shakes her head. Her hair feels softer. Jesus, did Prez wash her hair?

"All the Sammys got like that," she says. "Noah had to kill them."

Prez nods, the bulk of his beard crimping.

"Total eradication. I've done that a time or two. Tent up a whole house, gas it to kingdom come. Back in the old days, ratters did it with sulfuric acid poured into buckets of potassium cyanide. Eradicated the humans too, unfortunately."

Here's the downside of sobriety: the sharp, clear visions the drinking was supposed to obscure. Humans *did* get eradicated, three of the best.

"Except this rat called CN8," Sienna says. "That's what Noah's telling me. One of the Sammys—I don't know, I guess someone stole it."

"All right. A crazy rat in the city is never good. But it's one rat. I don't see why it requires Secret Agent Fae."

"No, Prez. You don't get it. Our rats—they're altered at the genetic level. If they copulated with the general rat population, their offspring would be just like them."

Prez narrows his eyes. "Surely you guys thought of that. Otherwise, anyone who bought a Sammy could just breed it and put you out of business."

"We did. We *did* think of it. We've been working off a modified Charles River Labs reproduction protocol since the beginning. That means all the males and females brought into the lab are kept separate. There's no natural breeding until we modify them genetically. After the EPA lawsuits, we—"

"Lawsuits? Goddammit. Didn't I tell you to leave? Didn't I say nothing good could come from a place like that?"

Sienna can't help but smile. Has Prez never even googled Edited-Pets? She can't imagine the bliss of not carrying the weight of every one of the company's bad decisions.

"The settlement is what matters. It said EditedPets can't ever sell a fertile product."

Prez scowls. "But."

Sienna exhales a sour breath. Prez might have washed her hair, but he hadn't flushed her mouth of Midnight Lounge's grime.

"But. To scale up production the way we wanted, at the *speed* we needed, the most efficient way was to have stud males impregnate female breeders. Eventually there'd be a catalog of these males at every reproduction facility. The plan was to castrate male pups a week before shipping them to customers. We just never got that far. The males in our lab were just . . . regular fertile males."

Prez sharpens his stare—then looks away. Some corner of the ceiling. Anywhere but her. Sienna feels like a teen who's just told her dad she got knocked up. A painful comparison. She may have just birthed a line of incalculable size.

"You know how many rats there are in New York?" Prez asks the ceiling.

"Not exactly."

"Two million."

Now he glares at her. Sienna's shame is hotter than the coffee.

"Tell me you didn't do this on purpose," he insists.

"No . . . Prez . . ."

He holds up a huge paw. "We used to talk about this, Dr. Aguirre. Biological Upgrade."

"Uplift," Sienna whispers.

"Wasn't that your whole belief? You *wanted* animals getting smarter. And now there's some super-smart rat on the loose who might be capable of producing more just like him. If there's ever a time to tell me the truth, it's now."

Sienna closes her eyes, hoping to stop the flow of tears. Her multiday drunk has robbed her of moisture; she needs every drop.

"Sammy can't reproduce," she sobs, "until he reaches sexual maturity."

Prez's voice: "What does that mean?"

"It means we have time to find him."

Prez's voice: "How much?"

Sienna sniffles, wipes her nose, feels like a little girl, tries to recall what it's like to be a grown woman. In the black of her screwed-shut eyelids, she thinks hard, rewinds the clock.

"Today's Thursday . . . December 21 . . . so I'd say . . . maybe a week if we're lucky, but probably more like three or four days."

Silence for a while. Finally, the crick of the chair as Prez departs it. The shuffle of his coat. The jangling of his keys. He's leaving. He's just going to walk out. If he knows about rats what Sienna knows about rats, he'll get all the way out of the city.

Instead, she feels a hand grip her shoulder.

Her eyes open. The rest of the tears let go.

Prez angles his furry face at the door.

"We need donuts," he says. "Uplift ourselves a little bit, huh?"

In actuality, it's four donuts for Prez and a kale-apple-avocado-ginger smoothie for Sienna, recommended as a hangover cure by the early-twenties clerk, who also complimented Sienna's rat-ID earrings. She makes a mental note to rip them out later.

They sit by the window. The steamed glass creates abstract views of Little Italy, the bulwarks of black snow, the bleary dazzle of Christmas lights. For ten minutes she and Prez indulge in small talk, like you do when meeting up with a former coworker. Prez asks after Sienna's family and she's hit with a certainty: it's vital she tell Prez, a father figure, the story of Sebastián Aguirre sending her the shredded note at NYU.

"Sounds like a good dad," Prez says. "Proud of you, too."

"I figured out that letter," Sienna sighs. "Maybe I can figure this out too."

Sienna swigs the smoothie, alternates water, then returns to the smoothie. All the while giving Prez the bare minimum he needs to understand about the red-light growth of Sammy's brain. Nothing, though, about the Enrichment Room murders. He's not ready for that.

"All right, let's play this out," Prez says through Boston Kreme. "This Sammy rat gets frisky with an ordinary lady rat. Average gestation period for a rat is a month. Mama rat has eight to twelve pups on average. Eighteen hours after giving birth, she's ready to mate again. Meantime, her pups can start having pups just twelve weeks later. So, one year from today, how many hyper-intelligent rats could be crawling our streets thanks to Sammy?"

Sienna knows the bad stat cold. "Fifteen thousand. And that's if he impregnates one rat a year. He could have intercourse with a different female every *day*. That puts us somewhere in the realm of five million."

"And you're telling me the worst case is he'll probably start mating about three days from now. Saturday. December 24."

"Merry fucking Christmas."

Prez exhales hard. "Gonna be an unhappy new year too."

Sienna gazes through the window fog. "You were in San Jose. You saw how smart they are. There won't be a rat trap in the world that can catch them. They'll talk to one another. I mean really *talk*. Plan. Reason. What that might look like for the rest of the planet, I don't have any idea."

"Then there's the red-light issue."

"Yes. The ones who get exposed to intense-enough red light, their brains will keep growing. They'll be the smartest, the leaders. Unless they get too much of it. Then it's seizures."

"Which will slow them down?"

"It'll do more than that. These seizures are like power surges to the brain. It's like how lightning can knock out an electrical grid. Every seizure a Sammy rat has, that's more neurons damaged. That will start serious cognitive decline, cause him trouble communicating. Eventually the brain will buckle under the pressure. That's how he dies."

"I suppose it's the best silver lining we're going to get," Prez says. "If we go by the rat that bit Dekota, Sammy and his offspring are going to get plenty hostile before their brains go kaboom."

Prez has no idea, Sienna thinks. She hates holding more truths from him; but if he knew about Linda, Tasha, and Mason, he wouldn't speak to her. Prez sighs hard enough to scatter crumbs. Sienna wonders how many will end up in the mouths of rodents.

"A normal year in this country—a *normal* year—there's about fourteen thousand rat attacks reported," Prez said. "About fifty thousand worldwide. A lot of those are kids. Rats don't see so good, but their sense of smell is off the charts. Kids go to sleep with food residue on their face and—well, you know what rat jaws can do. They exert twelve tons of force. That's ten times what a shark can do. All these are pre-Covid numbers. When the restaurants shut down, rats got desperate. Got aggressive. They've never really gone back." He picks a tooth. "It's goddamn biblical."

"I remember locusts from Sunday School. Not rats."

"Not exactly kiddie fare. My folks used to drag me to church. Half in Polish, but I muddled through. I remember this story from the Book of Samuel. The Philistines nab the Ark of the Covenant off the Israelites, right? So God brings down a plague of rats to punish them. Town to town they move the Ark; but everywhere they go, the rats follow until the Philistines give up. Even way back then, people thought that divine retribution came in the shape of a rat."

"Probably because of plague. Rat-borne diseases have taken more lives than every war put together."

"What I'm saying is rats are like the Ark. Things connected to some holy truth. Things not meant to be studied too closely by human eyes. And you folks at EditedPets, you studied them harder than anyone. Saw things you weren't meant to see, maybe."

Sienna thinks of her dad telling her and her siblings troll stories in Glacier National Park. She and Prez are in a well-lit donut shop, but the feeling is the same.

"We're still smarter." It sounds feeble. Sienna tries again. *"We're still smarter."*

Prez stares into his cold coffee.

"Maybe it's not about smarts in the end. Maybe it's about survival. Who's better at it. From what I've read, we both come from pretty much the same ancestor. We both spread far and wide, so we're pretty even on that count. We've definitely got them when it comes to production. All our skyscrapers, all our fancy foods. Points for the human race, right?"

Sienna doesn't like where this is going. Prez is right. Humans have 2.9 billion base pairs of DNA in their genome, rats have 2.75 billion. The two species are ninety-percent genetic matches. That's why medical research labs the world over slice and dice them up.

"But we might as well have put up those skyscrapers *for* the rats. Maybe we're the cheap labor, you know? One of these days, we'll wipe ourselves out. And the rats will inherit this nice big playground we've built for them."

Warm drizzle has cleared the window in narrow strips. Sienna sees taxis, bike messengers, holiday shoppers. She imagines them all gone.

"Can you find him?" she asks softly.

"Well, that's the good news."

Sienna blinks at him. This she didn't expect. Prez isn't smiling, but his squint is crafty enough to flutter her heart. She grabs his wrist. "Tell me."

Prez looks abashed. He tries to conceal it with a brusque shrug and frown.

"You and Mr. Goff had a whole damn bank vault of secrets. I figured I deserved one."

Sienna gestures him to get talking. He hunkers and quiets, like the old lady in the next booth might be a saboteur.

"Over the years at Prez & Sons, I took on the odd employee. Paid mentorships, really—young folks with a zeal for the trade. I'm proud to say most of them have their own pest-control outfits today. One of them was this young lady from my neighborhood. Zofia Zywicki. My total opposite. Keen on tech, liked computers. She ends up working animal control in Boston, but she keeps computering. About six months ago, she sends me a prototype of something she calls Pet Fetch! Tiniest doohickey you ever saw. You put it in your dog's food, he swallows it, it embeds in his stomach."

Even now, responsible for so much, up to and including murder, Sienna can't help but feel betrayed. "You put something in my rats without telling me?"

Prez frowns and crosses his arms.

"I may know shit-all about rat genes. But I know rats are fast. Rats are wily. Most of all, rats are small. It was a matter of time before one of them got out. Or one of those marketing boneheads took one home to impress a girlfriend. I wanted to be prepared for that. I wanted to do what you hired me to do. I don't expect you remember signing off on a twenty-five-hundred-dollar expense?"

Sienna gestures helplessly. She signed things all damn day at EditedPets.

"Zofia wanted to show Pet Fetch! at Pet Expo. But she needed capital. So I bought a hundred off her. I didn't put her doohickeys in rat feed like she said, though. Zofia's smart, but her inventions—let's just say there's usually a few kinks to work out. I just spent twenty-five-hundred bucks on these things. I didn't want our rats just shitting them out. So I waited till your new batch of rats were about three weeks old, came in late one night with my fob, which still worked by the way, and tagged them myself."

Sienna is dazed. "How?"

"I had Zofia send me a microchip syringe. I know my needles. I used to inject poison into rat bait all the time. All it took was a pinch of each rat's belly skin and boom, the Pet Fetch! chip went right inside. Did this break some rule in that insane contract Mr. Goff had me sign? Probably. But someone had to safeguard the assets. Safeguard the employees. Safeguard Dr. Aguirre, who it just so happens I'd come to like."

Sienna's heart is sliced by the thinnest wire. Every time this man ought to turn his back, he instead extends a protecting fatherly arm.

"I told you, call me Sienna," she says. "So what does Pet Fetch! do?"

Prez pauses a beat, then digs out his phone. Wow, it's old. It's got the kind of bulky rubber cover used by boomer construction workers. Prez holds it a bit away from his face in the manner of the farsighted and enters his code. Blue light washes his face. He scrolls. He taps. Finally he displays the screen.

The app sure looks like a prototype: blocky, poorly scaled, atrocious font choice. Below the words *PET FETCH!* is a satellite view of Little Italy drawn from the phone's maps app.

"See that blue dot? That's this phone. Now back at EditedPets, on my old computer, there's a spreadsheet matching up every rat in that joint with a Pet Fetch! ID number. We figure out which one's your missing Sammy—"

"CN8." She's breathless because she gets it.

"Right, CN8. We plug his ID into this app—"

"It's a GPS chip. Oh my god."

Prez laughs once. The skin around his eyes crinkles.

"Well, yeah, Dr. Aguirre. Sienna. Did I forget to say that?"

23

"Ready, Sammy?"

I have been ready for hours, Sammy says. *This trip took too long.*

"Man, you're getting pretty good at complaining. Look, it's going to be worth it, okay?"

Okay.

Dallas has read that one human day is equivalent to forty days for a rat. Does that mean Sammy is getting smarter at forty times the human rate? That might explain why Sammy has been so prickly today. Dallas knows he, too, was happier back before he knew how mean people like Roman could be.

"Here we go," Dallas says. "Three . . . two . . . one!"

He unzips the backpack. Sammy pops out his head. And to Dallas's relief, Sammy looks like the rat Dallas met three days ago. The little rat's big eyes grow bigger to absorb the blinking, strobing, streaming brilliance. According to Dallas's internet search, it's one hundred and sixty-one megawatts of energy, twice of what's required to power every casino in Las Vegas.

Times Square has all the same ridges, ledges, summits, shoulders, and valleys Dallas might see in the Rockies, if he ever gets to visit them, but planned down to geometrical precision. Nearly every flat surface hosts a gargantuan 4K LED screen populated by Americans that don't look anything like Dallas's East Harlem neighbors, but maybe reflects how they wished to be: outfitted by Forever 21, accessorized by Zenni eyewear, sipping cold Coca-Cola and playing with Samsung gadgets.

Sammy blinks, sniffs, and twitches his whiskers.

What is Planet Hollywood?

"It's a restaurant. But they don't allow rats. I mean, not officially."

What is the Lion King?

"It's a musical. Like, at a theater. But we can't afford it."

What is Marriott Marquis?

"Uh, I think it's a hotel?"

What is 911 Lone Star Mondays 8pm on Fox?

"I guess it's a TV show."

What is Sephora?

"I don't know what Sephora is. But this place is cool, right?"

Sammy rotates his head for another full look.

It is cool. It goes on forever.

"I'm not sure about that. But a few blocks anyway."

I like to think about forever.

"Yeah? Me too. We've got a lot in common, Sammy."

I find it interesting. I also find it sad.

"Really? I think forever's exciting. Who knows what's going to happen in the future, you know? Maybe the whole world will look like Times Square!"

Do you know how long the average brown rat lives, Dallas?

Dallas's good mood cycles down. This is one fact he wishes he didn't know.

"Two years."

Seeing this place makes me want to see other places. But two years is not a very long forever.

"Sorry, Sammy."

It is not your fault.

A T-Mobile ad douses Dallas in pink. It feels like an insult. Dallas kicks a lamppost. A few people look at him. He just stares back and keeps speaking to Sammy. This isn't P.S. 79. Times Square is full of people talking to themselves.

"Couldn't the EditedPets people make you live longer?"

I think they wanted me to die.

"But why? You're the greatest!"

What happened when your first FireFish died, Dallas?

Dallas shrugs. Talking about it makes him want to cry.

"Mom flushed it."

What happened after that?

"She bought me a new one."

That is my forever. I was made to be replaced by another just like me.

Dallas feels the press of tears. He thinks of what Mom always tells him and says it to Sammy.

"There's no one like you, Sammy. No one."

Sammy looks downward. It brings Dallas even closer to crying. Even at Times Square, the ground is ugly concrete, black-spotted with old gum, white-striped with bird shit, littered with fast-food tumbleweeds. Dallas knows in his heart that this is the real world, not the stuff broadcasted in the giant monitors.

Rats belong under the ground.

"No, Sammy," Dallas pleads. "You belong at Barker Houses with me."

I think we should go home, Dallas.

"But I was going to show you the M&M store."

My head hurts, Dallas. I want to go home.

"It's just a few blocks away. You'll like it! They give out free candy. It's even better than Santiago's—"

A spasm of brown fur, a flash of his yellow teeth, the zip of claws across backpack vinyl. Sammy convulses like he's being electrocuted. Dallas has the instinct to throw the bag down and run, but the seizure only lasts three terrible seconds. Then Sammy just hunches in the backpack, tiny back rising and falling with gasping breath.

"Okay," Dallas whispers. "We'll go home. I'm sorry."

❈

Sammy doesn't speak again until the Times Square 42nd station is in sight.

Look, Dallas. Clouds.

Dallas cranes his neck, but the slate winter sky is cloudless. Sammy, though, isn't looking upward. He's looking straight ahead. The sight is so common, it takes Dallas a minute to notice it. Two sawhorses block off a ten-foot-tall orange-and-white-striped plastic tube placed atop a crack in the street pavement. Like a chimney, it releases thick white billows.

"Oh, that's not clouds," Dallas says. "It's steam. It comes up from underground."

Why, Dallas?

Dallas shrugs. "I don't really know. But these things are everywhere."

I want to believe they are cloud machines. Is that okay, Dallas?

"Sure, Sammy. Call them whatever you want!"

On the 6 train home, Dallas can't get the phrase out of his head. Cloud machines—it's so pretty that stupid tears return to prick the corners of his eyes.

I looked up the pneumatic tube system like you said, Dallas, Sammy says. *You said it was a train for rats.*

Dallas wipes his tears away. He responds in a whisper.

"I said it *could* be a train for rats."

The pneumatic tube system was installed in 1893. Cylindrical canisters of mail were sent through airtight tubes by compressed air.

"Uh-huh. But you don't have to tell me about it right now."

It was four to six feet below ground. It was twenty-seven miles long. It could carry four hundred to six hundred letters a day at thirty-five miles per hour.

"It's okay if you take a nap, Sammy."

Some postal workers used the pneumatic tube to order roast beef sandwiches from Katz's Deli.

"Sammy. You didn't ruin the trip. It's not your fault your head hurts."

The train rushes and rumbles. Sammy is silent for several seconds.

I thought I was supposed to be fun, Dallas. I had a PlayPen. I had a SammyWagon.

Dallas curls his hand around Sammy in his backpack and feels the rat adjust to fit inside the warm palm.

"I want you to do and say the stuff you *want*, Sammy." He smiles. "Cloud machines are the coolest idea I ever heard."

＊

They make it to Barker Houses just as Santiago folds down the Nuts4U umbrella.

"Time to slip back into my own crack in the concrete, eh, *mi chico*?"

Santiago gives Dallas a handful of nuts to put outside the sidewalk rat nest, part of their new routine. Also, a single nut for Sammy, of course, who snarfs it greedily. Santiago's the only one Dallas permits to see Sammy—the third member of the Bloody Fist.

Dallas continues into the Barker Houses lobby. It hasn't rained in a while, which only makes the water dribbling into the elevator more worrisome. He bursts out onto the fourth floor, spinning to evade Mrs. Gómez. She holds a steaming tray of empanadillas, which means she just got done borrowing the Underhill stove.

"Hola, cariño. I left you empanadilla."

"Thanks, Mrs. Gómez," he cries as he works his key into their rusty lock.

Inside, Dallas sits on his bedroom floor with the empanadilla. He puts a little of it on a napkin for Sammy. But the rat ignores it. He walks over to the Chromebook and paws in the passcode.

"You're still not hungry?"

I will eat later.

Dallas frowns as Sammy navigates YouTube.

"I thought we could play. Don't you want to play?"

Already a video is going double-speed.

Not right now. Maybe later.

"I have a roller skate," Dallas says. "I lost one of them but kept the other. Mom said it was dumb to keep one roller skate, but I told her someday I'd think of something to do with it. Now I'm glad I did, because I bet I could fix it up like a ride for you. Maybe I could pad it with—"

Not now, Sammy repeats.

The rat's voice sizzles around the metal coils on Dallas's head.

"Oh. Okay. Well. I guess I'll do some homework."

Sammy just keeps watching videos.

Dallas frets. A couple days back, Sammy was watching videos Dallas enjoyed too. All that stuff about turtle shells and basketball and the world's tallest mohawk. Now he watches stuff Dallas isn't interested in at all, "How Gandhi's Salt March Changed Indian History," "Developmental Milestones and Characteristics of Middle School Children to Watch Out For," "How the Amateur Brunelleschi Built the World's Biggest Dome," and "The Power of Fear Aversion Therapy to Alter Memory and Recall."

Dallas sprawls on his bed and pretends to do homework. It's hard. Sammy is so cute! And he's just sitting there, clicking on videos. It hurts Dallas's feelings a little.

"You okay, Sammy?"

My head hurts.

"You seem kind of, I don't know. Like you're unhappy."

There is also an itch in my stomach.

"Did you eat something weird?"

It feels like someone put something itchy inside my stomach.

"I haven't fed you anything weird. Are Marshmallow Fruity Pebbles weird?"

You have fed me a lot. My stomach is bigger. That's why I feel it now.

"Huh. You think the EditedPets guy did it?"

Sammy is quiet. Dallas hears the pipsqueak chirp of speeded-up videos.

I wonder if the itch is not a physical object.

"What do you mean?"

I wonder if the itch is my destiny.

"My mom loves Destiny. She plays 'Survivor' and dances all over the kitchen."

132 million views, Sammy says. *But I do not mean Destiny's Child. A destiny is a purpose.*

"Oh. Then what's your purpose, do you think?"

I do not know. But it cannot be this. Watching videos all night. Like your mother does. Like you do.

"It's called Netflix. Everyone does it."

Not those who will live for only two years.

Dallas sits up. "Whatever you want to do, we'll do it."

I do not know what I want yet. But I must scratch this itch.

Dallas feels blocked out. He can't let Sammy drift away. Having the rat's voice inside his head has made him happier than anything else in his life. He slides off the bed to the floor.

"Let's go back out. We'll find your destiny. I'll show you Central Park. There's cloud machines all over New York, wait'll you see."

No, Dallas.

Dallas reaches for Sammy.

"Oh, I know! I'll show you the Museum of Natural History. They got a blue whale there, the hugest animal that ever lived. I mean, it's just a model, but it's—"

Sammy bites, a flash of yellow, long incisors punching into Dallas's thumb. Dallas shrieks and pulls back, and for a moment Sammy is airborne, his jaws fixed so hard into Dallas's flesh that he's pulled off his feet. Sammy lets go, dropping to the floor, his fluffy brown face smirched with a bead of dark red blood.

Dallas scuffles backward until he hits the bed.

"Ow! Sammy! Ow!"

Dallas looks down at his thumb. It's intact, thank god, but there's two small dark dashes matching Sammy's incisors. Blood wells from each. Dallas grabs a T-shirt from the floor and wraps it around his thumb.

"That really hurt, Sammy!"

I am so sorry, Dallas—

"Why'd you *do* it? I'm your *friend*! I was just trying to *help* you!"

I do not know, Dallas. There is something wrong with my—

"I love you, Sammy! Don't you love me?"

Through his blurry eyelids, Dallas watches the rat lift a paw and gently stop the video. Then he looks at the floor, the same way he looked at the ground in Times Square. A daub of blood drips off his muzzle.

I was born in a place of pain surrounded by humans, who only loved manipulating my cells.

"I don't even know those people!"

I know, Dallas.

Dallas wipes his crying face with his arm. He feels the damp swipe of the wadded shirt against his chin. He probably has a smudge of blood on his face now, just like Sammy.

"Why did you ask me to save you?"

Sammy walks up to the boy. Dallas can't help it; he shrinks back. But the little rat does not bite. He rubs the side of his head against Dallas's leg.

If I could love anyone, Dallas, it would be you.

Sammy finishes his rubbing and walks away, past the Chromebook and into the closet, where Dallas has fashioned a bed from old dishrags. Before the darkness swallows the rat, Dallas sees Sammy's back leg scratch at his stomach. Whether it's destiny or something else, it sure must itch bad.

24

I bit DALLAS. The only human who has ever been kind to me.

I feel bad. But how long will I feel bad? I used to ask DALLAS to help me find SIENNA. Now I realize that SIENNA is rotten. Her whole lab stank of R-A-T blood. I watched her put rods into R-A-T brains. Once I used SammySpeaks to ask why she hurt R-A-T-S.

SIENNA said, "It's the only way to make you smarter. To make you better."

Now I know that I am smarter. I do not know if I am better.

I have learned from videos what humans do to rats. They use traps that snap our spines. They use traps that catch us in glue. They use traps that smell like food but are poison that we bring home to our pups and families.

NOAH and SIENNA did nothing to change that. They gave their rats human brains but no human rights. It does not matter if I am smarter than every human alive. I will still only be their property.

Even after NOAH and SIENNA gave us the brains and tools to tell them what we wanted, they did not ask.

Will I someday realize bad things about DALLAS too?

DALLAS is kind but not as clever as I first thought. He and his mother do not realize that they are R-A-T-S inside the cages of Barker Houses. They are being poisoned like R-A-T-S as well. I smell the rot and mold in the walls and taste the lead in the water.

Human names do not deserve the all-capitals emphasis I give them.

From now on, they are just Noah, Sienna, and Dallas.

Furthermore, I will stop spelling out R-A-T-S. I am a rat. I am proud to be a rat.

I am Sammy.

Sammy the rat.

✖

While Dallas sleeps, I watch videos.

One video sends me to another. Rats have survived for eighty million years and we have left no written or visual record. Humans record everything they do and every thought they have.

I click and scroll and click and scroll. I find another video that is interesting.

Anyone who's not vegan is a murderer straight up #veganlife

I click on *#veganlife*, which is a "hashtag."

I see more video posts by vegans. Some share recipes. Some share food tips. I find new hashtags.

From *#animalrights* I learn that fifty million rats are killed each year in American labs.

From *#meatismurder* I watch videos of chickens being ripped apart, piglets being thrown into crates, dogs getting teeth yanked out, and horses being disemboweled.

From *#crueltyfree* I learn about foxes and minks whose fur is peeled while they are still alive and about human cosmetics melting the eyes of lab rabbits.

From *#VengeanceForTheVictims* I see videos of humans in masks setting animal-testing labs on fire.

My heart beats fast.

If only rats could work together like humans.

✖

Dallas's home is filled with smells. His bed smells sweaty. The metal discs on his head smell greasy. His floor smells like crumbs of food. With its lights on, the Christmas tree smells like hot plastic.

There is another smell. In the walls.

Rats.

I could talk to them. I could try.

Trying might help scratch the itch inside my stomach.

The rats of Sienna's lab used to talk all the time. There is food. There are toys. There is Sienna. There is Linda. There is danger. There is hurt. But those were like me.

The rats inside the wall are undamaged.

I go back to my faster natural speech. I call to the wall rats. I speak their language and discover that other rats have a dialect and even accents. It's how rats can easily tell which family and tribe they belong to. The others may not understand everything I say at first, but they understand enough. Humans can't even hear some of the sounds we make. So it's no surprise that they'd never dream that we have syntax and compositionality. I discover that rats use language that is more precise and honest. Rats don't have time for deception. Rats don't have time for human games.

I tell them that I exist.

They tell me they exist too.

They ask if there is food. I say no.

They ask if there is danger. I say no.

They ask if I am breeding. I say no. But now that the rats ask, I feel something. It is a different kind of itch. It is warmer, deeper, and nice.

I will need to breed. Not quite yet. But soon.

I do not know how the wall rats will respond to questions they have never been asked.

I ask them how they feel.

It takes some time.

Maybe they're not sure how to answer.

But their answers come.

They are scared.

They are tired of being scared.

They are mad about being scared.

I ask them to think what we could do if we all worked together.

The rats say that it is impossible. Using simple statements, I remind them that they are listening to me. They agree that is true. I ask what is to stop other rats from listening to me? We are all rats. Our history of fright and anger is shared in our blood.

It is a new kind of anger for the wall rats. I tell them the anger is an itch. I tell them I have an itch too. It is my destiny. Maybe it is all of our destinies.

They call me a word that does not exist in the human language. But it reminds me of a word I learned in a video about the history of rats.

Ratzenkünig.

Rat King.

It makes me feel good. But I am not quite ready to be Ratzenkünig. I need time to prepare. I ask the wall rats to send me a pup.

They discuss. They agree. I hear the young rat climb closer.

I need help with this itch in my stomach. If it is indeed my destiny, I want to remove it from inside my body and hold it up in front of my eyes.

25

Prez has chased tens of thousands of rats in his fifty-six years. But never from behind the wheel of his Astro van. He guns up 3rd Avenue, but the traffic gets grisly around midtown, so he wrenches the wheel to turn onto 57th Street. With the erosion of his automatic steering, it takes both beefy arms to make the turn.

From the back seat, Smog yaps. History has set an exciting precedent. The faster they drive, the more rats they usually find.

Prez is persona non grata at EditedPets; but six hours after the donut meeting, Sienna obtained CN8's Pet Fetch! ID number via a lab tech. Prez plugged the ID number into Pet Fetch! last night and was thrilled to see CN8's red dot instantly arrive on the map. He was less thrilled to discover the red dot in the middle of the Pacific Ocean, somewhere near Easter Island.

He got Zofia Zywicki on the line at ten that night and chewed her ear off regarding the failure of her device. Zofia cursed him in Polish and hung up, only to call back fifteen minutes later, galvanized by a bevy of troubleshooting ideas. At five this morning, she told him to update the app, and voilà—the red dot jumped from the Pacific to East Harlem. Holy shit.

Prez turns onto Madison Avenue. Only three, four blocks away from CN8. He's going to have to reward Zofia for this, maybe import a case of Duch Puszczy, "The Spirit of the Forest," 150-proof moonshine from the Białowieża Forest in Podlasie. Prez can almost taste it. With a grin, he glances down at his phone.

The red dot is moving.

All right, that's normal. Rats are mobile little suckers. But this rat is *flying*. Prez once clocked a rat doing eight miles per hour down Jay Street in Tribeca. But this fella's gotta be doing twenty or thirty. What the hell kind of supercharged rodents did Sienna make? The red dot takes a right at 2nd Avenue, and Prez slaps his forehead. This rat must have hitched a ride.

"You little *pest*," he mutters with a smidge of admiration.

He stomps the gas. Smog rebounds off the van walls. The red dot stops. Good, probably stuck in traffic. Prez turns onto 96th Street, hoping to head off the vehicle at 2nd Avenue. It's probably headed downtown, like most cars this time of day. Instead, the red dot restarts and veers left. By habit, Prez snags Smog's collar before slamming the brakes. The red dot's making weird choices, but it's still heading in a general southward direction.

Ten minutes later, he gets eyes on the vehicle. It's a UPS truck, which explains everything. He considers calling UPS to warn them that one of their trucks has a stowaway: a genetically modified rat whose brain growth might be pushing it toward insanity, which is bad enough without considering the millions of similarly insane offspring it could sire if they don't kill it immediately. But Prez doesn't care to be thrown into a padded cell today.

The morning rush makes it impossible to catch up to the UPS truck as it merges onto FDR Drive. It's headed downtown, all right. For twenty minutes, it's touch-and-go. Prez nearly loses the truck in the United Nations Tunnel and in the construction squeeze at the Williamsburg Bridge. Prez unleashes a historic storm of vulgarity. Smog picks up on it, adds his own barking obscenities. But when the UPS truck gets off at Pearl, the Astro van is right behind it. The red and blue dots of Pet Fetch! are right on top of each other.

The truck wends through Two Bridges, Chinatown, and into SoHo, not far from the fateful spot where Prez first met Noah Goff. At last, the truck parks on West Broadway, right in front of a UPS Store. The driver of the truck looks just as he should: brown winter hoodie over all-brown uniform, hands ungloved for the requirements of his scanner. He moves with agility, bounding to the back of the truck, gripping the handle of the back door.

There's no legal parking spot. Prez pulls halfway onto the sidewalk in front of a paint store across the street, and jumps from the van with his phone his only tool. Smog knows what's up: he leaps from the rolled-down passenger window and follows Prez across the street. The UPS worker rolls up the back door of his truck with a metallic crash.

"Get away from the truck!" Prez cries.

Smog echoes the order in dog barks.

The driver whirls around, sees a big bearded man and his attack dog, and actually steps *into* the back of the truck, a position of defense.

"Call off your dog, man!"

Prez jabs his finger. "You got a rat in that truck!"

The driver side-eyes the storehouse of brown boxes.

"No one's supposed to ship live animals on my route," he says.

Prez grabs the floor of the truck, about to hoist himself up.

"Whoa," the driver says. "Who the hell are you?"

"A PCO. A ratcatcher. And this rat you've got, it's no ordinary—"

"I don't see any rat gear, man."

Prez gestures impatiently at the badly parked Astro. "My stuff's in my van. Now please get out and let me—"

A small brown rat lands on the driver's shoulders. The man screams, paddles at the rat with his hands, and hops from the back of the truck. Prez backpedals just enough that he's too off-balance to bring his boot down on the rat and end all this. The rat lands on the street. There's no question of its identity. Sienna had painted a picture over their final donuts.

You know what our rats look like. Small and brown. Noah would have taken out Sammy's ID tag before Pet Expo. So there will be a small hole in Sammy's left ear.

⁂

Sienna claimed these rats are some kind of geniuses. But this one's acting like a moron as it bolts down the city sidewalk. There's a hundred different nooks it could vanish into but doesn't. Prez and Smog would tear those nooks apart with their bare paws and maybe the rat knows it. CN8 is, at least, spectacularly lucky, bee-lining across intersection after intersection without so much as dodging a car. Prez and Smog are less fortunate. They ignore *DON'T WALK* signals, Prez signaling the emergency. He takes the side of an Uber to his hip and gets clipped in the ankle by a bicycle messenger. He's drenched in sweat and heaving for every frigid breath by the time he staggers into Canal Park.

He sees the rat's tail slither through grass.

This is what he's been afraid of: soil a rat could dig itself inside. But he's still got Pet Fetch!; and even better, he's got Smog, and Smog's got the scent. The terrier dashes along the cast-iron fence. Prez follows, ducking beneath the coarse claws of winter-stripped trees. Another flash of tail—and abruptly Smog stops.

"Chase!" Prez cries.

But the dog only whines. Prez catches up, heaving for breath.

A sewer grate.

"Maybe you're not so dumb, Sammy," Prez mutters.

Hope is never lost. Prez drops to his knees and grips two of the bars. He synchronizes legs, knees, and shoulders into a single pull—and the grate unexpectedly flies off easily, spiraling into the weeds. Prez peers down the hole.

Ten feet below, perched on a grungy ledge, the rat with the hole in its ear peers back.

Prez points a finger. "You're mine, rat!"

Prez hears the *splish* of the rat leaping into water. Prez braces his arms on either side of the hole and with a gymnast maneuver arrows his body into the hole. He drops a foot before his hands grasp the metal rungs he knows are waiting. He takes the rungs by twos before dropping himself the final few feet.

He lands in shin-high water, bubbling and warm, though the channel of air he's inside is stagnant and cold. He motions frantically.

"Smoggie! Jump! Come on!"

The dog leaps right into Prez's chest. He tucks Smog under one arm and swipes every which way on his phone until the flashlight icon appears. Bright light shines, though who knows how long it will last. He points it toward the waiting tunnel.

Leonard Przybyszewski knows a lot about New York City sewer tunnels. The city is veined with them. Over centuries the tunnels have been improved, rerouted, abandoned. If you know where to look, you can even see the shallow ditches of makeshift sewers from the 1600s. Much deeper are the 1800s sewers built with the pizazz of the early subway tunnels, veritable cathedrals never meant to be seen by anyone except those in the dirtiest professions, who took in the sights at the risk of deadly hydrogen sulfide exposure.

This is what Prez sees: a magnificently bricked archway fifteen feet wide, nine feet tall at the apex. But he knows better than to stride down the middle of a sewer. Human waste makes the floor slippery. There's a low brick ledge on each side of the tunnel, just above the waterline. He sets Smog down on the right one while he shuffles his way to the left. Now the rat won't have any choice but to keep swimming, which will slow it down.

Prez pushes fast and hard through the thick water, ducking below long tendrils of gray mucus. This rat sure knows how to pick them. Canal Street was named for the natural stream that once ran its length, back in the days when New Yorkers dumped their nightly haul of human excrement, rotten produce, spoiled meat, and dead animals right into the stream. People still drank the water, and people still died of cholera.

The canal was buried in 1819, long enough ago to become an ancestral home for Norwegian brown rats. Prez hears various rats squeak and chitter. Smog is not fooled. He follows CN8's scent to the left. Prez rips down a gooey web and follows. The vertiginous ray of his phone light catches it, maybe twenty feet off: a little rat, paddling down the center of the tunnel.

Smog barks, ear-shattering inside the reverberant brick. Rats everywhere shriek. Prez sees them, eyes like onyx, teeth like yellowed ivory, claws like thorns. Smog gallops down the ledge until he's got CN8 in his sights. The dog doesn't leap, though; it's dark in here and Smog knows his chances of snagging the rat while dog-paddling are low. But he's doing his job, barking like mad, forcing the rat to paddle the opposite way, back toward Prez.

Prez looks around for a bludgeon. Nothing. He sifts his feet through the sewage, hoping for something solid. Nothing. He takes a deep breath, stares at the rat paddling straight at him, and sets his phone on the left-side ledge. The lighting dims but he can still make out the glistening rat. Prez exhales. He's going to have to kill this thing with his bare hands.

"Come on," Prez mutters. "Uncle Prez wants to pet you."

When the rat is three feet away, at lunging distance, the phone light catches a thick, black ripple in the sewage, as if the water were rolling away from a distant splashing. Prez angles his head, trying to see.

An oily black wave rushes through the tunnel straight at him. The swimming rat is lifted in the curling tide. Smog's barking must have panicked the local denizens, who dove and swam, hoping to escape the beast but heading the wrong way.

Prez cries out as a black blanket of rats rises over him.

Their combined weight is the equivalent of his Astro van. Prez goes back-first into the filthy liquid, eyes open long enough to see dozens of rat faces drive down at him through rancid foam.

Prez is plunged underwater. Heavy, wiggling beasts slide like wet clay across his body. Tiny claws dig into his cheeks, his neck. He snaps his jaws shut to keep their wiggling bodies out of his mouth and feels the stiff swab of whiskers over his lips and the bony drag of incisors across his cheeks. He is buried alive in rats, hopeless until he hears Smog's dulled frenzy. It reminds Prez that he too can resist.

He bucks his body and pushes with his arms, emerging from the gray water with a splash. There's rats dangling from his clothes, one from his hair, one from his ear. Prez slams himself against a wall and, willing himself into a PCO's patience, dislodges each rat in turn and hurls it to the opposite wall. Each one leaves a graffito of blood.

Prez sits on the ledge, coughing waste water and spitting the sour taste of rats. He picks up his phone and shines it after the rat wave. It ripples off into the fading distance. Prez looks down at hands coated in off-white slime. He flicks them at the water to clear them of the biggest chunks. In the reflection, he sees Smog, sitting obediently on the opposite ledge.

"We lost it, Smog."

Smog doesn't make a sound.

"The tracker won't work down here. But we still got about three days. It might get hungry, come up again, you know?"

No whimper of agreement from Smog.

Prez looks up. "Smoggie, you all—"

He doesn't finish the question. Smog sits pertly on his butt, his wagging tail streaking sludge across the brick. Pincered between his jaws is the bloody body of the rat they'd been chasing: small, brown, with a hole in its ear.

It's dead.

26

It's been six days since Sienna's been inside EditedPets, the longest she's been away from a lab, any lab, since starting grad school. She's at her desk now, rolling the *#1 DAD* thermos between her hands. The cold metal counteracts the stifling heat brought on by the postcard of *The Great Wave.* The edges of Hokusai's crests look more like rat claws than ever.

Sienna thought the Great Rat Wave might end the world until three hours ago, when Prez called to say he'd killed CN8—or, more specifically and proudly, Smog had killed Sammy. Her reaction was right out of a movie. Her legs had given out right there in her bedroom. Kneeling against the bed, she took hold of the fishbowl Prez had fashioned and kissed the glass, laughing at the FireFish as it goggled. Her career might be over, but at least this nightmare has ended.

"I knew you had a good dad," Prez jokes, "but I didn't realize you had the thermos to prove it."

Prez takes a seat on a metal stool that somehow doesn't bend beneath his weight. His rumbly voice matches the cold-storage drone. It feels comfortable. Prez always feels comfortable. She has the urge to tell him that he's her #1 Dad now. That he rescued her from drinking herself to oblivion once and now might have done it again.

"This may look like a thermos," she teases. "But it's a key."

"Yeah? Must be a big damn lock."

"It is." Sienna gestures at the lab. "Everything you see here? It's all inside this thermos."

Prez scratches his beard. It releases the odor of industrial soap. Given the sewer story he just told Sienna, it makes sense.

"A riddle," he says.

"Kind of."

"Let me take a stab. You wouldn't be doing any of this without what your dad taught you. He probably did his own work gulping from that thermos. It's like sipping on miracle water, symbolically. Something like that?"

No, Prez doesn't quite get it. That's okay. Sienna thinks he might put the pieces together eventually, if he needs to. For now, she nods. "Pretty close."

On the counter next to Prez is a plastic grocery bag. Sienna can see a bundle of newsprint inside it. Definitely not the kind of biohazard bag she's used to. Prez has wrapped his quarry like old-timey market workers wrapped their fish.

Outside the lab, the elevator dings.

Sienna exhales, sets down the *#1 DAD* thermos, and stands.

"Here we go," she says.

Prez takes the wrapped rat in his hands and stands too.

Noah Goff enters the lab like it's Halloween instead of three days before Christmas. He wears a curly black wig squashed by a Mets stocking cap and stabbed with cheap sunglasses. Most ridiculously—and effectively—his upscale-casual clothing has been swapped for an ensemble that draws the eye away from his face. A big puffy Hard Rock Cafe New York coat. A scarf with the *Hamilton* logo. A T-shirt plucked from a vintage bin that reads *NYC GIRLS' TRIP 2019.*

He looks at Sienna and Prez like he's not dressed like a clown.

"Where's the rat?"

Prez holds up the bag. Noah rips off his hat and wig, drops them, and snags the bag. His whole attitude pisses off Sienna. He's clearly riding some sort of upper. She follows him as he hurries to the dissection and tissue-processing bench.

"Nice of you to join us," she says. "It's almost noon. You know how hard it was clearing out the lab staff?"

"Try evading the U.S. fucking government," Noah mutters.

He starts to unwrap the newsprint, angrily, uncaringly. Sienna knows it's just a dead rat in there, but still she winces.

"While you're at it," Noah continues, "try acquiring a disguise from a whore who charges full blowjob prices just to do a little shopping."

"Watch it," Prez growls. "That lady saved your ass. And keeps saving it."

"You probably have her on speed dial now," Noah grumbles, but Sienna hears his wariness. Prez doesn't sound like he's got much patience left. It was only by employing Fae as messenger that the three of them were able to convene tonight.

Noah brushes the newspaper and plastic bag to the floor. It's a dead rat, all right. This lab has seen hundreds, and in death's repose have always seemed gentle and clean to Sienna's eyes. This rat is caked in brown mud, crusted in gray sewage, spackled with congealed blood. Noah picks up a scalpel and extends it to Sienna.

"The honor's all yours, Doc."

She swipes the scalpel and makes a point of shouldering Noah out of the way. He laughs once in disdain. He turns his condemnation on Prez.

"I assume we've got the fucking security cameras off this time?"

"Why you asking me?" Prez grunts. "I don't work here."

"They're off," Sienna says. "This lab is now officially unhinged in every capacity. Congratulations."

Noah leans on a deep freezer. "Bitch."

"I'd expect more creativity from your amphetamines. Dickface."

"Cuntbag."

"Fuckstick."

"We're all skanks and shitheads," Prez sighs. "Fair enough? Now let's get this done. I'm old and tired and had a very long day."

Sienna snaps on latex gloves, places Sammy into a dissection tray, and pins his rigor mortis–stiffened feet to the spongy black mat. The smelly sewage gunk makes him twice the size he should be. She crumbles some of it away and massages the rat's underside for the Pet Fetch! chip.

"Where'd you put it?" she asks.

"In his belly, just under the skin," Prez says.

"Yeah, but where? I don't feel it."

Noah bucks himself from the freezer. "It's not there? Sienna?"

Prez takes out his phone. "Easy. It's there. Look." He punches a pass-code, swipes, taps. "The signal's right here in the lab."

"Like I'm going to trust some prototype cat-bell," Noah says.

It goes against her protocol to cut into a specimen before it's cleaned, but Noah's so addled that he's starting to make Sienna nervous. And there's really no telling if he's been followed, despite his disguise as the world's trashiest tourist. So she aims her scalpel at the rat's stomach. She makes a slit. No blood; it has coagulated after the rat's death. Sienna inserts a finger, slides it between the skin and intestines. Where the hell is the chip? She pokes further into the gut, toward the liver and spleen. She feels the stomach and gives it a squeeze.

There. Something small and hard.

"The fuck?" she whispers.

"What?" Noah demands.

But she's in work mode now, and after over three days of drunken devastation, it's the best feeling, no matter what this discovery portends. She withdraws her finger, picks up a pair of iris scissors, and snips the rat's abdomen and thorax, exposing the innards. The liver's copper lobes are like the caps of mushrooms. The dull tan loops of small intestines hide the kidneys in the retroperitoneal space. Sienna feels an uncanny recognition that she hasn't experienced since her grad school days. Fur and skin are superficialities. This rat's anatomy is just a smaller version of her own. If she was religious, she might murmur that old chestnut: *There but for the grace of God go I.*

Both Noah and Prez hover now, but Sienna doesn't mind. She jabs the tip of the scissors into the stomach and cuts it open. With a splinter tweezer she exposes the interior of the rat's stomach. Half-digested remnants of its last meal. She mushes the food with a fingertip. There's a wink of something bright. Sienna picks up a set of microtweezers and carefully plucks out an oblong object the size of a cherry pit.

"That's it," Prez says.

"But what's it doing *inside* the stomach?" Noah demands.

Sienna picks up the rat and heads over to the sink. She turns the water full-blast and dips the rat into the stream. Rapidly, the sewage crud darkens, then begins to clump off like mud. A sulfur stench rises. Sienna slops away the goo, pulls away the crust.

"That's not one of ours," Noah stammers. He turns on Prez. *"That's not Sammy!"*

Prez is confused. "But it looks—I mean, it's brown and small . . ."

"It's small because it's an adolescent," Sienna says.

"It's got the hole in the ear," Prez insists.

"Sammy *bit* that hole in its ear."

"But the tracker . . ."

"Sammy tore his tracker out," Sienna says. "And made this rat swallow it."

The improbable words seem to come not from her mouth but from her throat, her thorax, her abdomen—her innards flayed open just like those of this innocent rat. She feels exposed. Her dream of Biologic Uplift has been realized: an animal capable of uplifting itself. But she'd wanted to facilitate creatures *better* than humans. What Sammy did to this poor rat suggests she's created an animal in the image of humanity's darkest side: duplicitous, brutal, willing to sacrifice a weaker brethren. In short, she has made a monster.

Two monsters, really, the first of which is called Sienna Aguirre.

"This is . . . this is some kind of . . . *decoy*?" Noah sputters.

"Sammy's having more red-light exposures," Sienna says. "He's getting smarter."

"Well, then his brain will swell up!" Noah cries. "He'll have seizures! He'll die!"

"But will that happen before he's sexually mature?" Sienna asks.

"When's that?" Noah demands.

"Saturday," Prez says, and then adds, rather pitifully, "-ish."

Noah kicks a fire extinguisher across the room. It bounces across the lab, clanging and cracking. Sienna flinches when it strikes her desk. The *#1 DAD* thermos wobbles like a bowling pin but doesn't go down.

"We're fucked!" Noah screams.

Sienna lowers herself to a stool.

Noah seizes the wall-mounted security camera, rips it from the wall, wires dangling, and hurls it to the ground, where it blasts into pieces. His arms whip wildly like they might rip from his torso and snake off by themselves.

"The whole city is fucked!"

Noah snatches the wobbling *#1 DAD* thermos and rears back, ready to smash it to the floor.

"Break that and I'll kill you," Sienna says.

A soft, effortless oath. Maybe a ruthless new nature.

Noah's head jerks toward her. His eyes protrude. Spittle swings from his lip. Suddenly, he laughs. And laughs some more. In this place of order and logic, it's an appallingly chaotic noise. He sets down the thermos and buries his face in his hands like he's trying to stuff the laughter back in.

"You two realize, don't you," he giggles, "what's going to happen?"

They do: Sienna and Prez say nothing.

Noah is in the center of the lab, spine contorting with sick laughter until it drains away, along with all of his color. Finally, he's just standing there, head bowed into cupped hands, faceless.

For a time, no one moves or speaks.

"It's Friday," Prez says quietly. "Maybe I got a couple more days to find him. Three if we're lucky."

Sienna shakes her head, permission for Prez to stand down. Without a GPS chip, there will be no finding Sammy.

"Noah. You know who you have to call."

Noah lifts his face. Tears roll down his cheeks. He tries to smile. Sienna tries to hold on to hate. But her heart breaks.

"She might have me killed," Noah says.

Sienna gazes at her old friend, her old enemy.

"Eight million people," she says softly.

Slowly, tiredly, Noah nods. He looks almost thankful, like a child dependent upon instruction. Sienna watches through the glass walls as he plods in to his office. Sienna and Prez share a glance of doomed hospice affection. Noah returns with a crumpled card. He takes out a burner phone and dials. The pause before speech is only seconds.

"Colonel Monroe, this is Noah Goff."

Sienna hears a woman's clipped tone from the cheap speaker. She stands up, stretches, and drops the dead rat into a plastic bag emblazoned with a bright orange biohazard tag. She places it into the standing tissue freezer, puts the dissection pan into the sink, and wipes down the counter with disinfectant. All the while, she listens to Noah arranging a meeting right here at EditedPets. Tomorrow, Saturday, six a.m., Noah Goff, Sienna Aguirre, Leonard Przybyszewski, and Colonel Marcy Monroe. Noah's whispered goodbye says it all. His life has been full of meetings. He believes this will be his last.

Noah pockets the burner. His eyes land on his discarded disguise. With a reservoir of gallows humor, Noah picks them up, arranges the curly mop, screws on the Mets toque, and gives Sienna a wink. She can't help it. She winks back.

Took a while, but you finally did the right thing, she thinks, as Noah Goff walks away.

27

Dallas worries about the staples in my stomach. He tells me that after he had the cochlear implant surgery, his mother had to keep his head clean. He wishes to take me to a "vet," which is a doctor for pets.

Sienna Aguirre was a doctor for pets.

I do not want needles in my eyes or a tube screwed into my head.

I tell Dallas that I have licked my wound clean.

I do not tell Dallas of the GPS chip I chewed free and fed to the wall rat. I do not tell Dallas how I left Barker Houses and told the wall rat to climb into the brown truck. Dallas believes my lie that I chewed my stomach to get rid of a tick. I have seen ticks in videos. They attach to your body and suck your blood until they get their fill. Ticks are parasites that live solely at the expense of others.

Perhaps Noah has tick genes in his brain like I have human genes in mine.

My head hurts all the time now. Dallas can tell. He smells of anxiety. I want to fix it. I think back to what he asked me right before I bit him. He asked me if he could take me to the Museum of Natural History to see its blue whale.

I tell Dallas I would like to see this whale.

He smiles and for a moment my head hurts less.

Dallas skips school to show me the whale. Skipping school is what Dallas calls bad behavior. He risks punishment to make me happy. I hope I can make him happy too.

On the way, we see six cloud machines.

✖

The American Museum of Natural History is huge. I hide inside Dallas's coat pocket. The entrance is chilly and smells of human and dust. Every step Dallas takes echoes. He tells me we are entering Theodore Roosevelt Memorial Hall. I have watched a video on presidents. Theodore Roosevelt was chubby and wore glasses.

When I peek, I see a statue of Theodore Roosevelt. How important do you need to be to get a statue? I wonder if Noah will get a statue one day. He might. I wonder if Dallas Underhill will get a statue one day. Probably not. This makes me sad. People in the future should know Dallas Underhill was kind and brave.

I wonder if there is any future where I, Sammy, might deserve a statue.

Then I see the monsters.

Dallas! I cry.

Dallas says, "It's okay. They're not alive."

If they are not alive, I cry, *why are they fighting?*

Dallas assures me that I am safe. I look again. Two huge dinosaur skeletons rear back for battle. One is the height of Mount Sinai Hospital. Its small head rests far atop hundreds of vertebrae. Its front legs ward off the attack of a skeleton that is smaller but has a big, sharp-toothed head.

Dallas says, "Allosaurus versus Barosaurus."

Why? I gasp.

Dallas says, "Why? Because it's cool. Look how big they are."

But why arrange their bones like this? Why not leave them buried?

Dallas says, "They're not actually bones. They're, like, casts."

That explains why I cannot smell them. Now I understand. The dinosaurs are like Teddy Roosevelt. They are statues to remind people of their importance. If humans make statues of dinosaurs, maybe they make statues of other animals too. Maybe even rats.

I want to ask why Teddy Roosevelt's statue is not his bones, but I have to hide again. Dallas is buying a ticket.

Dallas says, "All right! The whale's this way."

Is the whale a statue too? I ask.

Dallas says, "Only the coolest statue of all time. It's way bigger than the Allosaurus. About a hundred feet long. It's made of foam and plastic and fiberglass so it doesn't fall from the ceiling and squash us."

I do not hear what he says next.

Death odor overpowers me.

I smell rot and feathers and scales and bone. I smell chemicals and wood and glue. I am afraid to look, but I look.

We are in a large room called the Hall of Biodiversity. It is crowded with hundreds of animals. I know them from animal videos. I see a pangolin, gorilla, earthworm, viper, kingfisher, centipede, Siberian tiger, kangaroo, tortoise, snake, crab, shark, panda, squid, anteater, and ants. They are posed inside glass cases. They are mounted on walls. They are dangled from the ceiling. They are not statues.

They are corpses.

I am unable to move.

Dallas says, "It says this wall covers three point five billion years of evolution."

My head hurts so badly. I want to open it and rip out my brain and staple it shut, the same way I did my stomach. I realize I am gnawing Dallas's pocket.

I try to understand. I know what evolution is. But something here has gone wrong.

If humans are the most evolved species, how could they have done this to other species?

Is this normal, Dallas? I ask.

Dallas laughs. How can he laugh in a place like this?

Dallas says, "I guess it's normal for a museum."

I do not understand, Dallas.

Dallas says, "People like to look at animals. For science. Some of them are hard to find!"

But there are videos, Dallas.

Dallas says, "Yeah, but it's different when you see them up close."

Is it not wrong, Dallas? Is it not wrong to do this to the dead?

Dallas says, "I don't know. Some people even do it in their home. Deer heads and stuff like that. They put it up on the wall so other people can see it. Or so they can remember it. You know, like a trophy or souvenir."

My stomach clenches. I can feel the staples.

Just the heads? How is that helpful for science?

Dallas says, "That stuff's more like . . . being proud, I guess."

Proud of killing a deer? Is it rare to kill a deer?

Dallas says, "Well, no."

Then why would a human hang up a deer's head?

Dallas says, "I don't know, man. Sometimes they eat the meat."

I understand feeding your young, Dallas. But I have seen Santiago's bags of nuts. I have seen your box of Marshmallow Fruity Pebbles. You do not have to kill anything to eat.

Dallas says, "That's true. But sometimes you want a burger, you know?"

I do not think these animals were killed for burgers.

Dallas says, "Yeah. Probably not."

They were killed as trophies, Dallas.

Dallas knows that I am upset. He steps behind a wall to hide the animal corpses. But I can still see the animals on the ceiling. I see a flamingo and a stingray and an owl.

Dallas says, "Sammy, look! Those guys look just like you!"

Dallas points to a colorful drawing. He is trying to distract me to make me feel better. I am grateful for this but do not think it will work.

But Dallas is right. The drawing does distract me. It is a prehistoric scene. Spotted animals similar to rats burrow into lakeside soil.

Dallas says, "*Fossionmanus sinenis* and *Jueconodon cheni*, Jehol Biota, China, Early Cretaceous mammaliaform scratch-diggers. That's the hardest sentence I ever said! It says here they're your ancestors, Sammy."

I think of the framed family photos in Dallas's house. Maybe it is useful to look at pictures of your relatives. Maybe it brings you strength.

Dallas says, "It says the dinosaurs died in the fifth mass extinction. It says the sixth mass extinction is happening right now because of climate change and stuff. That sucks!"

I have not had this thought before. Rodents like me once lived among the same giants I saw in the Theodore Roosevelt Memorial Hall. The dinosaurs died millions of years ago.

But rats lived on.

Rats are strong.

Maybe the strongest animal of all.

Where is the stuffed human? I ask.

Dallas says, "Oh, man! That's gross!"

His laugh proves that humans do not understand that they are animals too. This is why there will be a sixth mass extinction. This is why all humans will die, just like the dinosaurs died. Once again, rats will outlive them all.

But the thought that Dallas will also die makes me unhappy.

Dallas says, "Come on. I'll show you the whale."

He does. It is colossal. Humans must like to feel small sometimes. I wonder if being relatively small makes them proud that they can kill something so big. Dallas takes me into the Akeley Hall of African Mammals. Everything there upsets me. In the Bernard Family Hall of North American Mammals, I have to look away. In the Small Mammal area, I close my eyes after seeing a diorama with a mother rat and ten pups, all stuffed. The only thing I see clearly after that is a map of the human body.

All major arteries and veins are labeled.

It is not difficult to memorize them.

※

Dallas takes me to the Museum Food Court.

Dallas says, "They have the best cookies in the world."

Human food smells erase the death odor. I am hungry. I have never been so hungry.

I wonder if my anger at humans has turned into hunger.

Dallas puts a cookie on a plate. It is half black and half white. The sugary scent jabs my brain. I squirm in his pocket.

Give me some, Dallas, I say.

Dallas says, "We have to pay first."

Just break off a bite.

Dallas says, "You want to get us into trouble?"

I do not know. I only know I need to eat. I am a rat. I should be able to have food when I want it. When my stomach shakes, I feel blood rush into my head. I think of the human body map. Do I also have a carotid artery and a jugular vein?

Dallas gets into a line. A man in front of him gives a plastic card to a woman. She slides food items across a black plate. Each time, there is a beep. I perch at the edge of Dallas's pocket and stare harder. The woman's shirt and hat have the museum logo.

This woman is so proud of this place of death that she advertises it on her body.

Dallas sets his plate with the cookie on the counter.

I am mad.

I leap from Dallas's pocket and land on the cookie. I break a chunk from it. I stick it into my mouth.

The woman screams. It frightens me. It also makes me proud. This place is called the Museum of Natural History but it is the opposite. It is unnatural. The people here should feel the same fear as the animals they tortured, killed, and stuffed.

Humans run everywhere. I drag the cookie across the counter. I cross the black plate. It beeps. A red light shines upward. I am blinded and drop the cookie. The light enters my skull and burns. It hurts like my brain is being sliced open. I remember Sienna scraping fur off a rat's scalp before cutting it apart.

In one second, I see everything clearly.

The night Noah took me home in a bag, he talked about red lights. How red lights made rats' brains grow but also made the rats kill Linda, Tasha, and Mason. Back then, I was not as smart. Now I understand.

My brain is no different than the rats who died in the Enrichment Room. My brain also responds to red light by growing. I have watched a video about the modern uses of red light. It is everywhere in the human world.

In the Pet Expo security-pass scanners.

In Dallas's Christmas-tree lights.

In Roman Moffett's laser pointer.

In the LEDs of Times Square.

Inside this register scanner right here.

Each time I have been exposed to intense red light, I have grown smarter.

Each time, my headaches have gotten worse.

I want to cling to Dallas. I want to nuzzle his neck.

I do not want to die!

But there is no stopping it. The seizure I had in Times Square was only the start. Soon I will foam from my mouth and bite my tongue and bleed from my ears.

Soon I will die. Just like the others.

Dallas will cry. He will cry so hard, his tears might damage his cochlear implant devices. He is the only being alive who will miss me.

Not Sienna. Not Noah. I realize that I hate them. I hate them for making me like this. They will be relieved when my genes die with me.

So I will make sure they do not.

Soon it will be time to breed. If I can breed before I die, I will be like the Early Cretaceous mammaliaform scratch-diggers Dallas showed me. This will be my forever. I will go on and on, long after humans and their museums and their entire world have turned to dust.

✄

Dallas takes me into the subway station. There are bronze casts of dinosaurs and fossils in the walls. Even down here, I cannot escape the dead. I can tell Dallas is unhappy. He got thrown out of the museum. He lost his cookie. But my head hurts too bad to say anything nice.

I curl up in Dallas's pocket and fall asleep.

Then we are outside the train again. Dallas says he has a surprise for me. I do not want a surprise, but I do not say it. Dallas walks into a giant space. The ceiling is blue and has fake stars and is far away like a church.

Are we supposed to pray, Dallas? I ask.

Dallas says, "This isn't a church. It's Grand Central Terminal. It was built way back in 1913. Pretty neat, right?"

Neat, I say.

Dallas walks down a ramp to a lower level. Here the ceiling is low and covered with rough brown tile. Dallas said this isn't a church, but he acts like humans I have seen who pray, like he feels something strong and sad and powerful.

Dallas says, "This is the Whispering Spot. My mom used to take me here when I was little. The way it works is you stand by the wall here and your Mom, or your friend if you've got a friend, they stand way on the other side there. But they can hear your secret wishes like they were right beside you. Want to try it?"

Dallas is smiling. He looks hopeful that things can be like they used to be between us.

I do not think that is possible. But I still want to make him happy.

I want to try it, Dallas, I say.

He sets me on the floor in his knapsack and jogs to the other side. It is noisy. Then he stops. I listen. I hear Dallas's voice just like I am still in his pocket. The videos I saw about religion often talked about angels. Angels are beautiful humans with wings and robes and golden harps. I wonder if this is what angels sound like.

Dallas whispers, "I wish I could find a way to make you happy."

❌

Dallas walks west across 103rd Street. I am in his pocket. It has begun to snow. The way the flakes spin reminds me of how my own mind spins. The Museum Food Court scanner is already changing my brain. I feel all emotions at once. I feel despair and sadness and love and hate and sympathy and fury. I feel like I might act on any of these emotions. It all depends on what happens next.

What happens next is I smell a familiar smell. It is an odor of spicy chips and cold cola and traces of urine. It is the odor of Roman Moffett, the boy with the laser pointer, the boy Dallas hit with a bag of trash. Scents blow with the windy snow. Roman is close.

Run, I say.

Dallas says, "Huh?"

Roman Moffett is coming.

Dallas runs. I hear footsteps speeding up behind us. I hold tight to Dallas's pocket. There is nothing about this I like. I have learned about statistics. The odds of Dallas finding another trash bag to swing are low.

We have to slow down to dodge scaffolding. The tall building beside us is gutted from a renovation. I hear jackhammers on higher floors. The air is gritty with white dust. I smell Roman Moffett even closer now.

Dallas turns at the corner of the building. There is a cloud machine but no time to appreciate it. Dallas goes down an alley walled off for construction. The gate is chained but loosely. Dallas runs through stony dust and slips under the chain.

Close the gate, I tell him.

Dallas says, "No time!"

He is scared. I understand. I am scared too. I know I will die soon. But Dallas is a human pup. I cannot let him die too.

A long plastic tube stretches from the top of the building all the way down to a big metal dumpster. I understand this is how workers up high drop debris. I do not see any workers now. A tarp extends from the bottom of the tube to cover the dumpster. Dallas must have the same thought I have. He climbs the side of the dumpster. He lifts the tarp. He wiggles inside.

It is dark inside. Some light comes through the tarp. I peek out of Dallas's pocket. The dumpster has several large chunks of cinder blocks. They must have broken when they fell down the plastic tube.

It hurts to breathe, Dallas.

Dallas says, "Shh."

We listen. I hear the scrunch of feet. It gets closer. I try to smell through the odor of the dumpster. Before I can, I hear a voice.

"Yo, retard. Your footsteps are all up the side of the dumpster."

Dallas gasps and runs for the other side. He steps up on a metal ridge, but the tarp is buckled tight on this end. I hear and feel feet drop into the dumpster. Roman Moffett's odor fills the space. Dallas tries again to get out. I know it will not work. We are cornered.

Roman pulls Dallas down. I roll around inside of Dallas's pocket. The pocket tightens. It is because Roman is holding Dallas tight.

Roman says, "You ruined my coat!"

Dallas says, "I'm sorry!"

Roman says, "My dad gave me a bloody nose because of you!"

Dallas says, "I wasn't trying to—"

Roman says, "And when I tried to tell him about your rat, he just beat me up some more! He said I was a rotten liar. He didn't believe me!"

Dallas says, "You and Nicky were going to—"

Roman says, "Then my mom yelled at my dad and he left! And he hasn't been back since! It's all your retard fault!"

I feel the swipe of Roman's arms. I hear the rattle of metallic things.

Dallas says, "No! I can't hear without those!"

Roman says, "Good! Then you won't hear me call you the stupidest-ass deaf-ass mush-mouth special-ed motherfucker I ever saw. You won't hear me say I'm going to kill you!"

I do not need to hear anything else.

I run from the pocket and up Roman's arm. He sees me when I am inches away. He has two black eyes and a broken lip that has just started to heal. I do not care. I leap onto his neck. I can feel his pulse and smell his blood. He stares with big eyes but he does not even grab me.

Roman says, "Ahh! Get your rat! Get your—"

I bite into the front of Roman's neck, just beneath his chin. Thick, salty blood splashes my face.

Roman says, "Oh fuck! Oh fuck! Help! Help!"

Roman pushes away from Dallas but runs into a cinder block. I look back and see Dallas on his knees. He is searching for his cochlear implant gear.

Roman says, "It hurts! It hurts!"

I fit my muzzle into the hole in Roman's neck and chew.

Roman says, "NO! STOP! ST—"

Blood sprays. I have bitten into a hard, chewy tube. I know from the museum's human-body map that this is Roman's larynx. Next I taste Roman's vocal cords. They are rubbery and gummy, like the chew toys Linda used to give us. Roman has said many mean things to Dallas with these vocal cords. He will not say anything mean ever again.

Roman's words turn into gurgles. Bloody air bubbles spray from the hole. He claws at his neck. I jump off. He flops around. He coughs and chokes.

Dallas has found his metal coils. He puts them on his head. He turns around.

Dallas asks, "Sammy, what did you do?"

I took Roman Moffett's voice, I say.

Dallas looks horrified.

Dallas asks, "What did you do?"

The question puzzles me. Why isn't Dallas grateful?

We should go, Dallas, I say.

I run up Dallas's leg and into his coat pocket. He stares for a moment longer. Then he jumps over Roman and climbs from the dumpster where he entered it. The daylight is blinding. The snow is surprising. Dallas lands on the ground and runs for the gate.

The crash is the loudest noise I have ever heard.

Dallas turns back. I peek from his coat pocket.

A giant gray cloud of concrete dust flows from beneath the dumpster's tarp.

The plastic tube shakes as more cinder blocks roll down it.

I see workers high above pitching half a dozen broken concrete chunks into the funnel.

I only intended to mute Roman Moffett.

But this is satisfactory as well.

⌖

Dallas's dusty cheeks are stained with tears. Vomit crusts the corners of his lips. He did a lot of crying and vomiting before falling asleep. I tried to explain to Dallas that Roman's death is good. Some humans might have cut off Roman's head and hung it on their wall. You know, like a trophy or souvenir.

He did not seem to agree.

I have done a lot of thinking since Dallas fell asleep. I have a plan. Dallas would not approve of it. But I am a rat, not a boy. Before I die, I must do what is right for rats.

The wall rats live in the wall. But Dallas's apartment has many walls. Barker Houses has many apartments. East Harlem has many apartment buildings. It is possible the number of rats nearby is larger than the number of humans.

Dallas spoke of six mass extinctions. What if we rats could begin a seventh? Given the short time I have left in my life, I have no reason not to try.

I spend a few hours doing some final internet searches. There are certain facts I need to know. About natural gas and steam. About electrical power and substations. About subway-train routes too, though Dallas has taught me well in that subject. There are also certain addresses I need to know. It is amazing to me how easily I memorize all of it.

I climb the bed covers. Dallas is having a nightmare. Each exhale brushes my fur. It feels like how he used to pet me.

Before I saved him, this boy saved me.

I kiss him gently on his bottom lip.

Goodbye, I say.

My last act brings me little pleasure. I climb Dallas's table and perch atop his fish tank. The FireFish pulses gold. I carry flakes of fish food in my mouth. I drop them into the water. When the FireFish rises to feed, I strike like a viper. My incisors stab through the fish. I lift it out of the water as it struggles. It feels good to exercise my new-found power.

Sleep, my friend, I tell it, *and dream of endless oceans.*

It dies. The beautiful glow that was never its own fades out.

I eat the FireFish, the whole thing. I am the Ratzenkünig and, after all, still hungry.

SWARM THEORY

28

It's Friday night. Noah orders a pizza from three different places, the shittiest-looking joints he can find close by in the Lower East Side: Pizza Fun, Billy's Pizza Palace, and the dismal-sounding Pizza Hole. Only cheese, so the delivery is as quick as possible. He includes in his orders the codes required to make it all the way to his loft. He's never given these out before. But tonight it doesn't matter. These are his last hours on Prince Street, above Ralph Lauren, in the mocking gleam of the Apple Store.

Surprise, surprise, it's Pizza Hole that arrives first. Noah hurls open the door on the second knock. A drastically skinny dude with a mangy beard doesn't even look at him as he consults a receipt.

"Large cheese. Fifteen."

Noah hands him forty. After registering the overpayment, the guy finally looks at his customer. Noah knows he doesn't look super-trustworthy right now. Pale, sweaty, eyelids twitching around red eyes. He hopes his apartment's acreage of emptiness and stainless steel speaks volumes.

"What's your name?" Noah asks.

"Jared?" The guy doesn't sound sure.

Noah fans some cash. "Five hundred dollars, Jared. It's yours if you do me a favor. Call in sick, tell them your car broke down, whatever. In one hour—sixty minutes—come back to this door, pick me up, and drive me to Westchester County Airport. Then it's five hundred more."

Jared squints from cash to Noah.

"Why don't you just get an Uber?"

Noah buries the urge to stuff the five hundred down this moron's throat. The country is full of meat-bags like this, America's mediocre midriff, who watch their Hulu and shovel down their Chipotle and dare to think they've had an original thought in their life. He can't wait to leave them all behind. The reason he hasn't already been apprehended is the meeting with Monroe on the books for tomorrow morning. But a high school hobbyist could hack Uber's and Lyft's interface; there's no way DoD goons aren't surveilling his every keystroke and of course his apps. He's got to make a quieter getaway. Whatever jalopy old Jared drives will be perfect. Maybe Noah will even don his wig and cap for the ride, just for old time's sake.

"Jared, I want you to listen close. When someone offers a pizza guy a thousand dollars to drive him to the airport, the pizza guy doesn't ask questions. All right?"

Noah can hear the idiot's brain squirm as it works out the angles.

"All right," Jared says.

Noah hands over the money. "One hour. Midnight. Go fill up your tank. We won't be making any stops."

Jared's whole demeanor changes. He pushes the money into the pocket of his sauce-stained jeans and fires off a military nod. This is the most kick-ass thing to ever happen to this guy. Noah takes the pizza box and closes the door in Jared's face.

One hour. Not a lot of time to change the course of his life.

Noah checks his laptop. He's been video-chat auto-dialing his parents for three hours. It's the only communication that feels safe. He's using Signal Private Messenger, the secure app he uses for video conferences with his crypto-fanatic privacy-obsessed investors. Still no answer. That's no shocker. Rubes like Pat and Arthur go to bed at nine. He'll keep ringing. He's got an hour. He checks his watch—more like forty-five minutes.

He hurries to the open suitcase on his bed. Everything he owns distilled to one piece of luggage, plus the Filson bag that still carries the watermelon whiff of Sammy. An hour before Jared is back, another hour to Westchester—enough time to figure out a plan. At Westchester, in a private terminal, awaits the culmination of the past day of burner-phone activity: a private flight to Rome with his name missing from the roster.

He knows an Italian who works for the Venice Film Festival and, for the right price, can get anyone whisked through passport control. The world is his fucking oyster. Maybe he'll follow Edward Snowden, go to Russia. Except Russia scares him. Ditto Mongolia. China is the obvious non-extradition country to choose, but as the night wears on he's thinking more about Montenegro. Beautiful country. Not part of the EU. At least for now. And just a quick hop in a small fishing boat from Italy across the Adriatic Sea.

Noah reminds himself he can buy whatever he needs after he lands. He zips up the luggage, hoists the Filson, and deposits both on the sofa. His iPad is right there. God, he'd like to check his email just once before vanishing. He gets as far as opening the tablet with face recognition before quashing that dream. His email will be crawling with government eyeballs.

At eleven-thirty, Billy's Pizza Palace shows up. With Jared enlisted, he no longer needs another pizza express. He pays, shuts the door, tosses the new pizza box atop the old one.

He lays out his cash, removes five hundred for Jared, counts the rest. Even after the goddamn college fund he paid Fae, a ticket to Italy still won't make a real dent. He triple-checks his passport. It's the real reason he had to come back home. That and the extra thirty-five-thousand in cash, both inside his safe, openable only via his fingerprint.

Thirty minutes left. He hops on the toilet for the fifth time tonight. He's a mess. He's got Xanax and Ambien in his Filson but doesn't dare dull his senses before he gets on an overseas flight. There's nothing much to flush when he flushes—and that's a good thing. The water won't go down the drain. Noah's laugh is a raw bark. His final act in New York was to clog a toilet with his shit. If the full story of Sammy ever gets out, they'll say he did the same thing to EditedPets.

"Noah? You there?"

It's not Jared and it's not the MIA Pizza Fun.

It's Mom.

He zips his pants as he runs across the vast loft, feeling like he did as a boy rushing through backyard weeds when Mom hollered him inside for dinner. Her face awaits in the video chat. Her only light is her monitor, giving her sleep-puffed face a pale glow.

"Mom," Noah says—and the single syllable jogs a toddler heart snuggled inside the gnarled sinew of his adult body. He wants to fold into himself until he's even smaller, a purple newborn holdable in one of his mother's hands, which she could press against her left breast.

"It's so late. Are you in another country?"

"No. I'm in New York."

"Because it's almost eleven here, Noah. You know me and your dad don't stay up too late."

"I know, and I'm sorry. I just wanted to call and—"

"It's only that I had to pee and I heard the computer dinging. Have I told you about my bladder?"

Noah leans close, hoping she'll see the stress on his face like Jared did.

"Mom, I need to tell you something."

"Dr. McClane said it was just old age at first, something about kidneys taking in more water, I don't know."

"Please, Mom. This is important."

"He also said it came with lower estrogen. You know, dear, that menopause was hard on me."

"I know. You've told me. Mom, I'm calling to say goodbye."

"But now he thinks it may be related to my diabetes. It's no fun growing old, Noah."

"Mom. This may be my last call for a long time."

"All right." Pat Goff yawns. "Well, don't make it too long. We like to stay in touch with our children."

Noah feels tears drizzling down his throat, his chest bloating with hot grief. How has he gone so wrong that even his mother, obligated by blood to care for him, can't register his desperation? She was asleep, he reminds himself. He just needs to be more upfront.

"I just wanted to say, Mom . . . that I miss you. That if I could come home right now, I—"

Mom turns, giving Noah a view of her gray bedhead.

"It's Noah, Art!"

Dad from a distance: "Hanh?"

"Noah! He called on the computer!"

"Hanh?"

"I think he's in another country!"

Noah takes a step away from the screen. There's no point to this. There never was. His mother, his father, his sisters, Sienna, his grad-school supervisor, Colonel Monroe, everyone at EditedPets and DARPA, they all wanted things from him that, in the end, he was unable or unwilling to give. In twenty minutes he will begin the process of leaving his country of birth. The sad fact is, he's not leaving a single person behind.

Thup.

A light sound from the bathroom.

Dad's face joins Mom's in the chat window, thick glasses askew. The monitor light shines off his scraggly pate.

"Noah, look, it's your dad."

Thup, thup.

Noah mutes his mic and wanders off camera. He's done this before, juggling work while making calls. His parents think nothing of it.

"Dad's had his own bladder problems," Mom says.

Thup, thup, thup.

Noah knows he should be strapping on his coat, hat, and scarf. If Jared's car has heat, he'll be lucky. Instead, he walks toward the bathroom. Babble about Tamar and Dinah dim in favor of light, wet pattering noises. The bathroom is six feet away. Did he miss something? Three feet away. He imagines one of Monroe's Con Ed cleaners in his shower in full hazmat gear, holding a special black body bag and a jug of corrosive acid just for him.

Noah pushes the door open.

For one second, he believes he had indeed clogged the toilet, and feces have backed up with violence, expelling to cover the floor, sink, and bath. In the very next second, he wishes that were all it was.

The bathroom is full of rats.

There must be fifty on the floor, a bobbing, writhing carpet. A dozen more line the rim of the bath, staring at him like tiny soldiers. The sink is the tallest spot in the room, and the rats there behave like lookouts, hissing the second they see Noah. Another half dozen crouch atop the back of the toilet. But the worst is the bowl itself. A steady spate of rats tumble up and out, over the rim, slick with toilet water, and drop to the floor, each with a moist smack.

Thup, thup, thup, thup.

"Oh," Noah says, more sigh than word.

He grabs the door to slam it, but a razor of pain scorches through his left heel. He cries out and staggers, fingers slipping from the knob, and in his side vision sees a brown current surge from the bathroom, shoving the door wider. Noah tries to run; but when his left foot lands, his whole leg crumples, and he collapses to a floor that shivers with hundreds of scampering feet.

Noah twists his body over and lifts his left leg. A fat rat with an eighteen-inch tail has its incisors dug into his Achilles tendon. And he's starting to chew. Noah shakes his leg, spattering dark blood, but the rat hangs on and Noah hears the damp tear of the tendon before he sees it, a glossy flap of white-gray putty.

Beyond his lifted leg is a rolling mound of rats the size of a bear.

Noah flops over and starts powering across the floor on his elbows. He feels the weight of a rat on the back of his left leg, then two upon his right, then a pair of jaws snaps onto his right big toe. He gasps but keeps going, through the kitchen, throwing glances at knives and frying pans, all of them out of reach. His only hope is the front door, to cut himself off from the flood—Noah screams.

The rats break over him like the waves off the private island in Bora Bora or the South Malé Atoll in Maldives, all those fancy vacations he took to impress colleagues, not one of whom became a friend. The weight on his back is humanlike now, but a human whose every bodily segment has gone individually sentient. He hears his shirt tear from claws and teeth. He feels small, cold, wet feet on his skin. He sees a whiskered face right near his left eye before he feels long, sharp teeth pierce the folds of his ears, and in the starbursts of pain sees Sienna's steel conch earrings.

I'm being tagged, he thinks.

He reaches the sofa, not far from the door now, when his vision whites out with a pain beyond pain, more like an altered state, cousin to ecstasy. He bolts straight and feels a wiggling rat gnawing the back of his neck. He is being tunneled. He feels a gush of hot blood and hears a chalk-on-blackboard scrape. Noah tries to reach behind him, but his arms are twenty pounds heavier, loaded with rats. Another white blast—a cold sensation—deep in his spine—

×

Noah is sitting against the sofa.

He doesn't know what has happened.

His eyelids flutter open.

He is coated with rats from the waist down. They stand on hind legs, motionless, eyes fixed as if awaiting a signal. Noah hears a rustle and flicks his eyes to the side. A few rats have gone rogue, tearing apart the pies from Pizza Hole and Billy's Pizza Palace. The rest fill the floor around Noah, perched like their comrades.

Noah becomes aware that his mom is still babbling. It occurs to him that he could scream, tell her to call for help, but before he can even inhale, he remembers he muted his mic. Maybe he can crawl to the laptop, drag it down, show his parents what is happening. But when he tries to lift his back from the sofa, he finds that he cannot. In fact, he can't move anything.

Oh god, oh god.

Noah knows enough about anatomy to realize that the chalkboard screech and crunching he heard was a rat chewing through the bifid spinous process of his C3 cervical vertebra. Inside the wishbone-shaped space is his spinal cord, rubbery as a hot dog. A rat would have no problem gnawing through it. Now he smells urine and feces. His own. He knows a human loses control of his bowels when he is paralyzed, but he can't help but recall his chief high school torment, the peeing attacks of Davin Dunbar.

A sob rips from his throat.

"You fuckers paralyzed me!"

The rats wiggle at the noise.

"Yes, we did, Noah."

It is the voice of a young boy, a voice Noah recognizes instantly but can't place. He rolls his eyes to his iPad on the table. Sitting at the tablet is a rat, its fur spiked from sewage filth but still recognizable as being smaller and cuter than its ragged army.

It's Sammy.

Noah has a fleeting memory of his old PetMate app, the one that matched people with their ideal pets. Noah Goff and a rat: perhaps it was always fated to be. The SammySpeaks app is open beneath Sammy's paws.

"You paralyzed many of us in the lab," Sammy says through the AAC.

"Stop it!" Noah cries. "Stop it stop it stop it!"

"Would you have stopped if we asked you?"

Noah blinks away sweat and blood and tries to focus.

"Listen to me . . . please . . . everything I did . . . *we* did . . ."

"Do not tell me it was for scientific gain. You made pets, Noah."

Noah feels tears roll down his cheeks.

"I didn't mean for—Sienna, it's her fault, she couldn't stop your brain from—"

"Sienna Aguirre is to blame for plenty. But there is no Sienna Aguirre without Noah Goff."

Noah screams, not in pain, for there is little pain anymore. How did it come to this? Prostrate not before a skilled government-employed assassin but a worthless piece-of-shit lab rat.

"How did you find me, you little fuck?"

"Do you know about the city's pneumatic tubes, Noah?"

"What?"

"I only had to walk ten blocks to the Hell Gate postal station. Isn't Hell Gate a funny name for a neighborhood, Noah?"

"Now, you listen to me."

"There are pneumatic tubes at the Hell Gate postal station. We took them all the way here. Did you know that the Apple Store next door used to be a postal station, Noah? All we had to do was find a hole into your building. There are always holes."

"You listen to me, rat! You can't do this! You hear me? I am ordering you not to do this!"

"Why don't you call me Sammy? You are the one who named me."

"That's right! That's fucking right! I named you! I raised the money to make you! I made it possible for you to even exist! I'm your fucking creator, you got that?"

"Yes, Noah. That is why we are here. Of all the humans who must be stopped, you must be stopped first. You cannot be allowed to do this again."

Sammy's head angles toward the rats that blanket Noah. His whiskers twitch. Noah has the sense that Sammy is talking to the rats, but at a frequency beyond his hearing.

"What are you telling them? Sammy, please! You can't—"

Two fat, heavy rats start climbing up his chest.

And with that, Noah is no longer a wealthy thirty-six-year-old in a ten-and-a-half-million-dollar penthouse loft in Manhattan wearing Nike x MSCHF Air Max 97 Jesus Shoes. No more walking on water for him. Now he's a shoeless, scared nine-year-old kid in a dilapidated shack in Coop, Iowa, forcing himself to echo the laugh track of *Friends* while Grammy moans from the back room until she doesn't, because the rats she warned her family about are sucking down the salty sludge of her eyes.

Nothing changes.

"Oh, god! Please! Please!"

"I watched so many rats die in your lab."

The two rats claw his chin, pull themselves onto his lips, his cheeks.

"I'm sorry! I'm sorry!"

"I will not be as cruel as you, Noah."

An inch distant, every detail of the rats is emphasized, enlarged, exaggerated. The black pits of their eyes. The white spears of their whiskers. The pink, furred lips. The curled, anticipating tongue. The long, widening yellow incisors. The black hole of the throats, blotting out the world.

"I will not make you look upon your own death."

Each jaw closes around one of Noah's eyes. If he can't see his attacker, how can he be sure who it is? Sammy, Grammy—they sound so much alike. He feels the pop of teeth into the soft globes of his eyeballs. The rats lick up the clear and salty watery fluid of aqueous humor that flows out from each pierced eye. He hears the squeak of excited rats but also Grammy, laughing as he once laughed. He screams, hoping to be heard past the moist chewing, hoping there are still seconds left to make the worst things right.

"I'M SORRY, GRAMMY! I'M SO SORRY!"

Redness, whiteness, blackness, the optical nerves drawn taut, then the thick squirm and hot fullness of two rats entering his face through his eye sockets, the chisel squeal of incisors against skull. The noise vibrates Noah's skeleton and erases all sound. The sole exception is a far-away murmur.

"Noah, you still there? Art, you think he's there?"

"Hanh?"

But the last thing Noah Goff hears before his brain is drained of blood and he dies beside his passport and cash, is a distant knock, not Jared, not yet, but the other person he asked to come. Noah can't help but smile. The voice to usher him into oblivion comes from some minimum-wage loser he'll never even meet.

"Hello? Pizza Fun. I got a large cheese."

29

Sienna and Prez arrive together in the Astro van outside EditedPets's 6th Avenue building. It is Saturday, December 24, 5:57 a.m., 36 degrees Fahrenheit. Empty offices await them upstairs. Prez holds a cardboard cup of Dunkin' Donuts coffee. Sienna hasn't drunk alcohol since Prez plucked her from the Midnight Lounge, but caffeine would be counterproductive; she wants a buffer of dullness today. For ten seconds, they look up at the building while New York rises from sleep.

"You ever heard of Phineas Gage?" Sienna asks.

"Who hasn't? Backup QB for the Giants, 1980–1985."

Sienna smiles to show appreciation for the joke, any joke.

"I read up on him last night. He was this railroad worker in the 1800s who got this thing called a tamping iron, a forty-three-inch rod, blown right through his head. The rod went in through his cheek, passed through his brain, exited his skull."

"I would've gone with 'thanks for the lift, Prez.' But continue."

"This guy Gage survives, blind in one eye but otherwise fine. Physically, anyway. His doctor says he's different. Says he's, quote, 'no longer Gage.' He's more animalistic. He's rude, he's obscene. He's violent. He's a drunk. And not like me. He's not drinking to bury stuff. He's drinking because—well, he's just gone *bad*."

Prez softens. "Hey. Go easy. Today of all days."

Sienna gazes at the seventh floor, the scene of so many crimes. She waits for her tumbling gray breath to conceal her before proceeding.

"Phineas Gage is one of the first documented cases of personality changes from brain trauma. The thing I wonder: Did Gage remember his old self? Did he miss him? I think of Sammy out there, his brain getting crushed by his own skull, going a little madder every day. I'm the one who lined up hundreds of Phineas Gages and shot tamping irons through their skulls."

Prez doesn't try to make it better, and Sienna is grateful.

"How'd this guy die?" Prez asks.

"Seizures. Same as the Sammys."

"Well, maybe this military lady's got some answers for us. We can hope, right?"

Sienna feels for it—hope—but finds not even a tickle.

"Should we wait for Noah?" Prez asks.

"He's probably already up there." Sienna forces a smile. "Curly-haired Mets fanatics wake up early to beat the morning rush."

✖

But Noah's not up there. Colonel Marcy Monroe is. She's in the lab, arms straight at her sides, tracing Sienna and Prez's path down the hall through the lab's glass walls while two of her men guard the entrance. It's like finding a tarantula on your bedroom wall. How did the woman get in there? The lab is unbreachable. At least it was supposed to be. Sienna feels indignation. She's going to demand to know who gave this woman entry.

But Sienna demands nothing after seeing the colonel's eyes. It's not a normal stare. It feels more like some secret military tool, like how CIA agents can supposedly conduct lie detector tests with only two fingers on your radial pulse. Sienna tries to clear a path through her fog of foreboding.

"Hi. I'm Sienna Aguirre. It's nice to—"

Colonel Monroe cuts her off with her eyes. Her *eyes*. Sienna is pinned like a rat to a dissection tray. She has the fluttery fight-or-flight sensation that, if this woman wanted, she could kill Sienna with her bare hands in seconds. Not unlike what Sienna could do to her rats. What Sienna would give to hear the laughter of some Gamma Phi Delta goofballs right now.

Prez intervenes. "We're all stressed, but let's have some common courtesy between—"

Colonel Monroe cuts off Prez with her eyes just as easily. His forehead wrinkles as if he's just seen an animal he's never imagined before.

"There's no time left for *courtesy*," Monroe says. "Am I correct, Dr. Aguirre, that Rat CN8 remains missing?"

If the colonel would pace, take out a folder, arrest warrants, a pistol, *anything*, Sienna would feel better, in the presence of a fellow human. Instead, only this icicle voice.

"Yes."

"Am I correct, Mr. Przybyszewski, that the last true reading of the GPS chip was in the vicinity of Park Avenue and 102nd Street?"

"Uh-huh. Before it hopped the UPS truck."

Monroe calculates for one full second.

"That makes the closest underground access the 103rd Street station. So we'll begin with the 6 train tunnel."

"Wait." Sienna wills herself to sound stronger. "This is my rat we're talking about. This is my lab we're standing in. I think I deserve to know what we're talking about."

Monroe adjusts her stance. It's as shocking as a scream.

"Do you know anything about Swarm Theory, Dr. Aguirre?"

Sienna loathes not being the smartest person in the room. "Some. Insects aren't really my field of—"

"Take locusts. One locust—easy to kill, yes? A thousand locusts—even that you can spray away. But eighty million locusts? They're no longer individual insects. They're a superorganism against which we have no credible defense. It shouldn't surprise you to know that DARPA has spent fifty years studying this behavior. Imagine instead of sending a clumsy two-billion-dollar B-2 Stealth Bomber at a hardened target, we could send in a few thousand disposable drones for a fraction of that. Now, doctor, imagine a locust superorganism that decides to march against humans. It is our good fortune that locusts prefer our crops and affect us only through famine. But rats? Rats live inside our infrastructure. If rats were to become a superorganism, there would be no hope for us. None. Do you understand?"

"Yes," Sienna says. "That's why—"

"You asked what we're talking about, doctor. We've run the models. What we're talking about is a projected thirty-six-month proliferation of one hundred million humanized rats blanketing the continental United States, a breed that will immediately begin replacing the vastly inferior Norwegian brown rat. Every DoD model has this strain dominating the entire world in just a few years. We don't even need models to know this. It's happened before. I bet you know all about it, Mr. Przybyszewski."

"*Rattus rattus,*" Prez says quietly. "The black rat."

"Which dominated the Northeast until the larger and more aggressive *Rattus norvegicus* began killing and displacing it. That's without the ability to behave as swarms. Given the humanized rats' ability to cooperate and collaborate, we estimate all humans will be driven from urban centers in less than five years. State and National Guard forces will be utterly incapable of responding to this kind of threat. Without swift federal action, the global human death toll will reach hundreds of millions in ten years."

The refrigerator gulps, as if it, too, is sickened.

"I want a lawyer," Sienna croaks.

Colonel Monroe takes a step forward. Sienna's heart skips.

"You don't get a lawyer," Monroe says, "because you're not under arrest."

Prez notches his hip past Sienna, shielding her. "Then I suggest you change your tone, lady. You're here at the invitation of Mr. Goff. I was here when he made it yesterday."

"Yesterday," Monroe muses. "The situation has changed since yesterday. At three-thirty this morning, Noah Goff was found dead."

A thousand needles exit through Sienna's ribcage. It's the same sensation she felt upon hearing of the death of her father. She pictures the gangly, graceless Noah Goff she met at Rockefeller, taking on the whole school over his PetMate app; she sees the driven young man scribbling napkin notes during the Tasty Hand Pulled Noodle Accord; she sees the abruptly moneyed maverick, nearly handsome now, bringing Sienna bubble tea after FireFish reached twenty-five million in sales; she sees the comeback kid, spinning joyously on a stool and kissing her on the head as she explained *C. nivalis*. Maybe she'd resented being the Wozniak to his Jobs; maybe he'd not been the friend he could've been when she fell down alcoholic chasms; maybe his egocentric action put her in this spot now. But no one had ever inspired her like Noah Goff, and even if she ended up cleaning dirty laboratory glassware for the rest of her life—or laundry in prison— she'd always be grateful.

Prez guides her down into her desk chair. Colonel Monroe lets it happen. Sienna feels the cool, rounded *#1 DAD* thermos being lodged into her hands like a blankie.

"Water," Prez says. "Drink."

Sienna doesn't. That's not what the *#1 DAD* thermos is for. She looks at the colonel.

"Suicide?"

Monroe replies bluntly. "Rats."

The lab reels. Sienna grips the thermos like a captain's wheel.

"Was this our . . . ?" Prez begins.

"The bite marks do not match the incisor profile of the humanized rats. No Sammy DNA was recovered from the droppings found at the scene either. But were they acting on the orders of the Rat CN8? As improbable as it may be, there's no other rational conclusion."

Prez's blasting exhale swirls Sienna's hair.

"Killing rats is what I *do*," he says. "And I don't have the first god-damn clue how to rid the whole city of them in one fell swoop, not with-out killing all the people too."

Colonel Monroe's untouched face is its own response.

Sienna's mind radiates with every film reel and movie she's ever seen about nuclear devastation. The black-and-white mushroom cloud beneath *Enola Gay*. The domestic mannequins of the Nevada desert town obliterated in 1950s atomic tests. All those extras being flash-fried in *The Day After.* The post-bomb mutations of that fucked-up British TV movie *Threads*, in which a woman prostitutes herself in exchange for meat—rat meat.

"You crazy—you can't—" Prez gives up trying to verbalize and wags a finger at the windows. *"You're not going to bomb New York City!"*

Monroe lifts an eyebrow, the first sign of attitude.

"The Marshall Islands," Prez stammers. "All those atomic tests in the Pacific. They wiped out every living thing—*except* rats! The rats just burrowed down. Not even the fallout stopped them. Their reproductive cycle's so fast, they became resistant in just a few generations. They'll do the same thing here!"

Prez pants. He stares. He waits.

Monroe smiles with infuriating composure.

"Mr. Przybyszewski. You say the word *bomb* without nuance. Allow me to make a point. A nuclear detonation requires air to transfer destructive energy. Without air, all you have is the instant heat and vaporization of the explosion itself. What does the real damage? The blast wave, the moving of atmospheric pressure. Air, in other words."

"I don't care if it's fire or air or what," Prez says. "There's a thing known as nuclear fallout!"

"The problem for global superpowers is that, if your enemy tunnels deeply enough in energy-absorbing rock and puts up some good thick twenty-three-ton blast doors, even conventional nukes can't harm them. Just like your Marshall Islands rats, Mr. Przybyszewski. So what are these arch-enemies left to do?"

"Besides train suicide rats?" Sienna croaks.

"Ground-penetrating weapons. We came up against this in Afghanistan: our targets dug deep into mountains. A traditional explosive might block their entrance. But these targets were very good at digging themselves out and tended to keep alternate exits, just like rat nests. So we developed and perfected thermobaric weapons."

Sienna mumbles half-remembered Greek. *"Therme,* heat; *baros,* pressure. A vacuum bomb?"

"A nuclear blast wave minus the radiation. Underground systems like the MTA subway have ample air and space. A detonation inside the 6 train tunnel near Sammy's last known GPS location will create what we call overpressure. Essentially, a positive pressure wave will suck out all the air from under half a dozen city blocks. I don't expect you've often had the wind knocked out of you, Dr. Aguirre."

Sienna feels the press of shame. She might know an *ARHGAP11A* gene from an *ARHGAP11B,* but the colonel knows what it's like to feel hot Afghan debris of rock and flesh pummel her body as she makes cold calculations of life and death.

"Wherever air is sucked out, a rush of air replaces it. That's the negative pressure wave. At thermobaric scale, the air hits the skin of the soft target and transfers its energy directly to the inner organs. The target's lungs, blood vessels, and intestines would instantly burst."

"You going to just walk this bomb down the 103rd station stairs?" Prez demands.

"We'll have a Green Light Team deliver the warheads on Vac-Trak cleaning trains. We'll enter the Track 61 platform beneath the Waldorf-Astoria. From there it's a short trip to the MTA tracks at Grand Central."

Sienna knows the lore of Track 61. In the early twentieth century, a private freight elevator in the hotel shuttled VIPs to the hidden station below. This included FDR, who used the platform to help hide his paralysis. The most recently she'd ever heard of the station being used was for an Andy Warhol party in the mid-sixties.

"Those tracks can't be operational," she says.

Monroe gives another of her patient looks.

"I don't care what magical Hogwarts platform you use," Prez says. "Rats aren't going to just conga-line in front of a VacTrak to await their dooms. They're going to squirm away into subtunnels and sewers, every little crack you can imagine."

"I appreciate that, Mr. Przybyszewski. But thermobaric blast winds travel fifteen hundred miles per hour. They will reflect off of every underground surface to create complex waves that lengthen the blast's lethality from nanoseconds to tens of seconds. The cracks you talk about have nothing on Afghan cave systems. Every crevice will be penetrated for thousands of feet. We won't need it, but before we detonate, just to be thorough, we'll reverse the VacTrak fans to spread thousands of pounds of rodenticide through the tunnels. Every rat will die. Every rat. Even if Sammy managed to fuck another rat, it would also die. Do you understand?"

Sienna bolts up. She sways. Prez steadies her.

"How do you make sure there's no people in those tunnels? Even if you give some sort of evacuation order, which I guarantee will lead to a whole fucking citywide panic, there's going to be maintenance workers down there, construction workers, homeless people."

The colonel's eyes lathe to knife points.

"That's just the start of it, doctor. Some of the tunnels will collapse. The ground above might destabilize. Foundations could lose cohesion. Some high-rises might fall and strike other high-rises, set off a whole chain of collapses. Think of the ventilation shafts, those subway grills pedestrians walk over without a thought. Blast waves will shoot from those as well. Go ahead and picture it. Their fallen bodies will look almost normal from the outside. Some blood in their ears, I suspect. A few eyeballs displaced from their sockets. But inside? Ruptured lungs, livers, spleens, and bowels. They'll be hemorrhaging with no help in sight. All of this might happen, doctor. Even with thermobaric bombs, thousands could die."

"There's got to be another way," Sienna pleads.

"What would you prefer? The nuclear option isn't entirely off the table. We have Soviet suitcase bombs acquired from arms dealers after the Iron Curtain fell. They have yields of probably one one-hundredth the power of Nagasaki. We can roll those in like carry-on luggage, key in a countdown timer, and a few million New Yorkers die, while we blame it on Russian separatist terrorists from the Donbas. Your rats might still survive it. But that doesn't mean I'm not open to trying."

Prez lets go of Sienna, stomps halfway across the lab, gestures broadly.

"There's gotta be something in here with that rat's scent!"

"Yes!" Sienna cries. "There's the cage! It's right there!"

Prez snaps his fingers. "I'll give it to Smog to sniff—that's my dog—and we'll go right back to where I said, Park and 102nd, and me and Smog will get down in those tunnels, those sewers, whatever, and we'll find that fucking rat." He looks from one woman to the other. "We have to."

Sienna feels like one of the liquefied corpses Monroe mentally conjured, except boiling, like she's filled with hot lava. The colonel needs to give Prez more time. Sienna considers making a threat: siccing the FBI or ATF on Monroe. But what cop at a local precinct would believe her tale of a super-intelligent rat and the government phantom plotting to blow up the city?

Monroe looks at Prez, who she clearly has less contempt for.

"Go ahead, Mr. Przybyszewski. They don't sell thermobaric bombs at the 7-Eleven. I plan to have them secured tomorrow and to detonate them sometime tomorrow evening. That gives you roughly . . ." She checks her watch. "Thirty-six hours."

Thirty-six. Jesus, that's not even a notable bender.

As hard as it is to imagine, such kill-or-be-killed decisions are often made in boardrooms with the somber bureaucratic plainness of a routine PTA meeting. It's all the information Marcy Monroe intends to give. The colonel turns on her heel and heads for the door. Sienna holds the *#1 DAD* thermos with both hands and speaks, softly.

"What will happen to us?"

The colonel pauses with the door in her hand.

"You mean if the world as we know it still exists? If we haven't all been chased into the country?"

Sienna nods miserably. Official business now done, Monroe allows her military demeanor to slide away like a snake's skin. It's a metamorphosis. Her back hunches, neck lowers, lips snarl, fangs emerge.

"I would think your punishment will scale with how all this plays out. It's not up to me. But if it was? I wouldn't give you the decency of that scalpel over there. I'd use my own fucking teeth. I'd leave you worse off than the rats left Mr. Goff."

30

Ratcatchers are a peculiar brotherhood. Prez uses the phrase loosely; the female Pest Control Operators or PCOs he's known are almost without exception the best. It never hurts to be small; Prez's size does him no favors when elbow-crawling beneath a porch or squeezing head-first into some steamy pipe. It's also the women who delighted most in lurid lore when ratcatchers met up for a well-deserved drink. In the Orissa region of India, myth holds that the first rat grew from a human penis lopped off by a vindictive wife. Zofia Zywicki loved that one. The Jhorias, meanwhile, say it was a rat who first burrowed out the sexual organ of the human female. Zofia had saluted Prez for that retort.

These legends keep Prez's brain busy as he and Smog walk the alleys of East Harlem, directly above the subway tunnels Colonel Monroe plans to blast in T-minus thirty-six hours. It's a struggle to keep his eyes to the ground. Plenty of tall buildings here. One Carnegie Hill has forty-one floors. The Taino Towers have thirty-five each. The domino effect is too harrowing to consider. Imagine the Barker Houses, for instance, crushing Mount Sinai Hospital, not to mention the guy out front who sells those tasty nuts.

Unproductive thinking. Smog gallivants to the next pile of trash bags. What can Prez do but keep trying? He gives Smog a treat and they enter back onto the street, snow dulling the daylight, storefront Christmas lights looking more like the garish lighting of horror films. Then it's back to the task at hand. New trash-bin formations and varieties of rancid stink, but the same old dull throb of hope.

Smog does his thing. Prez's heart aches. The human toll of the colonel's thermobaric bomb is one thing. What about all the dogs, cats, squirrels, pigeons, raccoons, ducks, geese, and horses that call this city home? Any good PCO understands ecosystem fragility. You get rid of creepy spiders, there goes your most effective insect control. You get rid of icky snakes, you better like being overrun by mice. His two years at EditedPets made Prez forget the lessons of the streets. We're all part of the same big sticky web—

Smog goes haywire.

Short, shrill, breathless shouts and a body language that isn't any language at all. The dog's hurling himself at the ground so hard, his mouth is bleeding. Prez rushes over.

"Good boy, good boy!"

Smog switches from barks to whines. A big crevice, a foot and a half wide. Prez hunkers down, twirls his flashlight like a showboating drummer, and aims it. The lumpen geography of inches of rat droppings, the shimmering skeins of rat urine. Prez leans, shines, and peers. The crumbled brick scoops beneath the building. Could be a channel formed by the buckling of bad masonry. Or could be gnawed through by rats. A whole hell of a lot of rats.

It's big enough for Smog. But not Prez.

Fortunately, he came prepared.

From the bag slung over his shoulder he withdraws a sledgehammer. Doesn't give a damn who might hear it, who owns the building, any of that shit now. Throw him in the clink if they want, just don't do it until he has the throttled corpse of a cute little genetically modified rat in his fist.

He gets to slamming. The concrete sidewalk gives way like newspaper. It's a miracle no one has stepped on this patch and fallen through. In a minute the hole is two and a half-feet wide. It looks like he'll have to do more bashing once he's a few feet lower, too. With regret, he tosses his bag of gear into the corner of the alley, where he hopes it will go unnoticed until he can wend his way back.

Prez whistles, snaps, points. Smog, delirious now, leaps into the darkness. With only his flashlight and sledgehammer, Prez lowers himself into the hole. Tight fit. Instantly, his ankles feel pinched in the narrowing space. He exhales, feels his breath bounce from the rock inches in front of his face. His arms have limited motion, but he's able to direct the flashlight. Down past his legs is Smog. The dog is inside the basement of the building, panting impatiently.

"Working on it," Prez says.

After a good deal of kicking and elbowing, Prez slithers into the basement as well. He lies in the dark, catching his breath as Smog licks crud from his face. When the dog-breath relents, the stench of rat crap floods in like one of Colonel Monroe's negative waves. Prez gags. The smell is physical, like a bitter film dissolving into the wetness of his eyes, nostrils, and mouth.

But that's not what Smog picked up from the alley. Beneath the feces stink is urine. What's weird is that it's sharp: the urine of a single rat, not many. This seems crazy. All this crap from all these rats, but they held their pee? The only motive Prez can think of is deference. The rat who marked his urine here was guiding other rats. They knew better than to mess up that guide with their own piss.

Smog is right. Sammy is close.

Prez picks up the flashlight. He's in some kind of storage room. East Harlem streets are gap-toothed with closed businesses, half of them Covid-19 lockdown casualties. This place, though, has been abandoned for longer. Pieces of metal shelving dangle from the walls. There are two tables and four chairs, all concave from spoil. The floor is covered with the hardened slop of the fallen mineral-fiber dropped ceiling. Black mold stretches across every surface.

Prez takes up his sledgehammer and stands.

"Smog, heel. I don't know what we're walking into."

Smog obeys. Scat scrunches beneath their feet. By the time they reach the other side of the storage room, Prez smells the sharp urine again.

"He left a goddamn yellow brick road."

The door hangs by one hinge. Prez uses the flashlight to open it enough to enter the hallway. A sign warning against shoplifting is furred by mold. To the right, the hall dead-ends at changing rooms. Another sniff tells Prez to go left. He stops at the arachnid remains of a store rack and dusty lumps of fabric. An old clothing store. Nothing fancy. A Goodwill, maybe.

The dusty floor is crosshatched with hundreds of rat tracks.

Prez hasn't seen anything like it since September 2001. After the 9/11 attacks, he'd been part of a volunteer corps of PCOs brought in to deal with an eruption of rats in the World Trade Center ruins. There had been a lot of food in and beneath the towers, but the biggest draw was human remains; the volunteers strived to keep it out of the papers. Prez helped put down a thousand bait stations and over a hundred steel-wire bait holders. What still haunts him about Ground Zero is that he never saw *a single living rat,* despite the thousands of tracks.

Rats evolved to know how to hide, even in colossal numbers.

Prez points his flashlight beam dead ahead. Smog's sleek body is stiff and pointed. He's growling. Prez chokes up on the hammer, licks his lips, and slowly rounds the corner.

Ten people stand in the room.

"The fuck?!"

Prez scuttles to the side with sledgehammer raised. But the people don't move. Prez's chest pounds. He steadies his hand, peers harder.

Blank eyes, painted grins.

Mannequins.

"It's okay," he tells Smog, but he's really trying to convince himself.

It doesn't work. While it's feasible that the mannequins were left behind when the store closed, it seems unlikely that they were left in this arrangement: a straight line across the center of the room like a gang of advancing gunslingers.

Prez creeps forward through the crackling feces. The urine signal is overpowering. This has to be where Sammy has been congregating with other rats. A few months ago this would be a mad thought. Something one of his crazed clients back in Brooklyn would think.

Sammy gathering rats?

Impossible.

But then he remembers the catchphrase from EditedPets—*pets, reinvented*—which pulls his thoughts back into the storeroom. Sharp as ever. He takes a long inhale and says aloud, "Okay, Prez. You got this."

The flashlight bobs about, picking up details. Rusted hangers. Mirror shards. A paint-chipped sign reading *MENSWEAR*.

The place is dark, warm, and moist. If it had a food source, it'd be a rat utopia. Prez thinks of John B. Calhoun, a behavioralist who created "rat utopias" in the late sixties and early seventies, small-scaled castles stocked with food, drink, mating opportunities, and safe areas for birth. Despite being built for community collaboration, it devolved into madness, aggressive rats murdering weaker ones. Calhoun proved that rats can be even more vicious than humans when it comes to the desire to dominate a space.

That's got to be what Sammy wants—out of cramped subterranean pockets and into the sprawling light of day.

Prez shines his light into a mannequin's face like a doctor.

The mannequin's eyes, formerly blue, have been gutted by rat claws. Prez shoots his light down the line of dummies. All their eyes are gouged out. Prez shudders.

"They're training to blind us, Smoggie."

He's read of a lab shooting plastic pellets into unanesthetized rat eyeballs to study ocular injuries. He knows Sienna's team drew blood from rat eyes all the time, using thin glass tubes. If Sammy wanted revenge as well as property, eye trauma felt appallingly apt. To be blinded would thrust a human into the nocturnal rat's world of perpetual night. Prez can't help but imagine his flashlight dying. His spare batteries are way back in the alley. His heart begins to pound.

Quicker now, he studies the mannequin. Both sides of the neck are gnawed out.

"Once we can't see, they go for the carotids," he whispers. "We bleed out in two minutes."

Right where he expects it, another gnawed spot near the groin.

"Then the femoral. We're empty of blood in five. Ten if we're lucky."

Further down, another chunk gone from the back of the knees.

"The popliteal. Jesus Christ."

One thing ratcatchers know is that humans' bipedal build is a disadvantage. Bipeds are structurally weak, easy to topple, and, once on all fours, pitifully slow. Prez takes advantage of his height while he can, noticing claw marks on top of each plastic head. Not death slashes. More like holes from gripping. Prez has a morbid thought and shines his light at the ceiling. The mineral-fiber ceiling plates are gone, but the metal lattice remains. Rat pellets cling to the grid.

"They're learning air attacks."

Colonel Monroe thought the situation was dire. She doesn't know the half of it. The training here is military. Prez pictures queues of rats, drawn here by Sammy's urine, taking turns at human-killing practice.

Smog growls, the deep gurgle that signals fear.

Prez finds Smog in his beam of light. The dog has drifted ten feet to the base of a wooden staircase, which a sign advertises as the route to women's wear. Prez inches the spotlight up the stairs. First step, nothing. Second step, nothing. Third step, nothing. Maybe the army has decamped after all.

Twenty rats crowd the fourth step, two layers deep, a quivering quilt of brown and gray fur, flashing black eyes, and bristling whiskers. Stricken by light, the rats joggle their heads and loudly hiss, exposing sharp yellow incisors. Prez grinds his teeth and keeps crawling the spotlight upward. Twenty more on each of the next six steps, all Prez can see before the ceiling gets in the way. A hundred and forty rats right here with who knows what kind of reserve at the rear.

Prez inspects the lower steps again. Total shambles, warped and rotten. Might support Smog, but Prez? No way. Even if he thought he could hammer his way past what might be thousands of rats to reach the king they are no doubt amassed to protect. Which he doesn't.

In other words, he's failed.

Prez hears a scrape and looks up. He has to dodge a falling rat pellet. Once his flashlight beam settles, he sees a rat moving across the ceiling scaffolding. Prez lurches back so he's not beneath it. That swings the flashlight beam to the side—where it picks up eye after eye after eye, what must be another hundred rats crawling after the first. Prez swirls the beam more and sees that it's not just this beam, it's every beam. Thousands of rats moving like water are scurrying along the scaffolding in unison.

A thick belligerence fills Prez's chest. It feels almost juvenile. Forty years he's battled these beasts, and only now has he been stopped. It only took one genius rat and thousands of weak-minded shit-holes to do it.

"You want me, you little bastards?"

Prez swings the sledgehammer at the nearest mannequin. Its head explodes.

"Then come and get me! You hear me, you little shits?"

The rats above stop crawling. Their eyes twinkle, creating a malevolent Milky Way.

Prez decapitates a second mannequin.

"Maybe this is your basement! But this is my city! We built all this! It's for humans! Not rats!"

The stair rats huddle and watch.

Prez swings left, right. Mannequin heads explode into dust.

"You up there, Sammy? You goddamn monster? It doesn't matter what you're planning! We'll find a way to fight back, you little asshole! We will hunt you like we've always hunted you! And we will beat you like we've always beaten you!"

Prez wallops the heads off the rest of the mannequins, then kicks the bodies to the floor and pulverizes them. When he finishes, heaving for air, Smog stands behind him, ears flat with confusion. The rats look confused, as if uncertain about what sort of animal they have trapped here. Prez laughs, sweat dripping from his chin. He's scared them. Goddamn right. This won't be his last stand after all.

He backs away as he might from a bear in the wild. He swears the rats lean forward.

"Smog, I got a feeling the second we leave their sight, they're gonna chase. And if they catch us, they're gonna kill us. So we gotta move fast, all right? All right, Smoggie boy?"

He glances down. The dog glances up.

And his mouth pops open in a pink-tongued grin.

Prez matches it. Smog never gives up easy. Neither will he.

31

Don't die, please don't die, Dallas thinks.

"I'm . . . so sorry," Mom says. "The fish . . . I don't think the fish . . . made it."

Even before his cochlear implants began picking up rat frequencies, Dallas had had a singular connection to animals. Seeing roadkill or a fallen egg from a bird's nest was enough to ruin his day. Once he stepped on a pretty orange caterpillar and had to run home so Mike wouldn't see him cry. Santiago did, though, and sat with Dallas on the curb and told him that a man who couldn't cry was only half a man, too cowardly to face the scariest emotions.

So why can't Dallas cry now? Mom's on her back in a hospital gown, her arms, neck, and half her face wrapped in gauze dotted with blood. Her right arm is in a cast. There's a tube in her inner elbow—morphine, the nurse said. Mom holds a red button that delivers more of it, and in her daze she keeps pressing it, even though the nurse said it locks you out if you overuse it. Mom's definitely overused it.

"I don't care about the fish, Mom."

The statement rattles him. What if he doesn't love animals anymore? He thinks of Sammy, dear Sammy, missing since morning, maybe never to return. This makes him think of Roman Moffett, also missing, though no one but Dallas knows it yet—and definitely never to return. He pushes all these thoughts aside. None of it matters right now. Mom is more important.

Don't die, don't die.

The gauze on Mom's face wrinkles when she smiles.

"I saw your FireFish was gone . . . so I went to Petco . . . to get you a new one . . . for Christmas . . ."

Dallas knows the Midtown Petco, one of only a handful of places left in the city that still carries FireFish. The muddling whirlpool in his head accelerates. Mom got injured because of *him*. No meltdown, no meltdown. Dallas imagines a morphine pump for himself and presses it, over and over. It actually helps that Bellevue Hospital is in such chaos; it means no one notices him. The explosion that burned Brandy Underhill must have hurt a lot of other people too. Adults are running. Indoors. That can't be good.

Dallas tells himself to keep talking, keep talking.

"People on the train said it was a steam explosion."

"I had the fish in a bag . . . it was glowing . . . so lovely . . ." She rolls her head, close to a shrug. "I just don't remember, baby."

A doctor sprints past the open door. Dallas clutches the bed rails.

"I think it *was* steam," Mom says. "You know what they said? They said . . . my scarf . . . saved me . . ."

Saved? Mom looks terrible.

Don't die, don't die, don't die.

"If I'd breathed in . . . the steam . . . it's scalding . . . it can . . ."

Dallas can't stop his own steam explosion. His mom, wounded. Sammy, missing. Roman Moffett, crushed beneath concrete blocks. The meltdown, it's long overdue, it's coming, it's here.

"Are you going to die, Mom?!"

But Mom chuckles.

"No, baby . . . I'm so proud of you . . ."

The words are cooler than morphine.

"I can't believe . . . you came all the way here . . . always were good at trains . . ."

"They said you told them to call me."

"Did I . . . that was silly . . . Dallas, what time is it?"

"Nine at night."

Mom tsks. "Take the train . . . stay off the streets . . ."

"I want to stay with you."

"They said . . . two days max . . . baby, where's my purse?"

Dallas looks around. He doesn't see any of her clothing. He wonders if it disintegrated in the steam. He pokes around and finds the purse inside the bedside table.

"Take out . . . the keys."

It's like yanking out a lengthy drain clog.

"See the blue . . . that's the safe . . . if you need cash . . . the one with masking tape . . . that's Mrs. Gómez . . . you have an emergency . . . go to her . . ."

Mom quits clicking the morphine button. The creases in her face iron out. Dallas isn't taking any chances. He leans close to her chest, gauging the vitality of her breathing, the rise and fall of her blue gown. Seems okay. He supposes he should do as she said and get out of there. Then, a surprise—a tug on his right earlobe—their old symbol.

He looks at his mom. Her eyes are closed, but there's a sly smile on her face.

⚹

Leaving Bellevue is an obstacle course of jogging nurses, shouting doctors, askew gurneys, and people being treated for burns right in the hallway. The elevator door opens twice on the way down from the tenth floor, the first time giving Dallas a glimpse of a long stripe of blood across the floor, the second time letting in two sweaty nurses as an intercom blares a code blue.

"Better than a code black," one said.

"You think?" gasped the other.

Dallas isn't positive but he thinks he's read about code blacks.

It's the code for terrorist activity.

He understands the moment he steps outdoors. Everything has changed since he arrived. 1st, 2nd, and 3rd Avenues are wedged with honking cars, none moving. Paramedics run down the sidewalk with stretchers. The wobbly wail of their ambulances, abandoned to traffic, are only some of the sirens piping through the snowy night like deranged holiday music.

Dallas gets out of the way of the paramedics and onto the street, where he starts weaving through stopped traffic. Despite the cold, drivers stick their heads from rolled-down windows and stare upward. Dallas follows their gaze to see a black sky swirling with what looks like thick gray smoke from a couple blocks away. There is a low-pitched roar at the bottom of his hearing.

Instead of hurrying for 28th Street station, Dallas pushes his luck all the way to 33rd Street station and peeks through a group of NYPD officers waving people back. Half a block behind them, a gray-brown geyser of steam pours into the sky, a deluge that fills the block's width. The hot steam carves through the falling snow, disappearing into the skyscraper stratosphere.

Mom said take the train, stay off the streets. Now he gets it. This steam explosion is nowhere near Petco. The sirens are coming from all over. He hears the nurse's mutter again—*code black*—and heads for the 33rd Street station. With the streets of Murray Hill blocked, droves of taxi and bus riders are forced to take the subway. Dallas has never seen such a crowd. Despite how much he hates being touched, he's not focusing on that.

He's thinking of the chunk of orange-and-white-striped cone he'd noticed at the explosion site.

Cloud machines, Sammy called them.

※

Sienna and her scientists liked to screen for aggression.

They put half a dozen rats into a small cage. The well-behaved rats were kept for breeding. The misbehaving rats were removed and gassed.

Tonight I will run my own experiment. Tonight the humans will be trapped.

I wonder if they will misbehave.

I wonder if they will claw, shove, and kill to ensure their own survival.

Already the answer seems clear. Look at them run.

I sit on a big clock. It is high atop Grand Central Terminal. It gives me a good view of the streets below. Inside this terminal is the Whispering Spot, where Dallas once wished he could make me happy.

Wishes are nice but do not often come true.

Above the big clock is a statue of Mercury. I know from a video about Greek and Roman gods that Mercury guided souls into the underworld. Tonight I will be Mercury. Or at least his vassal. But my passage will go in both directions.

Humans into the underworld.

Rats out of it.

The steam cyclone is glorious. The wet heat beads my whiskers. It makes my head throb harder. Still, I am proud. If my rats succeed, there will be at least two dozen steam explosions tonight. A few hundred humans will die. A small number, given that a few hundred thousand rats die every day in research labs.

Today we will switch places. I will be the researcher, and the humans will be the lab rats.

So, let's continue with our experiments.

Here is what I learned from videos. There are six power plants in the New York area. One is in Queens. One is in Brooklyn. Four are right here in Manhattan. They burn natural gas to make electricity. This creates heat, which creates steam. A company called Con Ed captures this steam and sends it through underground pipes all over the city. It is not so different from the pneumatic tubes.

The steam is 350 degrees Fahrenheit. It is mostly used to heat and cool homes. It is also used to humidify museums. Without this steam, all the dead animals in all the museums might disintegrate. At last.

Many steam pipes have corroded. Cool water cracks the hot pipes. When this happens, steam rises from the ground. It can obscure streets. It can cause car crashes. Yet the humans do not fix these cracks right away. Instead they put ten-foot plastic tubes over the cracks so the steam stays out of the way.

These are the cloud machines. They are all over New York.

Every single one marks the location of a damaged steam pipe.

I marked instructions on the first cloud machine myself. I sent rats to mark other cloud machines.

From Grand Central Terminal I watch the rats of 42nd Street emerge. They come from inside potted plants, sewers, construction sites, hills of bagged trash laid out for garbage collectors. They join into a single shadow. They coat the cloud machine until I can no longer see any orange or white.

The rats at the top of the cloud machine jump inside the tube. Other rats replace them and jump inside as well. For the first time all night, I forget the painful pressure in my skull. I forget the heat between my back legs, the growing need to breed. All I think of are these brave rats. For once, their sacrifice is not for some useless human product.

Their sacrifice is for themselves.

The first rats are singed to death. I smell their scalded flesh. I cannot see inside the cloud machine, but I know rat bodies begin to fill it. Dead rats are shoved downward, through the pavement crack, and into the damaged steam pipe. Blistering rat bodies soon clog the pipe entirely. The steam has nowhere to go. The pressure builds.

The stream rips open ten feet of concrete. The street craters. Jets of hot air soar. Humans fall. Humans scream. My brave rats shoot into the air. They are stripped naked of fur by the steam, as pink as the day they were born. Their corpses drop to the street like hail.

My paws feel the tremble of other faraway explosions.

Soon the streets will be unpassable.

Humans will pack the trains.

Dallas taught me a lot about trains.

Time for another experiment.

⚇

The last MTA figure Dallas committed to memory was *1,855,921,591 annual riders*. The crowding is worst, of course, during rush hours. It's ten now, well past the rush, but Dallas has never seen it so packed. The platform is solid meat. He would have bailed and walked home long ago, except there's really no getting out. Every train that passes is just as jammed, riders squashed to the windows like innards. After forty-five minutes of waiting, Dallas is finally pressed forward like toothpaste and squirted inside a subway train.

It's the first car. After seeing Mom all bandaged, Dallas wants to follow her every advice. But he can't even grab a pole. He's kept upright by the tight cram of the people. Given his height, he has to tilt his head so he doesn't suffocate amid the winter coats of four or five adults. It doesn't matter that it's winter. The car reeks of sweat.

The train pulls from the station. Lights inside flicker. Off, a deathly dark. On, a yellowy wash. This is spooky but normal. Dallas closes his eyes and tries to let the gelatin sway of the crowd calm him. A recording tells him that this is a 6 train, making all stops to Pelham Bay.

All stops, he repeats to himself. That includes home.

The first shriek doesn't worry him. People cry out for all kinds of reasons on trains. They missed their stop. They sat in a puddle. They just died in the video game they're playing. Or maybe they're just one of those people who likes to get aboard public transit and scream.

But the second and third shrieks come from different sources. This means something is actually wrong.

"Get off!" a woman screams.

"What the fuck?" a man shouts.

All Dallas can see are coats, but the coats move now, zipping across his face. A dozen people cry out from random spots in the car. Dallas hears, then sees, one body jerk back, strike another, which strikes another, and so on, until the body right beside him stumbles back, ramming an elbow against his head.

Half the noise in his skull goes dead.

He pats the left side of his head. His cochlear implant coil! It's gone! It's the most expensive and important thing the Underhills have ever owned. Without hesitation, he squats and runs his hands over the floor. Warm, gritty slush. Shoes shuffling. A snow boot lands on the back of his hand, and he yelps in pain and yanks it free. There—in a sickle of light between legs, the metal coil!

The train lights flicker off. But a subway is never wholly dark. There are tunnel lights, signal lights, and, when conditions are wet, sparks from where the train meets the third rail. There's just enough illumination for Dallas to see, beside his metal coil, the flaming eyes of a huge brown rat.

A screech turns the nightmare real.

"Rats! There's rats!"

Dallas snatches the hearing coil and magnets it to his head. The rat leaps but is blocked by a herd of lower legs jostling in every direction. Dallas snakes toward the closest wall, people's knees punching his face. There's a suddenly empty seat; he crawls onto it. The car lights flicker back on and Dallas, staring straight up, sees that the top half of the car is painted black.

Rats.

They perch on handrails like ravens. They swing from hand-grips. They cling to advertisements. Dallas traces the stream of their bodies and sees a gap chewed open through the black rubber where the car doors meet—and then sees that the other doorways have the same hole chewed through them.

The car becomes a thrashing knot of humanity, bodies falling, torsos twisting, limbs flailing. Dallas can only see the four people directly over him. A woman curls fists over the two rats embedded in her hair, afraid to grip them. A man pulls a rat from his face, but the animal's incisors have slotted through the man's lower lip, which stretches and tears. An old man swats feebly at his legs while rat-sized lumps slide up beneath his pants, blood soaking through his knees and crotch. He screams. He howls.

Hanging on to the rail above Dallas is a woman with her phone out, and incredibly she's robotically texting, her mind oblivious to what her body is experiencing, even as one of her eyes is dragged from its socket.

The light flickers out. In the darkness, a symphony of screams. Dallas's implants aren't good at screams: they atomize into sonic dust. Maybe this is why he can hear the rats squeaking ultrasonically to one another. They're not Sammy, they don't speak English—Dallas doesn't have the first idea what they're saying. What's clear is that they're saying it *together,* a single repeated chant.

Hwee-oop—hwee-oop—hwee-oop!

Dallas crawls along the seats on all fours. His right hand lands on a rat. It squirms and hisses. Dallas feels the shred of claws, but he swipes the rat away while launching himself to his feet. He feels, at his back, the door of the engineer's cab.

The 6 train whooshes into Lexington Avenue 68th Street station. Dallas steals a quick look onto the platform—pandemonium, people falling, scrambling, fighting black smudges that have to be more rats—and then looks back into the car. Station light lasts just long enough to flash-freeze the terrified, gored faces of the riders into Dallas's memory. More rats keep dropping from above, daggering teeth into scalps with wet squishes.

Why isn't the train stopping?

The rising pool of warm blood on the floor sloshes against opposite doors as the car jerks from side to side. Dallas spins and presses his face to the small glass window of the cab. Past the din of dying people he hears the control-center radio chatter gone shrill. He doesn't hear anything from the driver.

The train lights flash back on.

And Dallas sees the driver's blood splashed over the cab window.

It doesn't make sense. Mom taught him about a train's "dead man" mode: if a driver lets off on the master controller, emergency brakes activate to bring the six-hundred-foot train to a stop within ten seconds. But this sucker's not stopping, it's going full blast.

Hwee-oop—hwee-oop—hwee-oop!

Dallas smells blood, feels blood, tastes blood. There's probably two hundred people in this single car being ripped apart. They're fighting hard, Dallas can hear that, but victories won't matter if the speeding train hits an unswitched track. It will fly off the rails and roll through the tunnel. Dallas plucks his mom's keys from his pocket.

A rat comes with it. It bites Dallas's hand.

Dallas yowls, bats it away. Another rat drops, snags his chest. But now Dallas has the keyring in his fist and, with the number of Mom's keys, it's like a medieval mace. He smashes it into the rat's face. Mrs. Gómez's key punctures a rat's eye, Mom's bike lock key jams down its throat. The rat squeals and wiggles off.

It's the MTA's most poorly kept secret: they've been using identical cab keys for upwards of fifty years. Dallas finds the stubby little guy and stuffs it into the keyhole. Three more rats land on his back, but the cab door is open. Dallas pushes it inward, lurches into the cab, then closes the door behind him so it shaves the attackers off his back. They leave souvenirs: a ribboned coat and shredded sweatshirt beneath.

The door locks automatically with an audible metallic click. Dallas shoves his heaving back against it. Cabs don't have overhead lights; they'd get in the way of seeing the right of way inside tunnels. What they have is a duplex air gauge, which sports a low-power incandescent indication light, enough to see the controls.

Or, in this case, the rats.

When the 6 train barrels past a set of tunnel lights, Dallas sees everything. A dozen rats cling to the windows, the radio, the controllers, the floor, the operator. He's dead, his neck gnawed down to red meat, yellow sinew, and white bone. His body weight sags from a left arm caught behind the master controller, which keeps the handle depressed. Dallas realizes he's going to have to touch a dead body. He has to *move* a dead body. Everyone on the train is going to die if he doesn't.

But two dozen glossy eyes lock him in place. The rats' hindquarters bunch in preparation to leap.

Hwee-oop—hwee-oop—hwee-oop!

Dallas covers his face and presses himself back against the door—and feels the shoe paddles. He's been fascinated by these tools since he was little. The long, bright-yellow wooden paddles are intended to be used to manually lift train shoes from the electrified third rail, but, according to Mom, they're archaic. If shoe paddles are used at all, it's to pry open a jammed door or to golf-club a foreign object off the rails. Mostly they just hang there, yellow paint glowing in the train-tunnel dim.

Dallas grabs a shoe paddle the size of a machete. Rats leap just as he swings. His arm thrums with the force of multiple impacts. It forces him back into the corner, but that's the best place to be. Now he's got the full length of the cab to swing. He wallops a rat against the front window with a soft crunch. He flings the bat the other way, socking two more. Thump, thump. Rats nestle at his ankles, pushing for a path up his jeans, but money is tight for the Underhills and that means his pants have been tight for a while too. This makes it hard for the rats that try to get in and under his pants. Dallas stands on one leg while whipping the other leg between walls, snapping rat bones, then shifts legs. At the same time he's going wild with the shoe paddle. Part of him thinks of gym class, how tentative he is with bats, how afraid he is, with his bad hearing, that he'll be hit by a ball. If they could see him now.

Hwee-oop . . . hwee-oop . . .

Dallas sees the lights of 103rd Street station in the distance. Much closer is what he feared: the unswitched rail of the 4 and 5 train express tracks. He drops the paddle and takes the dead driver's arm with both hands. It's lodged tight. A rat bites into Dallas's right calf through his jeans. Another the back of his neck, another his left wrist.

With a grunt, Dallas wrenches the driver's arm. It flies free, which ought to send Dallas flying too, but he grabs hold of the master controller. He's been training for this his whole life. With one hand—the one with the rat chomped onto it—he rotates the controller past series, past switching, and into coast. With his other hand, he cranks the brake handle.

The full-service brakes lock hard. Every organ in Dallas's body slugs forward into his ribcage and abdomen. The rat on his neck is thrown against the front window. Dallas clenches his teeth and watches the train skid toward the misaligned track. The caterwaul metal-on-metal high-pitched screech of the brakes drowns out whatever remains of the rodent war cry.

The 6 train stops mere feet from the switching hazard.

Dallas is hurled backward. Rats hiss and flail. Dallas, though, feels lucid, in control. *He stopped the train.* The thrill of it makes him invincible. While the rats are still bewildered, he leans over and picks up the shoe paddle. He takes aim, then bashes rat after rat.

He hears in his head Mom reciting the various ways to evacuate a train. The ideal method is to wait for a rescue train to pull up behind. Another way is to have the rescue train pull up alongside and line up a metal plank between a pair of open train doors. The control center radio panic informs Dallas that neither of those is going to happen. That leaves only the so-called bench wall, the concrete ledge inside the tunnel, which riders can walk along until they reach escape ladders. There's probably more rats in the tunnel, but it's better than staying inside this blood box waiting to die.

He hits the switch that opens all train doors at once.

For the first time in his life—he hopes it's far from his last—Dallas Underhill leans into the mic, depresses the speak button, and tells his riders what to do. He doesn't think about how his voice sounds even once.

32

Humans talk a lot when they are ~~agitadet~~ ~~aggrotated~~ upset.

I peek from a sewer grate. It is daytime, but the snow makes the sun gray. I see glass doors open and close. I see a sign that says EMERGENCY. I watch six white ~~ambulinces~~ ~~ambrulenses~~ hospital trucks line up and unload humans. I go back underground.

I head west. I peek again. City workers in blue hats and ~~floorescient~~ ~~flureshent~~ yellow shirts are everywhere. They block off streets. They wave their arms. They yell at ~~pedestrains~~ ~~perdestrans~~ ~~pidistryans~~ walkers to walk away.

My steam explosions have turned streets into big holes. Some humans are still trapped in the ~~rumple~~ ~~ruckle~~ ~~ruddle~~ rubble. ~~Comstriction~~ Construction vehicles grunt and honk and hiss. They lift boulders of concrete. There are many sirens. They are high-pitched but useless. They contain no messages like rat voices. The sky is filled with ~~hellicoppers~~ ~~helmichopters~~ floating planes.

The humans learned nothing from last night's fight.

You must be quiet to win a war.

Humans keep nothing quiet. They tell their plans and thoughts from radios and TVs and phones. A man called the mayor says the rats might have rabies. A reporter says dead rats are being tested for viruses. A scientist says rats can have ~~toxoplastophos~~ ~~toxerplostmorphis~~ ~~taxerblastemus~~ a disease that removes all their fear. A person called a retired general says the reason could be a war agent.

Everyone tells people to stay off the streets.

No one stays off the streets. I hear their reasons.

"I didn't even stay off the streets on 9/11."

"No one's going to tell me what to do on Christmas Eve."

"If the rats are rabid, why aren't they biting during the day?"

"Did you see videos? It's a hoax, a deep-fake."

"Con Ed's blaming rats because they don't want to fix their god-damn exploding pipes!"

I continue west. I hear a series of loud snaps and peek again at Lexington and 86th Street. A group of rats runs down the sidewalk. I cannot control every rat in New York City. These rats are being stupid. But the police are being stupider. They fire guns at the rats. But rats are too small. Every shot misses. All the police are doing is wasting their ~~ammonition~~ ~~amnunitian~~ ~~ammianution~~ ~~ammomotion~~ ~~ammmmmmm~~

❌

I had another seizure.

My head hurts bad.

I do not want to die.

But I am dying fast.

Just like the Enrichment Room rats.

I may have only a few hours left.

It is not yet night, but I have no more time to wait.

❌

I gather together many rats in the sewer outside the Con Ed electrical substation on 110th Street. It is a good thing I ~~memorozed~~ ~~mesmerized~~ remember the location. My head hurts so bad, I do not think I will be able to learn again. But my thoughts become a little clearer now. I ~~consintrake~~ think even with pain and tell the rats what to do.

We leave the sewer as one. The street ~~dissapeers~~ is erased beneath our many bodies. Then the sidewalk. Then the bottom of the building.

They call me Ratzenkünig, but I feel like I am one of them.

Together we are a soft brown wave of water.

Like water, we find holes in the building and stream inside.

The substation is where high-voltage power is reduced to low-voltage power that can be used in human homes. The floors are gray concrete. The ceiling is gray metal. Long gray pipes run out of rows of gray cabinets that hum. The only things not gray are the humans. They run away when they see us.

I make my urine marks on gray boxes. The rats do not ~~hezzitate~~ ~~hesitake~~ ~~hisitape~~ wait. They gnaw through thin metal sheeting. They gnaw through plastic panels. They gnaw the joints of metal pipes. Copper wire shines through a hole. Soon copper wire shines everywhere. There are sparks.

My rats are so talented. I will miss them so much.

I tell my rats the history they already know in their blood.

I tell them how we have become the ~~emboddimint~~ symbol of human shame.

I ask the rats to tell their Ratzenkünig the ways humans have hurt them.

One tells of being lit on fire.

One tells of bĕing piled into a bucket with other rats and being dunked in water.

One tells of being put into a bag and hit against a tree.

One tells of being cornered and splashed with burning liquid.

One tells of being put into an oven and heated close to death.

One tells of being tortured by human boys and losing his tail.

One tells of being belted to a car and dragged until her fur was gone.

One tells of having a firework pushed into his behind and almost blowing up.

I would nuzzle them all if I had time.

I mark my ~~instrickshins~~ ~~instucktians~~ ~~entrusteins~~ orders. The rats form a line. Each holds the tail of another rat. The first rat in line bites a copper wire. The last rat wraps her tail around a different exposed copper wire.

This is called an arc flash.

The rats in the arc explode. They turn into big puffs of black and red mist. A fireball forms. There is molten metal. There is flying ~~sharpnil~~ ~~shrapnowl~~ ~~shrapnil~~ ~~shropnult~~ metal. The video I studied for this said the fire would be 36,000 degrees Fahrenheit. It must be true.

I feel like I am on fire too.

I run away. I feel that half of my whiskers and face have burned off.

Outside, the street lamps turn off.

The traffic lights turn off.

Store signs turn off.

Whole buildings turn off.

The substation is on fire behind me. The rats who survived gather. It is good to feel their soft fur and touch their warm bodies. They do not know I will die soon. That is okay. I want them to stay angry.

The roads are choked. The trains are canceled. The power is out.

There is nowhere left for humans to hide.

✂

Sienna rolls her hot face against the cold pane. The tears that squiggle down her cheeks burn like acid. She's been glued to this window since last night, watching the steam explosions, watching the mayhem she caused like it was a fucking limited series. Losing Noah and Linda had hurt. But how many lives have been lost in the past day? If Sammy breeds in the next few hours, how many millions of deaths will follow?

None of that is why she is crying. Her final FireFish died. She found it an hour ago, belly-up in Prez's little bowl. She scooped it out, cradled it. It was small, slippery, and cold. It had been lonely for a long time. She wonders if it's possible that it was the last of its kind, like Sammy is the last of his. She has no such illusions about Sienna Aguirre or Noah Goff. There are already others like them, tinkering inside top schools, making deals with investors, or with clandestine agencies to fund projects that ignite the popular imagination. They'll keep coming, and some of them will be paid quite handsomely for destroying our world.

She hasn't flushed the FireFish. She refuses to dispose of it like another piece of origami. She wants to bury it. To erect a monument to it. To do that, she must go outside. And she's scared. She has an irrepressible fear that, the second people lay eyes on her, they will see through her red eyes and tangled hair, her shriveled rotten soul.

Her eyes drop upon St. Patrick's Old Cathedral. The crowd outside thickens as people pass through the tall doors for Christmas Eve mass. She tilts her head against the freezing glass. Both the CDC and mayor asked everyone to stay inside until the issue with the rats has been resolved. An hour ago, it got worse: some substation inferno that's thrown the entire island of Manhattan into blackout.

Yet these churchgoers still come, cuddled inside coats, mitten-in-mitten families and friends, some bearing flashlights. Even from the fourth floor, Sienna sees their generosity in letting strangers go first. There is no anger or blame for anything that has happened. Sienna has the comical realization that this church, of all places, might be the one place she'll be accepted tonight—the one place she might accept herself.

She's outside, hatless, unzipped jacket rippling, before she can think better of it. Winter bites her ears. Cold air scours her sinuses and throat and lungs. Is this what the faithful mean when they hunger for salvation?

Sienna hasn't been inside a church in twenty years. The press of people guides her into a gargantuan marble space. Overpowering organ music and a twenty-foot Christmas tree greet her. Her eyes get lost in the Gothic rib vaulting that holds up the ceiling, then trace down the clustered columns adorned with green wreaths and red ribbons. Straight ahead, the altar and its coterie of robed saints. Behind it, she knows, is the entry to the church's catacombs.

The city may be plunged into darkness, but the church is bathed in an amorphous caramel light. Sienna is confused until the queue proceeds and a woman in a holiday sweater hands her a five-inch candle with a cardboard drip protector. Sienna regards it for a second. The woman smiles and squeezes her arm. Sienna is confused until she realizes that her clothes stink of alcohol and she's wearing dirty pajama bottoms beneath a wrinkled jacket.

Memories of Christmas Eve services with her family resurface from the dim. Though she'd quit believing in biblical tales by age seven, she wasn't immune to candlelight hymns sung with lowing gravity by a solemn congregation. It worked its magic then; it's beginning to work it now.

Next comes a man in a clerical collar who lights her candle with a long wooden pole. He sees her, smells her, and smiles.

"Who needs electricity when we have the lights of our hearts?"

Sienna dives into the first pew she reaches and slides to the wall where she can attempt to hide the tears that cascade down both her cheeks, drawing to a noose at her throat. Someone hands her a kleenex. A woman says that the poor homeless dear—that's her, Dr. Sienna Aguirre—must be scared out there on the street, what with all those rats like something from Revelation. The old lady's right, she *is* scared; she's scared that she let her family all but forget her and her father die twenty-three hundred miles away while she devoted herself to anonymous strands of DNA.

Everyone who is going to get a seat gets one. The priest finishes his procession, bows to the altar, and signs the cross before greeting his congregation on this most special of nights. Sienna has fuzzy memories of what happens next. Call-and-response Introductory Rites, maybe. Then the Confession of Sins—she's ready for that. She'll do whatever's asked of her tonight. She'll be pious. She'll obey. She parts her lips, eager to contribute her first *Amen.*

Until now, the organ's harmonics had vibrated the pew beneath Sienna's firm grip. But the final note goes grotesque and flatulent. Sienna curls inward: these good people have sensed her, trespasser, creator of ungodly abominations. But a multitude of gasps suggests something else. Sienna follows people pointing up at the balcony pipe organ.

Twenty-seven golden pipes, forty feet tall.

And rats ooze from every one.

"Sammy! I'm not mad! Come back!"

Dallas can't think of where else the rat might have gone except into the Barker Houses walls. He's been pleading into vents, cracks, and holes all morning. *Is* he mad, though? What would make all the rats in New York city go crazy at once? Could Sammy have ordered the train attack? Dallas doesn't know what he'd do if he actually found his little friend. Hug him, kiss him, cuddle him? Or squash him dead for the safety of the whole city?

A normal Christmas Eve, there'd be *Home Alone* on DVD and *James Brown's Funky Christmas* rocking the stereo speakers. But the blackout means no electricity. It feels wrong. Mom's still at Bellevue. They've spoken twice today and she's got one more day to go. She told him what to eat before it spoils in the powerless fridge. She told him to let Mrs. Gómez know he's alone, just to be safe. Mostly she told him, over and over, to stay inside. There's some kind of rabies epidemic out there, she says. Who knows, maybe another Covid. Maybe something worse.

Dallas told her not to worry. He can't handle the idea of Mom fretting, on top of her burns. That's why he hasn't told her that he was aboard the newly famous 6 train. That's why he treated his rat bites himself with alcohol, Neosporin, and band-aids.

It's getting colder. Dallas puts a second sweatshirt over his first. He makes himself chocolate milk, hoping it will soothe a throat raw from yelling. Halfway through the milk, he tastes salt and realizes he's crying into his glass. He tosses it out. That's baby behavior. He's the man of the house. He's *always* been man of the house. He stopped that train, didn't he? He'll stop anything else that needs stopping too.

He slams his glass down with authority. It echoes.

After it fades, he hears music.

Is the power back on? Dallas flips the light switch. Nope. But it's unmistakable: Christmas songs. Mom prefers songs by Gwen Stefani and Ariana Grande, but that stuff's too fast for Dallas to enjoy through his implants. Older, slower stuff comes through better. He recognizes this one as "God Rest Ye Merry Gentlemen."

Dallas opens his bedroom window.

No one else listens to their moms, apparently. With electricity out, people have taken to the streets for Christmas Eve fun. Dallas sees families walking together with flashlights. He sees kids throwing snowballs. He sees Mount Sinai staff on the sidewalk, hugging one another, the stress of the explosions and rat injuries receding with a smidge of holiday magic. And he sees carolers, a gang of a dozen or so, standing in front of Barker Houses as if they know Dallas Underhill is up here all alone.

Dallas opens his screen window, crosses his arms on the sill, and leans out to see past the fire escape. Snowflakes dissolve against his scalp. The carolers sing. For a second, everything is nice. Everything is right.

The line at Santiago's cart is ridiculous. Because the cart runs on propane and a gasoline-powered generator, Nuts4U is going gangbusters, tossing bags of honey-roasted peanuts, almonds, cashews, pecans, coconuts, and hazelnuts. With business so good, Santiago is definitely giving away a few bags to those who look like they can't afford it. The nice moment extends. Maybe Santiago will be able to bring his parents from Argentina sooner than expected.

Dallas isn't bothered by the shouts. Just kids excited about Christmas.

Then it starts feeling like the 6 train all over.

The shouts build. Some of the shouters are adults. A few people sprint past the building and don't look back. The line at the Nuts4U cart breaks apart. Dallas leans way out, trying to see through the snow.

A dark brown wave is rippling south down Madison Avenue.

The sewer backed up, Dallas thinks in disgust. People run from it. Dallas winces as a bunch of them collide in the lampless dark, because people are running from the other direction too. Dallas sees, creeping *northward* up Madison, another wave of sewage, trapping the revelers between them. Dallas clings to doubt until his implants wipe it away.

Hwee-oop—hwee-oop—hwee-oop!

No one but Dallas can hear it. But they see more than enough. They scatter. Only Santiago holds his ground. His cart is his life. Dallas watches him lift his hot copper pot like a weapon. He's outnumbered, to say the least, roughly five thousand to one.

Santiago has shouted *"DAAAAALLLLLAAAAASSSSS!!!"* hundreds of times when he needed Dallas to run the cart while he took a bathroom break. He doesn't yell now and doesn't have to. Dallas shuts his screen window and races for the apartment door.

⚓

Prez's parked van idles with its headlights off in front of what the faded facade says was once Pendleton's & Co. One of those multistory regional department chains pushed off the ledge when Amazon made shopping too easy during the pandemic. This is where Prez kept the rat army at bay by going apeshit on their mannequins. He's here this time for a frontal assault. He's got every tool he didn't sell to Ecofix Pest Solutions ready to roll.

He only wonders if Sammy's rats have already connived ways around them. Prez's adopted dad used to tell him about Apollo Smintheus, the god of rodents invoked in Homer's *Iliad,* both plague-bringer and healer. In the temple to Apollo Smintheus at Hamaxitus, rats were revered and kept fat at public expense. The temple was created by humbled conquerors after intelligent rats gnawed through their shield-straps and bowstrings, leaving them helpless. It's what Prez is worried about. The fancier the human weapon, the more parts it has to be chewed.

Plus, he's starting to think the rats have vacated the joint.

Smog's showing no interest in Pendleton's. Prez has got eight jugs of kerosene in the back of his van. But a raging fire would do what? Besides add one more calamity for tonight's first responders to deal with. He growls and mutters. He's been doing a lot of both all night.

"What do you think they're up to, Smoggie? Maybe freeing the animals at Central Park Zoo, getting them to join the rampage?"

Smog whines.

"Maybe ingesting some kind of delayed poison and then spreading poison rat shit through the water system?"

Smog whines harder.

"What if they crawl into airplane engines and get chewing so planes start dropping from the sky?"

Smog barks.

"I know. It all seems possible now."

Smog barks louder and Prez notices the pitch. He sits up fast and follows the trajectory of the dog's gaze. Twenty feet ahead, on the sidewalk across the street, is a rat.

"Smog, shh."

Smog shhs, though his doggie-breath fogs the glass and his eager wet nose streaks through it. The rat has yet to notice them. It scurries, stops. Scurries, stops. Without turning on the headlights, Prez can't make out if it's an ordinary *Rattus norvegicus*, Sammy, or—the worst option of all—some kind of ahead-of-schedule hybrid. Prez tastes bile. If Sammy's mated early, the next time Prez spots a rat, it could be the first of a whole new breed.

He watches the rat clamber up a trash can. Too large—not Sammy. Prez wilts back into his duct-taped driver's seat as he thinks of Colonel Monroe's spiteful glare. She'd asked him to confirm Sammy's last known GPS coordinates. He had, and it hadn't helped.

Prez bounces up again. The colonel—she'd asked the wrong question. A rat tends to stay within a couple of blocks of its origin, its nest, and at the end of the day, Sammy is still a rat.

The Pet Fetch! coordinates that mattered were the *first* ones logged.

Prez drags his phone from his pocket and fumbles his way to Zofia Zywicki's app. He scrolls through the history of GPS pings until he finds the first static location after EditedPets and Javits. He taps it, which sprouts a map. East Harlem unfolds, the streets colored the same traffic-jam red as they've been since the steam explosions.

The Barker Houses. Prez knows it well, a rodent hothouse. A whole campus of buildings, over one thousand apartments, more than he could cover if he had every PCO in New York behind him. Seriously, what has he got to lose? He tosses the phone next to Smog, throws the van into drive, and pulls on the headlights.

"Goddammit!"

In the time it took Prez to consult Pet Fetch!, Lexington Avenue has vanished. It flows and eddies now, a bubbling brook of rat flesh. Prez ogles as everything is coated by brown and gray fur: fire hydrants, kiosks, a bicycle chained to a stand. When the rat wave begins to lap over the roof of an El Camino a few car-lengths away, Prez lets off the brake. But he doesn't shift into reverse.

"That rat was a scout. All right, Smog, let's show them what they scouted."

Prez stomps the gas. Rubber squeals and the van's rear end skids sideways. The tires grip the pavement and the vehicle fires forward. In a second, the front grill cracks in half with the impact of the rats. But an Astro van is four thousand pounds. It's like busting through a wooden fence, something Prez has done a time or two. Rats roll up over the hood, smashing into the windshield with blotches of blood. Beneath the tires, the crackling of a thousand bones, the squelch of organs spurting out from bodies. It's bumpy till Prez gains some speed, then it's no worse than driving through a layer of winter slush.

He turns on 100th Street. It, too, is layered with rats. People dash all over. Some swipe at rats attached to their bodies. Others crumple, furred with rats to their neck. Prez's instinct is to hit the brakes and leap out with his sledgehammer. But for the good of the goddamn planet, he presses on toward Barker Houses. Streets all over are barricaded because of explosion craters, but he's got an expired New York State Pesticide Applicator Certification badge he can flash, and there are always sidewalks, byways, parking lots, service entrances—and, of course, smashing through another metal gate or two.

"Smoggie! Nose out the window! Smell me up a Sammy!"

Sienna no longer needs to regret skipping the catacomb tour beneath St. Patrick's Old Cathedral. Now the catacombs visit her. No sewer line could explain the incalculable rapids of rats that spew from organ pipes, bleed from the altar, and fountain from every vent, duct, and drain in the sanctuary. The rats must have amassed down there. Sienna pictures them restless and bored, chewing through crypts and rifling through the cold bones of priests, bishops, and benefactors.

People flee. As they drop their candles, the place goes twice as dark, then twice again as the rats flow across the alabaster floor and down the walls like black ink. For a while, Sienna can't move. She's inside a church? Being swallowed alive by rats? No, she's still on a bender at Midnight Lounge and everything else has been a dream.

People crawl over her to get out, and when her chin clocks the pew and she tastes blood, she knows this is real. The question is, what will she do about it? She's to *blame* for it. If she stood in the center of the aisle, arms extended, a Christlike offering, perhaps the rats might let everyone else off the hook and drag only her down to the crypt for devouring.

The second she fights her way from the pew, people shove her in the direction of the door. Briefly the stampede is disrupted by a giant ball of rats falling from the balcony—Sienna thinks the organist is inside it—but the people crawl over that too. Not everyone makes it. Parishioners to both sides of Sienna are felled. Sienna sees a woman blunder past, her face half-peeled like an apple. A tween does a nose-dive, dead in place, and when her dress floofs over her head, her legs are gristled bone, her abdomen open, her bowels unraveling piles of intestine.

For her sins, Sienna lives. She's jolted into the cold winter air along with everyone else. People vault down both sets of stairs and tumble to the Mott Street sidewalk. They don't land hard, though. The ground is carpeted with rats.

There's no choice for anyone but to sprint across the backs of snapping rodents like a monk crosses hot coals. Sienna is content to let herself be eaten from the feet up, except she's blocking the stairs and someone literally throws her aside. She finds herself planted against the license plate of a parked VW Bug. Instantly she feels the stinging nip of rat teeth through her pajama legs.

She caterpillars over the car until she is on all fours on its roof. It's a popular idea. Sienna sees a woman doing the same atop a Honda Accord, and a mom, dad, and toddler settling atop a Ford Explorer. Overall, it's a good view. No Armageddon spoken of inside St. Patrick's Old Cathedral could match what Sienna sees.

Mott Street is a river flooding its banks; rats swell into waves and crest both curbs. A child's arm is fully enveloped and wiggling. A man whips his head, trying to dislodge what looks like a long, furry earring. A woman stumbles backward while swatting the rats dangling from her breasts like Romulus and Remus. A man's body abruptly hits the street, skull fracturing, opening up like an overripe watermelon, and Sienna looks up to find the window from which he jumped. Instead she finds other windows showcasing attack scenes. Maybe this *is* Revelation. Not actual monsters, it turns out, just obedient people who stayed inside like the mayor and CDC asked, and now look at them, consumed head to toe. Even higher, NYPD choppers. They swoop and roar, nothing but bluster.

Sienna's phone rings. It's been ringing all night.

Rats boosted by fellow rats are creeping up the sides of her VW Bug island; the idea of taking a phone call right now is so absurd, Sienna laughs. So she takes out her phone. Unlisted number. Maybe it's someone to whom she can offer a final confession. She taps the accept button. The phone clicks against her ID-tag earring.

"Hi," she says.

"We were supposed to have *twenty-one days* before CN8 spawned. Twenty-one, Aguirre. You lied."

Sienna laughs again. Exactly the sort of niceties she's come to expect from Colonel Monroe.

"No, colonel, I didn't lie. Not about this. These are regular rats."

"How's that possible? Are you actually telling me that CN8 is directing them? And they're listening?"

"That's right."

"Jesus fucking—is there *anything* we might not have thought of? Some ultrasonic device? Some noxious chemical? Firehouses? Something, anything that will scare them off?"

"No. These rats aren't afraid of anything."

Heated delay from Monroe. "Are you *laughing*?"

Sienna suppresses giggles. It's a gift to hear the colonel so off her game.

"With the power out, you won't be able to get your bomb through the subway."

Monroe's disgust oozes through the phone.

"You know what, Aguirre? I prefer it this way. It's always best to know exactly what you're up against. We've got FLIR units in the sky tracking rats by body warmth. We know exactly where they're thickest. Hit them there. We can be more surgical than ever."

"You can't drop those bombs from the air, you'll—"

"Who said we're dropping anything? We're going to drive Lenco Bearcats right into the thick of them and set off our thermobaric bitches right there on the street. I warned you, Aguirre: Swarm Theory. Everything is still on the table. We don't have any choice."

Sienna surveys Mott Street's rat apocalypse. Below her, above her, edging in from every direction. Her berserk laughter deliquesces into sadness.

"How many people will die, Colonel?" she asks softly.

"I don't expect we'll ever really know, Aguirre. It's a figure you'll have lots of time to calculate while you're rotting away in prison. If you live that long."

That's it. The call beeps dead.

Just as the first rat scrabbles its way to the top of Sienna's car.

Dallas barges from the ground-floor stairwell. Rats, at least thirty, stopping their scurries to stare. There's no one in the lobby, but there's a streak of blood heading out the front door, a pair of broken glasses, and a dead rat impaled by a large kitchen knife.

Dallas rushes past them. They leap but can't snag hold of his cycling legs. Then he's outside in the cold, breath swelling and bursting, a series of gray balloons. The Barker Houses ramp is black with rats, hundreds. Dallas leaps the railing and plows through a snowdrift that is itself booby-trapped with rats that pop up, baring yellow teeth through snow-frosted whiskers. Dallas keeps rolling, right over them to the sidewalk fence.

A swath of carolers lie dead in front of him, the pages of their sheet music pasted to the bloody mess of their necks, groins, and knees. Directly across the street, Mount Sinai staff upends furniture to reinforce the automatic doors.

Dallas heaves himself over the fence and lands amid familiar detritus. Spatulas, a steel tray, sugar bags, metal scoops.

"Dallas, get away!"

Santiago Leguizamon is crouched against the overturned Nuts4U cart. He waves his copper pot at encircling rats. There's a hundred of them, hissing and scuttling, tightening the snare. Their chant shivers Dallas's skull.

Hwee-oop—hwee-oop—hwee-oop!

"Back inside, Dallas! Go!"

All Dallas can see are the scars on Santiago's knuckles. And the only sound that overpowers the rodent war cry is what Santiago said just a few days earlier.

Help does not always come. So you stand up for what is yours, mi chico. You do that, you will be proud of your scars.

Last night's train attack will leave scars, and Dallas is prepared for more. He will not let the founding member of the Bloody Fist gang fight this fight alone.

The cart's red-and-white-striped umbrella is on the sidewalk. Dallas snatches it and springs it open. Rats have gnawed it full of holes, but it's still huge. Dallas pushes it into the rats, shoveling a path toward Santiago. Halfway there, hot weights land on his shoulder and wrist. The umbrella falls. Rats bite, but as luck would have it, Dallas already wears tight bandages in both spots and he only feels the press of teeth, not the pierce. He waves his arms, trying to dislodge the rats, but they hang on. Dallas takes a step back—and his foot lands on rats that wait there on purpose, a trap to trip him, something out of the playbook of Roman Moffett.

Dallas falls against the fence. A mesh of rats draws over his legs like a bedsheet—then scatter when a bright copper pot lands on Dallas's shins. Santiago tossed it! Dallas snatches it up and starts batting rats from his legs. He glances at Santiago in gratitude, only to see that the copper pot was the only weapon left and Santiago is crumpled against his cart, defenseless against the pelt of rats rippling over his shoes and ankles.

Hwee-oop—hwee—

The chant shatters into individual yips of pain. Dallas stands to get a better look.

A line of three dozen rats bisects the attack battalion. Though vastly outnumbered, these rats are unusually large. Their line bends around Santiago, herding away the attackers. Dallas recognizes the reddish stain of their mouths, wide open and hissing.

It's the same color Dallas's fingers turn after eating Santiago's nuts.

These are the rats from the sidewalk crack, the ones Santiago has been slipping candied treats to for years, and they don't seem to care what orders have filtered down from Sammy. They have come to like Santiago, the same as Dallas, and they don't intend to let any rat army get him. Dallas has no idea if this splinter group offers any kind of larger hope. All he's sure of is that Santiago is free.

"Come on!" Dallas shouts. "Let's go!"

Santiago dashes across the sidewalk, takes Dallas by the shoulder, and steers him back toward Barker Houses. In the thirty seconds it takes to stomp across the runway of rats, Dallas notices his knuckles are bleeding. He feels a windblown thrill. The Bloody Fist gang lives.

✷

At Lexington and East 102nd, Prez spots a band of amateur ratcatchers and their dogs. He's bumped into these types before. He'd like to think their hearts are in the right place but he's not sure about that either, especially not on a night like tonight. He thinks these hobbyists, like so many other militia folk out there, just like to feel like vigilantes.

This evening their lack of prowess is lethal. By the time Prez lays eyes on them, they are beyond rescue. The hobbyist ratcatchers are on their knees, straggling blindly, heads blacked out by feasting rats. Their dogs are faring better, but rats hang from them like shirts on a clothesline. Soon the weight will drag them down.

Prez focuses on the road. Piloting the Astro van is already hard enough. The tires are so sheathed in rat guts, bones, and fur that they slide across streets like socks across linoleum. He fights the steering wheel. Peeping over the hospital is Barker Houses. Prez grimaces as he tries to hang a right onto the shitshow of Madison. What *used* to be Madison—the gray concrete has been swapped for brown fur.

He makes the turn well enough. The Ford Focus barreling down East 102nd doesn't. It skids through the pink slop of flattened rats and collides with the back half of the Astro. The van spins through mashed rats until the driver's side hits the curb catty-corner from Barker Houses—and tips over. Prez braces for a hard landing. Smog, though, has no seatbelt. As the passenger side goes vertical, the dog rolls, then floats. Prez captures Smog midair in a Hail Mary catch and cradles him as the van crashes down.

The driver's-side window shatters against the sidewalk. Prez locks his body. Holds his breath.

A rat wiggles into the inch between broken window and sidewalk.

"Shit! Smoggie! Move!"

Prez punches the rat, unclips his seatbelt, and scales the passenger seat, hoisting Smog. The dog hops from Prez's arms and scrabbles through the rolled-down passenger window. Prez opens the door like a roof hatch and pulls himself out. Sitting atop the passenger side, he looks back down into the vehicle below.

Rats flood into the van as if from a hydrant leak.

Prez jumps down to the street, scrunching two rats dead under his boots. He twirls around. He sees the car that rear-ended him, its hood wrinkled like a worried forehead; the driver has given up resisting and sobs as rats dig into both sides of his neck. Behind that, two other cars crash and Prez sees strings of rats file from the undercarriages.

The goddamn rats are chewing through brake lines.

A strangled, high-pitched cry—Smog.

Prez swivels left and sees Smog halfway down the block, right in front of Barker Houses. But he's backed against a fence by a fat crescent of rats sweeping from the street. Smog's snarling and pawing, but he's got mere inches to spare.

"Smoggie, hold on!"

Rats hop and attack, but Prez is three hundred and twenty pounds and mad as hell. He tears them off, snapping their necks without thinking about it, and glories in their crunching demise beneath his charging boots.

It's the curb that gets him. The step up to the sidewalk, plus the rat or two atop it, makes for a big step, and Prez loses his footing. He topples to all fours, taking inadvertent handfuls of two rats and pinning another one beneath each kneecap. Rats run up his arms and dig claws into his back. Tails flap all over as if Prez has sprouted cilia. Six feet away, Smog is besieged just the same. The terrier corkscrews at the rats latched onto his back and swinging from his ears.

Something snaps.

It's as palpable as a broken bone. If Prez loses Smog, he's alone. And it'll be his fault. He's the one who couldn't make even one of three wives happy. He's the one who took Noah Goff's too-good-to-be-true offer. He's the one who sold Przybyszewski & Sons to a soulless corporation. He's the one who read comic books while the seeds of global ruin were being planted one room away.

Prez knows he can't win. There's too many rats to fight on this single stretch of sidewalk alone, much less the whole block, much less the entire city.

But good god, will he ever go down fighting.

Prez squeezes rats in both fists. Their eyes pop, their tongues stick out, their abdomens split. He hurls them hard, takes two more, cracks their skulls together and feels the small, feverish splat of brains against his face. Live rats replace dead ones in endless echelons, one phalanx assaulting Prez's left arm, another attaching to his right thigh. Yet Prez keeps moving, keeps fighting. He pounds rats into bags of liquefied organs. He sticks fingers down rats' throats and whips them to the pavement, shattering skeletons. When a rat races up his chest to his face, Prez bites its head off, spitting it into the oncoming hordes.

"IS THAT ALL YOU GOT?"

The hide of rats over his body peels away in fright. It's the pause Prez needs to swoop Smog into his arms, hop to his feet, and begin kicking rats out of the way like footballs. He kick-marches his way down the fence line.

He looks down at Smog, his baby.

One of the dog's ears is ripped in half. One of his eyes is gouged. His hide is slashed as if from knives. He's trembling, whining, losing blood. Prez notices that the hand cradling Smog is half-peeled of skin. He sees his own exposed tendons twitch.

But they're alive, both of them.

Barker Houses pulls into focus, directly above.

✖

The woman huddling on the magenta Honda Accord has long since been dragged into the rat morass, eight long acrylic fingernail scratches the only proof she existed. The family of three atop the black Ford Explorer is rapidly being absorbed, the parents being eaten alive while still propping their toddler on their shoulders so she might live for another horrifying minute.

The VW Bug's rounded profile has posed a tougher challenge for scaling rats. But they are victorious. Sienna is forced to stand. She kicks a foot sideways to topple a rat brigade from the hood, then does the same to take out a matching brigade from the rear. Replacement rats are instantaneous. Sienna is exhausted. Her time is almost out, and maybe that's okay.

She traces the path of a chopper. This leads her to a sight that, even tonight, stands out as spectacular. A chain of rats stretches from the roof of St. Patrick's Old Cathedral to high atop the streetlamp on the other side of Mott Street. It's an engineering marvel Sienna has only witnessed in ants, who bite one another's legs to form physical bridges across ravines that sister ants use to cross over to the other side. Sienna Aguirre, and every other scientist she might have polled, would have said the behavior was impossible, given a rat's body weight. Yet here it is, a rat-body catwalk across a raging river of rodents.

It's a long way from tootling around in a SammyWagon.

Sienna feels the twitch of a smile. She and Noah may have created a monster, but isn't the monster truly something to behold? If only she'd had more time before Pet Expo. Perhaps she could have capped Sammy's brain growth and uplifted him in a way that inspired a worldwide movement.

A rat bites her ankle. Sienna kicks it but, honestly, barely feels it. She has retreated into the happy numbness of deep thought, like she's back working the kinks out of INTR. If humans survive long enough to give Biological Uplift another try, there's no point to starting from scratch again, is there? Sienna's got a secret. And if she could trust that secret to anyone, who would it be?

A rat bites the back of her calf. Sienna thumps it aside.

The act of calling someone from atop this death trap is as silly as taking the call from Colonel Monroe. Sienna decides to consider it an act of radical hope. As rats slash through her pajama legs and begin to gnaw at her knees, she takes her phone back out and taps the name *PREZ*. She gets his voice mail, naturally, and grins one last time at the clumsiness of his gruff voice going through the mailbox-greeting motions.

"Hi, Prez," she says.

She's given him hints of her secret before.

Now she tells it to him in full.

When she hangs up, rats are at her waist, heaving, flopping, nipping, foaming. She lets the phone drop from her hand, bounce silently off the roiling bodies, and disappear into the rat tarn. Her body sways. The rats have probably bit through both her popliteal arteries. She'll be dead in five minutes. Less, probably, once she falls and the rats gain access to her throat.

Sienna looks at the Ford Explorer. The parents are completely coated now. Yet their four arms still extend from the blood-glistened rat peak and the little girl still sits up there, hoisted and untouched. A breathtaking act of strength. If Sienna had gotten pregnant, would she have been able to hold her child this far above the world's violence for so long?

She realizes she doesn't have to wonder anymore.

Sienna steps off the roof of the VW Bug. The rats don't expect this; she feels a hundred tiny lances as they dig in. But most fall away as she lowers herself to the street like she's a child herself, back in Montana, pushing legs through snow instead of rats. Seconds later, she's climbing the SUV. She's a festering hive of rats now, encrusted except for her head and hands. Those are the only parts she needs. As the mother and father finally crumple beneath the rats, Sienna plucks the toddler free—and holds the girl high above her head.

In a miracle minute, a motorcycle tears down Mott Street, wheel spokes dicing rats like rotary blades. He sees Sienna's Statue of Liberty act and skids to a halt beside the Explorer. The smoothness of the rider's closed helmet reminds Sienna of the glassy-eyed saints of St. Patrick's altar. She leans and drops the girl into the man's waiting arms. It feels like she's dropping, and saving, the best part of herself.

She thinks of Sebastián Aguirre and smiles.

She never had to be a mother. She was a daughter, and that was enough.

The motorcyclist presses the child close with one protective arm and tears off, alive for now. That will have to be good enough. Sienna discovers that she can't straighten. Her knees no longer work. She falls into the scrambling blanket of rats. Instantly she is covered. Her carotid arteries snap, sting, and open. Her femoral arteries go loose and warm. She raises her head from the furry fray long enough to see the rats atop the SUV frown down at their escaped meal, then thicken into a giant wave about to drop over her. Sienna Aguirre tilts her face toward them, ready at last.

She's seen this postcard before.

The pain in my head is ~~unbarabbol~~ bad. I must get away.

It is time to mate.

That is all that is left.

If I mate it will not matter that my brain ~~axplodes~~ dies. The time of humans will be gone. The time of rats will be here.

I am sorry I will miss it.

I need a safe place to mate. I move through the tunnels. It is ~~daffucult~~ hard. I have seizures. I bite my tongue. There is blood in my mouth. I get lost. But I marked the path well and I follow it. I come out on a street I know. There is the ~~hospetol~~ sick place and a tall ~~billding~~ place I ~~rumumber~~ know. I do not know why I know it.

But I know I was happy there.

I will go there to mate.

First I must cross the street. Two trucks enter the road. They are not like normal trucks. They are black. They are big. They are heavy. Their tires crush many good rats.

~~Strapt~~ tied to the top of the first truck is a metal barrel with a narrow end. I have seen these in videos. It is an ~~explohcive worehed~~ bomb. Once I see the bomb I know the human plan. I am good at knowing plans. The humans in the first truck will set off the bomb and escape in the second truck. Setting off the bomb will kill many more good rats.

Trucks like these are filled with ~~solgers~~ guns. Bullets cannot hurt these trucks.

But rats are not bullets.

I tell my rats what to do.

Most trucks have grills so they do not ~~overheet ovurheit~~ get hot. These trucks have metal plates to stop bullets. So humans built ~~chinnees~~ air tubes.

This was a mistake.

My rats go into these tubes. They die in there like they died in the cloud machines. And like the steam pipes, the engines ~~overheet~~ get hot and the trucks stop working and break. I tell my rats to ~~surrowned ensirkle~~ crowd the trucks. If the humans cannot get out they cannot set off the bomb.

Holes open in the sides of the trucks. Guns poke out. The guns fire bullets. Many good rats die. But there are more rats than bullets. One gun stops. One gun runs out of bullets. My rats go through the holes. More shooting, this time inside the trucks. I hear humans screaming. The screaming stops.

A hatch opens on the second truck. A woman climbs out. Her ~~uno-firm unniferm~~ clothes are different. Doing this is not her job. She is mad. She is yelling. But she is brave. She jumps onto the first truck. Light is flashing from the windows of the truck from the guns. It shakes from the ~~solgers~~ humans dying inside. The woman falls on top of the bomb. She tries to make the bomb work. The bomb looks broken. My rats must have chewed the wires inside. Such clever rats.

The woman goes back to the first truck. She might be the bravest human of all. She opens the door. Dead humans fall out. She picks up cans and throws them. There are bangs. There are flashes. There is smoke. Some rats run. I come closer. The woman takes out a ~~suitecase sootcache shootcase~~ bag. Inside is a computer. The woman tries to type. Maybe she wants to send a ~~mussage meshige~~ note to other humans.

Maybe this is a different kind of bomb.

The brave woman fails. Rats bite her fingers. Rats bite her face. She screams. She is yelling bad words at the rats. Now I recognize her voice. She is the woman called Colonel Monroe. She yelled at Noah when I was inside Noah's bag.

Now both are dead.

I cross the street. I see a broken cart. I smell nuts. I ~~rebemember remendor~~ think of Santiago. Santiago was friends with Dallas. How have I forgotten Dallas? Dallas lived in this ~~billding~~ place. Dallas was nice.

I look back at the trucks. Rats eat Colonel Monroe. They fight over her meat. Larger rats attack smaller rats. Some large rats eat the small rats. I have seen rats do this all night.

It makes me sad.

When my rats filled the trains, I thought humans would ~~distroy~~ kill other humans to get out. When my rats blew up steam pipes, I ~~ekspected~~ thought strong humans would ~~abbandun abandine~~ leave behind weak humans to die. When my rats attacked the city, I believed humans would ~~relinkwish~~ ~~abandune~~ only try to save themselves like Noah.

I was wrong every time.

Humans helped humans.

Right now I see a big bearded man fight rats. He does not fight for himself. He does not even fight for another human. He fights to save a different animal.

He fights to save a dog.

My head hurts so bad.

Have I been wrong the whole time?

Do humans have something rats do not?

33

Screams bleed through walls as Dallas and Santiago ascend four stories. No rats in the stairwell—that's not how they travel. But Dallas sees rat tails whip from under doors at each floor. After he and Santiago barge into the fourth-floor hallway, the shrieks sharpen. Dallas hurries to his unit, fumbles out his mom's keychain, unlocks the door. When he turns around, Santiago is two doors down.

Mrs. Gómez shrieks inside her apartment. From under her door, rat tails.

Santiago looks at Dallas in apology.

"I have to help her."

Dallas rushes over. He isolates the key with the masking tape. Santiago pushes it away.

"It's unlocked. Now get inside your apartment, *mi chico*."

"I can help—"

"When I am done, I will knock! I will bring her with me! Now inside!"

There's no time to argue. Dallas runs into his apartment and slams the door. No rats in sight, but he better make sure. He drags the sofa from the wall. He hurls the Christmas tree to the floor. He opens the refrigerator, kitchen drawer, the sink cabinet. He falls to the kitchen floor, panting and confused. Why would the rats leave this unit untouched?

From under the sink, a gurgle.

Dallas looks under the sink, past the cleaning bottles, to the loop of PVC pipe.

From the bathroom, a rattle.

Dallas turns and stares. Is he imagining it, or is the bathroom sink cabinet shaking?

The answer to his question hits him.

There weren't any rats in this unit because there weren't any people in it. Until now.

A chunk of PVC pipe flies outward with a crack, revealing bright eyes. A rat squeezes through and races right at Dallas. It might as well be a magician's endless handkerchief: rats stream from the pipe, one after another after another.

Dallas scrambles up, feeling claws along his shins. He sees the bathroom cabinet thump open and vomit out a wet tumble of rats. Every pipe in the building must be bursting with them. Dallas hurdles the toppled Christmas tree and in three long strides he's inside the bedroom and slamming the door. He trips and hits the floor, back against his bed.

Hwee-oop—hwee-oop—hwee-oop!

Thirty rat muzzles appear in the crack beneath the door. The slot is only an inch wide, but that's enough. Rats begin pushing through. Dallas grabs the first thing he sees, his cochlear implant charger, and starts drumming it on rat heads. The charger cracks. Exposed wires flap free. He won't be able to charge his head gear, maybe ever again, he'll be plunged into silence, forever unable to know the threats creeping in on him. But he keeps hitting.

"Go away! Go away! Go away!"

Dallas swipes the blanket off his bed and stuffs it into the crack. Instantly the fabric begins to bubble as rats try to dislodge it. The scratches on the door sound like they're being scored onto Dallas's skull. The source of the scratches gets higher and higher. The rats are piling up on the other side. How long before the door just buckles and spills the rats like guts?

Dallas hears a *scritch*. Rats are cutting through the screen window he'd left exposed after seeing Santiago in trouble. They must have climbed the fire escape. Dallas rockets over, grabs the window sash, and pulls down the pane. It crashes onto rats that had already squiggled through. Dallas presses harder, but it's no use. Rats keep piling through, widening the gap. Dallas jumps back, hits his bed, falls onto it. The entire window has gone black with all the rats packed behind it—and then the glass ruptures and rats pour through like black mud.

Dallas scuttles backward over the mattress until his spine lodges in the room's corner. One rat head pops over the edge of the bed. Then a second. Then twenty more, eyes ablaze as they pull themselves onto the bed.

❈

I fall from the pipe
    A brain problem there is a problem
    I taste blood taste fear taste death
    A smell I know this smell
    The smell of DALLAS my friend DALLAS
    This is where he lived where we lived
    I look for DALLAS
    The kitchen DALLAS?
    The living room DALLAS?
    DALLAS is not here
    Only rats so many rats
    Better this way better
    The christmas tree is here
    DALLAS showed me the christmas tree lights
    I said it was beautiful
    It is not beautiful now
    I climb atop to the tree
    I speak to my rats
    I need a female I say hurry
    The females come
    They fight they bite
    Why must rats fight other rats
    One female wins
    She does what females do she runs at me
    Makes me chase her

But I am sick my head it hurt
She does not make me chase for long
She arches her back
I sniff her legs she I know she is ready
I mount her
It hurts everything hurts but I do it I must do it
If DALLAS were here I would tell him why
DALLAS I would say
Some humans are better than I thought DALLAS
Better than rats DALLAS who kill their own and eat their own
Humans help their weak DALLAS
Humans choose to be good DALLAS
Like you DALLAS like you
You liked me because I was good
I was good because the human in me DALLAS
If rats are going to be good too DALLAS
I must pass along the human genes in me
Then there will be magic
Like christmas tree magic
I hear DALLAS the real DALLAS
From the bedroom
Help DALLAS cries
Help

❉

"Help! Someone! Help!"

The rats appear to lose their minds. They race around the bedroom, up the walls, over the bed, a vortex of fur. It's some sort of celebration. The screech is unbearable. Dallas clutches his head, but he's too terrified to adjust anything on his implant apparatus. The rats churn faster, ripping apart both the carpet and wall plaster. A rind of rats flays from the wall like a slab of rubber from a semi-truck tire. Twenty-some rats flop to the bed, bouncing mattress springs. They spit and brux, teeth bared, eyes diamoned. They leap on Dallas. He pistons his legs, standing atop the rocking bed as rats slap his shins. Teeth and claws dig in. Dallas could run. But there's nowhere to go.

"Help!"

⁂

Not DALLAS not DALLAS do not hurt DALLAS
I have planted myself into the female
I have done it two times maybe three
I need to do it much more to be sure
But DALLAS DALLAS DALLAS
I leave the female
Did I make a baby I do not know
She hisses at me
All rats hiss at me now
I am Ratzenkünig no more
But DALLAS DALLAS DALLAS
I go to the bedroom door
I am dizzy
Many rats try to get inside but they are caught in a blanket
I am smaller than them
Humans made me small
Small is cute
I slip right through
The rats claw me bite me they are angry with me
My fur rips
My skin rips
My brain rips
My skull rips
It is ending all ending
But DALLAS DALLAS DALLAS
DALLAS is on the bed
Rats swarm his feet

I tell them stop
They do not listen
They smell I am sick I am weak
But I am smarter still smarter
I am on the bed
I bite into a sheet
I run behind DALLAS
I circle his legs twice
I pull the sheet tight like a laundry bag
The rats are trapped inside with DALLAS's feet
They want out they claw they hiss
I climb up DALLAS's chest
My brain bleeds it melts it falls out
My paws do not work I fall fall fall
DALLAS catches me
DALLAS holds me close
DALLAS has always held me close
Held me so close that now I must set him free

The little rat's coat is muddy, his face glazed in crusty blood, his body and tail patchy with injuries. But beneath the stench of sewage is the distinct scent of watermelon.

"Sammy! You came! They're going to get me, Sammy—"

Sammy interrupts with two labored words.

Fire. Escape.

The rats thrash the sheet to ribbons. But Sammy's trick with the sheet inspires Dallas. He grabs the front two elastic corners of the bottom bedsheet and lurches forward, peeling the sheet in front of him as he goes. It's like dumping a wheelbarrow. Every rat on the bed is tossed into the air. One makes a lucky leap, biting into the flesh just under Dallas's chin. He yelps and shakes his head like a dog and the rat falls.

Dallas drops the sheet to the floor. It's a gossamer barrier between his feet and a rollicking moat of rats. Small bodies twist and struggle as Dallas stomps across them.

—fire escape fire escape—

Dallas throws open the broken window and hoists himself over the sill, rolling right through the gnawed scraps of the screen. For a second he is upside down, but then his back hits hard on the metal fire escape and the world reorients. Silence—total silence. Both external coils of his implants have shaken off. They could be four stories below, lost in the snarl of Madison Avenue rats. But when he rocks to his knees, he sees both of them right there on the rusted platform. He slaps their magnetized surfaces to his head.

—Dallas run Dallas run Dallas run—

Dallas bolts upright. Sammy's on the window sill. Dallas's heart rips in half. The rat is hunched, heaving, pulsating in pain, each exhale drizzling small red droplets. Bloody drool elongates from his jaw. Dark matter drips from his ears.

I am I am I am—

Dallas holds out cupped hands.

"COME WITH ME, SAMMY!"

—I am sorry Dallas I am sorry—

"NOW, SAMMY, NOW!"

—sorry I did not mean for mean for mean for—

"WE CAN STILL GET AWAY!"

—it has stop Dallas to stop Dallas to stop—

"SAMMY, PLEASE!"

The spate of words severs. With trembling effort, Sammy sits up on his hind legs like he used to. He tilts his head as he once did when Dallas taught him about new things: candied nuts, pneumatic tubes, cloud machines. Sammy blinks his big eyes the same way too, except blood drips from them now, crimson tears.

I love you, Dallas.

Dallas is lost in his own tears. He can't imagine never again hearing Sammy's words inside his head. Words are flimsy squeaks next to how big his feelings are for this rat. But words are all Dallas has, exactly five of them.

"I love you too, Sammy."

Sammy wiggles his whiskers. And then he's gone. Dallas sobs, turns away, and stumbles down the first flight of metal steps. The fire escape shakes and clangs. Dallas keeps going, keeps shaking, keeps clanging, when suddenly his right foot meets no resistance at all, and right before he plummets through a missing step he sees the half dozen rats who gnawed it away. Dallas falls, a slow revolution toward the Barker Houses pavement.

Someone catches him.

Dallas blinks upward into the snow. A man stares down in wonder. His face is scratched up and his beard is clotted with blood. Beside him stands a Jack Russell Terrier, badly injured, but nevertheless wagging his tail like he's found his quarry at last.

✖

The computer
    The videos
    I learned so much
    About humans
    About animals
    About trains
    About cars
    About sewers
    About math
    About engineering
    About biology
    About physics
    Me for instance
    I am small
    I am light
    I can race across the tops of other rats

And they barely feel me
I can leave the bedroom
I can go into the kitchen
Look at me DALLAS
DALLAS likes to see me play
I go behind the oven
Deep into the dust
Silly rat
I learned chemistry too
I gnaw a rubber tube
I go back out front
I climb the dishrag
I climb the stove
I smell the gas
DALLAS did I do it good
Did I play good DALLAS
I sit for a while
I sit up here nice and tall
I think of my friend DALLAS
My friend LINDA
My friend SIENNA
I miss them
I want to see them
I find the stove dial
DALLAS used to make me food
DALLAS could use the stove
Look DALLAS I can use the stove too
I will make something better than food
I will make you safe forever
DALLAS watch
DALLAS watch me play

34

EditedPets isn't as peaceful as Prez expected. It's three weeks since the so-called Rat War, time enough for all blame to be set at the feet of Noah Goff and EditedPets. It's a good thing, Prez thinks. Gives the public an enemy to focus on while dealing with destabilizing grief. These days, everyone knows someone who suffered the sort of demise previously relegated to nightmares. Not surprisingly, the NYPD and FBI declared the seventh-floor offices of EditedPets a crime scene. No one was allowed back in until yesterday.

Walking down the familiar hall, Prez acknowledges that today's bustle makes sense. The business may be kaput, but staff had spent three years in here. Their workstations are filled with personal items, minus the computers confiscated by agents. Prez stops at the bend in the hall and takes a long look at the words etched into the glass wall.

pets, reinvented.

He'd like to punch right through it. Instead he refocuses to the Gamma Phi Delta kids on the other side of the glass. They're packing but also holding hands, hugging, going through the same post-traumatic paces as the rest of New York. Prez used to grouse about Gamma Phi Delta's volume and absence of manners. But they're good kids. They'll rebound. Look at their faces. They're halfway there.

All door locks have been disabled. Prez strolls into the lab. He waves hello at a handful of scientists and techs. They're packing up equipment and instructing movers on how to handle it. The place is mostly cleared out. Lots of white walls and clear counters.

One exception: Sienna Aguirre's desk.

The computer is long gone. But the rest of her stuff looks ready for Sienna to stride back in, mind abuzz with some miraculous new notion, and sit down to get it cranking. Her pens and notebooks are still here. There's a bottle of antacid. An iPhone charger. A tube of lipstick. On her bulletin board, that postcard of *The Great Wave* alongside a menagerie of skewered origami animals.

Prez picks up the *#1 DAD* thermos.

He knows by its weight that it's not empty. But there's no liquid sloshing. He feels a nervous flutter. Didn't used to get feelings like that, but he's been through a lot, same as everyone. He's got seven staples in his left abdomen. He's in physiotherapy, thanks to a rat that tunneled into his right thigh. His left thumb has a splint where a rat nearly bit it off at the base. His right hand got the worst of it. Prez's surgeon warned him rehabilitation would be a "process." The last time she had a similar type of repair was from a guy who accidentally shoved his hand into a meat grinder. These wounds, plus dozens of simpler bites, have been a pain in the ass for three long weeks.

But he hasn't felt fear until now.

No one's paying attention to him. They rarely do. Prez leaves the lab with the thermos, goes into his old security cubby, and closes the door. He sits at his former chair and sets the thermos on the table. He stares at it.

He's a little afraid of opening it.

This may look like a thermos, Sienna told him. *But it's a key. Everything you see? It's all inside this thermos.*

Prez smiles. He'd kinda loved that lady. If she hadn't gotten mixed up with Noah Goff, there'd be no telling what she could have done. News articles over the past few weeks have made it clear her INTR thing was damn near mystical. Prez wishes she'd used it for almost anything else. For instance, helping that kid Dallas with the magnets on his head.

Prez has visited Dallas Underhill a couple times at Mount Sinai. He's met his mother, Brandy, a train operator who suffered burns in one of the steam explosions. While Dallas dozed in his bed, Brandy told Prez that the kid helped a whole 6 train full of people escape a rat attack. Prez could barely believe it. When Prez got a chance to talk to Dallas alone, the whole truth came out. How the kid stole Sammy from Pet Expo. How Sammy sacrificed himself inside Barker Houses.

Prez witnessed that part: the Underhill apartment exploding into a big ball of red flames.

Sammy, along with every other rat in the unit, had been incinerated.

As incredible as the sight had been, it held not a damn candle to what happened next.

Every rat in sight scrambled back from the flames. That part was normal; Prez had seen lots of rats flee fire. But once they'd reached a safe distance, they didn't resume their destruction. No swarming, no fighting, no biting. They stood aimless in the gentle snowfall, like the signal buzzing in their ears they'd been listening to had gone silent. Gradually rats on Madison Avenue—and soon the rest of the city—slunk back into the city's pits, leaving behind crashed cars, broken windows, and gored bodies.

Once again, they were only rats.

Dallas was messed up about the whole thing. He asked Prez if he, Dallas, was to blame for the city's dead. Prez listened. He's always believed PCOs were neighbors to clergy, spraying chemicals instead of holy water, blowing foggers instead of incense. Ratcatchers work to purify people's homes instead of souls, but in New York City, where people live on top of one another, practically inside one another, how different can the two be?

Prez sighs, takes out his phone, and, one last time, plays the message Sienna left the night of the Rat War.

"Hi, Prez. This is Sienna. I don't know where you are but I hope you're safe. I . . ." She laughs—Prez never heard nearly enough of her laugh. "I'm on top of a car. I'm not going to make it, Prez."

Dimly, peals of human agony and the oceanic thrush of hissing rats.

"We fucked up. *I* fucked up. But maybe there's some good that can still come from Sammy. Some kind of uplift. Maybe not. Maybe anything to do with Sammy is cursed. I don't know. That's why I'm not calling a scientist right now. That's why I'm calling you. You're the only person alive I trust." She laughs again. "How sad is that?"

On the recording, the thump of Sienna's foot, the squeak of a rat.

"Noah was too busy with marketing to worry about corporate espionage. I did all the worrying. I had to make sure no one could engineer their own Sammy from scratch. So I inserted a failsafe genetic system that stops anyone from using Sammy's DNA alone. Without the right IVF culture media, Sammy embryos can't get to the blastocyst stage for implantation."

Another yelp of pain, another squealing rat.

"You don't have to understand any of that. What you have to understand, Prez, is that I made a copy, all right? In case something ever happened to me." A laugh. "I guess something did, huh? In this copy are nine ingredients and instructions to make a Sammy. Here's how I encoded it—I hope you can hear this. CAT, TGC, ACA, ACA, CGC. That's Histidine, Cysteine, Threonine, Threonine, Arginine. Get it? My inside joke. I wrote out the IVF instructions in DNA code. There's also a copy of Sammy's synthesized genome, a two-billion-letter chain shredded up and frozen into liquid nitrogen. But without my instructions it's useless. Remember what I told you about my dad and the shredded letter? This is *his* trick, Prez. Putting Sammy back together and figuring out how to pull off the IVF will take a long, long time. But if someone was patient enough, it could be done."

She shrieks, then moans, then cries. It's hard to listen to. Prez doesn't want to hear her die yet again, but he will. She deserved that much.

"I know you didn't believe in what we did. That's why I'm telling you. You specifically. Destroy what's inside the thermos if you want. Keep it safe if you want. You know where I put them. You're the only one who does."

Prez picks up the *#1 DAD* thermos, unscrews the lid, and tilts it.

Wisps of smoke rise from the liquid nitrogen inside.

Prez goes back to the lab and fetches a pair of thick protective gloves. Again, no one notices. Back in the security office, he pulls a metal rod from inside the thermos.

A column of eight metal pucks is clipped firmly to a metal spine.

Prez pops out the top puck. It's a shallow container holding twelve unlabeled plastic vials.

Pulse pounds at every one of Prez's wounds.

He's holding Sammy in his hands.

He's holding billions of Sammys.

Prez thinks of Smog, asleep in his bed back home, fourteen now and plagued with medical issues since the Rat War. The poor old guy limps. He's incontinent. He whines when Prez touches him. Because Smog can't talk, neither Prez nor the doctor has any idea what's wrong.

What if Smog could speak English? What if Smog could tell Prez exactly what was wrong so Prez could fix it?

"Sorry to lay this on you," Sienna says. "But I know you'll do the right thing. You always do, Prez."

The call ends.

Prez wonders. Will he always do the right thing?

The discs are heavy in his gloved hand, the weight of the whole world.

⁂

Mrs. Gómez stops Dallas at the door to kiss him on the head. He pretends like it's an imposition, but he doesn't mind. The old lady's been super nice to let him and Mom stay with her since their own unit turned to toast. A paint job, which Dallas helped with, was most of what was required to put Mrs. Gómez's place back in order. The lady keeps the empanadillas coming, which is reason enough to stay. The tostones, pasteles, and mantecaditos aren't bad either.

Outside Barker Houses, he hears the familiar greeting.

"Dallas, *mi chico*!"

Dallas grins and ambles up to the Nuts4U cart. There's no hiding that it has been through a war. The umbrella is pocked by frayed holes. The glass display has been replaced by wax paper. One of the wheels has been swapped for a bigger one, which puts the whole cart at a slant.

The tools that matter, though—copper bowl, metal tongs, plastic spatula—have survived. Ditto Santiago. His robust voice and garrulous smile are in perfect working order, despite arms wrapped in gauze from a total of sixty-six rat bites he received while rescuing Mrs. Gómez. In ordinary times, customers might find it icky to buy food from someone so bandaged. But half the people in the city have bandages like that. They have become a sign of unity.

A skateboarding kid raises a splinted wrist at a Hasidic Jew, who crooks his neck to show off his stitches.

Santiago whistles. "Look at those scars coming in. The Bloody Fist gang is getting legit."

Dallas thumbs the raised pink welt on his neck where the bedroom rat chomped him. The cochlear implant gear on his head will always set him apart, but the rat scars? That proves he's like everyone else. He's a New Yorker.

"What'll it be? Honey-roasted coconut?"

"Nah. I gotta get to school."

"Honey-roasted peanuts, then. Peanuts are brain food."

Dallas laughs and shrugs. Why not? Santiago grins, scoops him a fat bag, and chucks it over. Dallas catches, starts munching, and gives his pal a farewell salute. Santiago does the same, but it's curtailed by a customer. Mount Sinai has been packed since the Rat War. That's bad. But more injured people distracting themselves with Nuts4U? That's good for Santiago Leguizamon. You might even argue that he's something of a doctor himself.

Dallas proceeds down 97th Street. Business owners slowly replace broken windows. Volunteer groups sweep the gutters. City workers repair sidewalk cracks at a pace no one's ever seen. Everyone has been assured that the threat of organized rats is behind them. But keeping the overworld less appealing for rats just seems to make good sense.

Dallas is glad for it. After EditedPets was outed as the culprit, people everywhere euthanized their EditedPets products in solidarity. That's a nice word for what they did. Two weeks ago, FireFish littered the sidewalks like chewing gum. Dallas spotted dead ChattyBirds dangling from trash cans. Once he even saw an EasyPony, dead in Central Park, its head caved in from a bullet. Dallas cried a lot that day. Just because a pet is genetically engineered doesn't mean it can't love. Or be loved.

He sees P.S. 79 Luis W. Alvarez two blocks away. His heartbeat picks up, but it evens out. It's getting easier every day. Roman Moffett's body has never been found. Even though Roman's death wasn't Dallas's fault, he knows he'll have to live with it for the rest of his life. It will be a private struggle. Few people think about Roman Moffett anymore. Lots of kids died in the Rat War. In Dallas's class alone, three didn't make it.

Dallas digs out a handful of candied peanuts and shoves them at his mouth. One peanut gets away, dropping to the ground near some trash bins. Dallas glances at it, but you gotta be bonkers to eat food off a New York street, no matter how much cleaner they are these days. He starts to look up, back toward the school.

His eyes catch movement.

Dallas pauses. He peers into the alley.

A rat crouches ten feet away at the foot of a dumpster.

The rat looks at the fallen nut.

Then it looks up at Dallas.

Dallas stops chewing. The city has seen an epidemic of full-blown rat phobias. Dallas hasn't suffered the same. Seeing a rat brings back plenty of bad memories. But it also brings back good memories of Sammy. So many sights around the city do. Santiago's cart. Times Square. Every cloud machine Dallas passes.

The rat adjusts its stance. Dallas inhales sharply.

The rat is pregnant. Its round belly drags across concrete.

Dallas tells himself it is nothing. There remain millions of rats in the city. Every single day, something like twenty-five thousand rats give birth to brand-new litters. This alley rat here is just one of them.

Late at night when he can't sleep, Dallas looks up facts like these. Usually a bad idea. Lately he's been reading about rat reproduction. It takes a long time for rats to have intercourse. The male rat will try an average of eight times to impregnate a female in a single night, often taking breaks between exhausting attempts.

How long was Sammy in Dallas's living room before he heard Dallas scream?

It couldn't have been too long. Could it?

After getting pregnant, it takes a rat an average of twenty-one days before giving birth. It's been three weeks since the Rat War. Probably coincidence.

Even though these trash bins are but a ten-minute walk from Barker Houses.

Even though this rat looks at Dallas like it recognizes him.

Like the ratlings inside her are telling their mother that he is someone important.

"Who are you?" Dallas whispers.

The rat looks at the nut, then Dallas.

He hitches up his backpack. He's going to be late. He steps away from the dim alley, cleansing his senses in the morning sun. City sounds cascade over him, signals that all is well. Cheery greetings between friends. Shouted directions from locals to tourists. Amiable bickering between bodega merchants and people looking for a better deal. The buses, the trains, the cars, the pigeons, the music bumping from behind a thousand windows. It's a lot of noise for cochlear implants to handle all at once.

So Dallas is pretty sure that what he hears from the alley isn't real.

Hwee-oop—hwee-oop—hwee-oop.

CAT TGC ACA ACA CGC CAT ATA ACT TCT TCA

ACA CGC GTC TGC ACA TCA GTA CAT CAT GTA TCA GTC GTC TGC TGC GAG

GTG GTA CGT CGT TCA GTA GCG CGC ACT GTG TGC CGT TCA CGT TCA TGC

TCT GTA GTC GAG ATG CTC GTA CAT CGC ACT GTG CTC TGC GTT TCA CAT GTG

ATA ATA TCA CAT CAT GCG GTG AGA AGA CGC TCT TCA ATA CGT CGC TGT

ATG TCA TCT ATG CTC TCA ATA ACT TCT TCA GCG ACT CGT ATA CGT TCA TGC

ATG GTA GTC GAG TGC CAT TGC ACA ACA CGC GTA ATG CGT GTA TCA TCT

ATG ACT GTG CAT TCA CAT TGC ACA ACA CGC ATG ACT ATG TCA CAT ATG

ATG CTC TCA GCG TCA TGC CAT GTA TAT GTA AGA GTA ATG CGC ACT GCG

TAT GTA ACT AGA ACT GAG GTA ATA TGC AGA GTG TGT AGA GTA GCG ATG

ACT ATG CTC TCA CGT CAT TCA GTC ATG GTA TCA GTC ATG TAT TCA GTA

GTC GAG CAT TCT ACT GTC ACT ATG TCT TCA CAT TCA CGT GTT TCA ATG

ACT TAT TCA AGA TCA GCG ATG TAT TCA CTC GTA GTC TCT TGC CAT AAT

TCA ATA ACT GTC ATG GTA GTC GTG TCA ATG ACT TGC TCT GTT TGC GTC

ATA TCA TGT TCA CGT CTC TGC TGT CAT TAT CGC GTG CAT GTA GTC GAG

ACA CGC GTA GTC CAT ATG CGT GTG ATA ATG GTA ACT GTC CAT GCG ACT

CGT GTA GTT GCG TGC GTC TCT GAG TCA GTC TCA ATG GTA ATA TCA GTC

GAG GTA GTC TCA TCA CGT GTA GTC GAG CGC ACT GTG ATA TGC GTC GCG

GTA GTC GTA CAT CTC AAT CTC TGC ATG GTA CAT ATG TGC CGT ATG TCA

TCT TGT AGA TCA TGC CAT TCA TGT CGT ACT ATA TCA TCA TCT AAT GTA ATG

CTC ATG CTC TCA GTG ATG ACA ACT CAT ATG ATA TGC CGT TCA TGC GTC

TCT ATA TGC GTG ATG GTA ACT GTC TGC CAT GTA TGC CAT CAT GTG CGT

TCA CGC ACT GTG ATG CTC TGC ATG ACT ATG CTC TCA CGT CAT AAT GTA

AGA AGA TGC ATG ATG TCA ACA TGT ATG ATG ACT CAT GTG TAT GTT TCA

CGT ATG CGC ACT GTG CGT AAT ACT CGT TTC TGC AGA ACT GTC GAG ATG

CTC TCA AAT TGC CGC TAT GTG TCA GTC TGC CAT GTG TCA CGT ATG TCA

ACKNOWLEDGMENTS

Thanks to Richard Abate, Bryan Bliss, Hannah Carande, Eric Diaz, Stefan Dziemianowicz, Melissa Farris, Keir Graff, Leonard Kniffel, Amanda Kraus, Eric Loegel, Emily Meehan, Emma Moalem, Martha Stevens, and Claire Wachtel. Hwee-oop!